SELECTED WRITINGS

V.I. LENIN

SELECTED WRITINGS

EDITED BY

VIJAY PRASHAD

Offset edition first published in August 2018
Digital print edition, January 2020

LeftWord Books
2254/2A Shadi Khampur
New Ranjit Nagar
New Delhi 110008
INDIA

LeftWord Books is the publishing division of
Naya Rasta Publishers Pvt. Ltd.

leftword.com

ISBN 978-93-80118-71-0

CONTENTS

EDITOR'S NOTE

The texts included in this volume have been matched against the Progress Publishers, Moscow editions of *Lenin Collected Works* (1973, 1974, 1977, 1978). Lenin's own notes are marked as such (—*Au.*). All other notes are by the Editors and Translators of *LCW*. Where the present edition has excerpted texts, this is indicated by ellipses in square brackets: [. . .].

COMRADE LENIN
Vijay Prashad

Vladimir Ilyich Ulyanov (1870-1924) was known by his pseudonym—Lenin. He was, like his siblings, a revolutionary, which in the context of Tsarist Russia meant that he spent long years in prison and in exile. Lenin helped build the Russian Social Democratic Labour Party both by his intellectual and his organisational work. Lenin's writings are not only his own words, but the summation of the activity and thoughts of the thousands of militants whose path crossed his own. It was Lenin's remarkable ability to develop the experiences of the militants into the theoretical realm that is on display in this volume. It is no wonder that the Hungarian Marxist György Lukács called Lenin "the only theoretician equal to Marx yet produced by the struggle for the liberation of the proletariat".

BUILDING A REVOLUTION

In 1896, when spontaneous strikes broke out in the St. Petersburg factories, the socialist revolutionaries were caught unawares. They did not know what to do. They were disoriented. Five years later, V.I. Lenin wrote, the "revolutionaries *lagged behind* this upsurge, both in their 'theories' and in their activity; they failed to establish a constant and continuous organisation capable of *leading* the whole movement". Lenin felt that this lag had to be rectified.

Most of Lenin's major writings followed this insight. Lenin worked out the contradictions of capitalism in Russia (*Development of Capitalism in Russia*, 1896), which allowed him to understand how the peasantry in the sprawling Tsarist Empire had a proletarian character. It was based on this that Lenin argued for the worker-peasant alliance against Tsarism and the capitalists. Lenin understood from his engagement with mass struggle and with his theoretical reading that the social democrats—as the most liberal section of the bourgeoisie and the aristocrats—were not capable of driving a bourgeois revolution let alone the movement that would lead to the emancipation of the peasantry and the workers. This work was done in *Two Tactics of Social Democracy in the Democratic Revolution* (1905). *Two Tactics* is perhaps the first major Marxist treatise that demonstrates the necessity for a socialist revolution, even in a "backward" country, where the workers and the peasants would need to ally to break the institutions of bondage.

These two texts show Lenin avoiding the view that the Russian Revolution could leapfrog capitalist development (as the populists—*narodniki*—suggested) or that it had to go through capitalism (as the liberal democrats argued). Neither path was possible nor necessary. Capitalism had already entered Russia—a fact that the populists did not acknowledge—and it could be overcome by a worker and peasant revolution—a fact that the liberal democrats disputed. The 1917 Revolution and the Soviet experiment proved Lenin's point.

Having established that the liberal elites would not be able to lead a worker and peasant revolution, or even a bourgeois revolution, Lenin turned his attention to the international situation. Sitting in exile in Switzerland, Lenin watched as the social democrats capitulated to the war-mongering in 1914 and delivered the working class to the world war. Frustrated by the betrayal of the social democrats, Lenin wrote an important text—*Imperialism*—which developed a clear-headed understanding of the growth of finance capital and monopoly firms as well as inter-capitalist and inter-imperialist conflict. It was in this text that Lenin explored the limitations of the socialist movements in the West—with the labour aristocracy providing a barrier to socialist militancy—and the potential for revolution in the East—where the "weakest link" in the imperialist chain might be found. Lenin's notebooks show that he read 148 books and 213 articles in English, French, German and Russian to clarify his thinking on contemporary imperialism. Clear-headed assessment of imperialism of this type ensured that Lenin developed a strong position on the rights of nations to self-determination, whether these nations were within the Tsarist Empire or indeed any other European empire. The kernel of the anti-colonialism of the USSR—developed in the Communist International (Comintern)—is found here.

The term "imperialism", so central to Lenin's expansion of the Marxist tradition, refers to the uneven development of capitalism on a global scale and the use of force to maintain that unevenness. Certain parts of the planet—mostly those that had a previous history of colonisation—remain in a position of subordination, with their ability to craft an independent national development agenda constrained by the tentacles of foreign political, economic, social and cultural power. In our time, new theories have emerged that suggest that the new conditions no longer can be sustained by the Leninist theory of imperialism. Antonio Negri and Michael Hardt, for instance, argue that there is no geo-political rivalry left, that there is only the extension of the sovereignty of the constitution of the United States on a world-scale. This is what they call Empire. What the people—the multitude—must do, they suggest, is to contest the terms of this constitution but not the fact of its global aspiration. Others argue that the world has flattened, so that there is no longer a Global North that oppresses a Global South, that the elites of both regions are part of a global capitalist order. This is the kind of theory that Karl Kautsky advanced in the name of "ultra-imperialism". Lenin responded sharply to Kautsky and this theory of "ultra-imperialism", saying that Kautsky noted that "the rule of finance capital lessens the unevenness and contradictions inherent in the world economy, whereas in reality it increases them". Elements of Lenin's text are, of course, dated—it was written a hundred years ago—and would require careful reworking. But the essence of the theory is valid—the insistence on the tendency of capitalist firms to become monopolies, the ruthlessness with which finance capital drains the wealth of the Global South and the use of force to contain the ambitions of countries of the South to chart their own development agenda.

Finally, Lenin spent the period from 1893 to 1917 studying carefully the limitations of the party of the old type—the social democratic party. Our volume contains Lenin's text *Our Programme*—in which he makes the point that the party must be involved in continuous activity and not rely upon spontaneous or initial [*stikhiinyi*] outbreaks. This continuous activity would bring the party into intimate and organic touch with the working class and the peasantry as well as help to germinate the protests that then might take on a mass character. It was this consideration that led Lenin to work out his understanding of the revolutionary party in *What Is To Be Done?* (1902). The extracts in this volume present the bold ideas of the party that Lenin developed, including the role of the class-conscious workers as the vanguard of the party and the importance of political agitation amongst workers to develop a genuinely powerful political consciousness against *all* tyranny and *all* oppression. The workers need to *feel* the intensity of the brutality of the system and of the importance of solidarity.

These texts—from 1896 to 1916—prepared the terrain for the Bolsheviks and Lenin to understand how to operate during the struggles in 1917. It is a measure of Lenin's confidence in the masses and to his theory that Lenin wrote his audacious pamphlet—*Can the Bolsheviks Retain State Power?*—which is reproduced here. This was written a few weeks before the seizure of power.

BUILDING A STATE

The last section in this volume—*Socialist Construction*—collects Lenin's writings and speeches as the Bolsheviks tried to build a socialist state and society in the former Tsarist empire. Half of Lenin's collected works hold these writings and speeches from six years (whereas the other half collect work from over twenty-four years). An immense amount of writing was necessary as Lenin and his comrades tried to understand what they were doing in uncharted territory. A close reading of *State and Revolution* (1917) anticipates the problems faced by the Soviets in their new task—they could not only inherit the state structure, but had to "smash the state", build a new set of institutions and a new institutional culture, create a new attitude by the cadre towards the state and society.

The most important text here is *The Immediate Tasks of the Soviet Government* (April 1918), which lays out the agenda for the USSR in its first few years. The other texts show Lenin's general attitude towards state construction and to the challenges faced by the USSR—surrounded by hostile powers—in this period. Lenin's *Better Fewer, But Better* (1923), written towards the end of his life, is one of the most honest and reasonable texts on the problems faced by the new government and society.

In his last public appearance—at the Moscow Soviet on November 20, 1922—one can see Lenin's personality in full display. There is Lenin's confidence and his humanness. There is Lenin's honesty and his ambition,

> We still have the old machinery, and our task now is to remould it along new lines. We cannot do so at once, but we must see to it that the Communists we have are properly placed. What we need is that they, the Communists, should control the machinery they are assigned to, and not, as so often happens with us, that the machinery should control them. We should make no secret of it and speak of it frankly. Such are the tasks and the difficulties that confront us—and that at a moment when we have set out on our practical path, when we must not approach socialism as if it were an icon painted in festive colours. We need to take the right direction, we need to see that everything is checked, that the masses, the entire population, check the path we follow and say, "Yes, this is better than the old system". That is the task we have set ourselves. Our Party, a little group of people in comparison with the country's total population, has tackled this job. This tiny nucleus has set itself the task of remaking everything, and it will do so. We have proved that this is no utopia but a cause which people live by. We have all seen this. This has already been done. We must remake things in such a way that the great majority of the masses, the peasants and workers, will say, "It is not

> you who praise yourselves, but we. We say that you have achieved splendid results, after which no intelligent person will ever dream of returning to the old". We have not reached that point yet . . . Socialism is no longer a matter of the distant future, or an abstract picture, or an icon. Our opinion of icons is the same—a very bad one. We have brought socialism into everyday life and must here see how matters stand. That is the task of our day, the task of our epoch.

READING LENIN

Nothing Lenin wrote over the course of the last thirty years of his life was written for posterity. Lenin wrote in the midst of events, in the middle of arguments. For the first-time reader there is something bracing about the text, but also something bewildering. What is bracing is that Lenin is on the fly—he writes as if he has somewhere to go, a demonstration or a meeting. What is difficult is that Lenin is in the middle of a debate—against Bernstein here or Kautsky there. It is hard to know the terms of the debate or even to follow what it is in the other person that forced Lenin to respond. Renegade Kautsky, writes Lenin, and you must accept it as such. The text is rushed. The reader leans over Lenin's shoulder, watching his pen rush across the page, his notes sprawled over his desk and on the floor.

To annotate Lenin's work is to miss the point—which is why this selection comes to you without an immense scholarly apparatus. It is not so important to understand precisely the debates that detain Lenin as it is to watch him use his experience as a political leader to sort through ideological debates and find a way forward. We would like the first-time reader to be patient, to go through the text, to find what is useful and to make notes towards learning more about the debates.

Lenin's theoretical landscape is determined by the requirements of the revolutionary movement at a particular conjuncture. He writes about the vanguard party because he is in a debate with others about how to deal with spontaneous uprisings. He writes of imperialism because he is trying to understand why the social democrats voted for the war. But Lenin does not descend to the slogans of his time. He rises above them—looking at the theoretical principles that lie beneath these slogans. But he does not rise too far away from the political debates of his time. Lenin moves craftily from theory to tactics, from Marxist thought to revolutionary activity. It is as important to learn from these texts Lenin's *style* of writing as much as what Lenin is saying.

BOOKS

Lenin wrote hundreds of books and pamphlets, delivered thousands of speeches and reports over the course of his life. His collected works—in Russian—comprise 54 volumes—each volume at around 650 pages. In English, this work appeared in 45 volumes from Progress Publishers in Moscow. To make Lenin's work accessible, Progress Publishers and other publishing houses produced smaller, cheaper editions of some of Lenin's most important texts—*What Is To Be Done?* (1902), *Imperialism* (1916) and *State and Revolution* (1917). For ease of study, Progress Publishers released a three-volume set of Lenin's writings and speeches in 1963. In 1968, Progress Publishers published a selection from Lenin in one volume. With the collapse of the Soviet Union in 1991, Progress Publishers went out of business and these books vanished from the shelves of bookstores and—increasingly—of militants.

LeftWord Books has taken it in hand to produce reasonably priced editions of Marxist classics. We have already published Lenin's *Imperialism* (2000, with an introduction by Prabhat Patnaik) as well as a volume of Lenin's writings and speeches from 1917 entitled *Revolution!* (2017, with an introduction by Prakash Karat). We have now produced a selected volume of Lenin's writings. This is a formidable task. The 1968 edition from Progress Publishers ran for almost 800 pages. A book that size would not only be enormous but also expensive. It would undermine the purpose of such a book, namely to get it into the hands of those who want to study Lenin's writings and to understand the dilemmas that he faced in his time. It has taken a great deal of effort to produce this selection. There is no way to be perfectly happy with what has been chosen and what has been left out. If you have suggestions to improve this volume for our next printing, please write to vijay@leftword.com.

LENINISM AND THE LIBERATION OF OPPRESSED PEOPLES

Ho Chi Minh

On April 22, 1870, in old despotic Russia, there was born the future leader and talented teacher of the toiling masses and oppressed people throughout the world—Vladimir Ilyich Lenin.

At the end of the nineteenth and the beginning of the twentieth century, capitalism reached its highest and ultimate development—imperialism—and ushered in the era of proletarian revolution. The man who skilfully continued Marx's and Engels's great work in the new historical conditions was V.I. Lenin.

Struggling uncompromisingly with the reformists and all kinds of distortionists of Marxism, Lenin brought scientific socialism to a new stage. He enriched Marxism, the great ideological weapon of the proletariat, and greatly contributed to the formulation of the theory of proletarian dictatorship. He developed the Marxist principle on the worker-peasant alliance, the national and colonial question, proletarian internationalism, the building and strengthening of a new type of proletarian party, which is the only organisation capable of leading the multiform struggle of the working class and enslaved peoples. Lenin established a new theory of socialist revolution and demonstrated the possibilities of the triumph of socialism in a single country.

Lenin helped the working people, who were suffering from imperialist oppression, to realise in a more comprehensive manner the law of social development, the requirements and objective conditions of the political struggle in every stage of the proletarian revolution, and the whole liberation movement. He acquainted the oppressed masses with the intricate and complex developments of our times. He gave them the miraculous weapon to fight for their emancipation—the theory and tactics of Bolshevism.

The Russian Communist Party founded by Lenin set a bright example to the world's people. Under the clear-sighted leadership of the great Lenin, the talented strategist and tactician, the Communist Party led the Russian proletariat to seize power and establish the first state of the working masses; the founding of this state ushered in a new era in the history of mankind. In the eyes of the peoples loving peace and democracy, the Soviet Union is an unshakeable bulwark of independence and freedom. After World War II, the mighty camp of peace, democracy, and socialism headed by the Soviet Union took shape, in opposition to imperialism.

Lenin's popularity and doctrine are closely linked to all the successes of the camp of peace and democracy which stretches from the Elbe River to the Pacific Ocean. And from the arctic pole to the tropics. This is why all the oppressed and unfortunate people regard Lenin's banner, which is now being held aloft by the Communists of all countries, as a symbol of faith and a torchlight of hope.

The heroic struggle waged by the Soviet people to build Communism is now encouraging all the peoples and showing them the way to attain a living worthy of man.

The consistent peace policy of the Soviet Government, clearly embodied in the decree signed by Lenin and promulgated immediately after the triumph of the socialist revolution, is now stimulating the broad masses of people to struggle for the defence and strengthening of peace against the warmongers headed by U.S. imperialists.

The principles laid down by Lenin on the people's right to self-determination, peaceful coexistence, noninterference into the internal affairs of other countries—equality and relations beneficial to the parties concerned, principles which are the bases of the Soviet Union's foreign policy—are now showing the of colonial and dependent countries the path of struggle for national reunification and independence.

For the Asian peoples as well as for the peoples throughout the world who are fighting for peace, independence, democracy, and socialism, Leninism is like the sun which brings with it a cheerful life. Lenin always attached great importance to the movement for national liberation waged by the Asian peoples, and regarded it as part and parcel of the struggle put up by the toiling masses throughout the world against the imperialist oppressors. Lenin made it clear that the awakening of Asia and the first struggle waged by the advanced proletariat in Europe to seize power marked a new era in world history, an era which began with the twentieth century. In 1913, V.I. Lenin wrote: "The whole of Europe takes the leading place; the entire bourgeoisie in Europe is colluding with all the reactionary forces and medieval forces in China.

"But all young Asia, that is, hundreds of millions of toiling masses in Asia, has the proletariat of all civilised countries as a firm ally. No force in the world is able to check the victory of the proletariat in the liberation of the European and Asian peoples."

Today, in the midst of the twentieth century, the "young Asia" referred to by Lenin is precisely the People's Republic of China, the People's Republic of Mongolia, the People's Democratic Republic of Korea, and the Democratic Republic of Viet-Nam. In other regions of Asia, similar young forces are rising to struggle for national liberation. These scientific previsions of the great revolutionary strategist have been substantiated so swiftly that the imperialist camp becomes anxious and fearful!

If, under the leadership of the Marxist-Leninist parties, the enslaved peoples of Asia have recorded practical successes, it is because they have followed Lenin's great teachings.

In his appeal to the revolutionaries in the East, Lenin wrote: "You have before you a task which was unknown to the Communists in the world: relying on the theory and common practice of Communism and applying them to specific conditions in which do not exist in Europe, you must know how to use them in the conditions in which the peasants are the basic masses and the task is not to struggle against capitalism but against medieval vestiges."

This is an instruction most valuable for a country like ours, in which 90 per cent of the population live on agriculture, and a great deal of the vestiges of rotten feudalism and mandarinate still exists.

Under the leadership of the glorious Communist Party of China and of comrade Mao Tse-tung, its clear-sighted leader, the victory of the great Revolution in China was the triumph of Leninist thinking. It is precisely for this reason that comrade Mao Tse-tung said that the gun report of the October Revolution has brought Marxism-Leninism to China, and 600 million people are once and for all freed from the grip of imperialism.

Applying Leninism to internationalism, the Soviet Union, where socialism has triumphed, has constantly given great moral assistance to the national liberation movement in colonial and dependent countries. Particularly with her consistent peace policy and due to her great prestige all over the world, the Soviet Union has greatly helped the Korean and Vietnamese peoples to defend their fatherlands against the danger wrought by the U.S. imperialists and their allies. The diplomatic activities of the Soviet Union were a deciding factor in bringing the wars in Korea and Viet-Nam to an end.

Educated in the spirit of proletarian internationalism, the Vietnamese people highly appreciate the moral support of the peoples throughout the world, including the French toiling people who have been fighting to put an end to the war in Indochina.

* * *

Lenin bequeathed to us, as to all the Communist and workers' parties, an invaluable treasure which was his ideology: organisational principles, theory, and tactics of a revolutionary party. Leninism is a powerful ideological force which guides our Party and makes it possible to become the highest organisation of the toiling masses and the embodiment of the intelligence, dignity, and conscience of our people.

Under the banner of Leninism, the Viet-Nam Workers' Party has won the confidence of our people and is considered as their vanguard party. Our Party has known how to make use of the potentialities and creative initiative of our people, who never resigned themselves to the yoke of slavery and colonialism.

Lenin embodied the unity of mind within the Party, the solidarity of its ranks, the respect of revolutionary discipline, the unshakeable faith in the great cause of Communism and firm confidence in the final victory. All this is now an encouragement for the Viet-Nam Workers' Party, which has daily and hourly applied the principle of criticism and self-criticism and regarded it as the miraculous method to correct mistakes and shortcomings and to struggle against the manifestations of subjectivism and complacency. Our Party has no other interests than those of our people and our Fatherland; therefore, it attaches great importance to raising the level of its work. While doing its utmost to fulfill its tasks, our Party has constantly studied Leninism in order to raise its combativeness, political dynamism, the unity in organisation, and the ideological level of the Party members.

Our people and Party members were steeled in the flame of the long and hard struggle for national salvation and suffered untold hardship and suffering. For over eight years, our people and Party waged a historic struggle which ended victoriously in favour of the Vietnamese people and in the reestablishment of peace in Indochina. The Geneva Agreement demonstrated that the struggle for national liberation waged by the Vietnamese people and the brother peoples of Laos and Cambodia and their lofty sacrifice and heroism have been internationally recognised.

Today, while peace has been restored, we are continuing to fight for the correct implementation of the Geneva Agreement. According to figures already checked, we have recently been able to affirm that the other side has violated the Agreement 2,114 times, including 467 times in South Viet-Nam. Here are some shocking figures: 806 dead, 3,501 wounded, and 12, 741 persons arrested groundlessly.

Last year, in September, the Viet-Nam Workers' Party passed many resolutions on our people's action aimed at strictly implementing the

Geneva Agreement and opposing all manoeuvres to sabotage it. Our main tasks are: to consolidate peace, complete land reform, work with might and main in order to improve our economic life, stabilise our livelihood in every respect in the territory north of the 17th parallel, and continue the political struggle waged by the entire people. We have put forth the following slogans for our struggle: to consolidate peace, achieve national reunification, gain complete independence, and popularise democracy throughout the country.

Today we are struggling to carry through these fundamental tasks. At the same time, we cannot ignore that, after the conferences held by the imperialists in Manila and Bangkok,[1] a new situation has arisen in Asia. Today the United States has openly intervened in Indochina's affairs and has carried out many more manoeuvres to torpedo the Geneva Agreement.

For the realisation of their goal, the imperialists and their henchmen of all kinds are nurturing the dark scheme of permanently dividing our country, placing South Viet-Nam under their sway, checking all democratic forces, and sabotaging the 1956 general elections.

In these conditions, our struggle shifts now from the stage of armistice to that of political struggle to check the enemy's plot to rekindle war and to achieve national reunification by nationwide elections scheduled for July 1956.

Peace, reunification, national independence, and democracy are problems which are closely linked together. If there is no consolidation of peace, there is no possibility of reunifying Viet-Nam through general elections. Inversely, if there is no national reunification by means of general elections, there is no possibility of establishing a firm basis for peace.

The recent developments and the examination of the political situation enable our Party to see clearly that the struggle for peace, independence, and democracy waged by the Vietnamese people will encounter a lot of difficulties. However, our Party is firmly confident in the final victory.

[1] At a conference in Manila in September 1954 in the wake of the D.R.V.N.'s victory over France, the United States, Great Britain, France, Australia, New Zealand, the Philippines, Thailand, and Pakistan established the Southeast Asia Treaty Organization (SEATO). This political and military alliance, designed to provide protection specifically for Laos, Cambodia, and South Viet-Nam, has thus far not been brought into the Viet-Nam conflict. In recent years, France and Pakistan have not been active in the organization.—*Ed.*

From the most powerful Leninist doctrine, we draw a great strength to fulfill our sacred task of securing peace, reunification, independence, and democracy and to win victory for socialism.

Part I

Marxism

THE HISTORICAL DESTINY OF THE DOCTRINE OF KARL MARX (1913)

The chief thing in the doctrine of Marx is that it brings out the historic role of the proletariat as the builder of socialist society. Has the course of events all over the world confirmed this doctrine since it was expounded by Marx?

Marx first advanced it in 1844. The *Communist Manifesto* of Marx and Engels, published in 1848, gave an integral and systematic exposition of this doctrine, an exposition which has remained the best to this day. Since then world history has clearly been divided into three main periods: (1) from the revolution of 1848 to the Paris Commune (1871); (2) from the Paris Commune to the Russian revolution (1905); (3) since the Russian revolution.

Let us see what has been the destiny of Marx's doctrine in each of these periods.

I

At the beginning of the first period Marx's doctrine by no means dominated. It was only one of the very numerous groups or trends of socialism. The forms of socialism that did dominate were in the main akin to our Narodism: incomprehension of the materialist basis of historical movement, inability to single out the role and significance of each class in capitalist society, concealment of the bourgeois nature of democratic reforms under diverse, quasi-socialist phrases about the "people", "justice", "right", and so on.

The revolution of 1848 struck a deadly blow at all these vociferous, motley and ostentatious forms of *pre*-Marxian socialism. In all countries, the revolution revealed the various classes of society *in action*. The shooting of the workers by the republican bourgeoisie in Paris in the June days of 1848 finally revealed that the proletariat *alone* was socialist by nature. The liberal bourgeoisie dreaded the independence of this class a hundred times more than it did any kind of reaction. The craven liberals grovelled before reaction. The peasantry were content with the abolition of the survivals of feudalism and joined the supporters of order, wavering but occasionally between *workers' democracy and bourgeois liberalism.*

All doctrines of *non*-class socialism and *non*-class politics proved to be sheer nonsense.

The Paris Commune (1871) completed this development of bourgeois changes; the republic, i.e., the form of political organisation in which class relations appear in their most unconcealed form, owed its consolidation solely to the heroism of the proletariat.

In all the other European countries, a more tangled and less complete development led to the same result—a bourgeois society that had taken definite shape. Towards the end of the first period (1848-71), a period of storms and revolutions, pre-Marxian socialism was *dead*. Independent *proletarian* parties came into being: the First International (1864-72) and the German Social-Democratic Party.

II

The second period (1872-1904) was distinguished from the first by its "peaceful" character, by the absence of revolutions. The West had finished with bourgeois revolutions. The East had not yet risen to them.

The West entered a phase of "peaceful" preparations for the changes to come. Socialist parties, basically proletarian, were formed everywhere, and learned to use bourgeois parliamentarism and to found their own daily press, their educational institutions, their trade unions and their co-operative societies. Marx's doctrine gained a complete victory and *began to spread*. The selection and mustering of the forces of the proletariat and its preparation for the coming battles made slow but steady progress.

The dialectics of history were such that the theoretical victory of Marxism compelled its enemies to *disguise themselves* as Marxists. Liberalism, rotten within, tried to revive itself in the form of socialist *opportunism*. They interpreted the period of preparing the forces for great battles as renunciation of these battles. Improvement of the conditions of the slaves to fight against wage slavery they took to mean the sale by the slaves of their right to liberty for a few pence. They cravenly preached "social peace" (i.e., peace with the slave-owners), renunciation of the class struggle, etc. They had very many adherents among socialist members of parliament, various officials of the working-class movement, and the "sympathising" intelligentsia.

III

However, the opportunists had scarcely congratulated themselves on "social peace" and on the non-necessity of storms under "democracy" when a new source of great world storms opened up in Asia. The Russian revolution was followed by revolutions in Turkey, Persia and China. It is in this era of storms and their "repercussions" in Europe that we are now living. No matter what the fate of the great Chinese republic, against which various "civilised" hyenas are now whetting their teeth, no power on earth can restore the old serfdom in Asia or wipe out the heroic democracy of the masses in the Asiatic and semi-Asiatic countries.

Certain people who were inattentive to the conditions for preparing and developing the mass struggle were driven to despair and to anarchism by the lengthy delays in the decisive struggle against capitalism in Europe. We can now see how short-sighted and faint-hearted this anarchist despair is.

The fact that Asia, with its population of eight hundred million, has been drawn into the struggle for these same European ideals should inspire us with optimism and not despair.

The Asiatic revolutions have again shown us the spinelessness and baseness of liberalism, the exceptional importance of the independence of the democratic masses, and the pronounced demarcation between the proletariat and the bourgeoisie of all kinds. After the experience both of Europe and Asia, anyone who speaks of *non*-class politics and *non*-class socialism, ought simply to be put in a cage and exhibited alongside the Australian kangaroo or something like that.

After Asia, Europe has also begun to stir, although not in the Asiatic way. The "peaceful" period of 1872-1904 has passed, never to return. The high cost of living and the tyranny of the trusts are leading to an unprecedented sharpening of the economic struggle, which has set into movement even the British workers who have been most corrupted by liberalism. We see a political crisis brewing even in the most "diehard", bourgeois-Junker country, Germany. The frenzied arming and the policy of imperialism are turning modern Europe into a "social peace" which is more like a gunpowder barrel. Meanwhile the decay of *all* the bourgeois parties and the maturing of the proletariat are making steady progress.

Since the appearance of Marxism, each of the three great periods of world history has brought Marxism new confirmation and new triumphs. But a still greater triumph awaits Marxism, as the doctrine of the proletariat, in the coming period of history.

THE THREE SOURCES AND THREE COMPONENT PARTS OF MARXISM (1913)

Throughout the civilised world the teachings of Marx evoke the utmost hostility and hatred of all bourgeois science (both official and liberal), which regards Marxism as a kind of "pernicious sect".[1] And no other attitude is to be expected, for there can be no "impartial" social science in a society based on class struggle. In one way or another, *all* official and liberal science *defends* wage-slavery, whereas Marxism has declared relentless war on that slavery. To expect science to be impartial in a wage-slave society is as foolishly naïve as to expect impartiality from manufacturers on the question of whether workers' wages ought not to be increased by decreasing the profits of capital.

But this is not all. The history of philosophy and the history of social science show with perfect clarity that there is nothing resembling "sectarianism" in Marxism, in the sense of its being a hidebound, petrified doctrine, a doctrine which arose *away from* the high road of the development of world civilisation. On the contrary, the genius of Marx consists precisely in his having furnished answers to questions already raised by the foremost minds of mankind. His doctrine emerged as the direct and immediate *continuation* of the teachings of the greatest representatives of philosophy, political economy and socialism.

The Marxist doctrine is omnipotent because it is true. It is compreh-

[1] This article was published in 1913 in *Prosveshcheniye* No. 3, dedicated to the Thirtieth Anniversary of Marx's death.

Prosveshcheniye (Enlightenment) was a Bolshevik social, political and literary monthly published legally in St. Petersburg from December 1911 onwards. Its inauguration was proposed by Lenin to replace the Bolshevik journal *Mysl* (Thought), a Moscow publication banned by the tsarist government. Lenin directed the work of the journal from abroad and wrote the following articles for it: "Fundamental Problems of the Election Campaign", "Results of the Election", "Critical Remarks on the National Question", "The Right of Nations to Self-Determination", and others.

The journal was suppressed by the tsarist government in June 1914, on the eve of the First World War. Publication was resumed in the autumn of 1917 but only one double number appeared; this number contained two articles by Lenin: "Can the Bolsheviks Retain State Power?" and "A Review of the Party Programme".

ensive and harmonious, and provides men with an integral world outlook irreconcilable with any form of superstition, reaction, or defence of bourgeois oppression. It is the legitimate successor to the best that man produced in the nineteenth century, as represented by German philosophy, English political economy and French socialism.

It is these three sources of Marxism, which are also its component parts that we shall outline in brief.

I

The philosophy of Marxism is *materialism*. Throughout the modern history of Europe, and especially at the end of the eighteenth century in France, where a resolute struggle was conducted against every kind of medieval rubbish, against serfdom in institutions and ideas, materialism has proved to be the only philosophy that is consistent, true to all the teachings of natural science and hostile to superstition, cant and so forth. The enemies of democracy have, therefore, always exerted all their efforts to "refute", undermine and defame materialism, and have advocated various forms of philosophical idealism, which always, in one way or another, amounts to the defence or support of religion.

Marx and Engels defended philosophical materialism in the most determined manner and repeatedly explained how profoundly erroneous is every deviation from this basis. Their views are most clearly and fully expounded in the works of Engels, *Ludwig Feuerbach* and *Anti-Dühring*, which, like the *Communist Manifesto*, are handbooks for every class-conscious worker.

But Marx did not stop at eighteenth-century materialism: he developed philosophy to a higher level. He enriched it with the achievements of German classical philosophy, especially of Hegel's system, which in its turn had led to the materialism of Feuerbach. The main achievement was *dialectics*, i.e., the doctrine of development in its fullest, deepest and most comprehensive form, the doctrine of the relativity of the human knowledge that provides us with a reflection of eternally developing matter. The latest discoveries of natural science—radium, electrons, the transmutation of elements—have been a remarkable confirmation of Marx's dialectical materialism despite the teachings of the bourgeois philosophers with their "new" reversions to old and decadent idealism.

Marx deepened and developed philosophical materialism to the full, and extended the cognition of nature to include the cognition of *human society*. His *historical materialism* was a great achievement in scientific thinking. The chaos and arbitrariness that had previously reigned in views on history and politics were replaced by a strikingly integral and harmonious scientific theory, which shows how, in consequence of the growth of productive forces, out of one system of social life another and higher system develops—how capitalism, for instance, grows out of feudalism.

Just as man's knowledge reflects nature (i.e., developing matter), which exists independently of him, so man's *social knowledge* (i.e., his various views and doctrines—philosophical, religious, political and so forth) reflects the *economic system* of society. Political institutions are a superstructure on the economic foundation. We see, for example, that the various political forms of the modern European states serve to strengthen the domination of the bourgeoisie over the proletariat.

Marx's philosophy is a consummate philosophical materialism which has provided mankind, and especially the working class, with powerful instruments of knowledge.

II

Having recognised that the economic system is the foundation on which the political superstructure is erected, Marx devoted his greatest attention to the study of this economic system. Marx's principal work, *Capital*, is devoted to a study of the economic system of modern, i.e., capitalist, society.

Classical political economy, before Marx, evolved in England, the most developed of the capitalist countries. Adam Smith and David Ricardo, by their investigations of the economic system, laid the foundations of the *labour theory of value*. Marx continued their work; he provided a proof of the theory and developed it consistently. He showed that the value of every commodity is determined by the quantity of socially necessary labour time spent on its production.

Where the bourgeois economists saw a relation between things (the exchange of one commodity for another) Marx revealed a *relation between people*. The exchange of commodities expresses the connection between individual producers through the market. *Money* signifies that the connection is becoming closer and closer, inseparably uniting the entire economic life of the individual producers into one whole. *Capital* signifies a further development of this connection: man's labour-power becomes a commodity. The wage-worker sells his labour-power to the owner of land, factories and instruments of labour. The worker spends one part of the day covering the cost of maintaining himself and his family (wages), while the other part of the day he works without remuneration, creating for the capitalist *surplus-value*, the source of profit, the source of the wealth of the capitalist class.

The doctrine of surplus-value is the corner-stone of Marx's economic theory.

Capital, created by the labour of the worker, crushes the worker, ruining small proprietors and creating an army of unemployed. In industry, the victory of large-scale production is immediately apparent, but the same phenomenon is also to be observed in agriculture, where the superiority of large-scale capitalist agriculture is enhanced, the use of machinery increases and the peasant economy, trapped by money-capital, declines and falls into ruin under the burden of its backward technique. The decline of small-scale production assumes different forms in agriculture, but the decline itself is an indisputable fact.

By destroying small-scale production, capital leads to an increase in productivity of labour and to the creation of a monopoly position for the associations of big capitalists. Production itself becomes more and more social—hundreds of thousands and millions of workers become bound together in a regular economic organism—but the product of this collective labour is appropriated by a handful of capitalists. Anarchy of production, crises, the furious chase after markets and the insecurity of existence of the mass of the population are intensified.

By increasing the dependence of the workers on capital, the capitalist system creates the great power of united labour.

Marx traced the development of capitalism from embryonic commodity economy, from simple exchange, to its highest forms, to large-scale production.

And the experience of all capitalist countries, old and new, year by year demonstrates clearly the truth of this Marxian doctrine to increasing numbers of workers.

Capitalism has triumphed all over the world, but this triumph is only the prelude to the triumph of labour over capital.

III

When feudalism was overthrown and "*free*" capitalist society appeared in the world, it at once became apparent that this freedom meant a new system of oppression and exploitation of the working people. Various socialist doctrines immediately emerged as a reflection of and protest against this oppression. Early socialism, however, was *utopian* socialism. It criticised capitalist society, it condemned and damned it, it dreamed of its destruction, it had visions of a better order and endeavoured to convince the rich of the immorality of exploitation.

But utopian socialism could not indicate the real solution. It could not explain the real nature of wage-slavery under capitalism, it could not reveal the laws of capitalist development, or show what *social force* is capable of becoming the creator of a new society.

Meanwhile, the stormy revolutions which everywhere in Europe, and especially in France, accompanied the fall of feudalism, of serfdom, more and more clearly revealed the *struggle of classes* as the basis and the driving force of all development.

Not a single victory of political freedom over the feudal class was won except against desperate resistance. Not a single capitalist country evolved on a more or less free and democratic basis except by a life-and-death struggle between the various classes of capitalist society.

The genius of Marx lies in his having been the first to deduce from this the lesson world history teaches and to apply that lesson consistently. The deduction he made is the doctrine of the *class struggle*.

People always have been the foolish victims of deception and self-deception in politics, and they always will be until they have learnt to seek out the *interests* of some class or other behind all moral, religious, political and social phrases, declarations and promises. Champions of reforms and improvements will always be fooled by the defenders of the old order until they realise that every old institution, however barbarous and rotten it may appear to be, is kept going by the forces of certain ruling classes. And there is *only one* way of smashing the resistance of those classes, and that is to find, in the very society which surrounds us, the forces which can—and, owing to their social position, *must*—constitute the power capable of sweeping away the old and creating the new, and to enlighten and organise those forces for the struggle.

Marx's philosophical materialism alone has shown the proletariat the way out of the spiritual slavery in which all oppressed classes have hitherto languished. Marx's economic theory alone has explained the true position of the proletariat in the general system of capitalism.

Independent organisations of the proletariat are multiplying all over the world, from America to Japan and from Sweden to South Africa. The proletariat is becoming enlightened and educated by waging its class struggle; it is ridding itself of the prejudices of bourgeois society; it is rallying its ranks ever more closely and is learning to gauge the measure of its successes; it is steeling its forces and is growing irresistibly.

MARXISM AND REVISIONISM (1908)

There is a well-known saying that if geometrical axioms affected human interests attempts would certainly be made to refute them. Theories of natural history which conflicted with the old prejudices of theology provoked, and still provoke, the most rabid opposition. No wonder, therefore, that the Marxian doctrine, which directly serves to enlighten and organise the advanced class in modern society, indicates the tasks facing this class and demonstrates the inevitable replacement (by virtue of economic development) of the present system by a new order—no wonder that this doctrine has had to fight for every step forward in the course of its life.

Needless to say, this applies to bourgeois science and philosophy, officially taught by official professors in order to befuddle the rising generation of the propertied classes and to "coach" it against internal and foreign enemies. This science will not even hear of Marxism, declaring that it has been refuted and annihilated. Marx is attacked with equal zest by young scholars who are making a career by refuting socialism, and by decrepit elders who are preserving the tradition of all kinds of outworn "systems". The progress of Marxism, the fact that its ideas are spreading and taking firm hold among the working class, inevitably increase the frequency and intensity of these bourgeois attacks on Marxism, which becomes stronger, more hardened and more vigorous every time it is "annihilated" by official science.

But even among doctrines connected with the struggle of the working class, and current mainly among the proletariat, Marxism by no means consolidated its position all at once. In the first half-century of its existence (from the 1840s on) Marxism was engaged in combating theories fundamentally hostile to it. In the early forties Marx and Engels settled accounts with the radical Young Hegelians whose viewpoint was that of philosophical idealism. At the end of the forties the struggle began in the field of economic doctrine, against Proudhonism. The fifties saw the completion of this struggle in criticism of the parties and doctrines which manifested themselves in the stormy year of 1848. In the sixties the struggle shifted from the field of general theory to one closer to the direct labour movement: the ejection of Bakuninism from the International. In the early seventies the stage in Germany was occupied for a short while by the Proudhonist Mühlberger, and in the late seventies by the positivist Dühring. But the influence of both on the proletariat was already absolutely insignificant. Marxism was already gaining an unquestionable victory over all other ideologies in the labour movement.

By the nineties this victory was in the main completed. Even in the Latin countries, where the traditions of Proudhonism held their ground longest of all, the workers' parties in effect built their programmes and their tactics on Marxist foundations. The revived international organisation of the labour movement—in the shape of periodical international congresses—from the outset, and almost without a struggle, adopted the Marxist standpoint in all essentials. But after Marxism had ousted all the more or less integral doctrines hostile to it, the tendencies expressed in those doctrines began to seek other channels. The forms and causes of the struggle changed, but the struggle continued. And the second half-century of the existence of Marxism began (in the nineties) with the struggle of a trend hostile to Marxism within Marxism itself.

Bernstein, a one-time orthodox Marxist, gave his name to this trend by coming forward with the most noise and with the most purposeful expression of amendments to Marx, revision of Marx, revisionism. Even in Russia where—owing to the economic backwardness of the country and the preponderance of a peasant population weighed down by the relics of serfdom—non-Marxist socialism has naturally held its ground longest of all, it is plainly passing into revisionism before our very eyes. Both in the agrarian question (the programme of the municipalisation of all land) and in general questions of programme and tactics, our Social-Narodniks are more and more substituting "amendments" to Marx for the moribund and obsolescent remnants of their old system, which in its own way was integral and fundamentally hostile to Marxism.

Pre-Marxist socialism has been defeated. It is continuing the struggle, no longer on its own independent ground, but on the general ground of Marxism, as revisionism. Let us, then, examine the ideological content of revisionism.

In the sphere of philosophy revisionism followed in the wake of bourgeois professorial "science". The professors went "back to Kant"—and revisionism dragged along after the neo-Kantians. The professors repeated the platitudes that priests have uttered a thousand times against philosophical materialism—and the revisionists, smiling indulgently, mumbled (word for word after the latest *Handbuch*) that materialism had been "refuted" long ago. The professors treated Hegel as a "dead dog",[1]

[1] Lenin quotes from K. Marx's afterword to the second edition of Volume One

and while themselves preaching idealism, only an idealism a thousand times more petty and banal than Hegel's, contemptuously shrugged their shoulders at dialectics—and the revisionists floundered after them into the swamp of philosophical vulgarisation of science, replacing "artful" (and revolutionary) dialectics by "simple" (and tranquil) "evolution". The professors earned their official salaries by adjusting both their idealist and their "critical" systems to the dominant medieval "philosophy" (i.e., to theology)—and the revisionists drew close to them, trying to make religion a "private affair", not in relation to the modern state, but in relation to the party of the advanced class.

What such "amendments" to Marx really meant in class terms need not be stated: it is self-evident. We shall simply note that the only Marxist in the international Social-Democratic movement to criticise the incredible platitudes of the revisionists from the standpoint of consistent dialectical materialism was Plekhanov. This must be stressed all the more emphatically since profoundly mistaken attempts are being made at the present time to smuggle in old and reactionary philosophical rubbish disguised as a criticism of Plekhanov's tactical opportunism.[2]

Passing to political economy, it must be noted first of all that in this sphere the "amendments" of the revisionists were much more comprehensive and circumstantial; attempts were made to influence the public by "new data on economic development". It was said that concentration and the ousting of small-scale production by large-scale production do not occur in agriculture at all, while they proceed very slowly in commerce and industry. It was said that crises had now become rarer and weaker, and that cartels and trusts would probably enable capital to eliminate them altogether. It was said that the "theory of collapse" to which capitalism is heading was unsound, owing to the tendency of class antagonisms to become milder and less acute. It was said, finally, that it would not be amiss to correct Marx's theory of value, too, in accordance with Böhm-Bawerk.[3]

of *Capital* (see K. Marx and F. Engels, *Selected Works*, Vol. I, Moscow, 1958, p. 456).

[2] See *Studies in the Philosophy of Marxism* by Bogdanov, Bazarov and others. This is not the place to discuss the book, and I must at present confine myself to stating that in the very near future I shall prove in a series of articles, or in a separate pamphlet, that everything I have said in the text about neo-Kantian revisionists essentially applies also to these "new" neo-Humist and neo-Berkeleyan revisionists.—*Au.* (See *Lenin Collected Works* [henceforth *LCW*], Vol. 14, 1977).

[3] *Böhm-Bawerk, E.*—an Austrian bourgeois economist.

The fight against the revisionists on these questions resulted in as fruitful a revival of the theoretical thought in international socialism as did Engels's controversy with Dühring twenty years earlier. The arguments of the revisionists were analysed with the help of facts and figures. It was proved that the revisionists were systematically painting a rose-coloured picture of modern small-scale production. The technical and commercial superiority of large-scale *production* over small-scale production not only in industry, but also in agriculture, is proved by irrefutable facts. But commodity production is far less developed in agriculture, and modern statisticians and economists are, as a rule, not very skillful in picking out the special branches (sometimes even the operations) in agriculture which indicate that agriculture is being progressively drawn into the process of *exchange* in world economy. Small-scale production maintains itself on the ruins of natural economy by constant worsening of diet, by chronic starvation, by lengthening of the working day, by deterioration in the quality and the care of cattle, in a word, by the very methods whereby handicraft production maintained itself against capitalist manufacture. Every advance in science and technology inevitably and relentlessly undermines the foundations of small-scale production in capitalist society; and it is the task of socialist political economy to investigate this process in all its forms, often complicated and intricate, and to demonstrate to the small producer the impossibility of his holding his own under capitalism, the hopelessness of peasant farming under capitalism, and the necessity for the peasant to adopt the standpoint of the proletarian. On this question the revisionists sinned, in the scientific sense, by superficial generalisations based on facts selected one-sidedly and without reference to the system of capitalism as a whole. From the political point of view, they sinned by the fact that they inevitably, whether they wanted to or not, invited or urged the peasant to adopt the attitude of a small proprietor (i.e., the attitude of the bourgeoisie) instead of urging him to adopt the point of view of the revolutionary proletarian.

The position of revisionism was even worse as regards the theory of crises and the theory of collapse. Only for a very short time could people, and then only the most short-sighted, think of refashioning the foundations of Marx's theory under the influence of a few years of industrial boom and prosperity. Realities very soon made it clear to the revisionists that crises were not a thing of the past: prosperity was followed by a crisis. The forms, the sequence, the picture of particular crises changed, but crises remained an inevitable component of the capitalist system. While uniting production, the cartels and trusts at the same time, and in a way that was obvious to all, aggravated the anarchy of production, the insecurity of existence of the proletariat and the oppression of capital, thereby intensifying class antagonisms to an unprecedented degree. That capitalism is heading for a break-down—in the sense both of individual political and economic crises and of the complete collapse of the entire capitalist system—has been made particularly clear, and on a particularly large scale, precisely by the new giant trusts. The recent financial crisis in America and the appalling increase of unemployment all over Europe, to say nothing of the impending industrial crisis to which many symptoms are pointing—all this has resulted in the recent "theories" of the revisionists having been forgotten by everybody, including, apparently, many of the revisionists themselves. But the lessons which this instability of the intellectuals had given the working class must not be forgotten.

As to the theory of value, it need only be said that apart from the vaguest of hints and sighs, *à la* Böhm-Bawerk, the revisionists have contributed absolutely nothing, and have therefore left no traces whatever on the development of scientific thought.

In the sphere of politics, revisionism did really try to revise the foundation of Marxism, namely, the doctrine of the class struggle. Political freedom, democracy and universal suffrage remove the ground for the class struggle—we were told—and render untrue the old proposition of the *Communist Manifesto* that the working men have no country. For, they said, since the "will of the majority" prevails in a democracy, one must neither regard the state as an organ of class rule, nor reject alliances with the progressive, social-reform bourgeoisie against the reactionaries.

It cannot be disputed that these arguments of the revisionists amounted to a fairly well-balanced system of views, namely, the old and well-known liberal-bourgeois views. The liberals have always said that bourgeois parliamentarism destroys classes and class divisions, since the right to vote and the right to participate in the government of the country are shared by all citizens without distinction. The whole history of Europe in the second half of the nineteenth century, and the whole history of the Russian revolution in the early twentieth, clearly show how absurd such views are. Economic distinctions are not mitigated but aggravated and intensified under the freedom of "democratic" capitalism. Parliamentarism does not eliminate, but lays bare the innate character even of the most democratic bourgeois republics as organs of class oppression. By helping to enlighten and to organise immeasurably wider masses of the population than those which previously took an active part in political events, parliamentarism does not make for the elimination of crises and political revolutions, but for the maximum intensification of civil war during such revolutions. The events in Paris in the spring of 1871 and the events in Russia in the winter of 1905 showed as clearly as could be how inevitably this intensification comes about. The French bourgeoisie without a moment's hesitation made a deal with the enemy of the whole nation, with the foreign army which had ruined its country, in order to crush the proletarian movement. Whoever does not understand the inevitable inner dialectics of parliamentarism and bourgeois democracy—which leads to an even sharper decision of the argument by mass violence than formerly—will never be able on the basis of this parliamentarism to conduct propaganda and agitation consistent in principle, really preparing the working-class masses for victorious participation in such "arguments". The experience of alliances, agreements and blocs with the social-reform liberals in the West and with the liberal reformists (Cadets) in the Russian revolution, has convincingly shown that these agreements only blunt the consciousness of the masses, that they do not enhance but weaken the actual significance of their struggle, by linking fighters with elements who are least capable of fighting and most vacillating and treacherous. Millerandism in France—the biggest experiment in applying revisionist political tactics on a wide, a really national scale—has provided a practical appraisal of revisionism that will never be forgotten by the proletariat all over the world.

A natural complement to the economic and political tendencies of revisionism was its attitude to the ultimate aim of the socialist movement. "The movement is everything, the ultimate aim is nothing"—this catch-phrase of Bernstein's expresses the substance of revisionism better than many long disquisitions. To determine its conduct from case to case, to adapt itself to the events of the day and to the chopping and changing of petty politics, to forget the primary interests of the proletariat and the basic features of the whole capitalist system, of all capitalist evolution, to sacrifice these primary interests for the real or assumed advantages of the moment—such is the policy of revisionism. And it patently follows from the very nature of this policy that it may assume an infinite variety of forms, and that every more or less "new" question, every more or less unexpected and unforeseen turn of events, even though it change the basic line of development only to an insignificant degree and only for the briefest period, will always inevitably give rise to one variety of revisionism or another.

The inevitability of revisionism is determined by its class roots in modern society. Revisionism is an international phenomenon. No thinking socialist who is in the least informed can have the slightest doubt that the relation between the orthodox and the Bernsteinians in Germany, the Guesdists and the Jaurèsists (and now particularly the Broussists) in France, the Social Democratic Federation and the Independent Labour Party in Great Britain, Brouckère and Vandervelde in Belgium, the Integralists and the Reformists in Italy, the Bolsheviks and the Mensheviks in Russia, is everywhere essentially similar, notwithstanding the immense variety of national conditions and historical factors in the present state of all these countries. In reality, the "division" within the present international socialist movement is now proceeding along the *same* lines in all the various countries of the world, which testifies to a tremendous advance compared with thirty or forty years ago, when heterogeneous trends in the various countries were struggling within the one international socialist movement. And that "revisionism from the left" which has taken shape in the Latin countries as "revolutionary syndicalism",[4] is also adapting itself to Marxism, "amending" it: Labriola in Italy and Lagardelle in France frequently appeal from Marx who is understood wrongly to Marx who is understood rightly.

We cannot stop here to analyse the ideological content of *this* revisionism, which as yet is far from having developed to the same extent as opportunist revisionism: it has not yet become international, has not yet stood the test of a single big practical battle with a socialist party in any single country. We confine ourselves therefore to that "revisionism from the right" which was described above. Wherein lies its inevitability in capitalist society? Why is it more profound than the differences of national peculiarities and of degrees of capitalist development? Because in every capitalist country, side by side with the proletariat, there are always broad strata of the petty bourgeoisie, small proprietors. Capitalism arose and is constantly arising out of small production. A number of new "middle strata" are inevitably brought into existence again and again by capitalism (appendages to the factory, work at home, small workshops scattered all over the country to meet the requirements of big industries, such as the bicycle and automobile industries, etc.). These new small producers are

[4] "*Revolutionary syndicalism*"—a petty-bourgeois semi-anarchist trend that made its appearance in the labour movement of a number of West-European countries at the close of the nineteenth century.

The syndicalists saw no need for the working class to engage in political struggle, they repudiated the leading role of the Party and the dictatorship of the proletariat. They believed that by organising a general strike of the workers the trade unions (in France—syndicats) could, without a revolution, overthrow capitalism and take over control of production.

just as inevitably being cast again into the ranks of the proletariat. It is quite natural that the petty-bourgeois world-outlook should again and again crop up in the ranks of the broad workers' parties. It is quite natural that this should be so and always will be so, right up to the changes of fortune that will take place in the proletarian revolution. For it would be a profound mistake to think that the "complete" proletarianisation of the majority of the population is essential for bringing about such a revolution. What we now frequently experience only in the domain of ideology, namely, disputes over theoretical amendments to Marx; what now crops up in practice only over individual side issues of the labour movement, as tactical differences with the revisionists and splits on this basis—is bound to be experienced by the working class on an incomparably larger scale when the proletarian revolution will sharpen all disputed issues, will focus all differences on points which are of the most immediate importance in determining the conduct of the masses, and will make it necessary in the heat of the fight to distinguish enemies from friends, and to cast out bad allies in order to deal decisive blows at the enemy.

The ideological struggle waged by revolutionary Marxism against revisionism at the end of the nineteenth century is but the prelude to the great revolutionary battles of the proletariat, which is marching forward to the complete victory of its cause despite all the waverings and weaknesses of the petty bourgeoisie.

Part II

Social Democracy

OUR PROGRAMME
(1899)

International Social-Democracy is at present in a state of ideological wavering. Hitherto the doctrines of Marx and Engels were considered to be the firm foundation of revolutionary theory, but voices are now being raised everywhere to proclaim these doctrines inadequate and obsolete. Whoever declares himself to be a Social-Democrat and intends to publish a Social-Democratic organ must define precisely his attitude to a question that is preoccupying the attention of the German Social-Democrats and not of them alone.

We take our stand entirely on the Marxist theoretical position: Marxism was the first to transform socialism from a utopia into a science, to lay a firm foundation for this science, and to indicate the path that must be followed in further developing and elaborating it in all its parts. It disclosed the nature of modern capitalist economy by explaining how the hire of the labourer, the purchase of labour-power, conceals the enslavement of millions of propertyless people by a handful of capitalists, the owners of the land, factories, mines, and so forth. It showed that all modern capitalist development displays the tendency of large-scale production to eliminate petty production and creates conditions that make a socialist system of society possible and necessary. It taught us how to discern, beneath the pall of rooted customs, political intrigues, abstruse laws, and intricate doctrines—the *class struggle*, the struggle between the propertied classes in all their variety and the propertyless mass, the *proletariat*, which is at the head of all the propertyless. It made clear the real task of a revolutionary socialist party: not to draw up plans for refashioning society, not to preach to the capitalists and their hangers-on about improving the lot of the workers, not to hatch conspiracies, *but to organise the class struggle of the proletariat and to lead this struggle, the ultimate aim of which is the conquest of political power by the proletariat and the organisation of a socialist society.*

And we now ask: Has anything new been introduced into this theory by its loud-voiced "renovators" who are raising so much noise in our day and have grouped themselves around the German socialist Bernstein? *Absolutely nothing.* Not by a single step have they advanced the science which Marx and Engels enjoined us to develop; they have not taught the proletariat any new methods of struggle; they have only retreated, borrowing fragments of backward theories and preaching to the proletariat, not the theory of struggle, but the theory of concession—concession to the most vicious enemies of the proletariat, the governments and bourgeois parties who never tire of seeking new means of baiting the socialists. Plekhanov, one of the founders and leaders of Russian Social-Democracy, was entirely right in ruthlessly criticising Bernstein's latest "critique"[1]; the views of Bernstein have now been rejected by the representatives of the German workers as well (at the Hannover Congress).[2]

We anticipate a flood of accusations for these words; the shouts will rise that we want to convert the socialist party into an order of "true believers" that persecutes "heretics" for deviations from "dogma", for every independent opinion, and so forth. We know about all these fashionable and trenchant phrases. Only there is not a grain of truth or sense in them. There can be no strong socialist party without a revolutionary theory which unites all socialists, from which they draw all their convictions, and which they apply in their methods of struggle and means of action. To defend such a theory, which to the best of your knowledge you consider to be true, against unfounded attacks and attempts to corrupt it is not to imply that you are an enemy of *all* criticism. We do not regard Marx's theory as something completed and inviolable; on the contrary, we are convinced that it has only laid the foundation stone of the science which socialists *must* develop in all directions if they wish to keep pace with life. We think that an *independent* elaboration of Marx's theory is especially essential for Russian socialists; for this theory provides only general *guiding* principles, which, *in particular*, are applied in England differently than in France, in France differently than in Germany, and in Germany differently than in Russia. We shall therefore gladly afford space in our paper for articles on theoretical questions and we invite all comrades openly to discuss controversial points.

What are the main questions that arise in the application to Russia of the programme common to all Social-Democrats? We have stated that the essence of this programme is to organise the class struggle of

[1] The reference is to Plekhanov's article, "Bernstein and Materialism", published in issue No. 44 of *Neue Zeit* (New Times), organ of the German Social-Democrats, in July 1898.

[2] The *Hannover Congress* of the German Social-Democrats was held in 1899 from September 27 to October 2 (October 9-14). In the discussion of the chief point on the agenda, "The Attack on the Fundamental Views and Tactics of the Party", the Congress voted against Bernstein's revisionist views, without, however, subjecting them to an extensive criticism.

the proletariat, and to lead this struggle, the ultimate aim of which is the conquest of political power by the proletariat and the establishment of a socialist society. The class struggle of the proletariat comprises the economic struggle (struggle against individual capitalists or against individual groups of capitalists for the improvement of the workers' condition) and the political struggle (struggle against the government for the broadening of the people's rights, i.e., for democracy, and for the broadening of the political power of the proletariat). Some Russian Social-Democrats (among them apparently those who direct *Rabochaya Mysl*) regard the economic struggle as incomparably the more important and almost go so far as to relegate the political struggle to the more or less distant future. This standpoint is utterly false. All Social-Democrats are agreed that it is necessary to organise the economic struggle of the working class, that it is necessary to carry on agitation among the workers on this basis, i.e., to help the workers in their day-to-day struggle against the employers, to draw their attention to every form and every case of oppression and in this way to make clear to them the necessity for combination. But to forget the political struggle for the economic would mean to depart from the basic principle of international Social-Democracy, it would mean to forget what the entire history of the labour movement teaches us. The confirmed adherents of the bourgeoisie and of the government which serves it have even made repeated attempts to organise purely economic unions of workers and to divert them in this way from "politics", from socialism. It is quite possible that the Russian Government, too, may undertake something of the kind, as it has always endeavoured to throw some paltry sops or, rather, sham sops, to the people, only to turn their thoughts away from the fact that they are oppressed and without rights. No economic struggle can bring the workers any lasting improvement, or can even be conducted on a large scale, unless the workers have the right freely to organise meetings and unions, to have their own newspapers, and to send their representatives to the national assemblies, as do the workers in Germany and all other European countries (with the exception of Turkey and Russia). But in order to win these rights it is necessary to wage a *political struggle.* In Russia, not only the workers, but all citizens are deprived of political rights. Russia is an absolute and unlimited monarchy. The tsar alone promulgates laws, appoints officials and controls them. For this reason, *it seems* as though in Russia the tsar and the tsarist government are independent of all classes and accord equal treatment to all. But *in reality* all officials are chosen exclusively from the proper tied class and all are subject to the influence of the big capitalists, who make the ministers dance to their tune and who achieve whatever they want. The Russian working class is burdened by a double yoke; it is robbed and plundered by the capitalists and the landlords, and to prevent it from fighting them, the police bind it hand and foot, gag it, and every attempt to defend the rights of the people is persecuted. Every strike against a capitalist results in the military and police being let loose on the workers. Every economic struggle necessarily becomes a political struggle, and Social-Democracy must indissolubly combine the one with the other into a *single class struggle of the proletariat.* The first and chief aim of such a struggle must be the conquest of political rights, *the conquest of political liberty.* If the workers of St. Petersburg alone, with a little help from the socialists, have rapidly succeeded in wringing a concession from the government—the adoption of the law on the reduction of the working day[3]—then the Russian working class as a whole, led by a single Russian Social-Democratic Labour Party, will be able, in persistent struggle, to win incomparably more important concessions.

The Russian working class is able to wage its economic and political struggle alone, even if no other class comes to its aid. But in the political struggle the workers do not stand alone. The people's complete lack of rights and the savage lawlessness of the bashi-bazouk officials rouse the indignation of all honest educated people who cannot reconcile themselves to the persecution of free thought and free speech; they rouse the indignation of the persecuted Poles, Finns, Jews, and Russian religious sects; they rouse the indignation of the small merchants, manufacturers, and peasants, who can nowhere find protection from the persecution of officials and police. All these groups of the population are incapable, separately, of carrying on a persistent political struggle. But when the working class raises the banner of this struggle, it will receive support from all sides. Russian Social-Democracy will place itself at the head of all fighters for the rights of the people, of all fighters for democracy, and it will prove invincible!

These are our fundamental views, and we shall develop them

[3] The law of June 2 (14), 1897, establishing an eleven-and-a-half-hour day for industrial enterprises and railway workshops. Prior to this the working day in Russia had not been regulated and was as long as fourteen or fifteen hours. The tsarist government was forced to issue the June 2 law because of pressure on the part of the working-class movement headed by the Leninist "League of Struggle for the Emancipation of the Working Class". Lenin made a detailed analysis and criticism of the law in a pamphlet entitled *The New Factory Law* (see *LCW*, Vol. 2, 1972, pp. 267-315).

systematically and from every aspect in our paper. We are convinced that in this way we shall tread the path which has been indicated by the Russian Social-Democratic Labour Party in its published *Manifesto*.

WHERE TO BEGIN?
(1901)

In recent years the question of "what is to be done" has confronted Russian Social-Democrats with particular insistence. It is not a question of what path we must choose (as was the case in the late eighties and early nineties), but of what practical steps we must take upon the known path and how they shall be taken.[1] It is a question of a system and plan of practical work. And it must be admitted that we have not yet solved this question of the character and the methods of struggle, fundamental for a party of practical activity, that it still gives rise to serious differences of opinion which reveal a deplorable ideological instability and vacillation. On the one hand, the "Economist" trend, far from being dead, is endeavouring to clip and narrow the work of political organisation and agitation. On the other, unprincipled eclecticism is again rearing its head, aping every new "trend", and is incapable of distinguishing immediate demands from the main tasks and permanent needs of the movement as a whole. This trend, as we know, has ensconced itself in *Rabocheye Dyelo*.[2] This journal's latest statement of "programme", a bombastic article under the bombastic title "A Historic Turn" ("*Listok*" *Rabochevo Dyela*, No. 6[3]), bears out with special emphasis the characterisation we have given. Only yesterday there was a flirtation with "Economism", a fury over the resolute condemnation of *Rabochaya Mysl*,[4] and Plekhanov's presentation of the

[1] *"Where To Begin"* was published in *Iskra* and reissued by local Social-Democratic organisations as a separate pamphlet. The Siberian Social-Democratic League printed 5,000 copies of the pamphlet and distributed it throughout Siberia. The pamphlet was also distributed in Samara, Tambov, Nizhni-Novgorod, and other Russian cities.

[2] *Rabocheye Dyelo* (The Workers' Cause)—a journal with "Economist" views, organ of the Union of Russian Social-Democrats Abroad. It appeared irregularly and was published in Geneva from April 1899 to February 1902 under the editorship of B.N. Krichevsky, A.S. Martynov, and V.P. Ivanshin. Altogether 12 numbers appeared in nine issues.

Lenin criticised the views of the *Rabocheye Dyelo* group in his *What Is To Be Done?* (see *LCW*, Vol. 5, 1977, pp. 347-529).

[3] "*Listok*" *Rabochevo Dyela* (*Rabocheye Dyelo* Supplement)—*of* which eight numbers were issued in Geneva, at irregular intervals, between June 1900 and July 1901.

[4] *Rabochaya Mysl* (Workers' Thought)—an "Economist" newspaper, organ of the Union of Russian Social-Democrats Abroad, published from October

question of the struggle against autocracy was being toned down. But today Liebknecht's words are being quoted: "If the circumstances change within twenty-four hours, then tactics must be changed within twenty-four hours." There is talk of a "strong fighting organisation for direct attack, for storming the autocracy; of "broad revolutionary political agitation among the masses" (how energetic we are now—both revolutionary and political!); of "ceaseless calls for street protest"; of "street demonstrations of a pronounced [*sic!*] political character"; and so on, and so forth.

We might perhaps declare ourselves happy at *Rabocheye Dyelo*'s quick grasp of the programme we put forward in the first issue of *Iskra*,[5]

1897 to December 1902. Altogether 16 issues appeared: numbers 3 to 11 and number 16 were published in Berlin, the remaining numbers in St. Petersburg. It was edited by K.M. Takhtarev and others.

Lenin characterised the paper's views as a Russian variety of international opportunism and criticised them in a number of his articles published in *Iskra* and in other works including *What Is To Be Done?*

[5] The reference is to the article "The Urgent Tasks of Our Movement", which was published as the leading article in *Iskra*, No. 1, December 1900 (see *LCW*, Vol. 4, 1977, pp. 366-71).

Iskra (The Spark)—the first All-Russian illegal Marxist newspaper, founded by Lenin in 1900. The foundation of a militant organ of revolutionary Marxism was the main task confronting Russian Social-Democrats at the time.

Since the publication of a revolutionary newspaper in Russia was impossible, owing to police persecution, Lenin, while still in exile in Siberia, worked out all the details of a plan to publish the paper abroad. When his term of exile ended in January 1900, be immediately began to put his plan into effect. In February, he conducted negotiations with Vera Zasulich, who had come illegally to St. Petersburg from abroad, on the participation of the Emancipation of Labour group in the publication of an All-Russian Marxist newspaper. The so-called Pskov Conference was held in April, with V.I. Lenin, L. Martov (Y.O. Tsederbaum), A.N. Potresov, S.I. Radchenko, and the "legal Marxists" (P.B. Struve and M.I. Tugan-Baranovsky) participating. The conference heard and discussed Lenin's draft editorial declaration on the programme and the aims of the All-Russian newspaper (*Iskra*) and the scientific and political magazine (*Zarya*). Lenin visited a number of Russian cities—St. Petersburg, Riga, Pskov, Nizhni-Novgorod, Ufa, and Samara—establishing contact with Social-Democratic groups and individual Social-Democrats and obtaining their support for *Iskra*. In August, when Lenin arrived in Switzerland, he and Potresov held a conference with the Emancipation of Labour group on the programme and the aims of the newspaper and the magazine, on possible contributors, on the composition of Editorial Board, and on the problem of residence. For an account of the founding of *Iskra* see the article "How the 'Spark' was Nearly Extinguished" (see *LCW*, Vol. 4, 1977, pp. 333-49).

calling for the formation of a strong well-organised party, whose aim is not only to win isolated concessions but to storm the fortress of the

---

The first issue of Lenin's *Iskra* was published in Leipzig in December 1900; the ensuing issues were published in Munich; from July 1902 it was published in London; and from the spring of 1903 in Geneva.

The Editorial Board consisted of V.I. Lenin, G.V. Plekhanov, L. Martov, P.B. Axelrod, A.N. Potresov, and V.I. Zasulich. The first secretary of the Editorial Board was I.G. Smidovich-Leman. From the spring of 1901 the post was taken over by N.K. Krupskaya, who was also in charge of all correspondence between *Iskra* and Russian Social-Democratic organisations. Lenin was actually Editor-in-Chief and the leading figure in *Iskra.* He published his articles on all important questions of Party organisation and the class struggle of the proletariat in Russia and dealt with the most important events in world affairs.

Iskra became, as Lenin had planned, a rallying centre for the Party forces, a centre for the training of leading Party workers. In a number of Russian cities (St. Petersburg, Moscow, Samara, and others) groups and committees of the Russian Social-Democratic Labour Party (R.S.D.L.P.) were organised along Lenin's *Iskra* line. *Iskra* organisations sprang up and worked under the direct leadership of Lenin's disciples and comrades-in-arms: N.E. Bauman, I.V. Babusbkin, S.I. Gusev, M.I. Kalinin, G.M. Krzhizhanovsky, and others. The newspaper played a decisive role in the struggle for the Marxist Party, in the defeat of the "Economists", and in the unification of the dispersed Social-Democratic study circles.

On the initiative and with the direct participation of Lenin, the Editorial Board drew up a draft programme of the Party (published in *Iskra*, No. 21) and prepared the Second Congress of the R.S.D.L.P., which was held in July and August 1903. By the time the Congress was convened the majority of the local Social-Democratic organisations in Russia had joined forces with *Iskra*, approved its programme, organisational plan, and tactical line, and accepted it as their leading organ. By a special resolution, which noted the exceptional role played by *Iskra* in the struggle to build the Party, the Congress adopted the newspaper as the central organ of the R.S.D.L.P. and approved an editorial board consisting of Lenin, Plekhanov, and Martov. Despite the decision of the Congress, Martov refused to participate, and Nos. 46 to 51 were edited by Lenin and Plekhanov. Later Plekhanov went over to the Menshevik position and demanded that all the old Menshevik editors, notwithstanding their rejection by the Congress, be placed on the Editorial Board. Lenin could not agree to this, and on October 19 (November 1, new style), 1903, he left the *Iskra* Editorial Board to strengthen his position in the Central Committee and from there to conduct a struggle against the Menshevik opportunists. Issue No. 52 of *Iskra* was edited by Plekhanov alone. On November 13 (26), 1903, Plekhanov, on his own initiative and in violation of the will of the Congress, co-opted all the old Menshevik editors on to the Editorial Board. Beginning with issue No. 52, the Mensheviks turned *Iskra* into their own, opportunist, organ.

autocracy itself; but the lack of any set point of view in these individuals can only dampen our happiness.

Rabocheye Dyelo, of course, mentions Liebknecht's name in vain. The tactics of agitation in relation to some special question, or the tactics with regard to some detail of party organisation may be changed in twenty-four hours; but only people devoid of all principle are capable of changing, in twenty-four hours, or, for that matter, in twenty-four months, their view on the necessity—in general, constantly, and absolutely—of an organisation of struggle and of political agitation among the masses. It is ridiculous to plead different circumstances and a change of periods: the building of a fighting organisation and the conduct of political agitation are essential under any "drab, peaceful" circumstances, in any period, no matter how marked by a "declining revolutionary spirit"; moreover, it is precisely in such periods and under such circumstances that work of this kind is particularly necessary, since it is too late to form the organisation in times of explosion and outbursts; the party must be in a state of readiness to launch activity at a moment's notice. "Change the tactics within twenty-four hours"! But in order to change tactics it is first necessary to have tactics; without a strong organisation skilled in waging political struggle under all circumstances and at all times, there can be no question of that systematic plan of action, illumined by firm principles and steadfastly carried out, which alone is worthy of the name of tactics. Let us, indeed, consider the matter; we are now being told that the "historic moment" has presented our Party with a "completely new" question—the question of terror. Yesterday the "completely new" question was political organisation and agitation; today it is terror. Is it not strange to hear people who have so grossly forgotten their principles holding forth on a radical change in tactics?

Fortunately, *Rabocheye Dyelo* is in error. The question of terror is not a new question at all; it will suffice to recall briefly the established views of Russian Social-Democracy on the subject.

In principle we have never rejected, and cannot reject, terror. Terror is one of the forms of military action that may be perfectly suitable and even essential at a definite juncture in the battle, given a definite state of the troops and the existence of definite conditions. But the important point is that terror, at the present time, is by no means suggested as an operation for the army in the field, an operation closely connected with and integrated into the entire system of struggle, but as an independent form of occasional attack unrelated to any army. Without a central body and with the weakness of local revolutionary organisations, this, in fact, is all that terror can be. We, therefore, declare emphatically that under the present conditions such a means of struggle is inopportune and unsuitable; that it diverts the most active fighters from their real task, the task which is most important from the standpoint of the interests of the movement as a whole; and that it disorganises the forces, not of the government, but of the revolution. We need but recall the recent events. With our own eyes we saw that the mass of workers and "common people" of the towns pressed forward in struggle, while the revolutionaries lacked a staff of leaders and organisers. Under such conditions, is there not the danger that, as the most energetic revolutionaries go over to terror, the fighting contingents, in whom alone it is possible to place serious reliance, will be weakened? Is there not the danger of rupturing the contact between the revolutionary organisations and the disunited masses of the discontented, the protesting, and the disposed to struggle, who are weak precisely because they are disunited? Yet it is this contact that is the sole guarantee of our success. Far be it from us to deny the significance of heroic individual blows, but it is our duty to sound a vigorous warning against becoming infatuated with terror, against taking it to be the chief and basic means of struggle, as so many people strongly incline to do at present. Terror can never be a regular military operation; at best it can only serve as one of the methods employed in a decisive assault. But can we *issue the call* for such a decisive assault at the present moment? *Rabocheye Dyelo* apparently thinks we can. At any rate, it exclaims: "Form assault columns!" But this, again, is more zeal than reason. The main body of our military forces consists of volunteers and insurgents. We possess only a few small units of regular troops, and these are not even mobilised; they are not connected with one another, nor have they been trained to form columns of any sort, let alone assault columns. In view of all this, it must be clear to anyone who is capable of appreciating the general conditions of our struggle and who is mindful of them at every "turn" in the historical course of events that at the present moment our slogan cannot be "To the assault", but has to be, "Lay siege to the enemy fortress". In other words, the immediate task of our Party is not to summon all available forces for the attack right now, but to call for the formation of a revolutionary organisation capable of uniting all forces and guiding the movement in actual practice and not in name alone, that is, an organisation ready at any time to support every protest and every outbreak and use it to build up and consolidate the fighting forces suitable for the decisive struggle.

The lesson of the February and March events[6] has been so impressive that no disagreement in principle with this conclusion is now likely to be encountered. What we need at the present moment, however, is not a solution of the problem in principle but a practical solution. We should not only be clear on the nature of the organisation that is needed and its precise purpose, but we must elaborate a definite *plan* for an organisation, so that its formation may be undertaken from all aspects. In view of the pressing importance of the question, we, on our part, take the liberty of submitting to the comrades a skeleton plan to be developed in greater detail in *a pamphlet now in preparation for print.*[7]

In our opinion, the starting-point of our activities, the first step towards creating the desired organisation, or, let us say, the main thread which, if followed, would enable us steadily to develop, deepen, and extend that organisation, should be the founding of an All-Russian political newspaper. A newspaper is what we most of all need; without it we cannot conduct that systematic, all-round propaganda and agitation, consistent in principle, which is the chief and permanent task of Social-Democracy in general and, in particular, the pressing task of the moment, when interest in politics and in questions of socialism has been aroused among the broadest strata of the population. Never has the need been

[6] This passage refers to the mass revolutionary actions of students and workers—political demonstrations, meetings, strikes—that took place in February and March 1901, in St. Petersburg, Moscow, Kiev, Kharkov, Kazan, Yaroslavl, Warsaw, Belostok, Tomsk, Odessa, and other cities in Russia.

The student movement of 1900-01, which began with academic demands, acquired the character of revolutionary action against the reactionary policy of the autocracy; it was supported by the advanced workers and it met with a response among all strata of Russian society. The direct cause of the demonstrations and strikes in February and March 1901, was the drafting of 183 Kiev University students into the army as a punitive act for their participation in a students' meeting (see *LCW*, Vol. 4, 1977, pp. 414-19). The government launched a furious attack on participants in the revolutionary actions; the police and the Cossacks dispersed demonstrations and assaulted the participants; hundreds of students were arrested and expelled from colleges and universities. On March 4 (17), 1901, the demonstration in the square in front of the Kazan Cathedral, in St. Petersburg, was dispersed with particular brutality. The February-March events were evidence of the revolutionary upsurge in Russia; the participation of workers in the movement under political slogans was of tremendous importance.

[7] The reference is to Lenin's work *What Is To Be Done? Burning Questions of Our Movement* (see *LCW*, Vol. 5, 1977, pp. 347-529).

felt so acutely as today for reinforcing dispersed agitation in the form of individual action, local leaflets, pamphlets, etc., by means of generalised and systematic agitation that can only be conducted with the aid of the periodical press. It may be said without exaggeration that the frequency and regularity with which a newspaper is printed (and distributed) can serve as a precise criterion of how well this cardinal and most essential sector of our militant activities is built up. Furthermore, our newspaper must be All-Russian. If we fail, and as long as we fail, to combine our efforts to influence the people and the government by means of the printed word, it will be utopian to think of combining other means, more complex, more difficult, but also more decisive, for exerting influence. Our movement suffers in the first place, ideologically, as well as in practical and organisational respects, from its state of fragmentation, from the almost complete immersion of the overwhelming majority of Social-Democrats in local work, which narrows their outlook, the scope of their activities, and their skill in the maintenance of secrecy and their preparedness. It is precisely in this state of fragmentation that one must look for the deepest roots of the instability and the waverings noted above. The *first* step towards eliminating this shortcoming, towards transforming diverse local movements into a single, All-Russian movement, must be the founding of an All-Russian newspaper. Lastly, what we need is definitely a *political* newspaper. Without a political organ, a political movement deserving that name is inconceivable in the Europe of today. Without such a newspaper we cannot possibly fulfill our task—that of concentrating all the elements of political discontent and protest, of vitalising thereby the revolutionary movement of the proletariat. We have taken the first step, we have aroused in the working class a passion for "economic", factory exposures; we must now take the next step, that of arousing in every section of the population that is at all politically conscious a passion for *political* exposure. We must not be discouraged by the fact that the voice of political exposure is today so feeble, timid, and infrequent. This is not because of a wholesale submission to police despotism, but because those who are able and ready to make exposures have no tribune from which to speak, no eager and encouraging audience, they do not see anywhere among the people that force to which it would be worthwhile directing their complaint against the "omnipotent" Russian Government. But today all this is rapidly changing. There is such a force—it is the revolutionary proletariat, which has demonstrated its readiness, not only to listen to and support the summons to political struggle, but boldly to engage in battle. We are now in a position to provide a tribune for the nationwide exposure of the tsarist government, and it is our duty to do this. That tribune must be a Social-Democratic newspaper. The Russian working class, as distinct from the other classes and strata of Russian society, displays a constant interest in political knowledge and manifests a constant and extensive demand (not only in periods of intensive unrest) for illegal literature. When such a mass demand is evident, when the training of experienced revolutionary leaders has already begun, and when the concentration of the working class makes it virtual master in the working-class districts of the big cities and in the factory settlements and communities, it is quite feasible for the proletariat to found a political newspaper. Through the proletariat the newspaper will reach the urban petty bourgeoisie, the rural handicraftsmen, and the peasants, thereby becoming a real people's political newspaper.

The role of a newspaper, however, is not limited solely to the dissemination of ideas, to political education, and to the enlistment of political allies. A newspaper is not only a collective propagandist and a collective agitator, it is also a collective organiser. In this last respect it may be likened to the scaffolding round a building under construction, which marks the contours of the structure and facilitates communication between the builders, enabling them to distribute the work and to view the common results achieved by their organised labour. With the aid of the newspaper, and through it, a permanent organisation will naturally lake shape that will engage, not only in local activities, but in regular general work, and will train its members to follow political events carefully, appraise their significance and their effect on the various strata of the population, and develop effective means for the revolutionary party to influence these events. The mere technical task of regularly supplying the newspaper with copy and of promoting regular distribution will necessitate a network of local agents of the united party, who will maintain constant contact with one another, know the general state of affairs, get accustomed to performing regularly their detailed functions in the All-Russian work, and test their strength in the organisation of various revolutionary actions. This network of agents[8] will form the skeleton of precisely the kind of organisation we need—one that is sufficiently large to embrace the whole country; sufficiently broad and many-sided to

[8] It will be understood, of course, that these agents could work successfully only in the closest contact with the local committees (groups, study circles) of our Party. In general, the entire plan we project can, of course, be implemented only with the most active support of the committees which have on repeated occasions attempted to unite the Party and which, we are sure, will achieve this unification—if not today, then tomorrow, if not in one way, then in another.—*Au.*

effect a strict and detailed division of labour; sufficiently well tempered to be able to conduct steadily *its own* work under any circumstances, at all "sudden turns", and in face of all contingencies; sufficiently flexible to be able, on the one hand, to avoid an open battle against an overwhelming enemy, when the enemy has concentrated all his forces at one spot, and yet, on the other, to take advantage of his unwieldiness and to attack him when and where he least expects it. Today we are faced with the relatively easy task of supporting student demonstrations in the streets of big cities; tomorrow we may, perhaps, have the more difficult task of supporting, for example, the unemployed movement in some particular area, and the day after to be at our posts in order to play a revolutionary part in a peasant uprising. Today we must take advantage of the tense political situation arising out of the government's campaign against the Zemstvo; tomorrow we may have to support popular indignation against some tsarist bashi-bazouk on the rampage and help, by means of boycott, indictment, demonstrations, etc., to make things so hot for him as to force him into open retreat. Such a degree of combat readiness can be developed only through the constant activity of regular troops. If we join forces to produce a common newspaper, this work will train and bring into the foreground, not only the most skilful propagandists, but the most capable organisers, the most talented political party leaders capable, at the right moment, of releasing the slogan for the decisive struggle and of taking the lead in that struggle.

In conclusion, a few words to avoid possible misunderstanding. We have spoken continuously of systematic, planned preparation, yet it is by no means our intention to imply that the autocracy can be overthrown only by a regular siege or by organised assault. Such a view would be absurd and doctrinaire. On the contrary, it is quite possible, and historically much more probable, that the autocracy will collapse under the impact of one of the spontaneous outbursts or unforeseen political complications which constantly threaten it from all sides. But no political party that wishes to avoid adventurous gambles can base its activities on the anticipation of such outbursts and complications. We must go our own way, and we must steadfastly carry on our regular work, and the less our reliance on the unexpected, the less the chance of our being caught unawares by any "historic turns".

WHAT IS TO BE DONE?
BURNING QUESTIONS OF OUR MOVEMENT
(1902)

In the previous chapter we pointed out how *universally* absorbed the educated youth of Russia was in the theories of Marxism in the middle of the nineties.[1] In the same period the strikes that followed the famous St Petersburg industrial war of 1896 assumed a similar general character. Their spread over the whole of Russia clearly showed the depth of the newly awakening popular movement, and if we are to speak of the "spontaneous element" then, of course, it is this strike movement which, first and foremost, must be regarded as spontaneous. But there is spontaneity and spontaneity. Strikes occurred in Russia in the seventies and sixties (and even in the first half of the nineteenth century), and they were accompanied by the "spontaneous" destruction of machinery, etc. Compared with these "revolts", the strikes of the nineties might even be described as "conscious", to such an extent do they mark the progress which the working-class movement made in that period. This shows that the "spontaneous element", in essence, represents nothing more nor less than consciousness in an *embryonic form*. Even the primitive revolts expressed the awakening of consciousness to a certain extent. The workers were losing their age-long faith in the permanence

[1] Lenin's work *What Is To Be Done?* was written at the end of 1901 and early in 1902. In "Where To Begin", published in *Iskra*, No. 4 (May 1901), Lenin said that the article represented "a skeleton plan to be developed in greater detail in a pamphlet now in preparation for print".

Lenin began the actual writing of the book in the autumn of 1901. In his "Preface to the Pamphlet Documents of the 'Unity' Conference", written in November 1901, Lenin said that the book was in preparation "to be published in the near future". In December Lenin published (in *Iskra*, No. 12) his article "A Talk with Defenders of Economism", which he later called a conspectus of *What Is To Be Done?* He wrote the Preface to the book in February 1902 and early in March the book was published by Dietz in Stuttgart. An announcement of its publication was printed in *Iskra*, No. 18, March 10, 1902.

In republishing the book in 1907 as part of the collection *Twelve Years*, Lenin omitted Section A of Chapter V, "Who Was Offended by the Article 'Where to Begin'", stating in the Preface that the book was being published with slight abridgements representing the omission solely of details of the organisational relationships and minor polemical remarks. Lenin added five footnotes to the new edition.

of the system which oppressed them and began. . . I shall not say to understand, but to sense the necessity for collective resistance, definitely abandoning their slavish submission to the authorities. But this was, nevertheless, more in the nature of outbursts of desperation and vengeance than of *struggle*. The strikes of the nineties revealed far greater flashes of consciousness; definite demands were advanced, the strike was carefully timed, known cases and instances in other places were discussed, etc. The revolts were simply the resistance of the oppressed, whereas the systematic strikes represented the class struggle in embryo, but only in embryo. Taken by themselves, these strikes were simply trade union struggles, not yet Social-Democratic struggles. They marked the awakening antagonisms between workers and employers; but the workers, were not, and could not be, conscious of the irreconcilable antagonism of their interests to the whole of the modern political and social system, i.e., theirs was not yet Social-Democratic consciousness. In this sense, the strikes of the nineties, despite the enormous progress they represented as compared with the "revolts", remained a purely spontaneous movement.

We have said that *there could not have been* Social-Democratic consciousness among the workers. It would have to be brought to them from without. The history of all countries shows that the working class, exclusively by its own effort, is able to develop only trade-union consciousness, i.e., the conviction that it is necessary to combine in unions, fight the employers, and strive to compel the government to pass necessary labour legislation, etc.[2] The theory of socialism, however, grew out of the philosophic, historical, and economic theories elaborated by educated representatives of the propertied classes, by intellectuals. By their social status the founders of modern scientific socialism, Marx and Engels, themselves belonged to the bourgeois intelligentsia. In the very same way, in Russia, the theoretical doctrine of Social-Democracy arose altogether independently of the spontaneous growth of the working-class movement; it arose as a natural and inevitable outcome of the development of thought among the revolutionary socialist intelligentsia. In the period under discussion, the middle nineties, this doctrine not only represented the completely formulated programme

[2] Trade-unionism does not exclude "politics" altogether, as some imagine. Trade unions have always conducted some political (but not Social-Democratic) agitation and struggle. We shall deal with the difference between trade-union politics and Social-Democratic politics in the next chapter.—*Au.*

of the Emancipation of Labour group, but had already won over to its side the majority of the revolutionary youth in Russia.

Hence, we had both the spontaneous awakening of the working masses, their awakening to conscious life and conscious struggle, and a revolutionary youth, armed with Social-Democratic theory and straining towards the workers. In this connection it is particularly important to state the oft-forgotten (and comparatively little-known) fact that, although the *early* Social-Democrats of that period *zealously carried on economic agitation* (being guided in this activity by the truly useful indications contained in the pamphlet *On Agitation*,[3] then still in manuscript), they did not regard this as their sole task. On the contrary, *from the very beginning* they set for Russian Social-Democracy the most far reaching historical tasks, in general, and the task of overthrowing the autocracy, in particular.

[. . .]

And so, we have become convinced that the fundamental error committed by the "new trend" in Russian Social-Democracy is its bowing to spontaneity and its failure to understand that the spontaneity of the masses demands a high degree of consciousness from us Social-Democrats. The greater the spontaneous upsurge of the masses and the more widespread the movement, the more rapid, incomparably so, the demand for greater consciousness in the theoretical, political, and organisational work of Social-Democracy.

The spontaneous upsurge of the masses in Russia proceeded (and continues) with such rapidity that the young Social-Democrats proved unprepared to meet these gigantic tasks. This unpreparedness is our common misfortune, the misfortune of *all* Russian Social-Democrats.

[3] The pamphlet *On Agitation* was written by A. Kremer (later an organiser of the Bund) and edited by Y.O. Tsederbaum (Martov) in Vilno in 1894; it was at first circulated in handwritten and hectographed copies, but at the end of 1897 it was printed in Geneva and supplied with a preface and a concluding piece by P.B. Axelrod. The pamphlet summarised the experiences gained in Social-Democratic work in Vilno and exerted a great influence on Russian Social-Democrats, since it called on them to reject narrow study-circle propaganda and to go over to mass agitation among the workers on issues of their everyday needs and demands. It exaggerated the role of the purely economic struggle, however, to the detriment of political agitation on issues of general democratic demands, and was the embryo of the future "Economism". P.B. Axelrod noted the one-sidedness of the "Vilno Economism" in his concluding piece to the Geneva edition; G.V. Plekhanov made a critical analysis of the pamphlet *On Agitation* in his *Once More on Socialism and the Political Struggle.*

The upsurge of the masses proceeded and spread with uninterrupted continuity; it not only continued in the places where it began, but spread to new localities and to new strata of the population (under the influence of the working-class movement, there was a renewed ferment among the student youth, among the intellectuals generally, and even among the peasantry).

[. . .]

Revolutionary Social-Democracy has always included the struggle for reforms as part of its activities. But it utilises "economic" agitation for the purpose of presenting to the government, not only demands for all sorts of measures, but also (and primarily) the demand that it cease to be an autocratic government. Moreover, it considers it its duty to present this demand to the government on the basis, not of the economic struggle *alone*, but of all manifestations in general of public and political life. In a word, it subordinates the struggle for reforms, as the part to the whole, to the revolutionary struggle for freedom and for socialism.

[. . .]

[T]he propagandist, dealing with, say, the question of unemployment, must explain the capitalistic nature of crises, the cause of their inevitability in modern society, the necessity for the transformation of this society into a socialist society, etc. In a word, he must present "many ideas", so many, indeed, that they will be understood as an integral whole only by a (comparatively) few persons. The agitator, however, speaking on the same subject, will take as an illustration a fact that is most glaring and most widely known to his audience, say, the death of an unemployed worker's family from starvation, the growing impoverishment, etc., and, utilising this fact, known to all, will direct his efforts to presenting *a single idea* to the "masses", e.g., the senselessness of the contradiction between the increase of wealth and the increase of poverty; he will strive *to rouse* discontent and indignation among the masses against this crying injustice, leaving a more complete explanation of this contradiction to the propagandist. Consequently, the propagandist operates chiefly by means of the *printed* word; the agitator by means of the *spoken* word. The propagandist requires qualities different from those of the agitator. Kautsky and Lafargue, for example, we term propagandists; Bebel and Guesde we term agitators.

[. . .]

In reality, it is possible to "raise the activity of the working masses" *only* when this activity *is not restricted* to "political agitation on an economic basis". A basic condition for the necessary expansion of political agitation is the organisation of *comprehensive* political exposure. *In no way* except by means of such exposures can the masses be trained in political consciousness and revolutionary activity. Hence, activity of this kind is one of the most important functions of international Social-Democracy as a whole, for even political freedom does not in any way eliminate exposures; it merely shifts somewhat their sphere of direction. Thus, the German party is especially strengthening its positions and spreading its influence, thanks particularly to the untiring energy with which it is conducting its campaign of political exposure. Working-class consciousness cannot be genuine political consciousness unless the workers are trained to respond to *all* cases of tyranny, oppression, violence, and abuse, no matter *what class* is affected—unless they are trained, moreover, to respond from a Social-Democratic point of view and no other. The consciousness of the working masses cannot be genuine class-consciousness, unless the workers learn, from concrete, and above all from topical, political facts and events to observe *every* other social class in *all* the manifestations of its intellectual, ethical, and political life; unless they learn to apply in practice the materialist analysis and the materialist estimate of *all* aspects of the life and activity of *all* classes, strata, and groups of the population. Those who concentrate the attention, observation, and consciousness of the working class exclusively, or even mainly, upon itself alone are not Social-Democrats; for the self-knowledge of the working class is indissolubly bound up, not solely with a fully clear theoretical understanding—or rather, not so much with the theoretical, as with the practical, understanding—of the relationships between *all* the various classes of modern society, acquired through the experience of political life. For this reason the conception of the economic struggle as the most widely applicable means of drawing the masses into the political movement, which our Economists preach, is so extremely harmful and reactionary in its practical significance. In order to become a Social-Democrat, the worker must have a clear picture in his mind of the economic nature and the social and political features of the landlord and the priest, the high state official and the peasant, the student and the vagabond; he must know their strong and weak points; he must grasp meaning of all the catchwords and sophisms by which each class and each stratum *camouflages* its selfish strivings and its real "inner workings"; he must understand what interests are reflected by certain institutions and certain laws and how they are reflected. But this "clear picture" cannot be obtained from any book. It can be obtained only from living examples and from exposures that follow close upon what is going on about us at a given moment; upon what is being discussed, in whispers perhaps, by each one in his own way; upon what finds expression in such and such events, in such and such statistics, in such and such court sentences, etc., etc. These comprehensive political exposures are an essential and *fundamental* condition for training the masses in revolutionary activity.

Why do the Russian workers still manifest little revolutionary activity in response to the brutal treatment of the people by the police, the persecution of religious sects, the flogging of peasants, the outrageous censorship, the torture of soldiers, the persecution of the most innocent cultural undertakings, etc.? Is it because the "economic struggle" does not "stimulate" them to this, because such activity does not "promise palpable results", because it produces little that is "positive"? To adopt such an opinion, we repeat, is merely to direct the charge where it does not belong, to blame the working masses for one's own philistinism (or Bernsteinism). We must blame ourselves, our lagging behind the mass movement, for still being unable to organise sufficiently wide, striking, and rapid exposures of all the shameful outrages. When we do that (and we must and can do it), the most backward worker will understand, *or will feel*, that the students and religious sects, the peasants and the authors are being abused and outraged by those same dark forces that are oppressing and crushing him at every step of his life. Feeling that, he himself will be filled with an irresistible desire to react, and he will know how to hoot the censors one day, on another day to demonstrate outside the house of a governor who has brutally suppressed a peasant uprising, on still another day to teach a lesson to the gendarmes in surplices who are doing the work of the Holy Inquisition, etc. As yet we have done very little, almost nothing, *to bring* before the working masses prompt exposures on all possible issues. Many of us as yet do not recognise this as our *bounden duty* but trail spontaneously in the wake of the "drab everyday struggle", in the narrow confines of factory life.

[. . .]

Class political consciousness can be brought to the workers *only from without*, that is, only from outside the economic struggle, from outside the sphere of relations between workers and employers. The sphere from which alone it is possible to obtain this knowledge is the sphere of relationships of *all* classes and strata to the state and the government, the sphere of the interrelations between *all* classes. For that reason, the reply to the question as to what must be done to bring political knowledge to the workers cannot be merely the answer with which, in the majority of cases, the practical workers, especially those inclined towards Economism, mostly content themselves, namely: "To go among the workers." To bring political knowledge to the *workers* the Social-Democrats must *go among all classes of the population*; they must dispatch units of their army *in all directions*.

[...]

Let us take the type of Social-Democratic study circle that has become most widespread in the past few years and examine its work. It has "contacts with the workers" and rests content with this, issuing leaflets in which abuses in the factories, the government's partiality towards the capitalists, and the tyranny of the police are strongly condemned. At workers' meetings the discussions never, or rarely ever, go beyond the limits of these subjects. Extremely rare are the lectures and discussions held on the history of the revolutionary movement, on questions of the government's home and foreign policy, on questions of the economic evolution of Russia and of Europe, on the position of the various classes in modern society, etc. As to systematically acquiring and extending contact with other classes of society, no one even dreams of that. In fact, the ideal leader, as the majority of the members of such circles picture him, is something far more in the nature of a trade-union secretary than a socialist political leader. For the secretary of any, say English, trade union always helps the workers to carry on the economic struggle, he helps them to expose factory abuses, explains the injustice of the laws and of measures that hamper the freedom to strike and to picket (i.e., to warn all and sundry that a strike is proceeding at a certain factory), explains the partiality of arbitration court judges who belong to the bourgeois classes, etc., etc. In a word, every trade-union secretary conducts and helps to conduct "the economic struggle against the employers and the government". It cannot be too strongly maintained that *this is still not* Social-Democracy, that the Social-Democrat's ideal should not be the trade-union secretary, but *the tribune of the people*, who is able to react to every manifestation of tyranny and oppression, no matter where it appears, no matter what stratum or class of the people it affects; who is able to generalise all these manifestations and produce a single picture of police violence and capitalist exploitation; who is able to take advantage of every event, however small, in order to set forth *before all* his socialist convictions and his democratic demands, in order to clarify for *all* and everyone the world-historic significance of the struggle for the emancipation of the proletariat.

[...]

For it is not enough to call ourselves the "vanguard", the advanced contingent; we must act in such a way that *all* the other contingents recognise and are obliged to admit that we are marching in the vanguard. And we ask the reader: Are the representatives of the other "contingents" such fools as to take our word for it when we say that we are the "vanguard"? Just picture to yourselves the following: a Social-Democrat comes to the "contingent" of Russian educated radicals, or liberal constitutionalists, and says, We are the vanguard; "the task confronting us now is, as far as possible, to lend the economic struggle itself a political character". The radical, or constitutionalist, if he is at all intelligent (and there are many intelligent men among Russian radicals and constitutionalists), would only smile at such a speech and would say (to himself, of course, for in the majority of cases he is an experienced diplomat): "Your 'vanguard' must be made up of simpletons. They do not even understand that it is our task, the task of the progressive representatives of bourgeois democracy to lend the workers' economic struggle *itself* a political character. Why, we too, like the West-European bourgeois, want to draw the workers into politics, *but only into trade-unionist, not into Social-Democratic politics*. Trade-unionist politics of the working class is precisely *bourgeois politics* of the working class, and this 'vanguard's' formulation of its task is the formulation of trade-unionist politics! Let them call themselves Social-Democrats to their heart's content, I am not a child to get excited over a label. But they must not fall under the influence of those pernicious orthodox doctrinaires, let them allow 'freedom of criticism' to those who unconsciously are driving Social-Democracy into trade-unionist channels."

[. . .]

But if "we" desire to be front-rank democrats, we must make it our concern *to direct* the thoughts of those who are dissatisfied only with conditions at the university, or in the Zemstvo, etc., to the idea that the entire political system is worthless. *We* must take upon ourselves the task of organising an all-round political struggle under the leadership of *our* Party in such a manner as to make it possible for all oppositional strata to render their fullest support to the struggle and to our Party. *We* must train our Social-Democratic practical workers to become political leaders, able to guide all the manifestations of this all-round struggle, able at the right time to "dictate a positive programme of action" for the aroused students, the discontented Zemstvo people, the incensed religious sects, the offended elementary school-teachers, etc., etc.

[. . .]

Iskra desires *to elevate* the trade-unionist politics of the working class (to which, through misconception, through lack of training, or through conviction, our practical workers frequently confine themselves) to the level of Social-Democratic politics. *Rabocheye Dyelo*, however, desires *to degrade* Social-Democratic politics to trade-unionist politics. Moreover, it assures the world that the two positions are "entirely compatible within the common cause". *O, sancta simplicitas!*

TWO TACTICS OF SOCIAL DEMOCRACY IN THE DEMOCRATIC REVOLUTION (1905)

The degree of Russia's economic development (an objective condition), and the degree of class-consciousness and organisation of the broad masses of the proletariat (a subjective condition inseparably bound up with the objective condition) make the immediate and complete emancipation of the working class impossible.[1] Only the most ignorant people can close their eyes to the bourgeois nature of the democratic revolution which is now taking place; only the most naïve optimists can forget how little as yet the masses of the workers are informed about the aims of socialism and the methods of achieving it. We are all convinced that the emancipation of the working classes must be won by the working classes themselves; a socialist revolution is out of the question unless the masses become class-conscious and organised, trained, and educated in an open class struggle against the entire bourgeoisie. Replying to the anarchists' objections that we are putting off the socialist revolution, we say: we are not putting it off, but are taking the first step towards it in the only possible way, along the only correct path, namely, the path of a democratic republic. Whoever wants to reach socialism by any other path than that of political democracy, will inevitably arrive at conclusions that are absurd and reactionary both in the economic and the political sense. If any workers ask us at the appropriate moment why we should not go ahead and carry out our maximum programme we shall answer

[1] *Two Tactics of Social-Democracy in the Democratic Revolution* was written by Lenin in Geneva, in June-July 1905. The book was published in late July 1905, in Geneva, by the Central Committee of the R.S.D.L.P. It was twice republished in Russia in the same year, once by the Central Committee of the R.S.D.L.P., and the second time by the Moscow Committee of the Party, this time in 10,000 copies.

The book was illegally distributed throughout the country—particularly in St. Petersburg, Moscow, Kazan, Tiflis and Baku. On February 19, 1907, it was banned by the St. Petersburg Press Department, and on December 22 of the same year the St. Petersburg Court issued an injunction for its destruction.

In 1907 Lenin had *Two Tactics* published in the miscellany *Twelve Years*, supplementing the book with new notes. The material prepared by Lenin for this book, his plans, précis, and other notes, were published in *Lenin Miscellany V*, pp. 315-20, and *XVI*, pp. 151-56.

by pointing out how far from socialism the masses of the democratically-minded people still are, how undeveloped class antagonisms still are, and how unorganised the proletarians still are. Organise hundreds of thousands of workers all over Russia; get the millions to sympathise with our programme! Try to do this without confining yourselves to high-sounding but hollow anarchist phrases—and you will see at once that achievement of this organisation and the spread of this socialist enlightenment depend on the fullest possible achievement of democratic transformations.

[. . .]

Let us return to the resolution on a provisional government. We have shown that new-Iskrist tactics does not push the revolution forward—the possibility of which they would like to ensure by their resolution—but pull it back. We have shown that it is precisely this tactics that *ties the hands* of Social-Democracy in the struggle against the inconsistent bourgeoisie and does not prevent its being dissolved in bourgeois democracy. The false premises of the resolution naturally lead to the following false conclusion: "Therefore, Social-Democracy must not set itself the aim of seizing or sharing power in the provisional government, but must remain the party of extreme revolutionary opposition." Consider the first half of this conclusion, which contains a statement of aims. Do the new-Iskrists declare that the revolution's decisive victory over tsarism is the aim of Social-Democratic activity? They do. They are unable correctly to formulate the conditions of a decisive victory, and lapse into the [liberal] *Osvobozhdeniye* formulation, but they do set themselves this aim. Further, do they associate a provisional government with insurrection? Yes, they do so directly by stating that a provisional government "will emerge from a victorious popular insurrection". Finally, do they set themselves the aim of guiding the insurrection? Yes, they do. Like Mr. Struve they evade the admission that an insurrection is an urgent necessity, but at the same time, unlike Mr. Struve, they say that "Social-Democracy strives to *subordinate* it (the insurrection) to its influence and *leadership* and to use it in the interests of the working class".

How nicely this hangs together, does it not? We set ourselves the *aim* of subordinating the insurrection of both the proletarian and *non-proletarian* masses to our influence and our leadership, and of using it in our interests. Hence, we set ourselves the aim of leading, in the insurrection, both the proletariat, and the revolutionary bourgeoisie and petty bourgeoisie ("the non-proletarian groups"), i.e., of "*sharing*" the leadership of the insurrection between the Social-Democracy and the revolutionary bourgeoisie. We set ourselves the aim of securing *victory* for the insurrection, which is to lead to the establishment of a provisional government ("which will emerge from a victorious popular insurrection"). *Therefore*... therefore we must not set ourselves the aim of seizing power or of sharing it in a provisional revolutionary government!!

[. . .]

The basic idea here is the one repeatedly formulated by *Vperyod*, which has stated that we must not be afraid (as Martynov is) of Social-Democracy's complete victory in a democratic revolution, i.e., of a revolutionary-democratic dictatorship of the proletariat and the peasantry, for such a victory will enable us to rouse Europe; after throwing off the yoke of the bourgeoisie, the socialist proletariat of Europe will in its turn help us to accomplish the socialist revolution. But see how the new-*Iskra* rendering impairs this idea. We shall not dwell on details; on the absurd assumption that power could "fall" into the hands of a class-conscious party which considers seizure of power harmful tactics; on the fact that in Europe the conditions for socialism have reached not a certain degree of maturity, but maturity in general; on the fact that our Party programme knows no socialist reforms, but only the socialist revolution. Let us take the principal and basic difference between *Vperyod*'s idea and the one presented in the resolution. *Vperyod* set the revolutionary proletariat of Russia an active task: winning the battle for democracy and using this victory to bring the revolution into Europe. The resolution fails to grasp this link between our "decisive victory" (not in the new-*Iskra* sense) and the revolution in Europe, and, therefore, it does not speak of the tasks of the proletariat or the prospects of the *latter*'s victory, but of one of the possibilities in general: "in the event of the revolution spreading. . . ." *Vperyod* pointedly and definitely indicated—and this was incorporated in the resolution of the Third Congress of the Russian Social-Democratic Labour Party—how "governmental power" can and must "be utilised" in the interests of the proletariat, bearing in mind what can be achieved immediately, at a given stage of social development, and what must first be achieved as a democratic prerequisite of the struggle for socialism. Here, too, the resolution lags hopelessly behind when it states: "will be able to prepare itself to utilise", but fails to say *how* it will be able, *how* it will prepare itself, and to utilise *for what purpose*. We have no doubt, for instance, that the new-Iskrists may be "able to prepare themselves to utilise" their leading position in the Party, but the point is that so far their experience of that utilisation, their preparation, does not hold out much hope of possibility becoming reality. . . .

Vperyod stated quite definitely wherein lies the real "possibility of retaining power"—namely, in the revolutionary-democratic dictatorship of the proletariat and the peasantry; in their joint mass strength, which is capable of outweighing all the forces of counter-revolution; in the inevitable concurrence of their interests in *democratic* reforms. Here, too, the resolution of the Conference gives us nothing positive; it merely evades the issue. Surely, the possibility of retaining power in Russia must be determined by the composition of the social forces in Russia herself, by the circumstances of the democratic revolution now taking place in our country. A victory of the proletariat in Europe (it is still quite a far cry from bringing the revolution into Europe to the victory of the proletariat) will give rise to a desperate counter-revolutionary struggle on the part of the Russian bourgeoisie—yet the resolution of the new-Iskrists does not say a word about this counter-revolutionary force whose significance was appraised in the resolution of the R.S.D.L.P.'s Third Congress. If, in our fight for a republic and democracy, we could not rely upon the peasantry as well as upon the proletariat, the prospect of our "retaining power" would be hopeless. But if it is not hopeless, if the "revolution's decisive victory over tsarism" opens up such a possibility, then we must indicate it, call actively for its transformation into reality, and issue practical slogans not only *for the contingency* of the revolution being brought into Europe, but also for the *purpose* of taking it there. The reference made by tail-ist Social-Democrats to the "limited historical scope of the Russian revolution" merely serves to cover up their limited understanding of the aims of this democratic revolution, and of the proletariat's leading role in it!

[. . .]

The proletariat must carry the democratic revolution to completion, allying to itself the mass of the peasantry in order to crush the autocracy's resistance by force and paralyse the bourgeoisie's instability. The proletariat must accomplish the socialist revolution, allying to itself the mass of the semi-proletarian elements of the population, so as to crush the bourgeoisie's resistance by force and paralyse the instability of the peasantry and the petty bourgeoisie.

[. . .]

The depth of the rift among present-day Social-Democrats on the question of the path to be chosen can at once be seen by comparing the

Caucasian resolution of the new-*Iskra* supporters with the resolution of the Third Congress of the Russian Social-Democratic Labour Party. The Congress resolution says: the bourgeoisie is inconsistent and will without fail try to deprive us of the gains of the revolution. Therefore, make more energetic preparations for the fight, comrades and workers! Arm yourselves, win the peasantry over to your side! We shall not, without a struggle, surrender our revolutionary gains to the self-seeking bourgeoisie. The resolution of the Caucasian new-*Iskra* supporters says: the bourgeoisie is inconsistent and may recoil from the revolution. Therefore, comrades and workers, please do not think of joining a provisional government, for, if you do, the bourgeoisie will certainly recoil, and the sweep of the revolution will thereby be diminished!

One side says: advance the revolution to its consummation despite resistance or passivity on the part of the inconsistent bourgeoisie.

The other side says: do not think of independently advancing the revolution to completion, for if you do, the inconsistent bourgeoisie will recoil from it.

Are these not two diametrically opposite paths?

[...]

In its social and economic essence, the democratic revolution in Russia is a bourgeois revolution. It is, however, not enough merely to repeat this correct Marxist proposition. It has to be properly understood and properly applied to political slogans. In general, all political liberty founded on present-day, i.e., capitalist, relations of production is bourgeois liberty. The demand for liberty expresses primarily the interests of the bourgeoisie. Its representatives were the first to raise this demand. Its supporters have everywhere used like masters the liberty they acquired, reducing it to moderate and meticulous bourgeois doses, combining it with the most subtle suppression of the revolutionary proletariat in peaceful times, and with savage suppression in times of storm.

But only rebel Narodniks, anarchists, and Economists could conclude therefrom that the struggle for liberty should be negated or disparaged. These intellectualist-philistine doctrines could be foisted on the proletariat only for a time and against its will. The proletariat has always realised instinctively that it needs political liberty, needs it more than anyone else, although the immediate effect of that liberty will be to strengthen and organise the bourgeoisie. It is not by evading the class struggle that the proletariat expects to find its salvation, but by developing it, by extending its scope, its consciousness, organisation, and resoluteness. Whoever disparages the tasks of the political struggle transforms the Social-Democrat from a tribune of the people into a trade union secretary. Whoever disparages the proletarian tasks in a democratic bourgeois revolution transforms the Social-Democrat from a leader of the people's revolution into a leader of a free labour union.

Yes, the *people*'s revolution. Social-Democracy has fought, and is quite rightly fighting, against the bourgeois-democratic abuse of the word "people". It demands that this word shall not be used to cover up failure to understand class antagonisms within the people. It insists categorically on the need for complete class independence for the party of the proletariat. However, it does not divide the "people" into "classes" so that the advanced class will become locked up within itself, will confine itself within narrow limits and emasculate its activity for fear that the economic rulers of the world will recoil; it does that so that the advanced class, which does not suffer from the half-heartedness, vacillation, and indecision of the intermediate classes, should fight with all the greater energy and enthusiasm for the cause of the whole people, at the head of the whole people.

[. . .]

Revolutions are the locomotive of history, said Marx.[2] Revolutions are festivals of the oppressed and the exploited. At no other time are the mass of the people in a position to come forward so actively as creators of a new social order, as at a time of revolution. At such times the people are capable of performing miracles, if judged by the limited, philistine yardstick of gradualist progress. But it is essential that leaders of the revolutionary parties, too, should advance their aims more comprehensively and boldly at such a time, so that their slogans shall always be in advance of the revolutionary initiative of the masses, serve as a beacon, reveal to them our democratic and socialist ideal in all its magnitude and splendour, and show them the shortest and most direct route to complete, absolute, and decisive victory.

[2] See K. Marx and F. Engels, *Selected Works*, Moscow, 1958, Vol. I, p. 217.

PARTY ORGANISATION AND PARTY LITERATURE (1905)

The new conditions for Social-Democratic work in Russia which have arisen since the October revolution have brought the question of party literature to the fore. The distinction between the illegal and the legal press, that melancholy heritage of the epoch of feudal autocratic Russia, is beginning to disappear. It is not yet dead, by a long way. The hypocritical government of our Prime Minister is still running amuck, so much so that *Izvestia Soveta Rabochikh Deputatov*[1] is printed "illegally"; but apart from bringing disgrace on the government, apart from striking further moral blows at it, nothing comes of the stupid attempts to "prohibit" that which the government is powerless to thwart.

So long as there was a distinction between the illegal and the legal press, the question of the party and non-party press was decided extremely simply and in an extremely false and abnormal way. The entire illegal press was a party press, being published by organisations and run by groups which in one way or another were linked with groups of practical party workers. The entire legal press was non-party—since parties were banned—but it "gravitated" towards one party or another. Unnatural alliances, strange "bed-fellows" and false cover-devices were inevitable. The forced reserve of those who wished to express party views merged with the immature thinking or mental cowardice of those who had not risen to these views and who were not, in effect, party people.

An accursed period of Aesopian language, literary bondage, slavish speech, and ideological serfdom! The proletariat has put an end to this foul atmosphere which stifled everything living and fresh in Russia. But so far the proletariat has won only half freedom for Russia.

The revolution is not yet completed. While tsarism is *no longer* strong enough to defeat the revolution, the revolution is *not yet* strong enough to defeat tsarism. And we are living in times when everywhere and in everything there operates this unnatural combination of open,

[1] *Izvestia Soveta Rabochikh Deputatov* (Bulletin of the Soviet of Workers' Deputies)—an official newspaper of the St. Petersburg Soviet of Workers' Deputies. It appeared from October 17 (30) to December 14 (27), 1905. Being in effect an information bulletin, it had no permanent staff and was printed by the workers themselves in the printing-works of various bourgeois papers. Altogether ten issues were brought out. Issue No. 11 was seized by the police while being printed.

forthright, direct and consistent party spirit with an underground, covert, "diplomatic" and dodgy "legality". This unnatural combination makes itself felt even in our newspaper: for all Mr. Guchkov's[2] witticisms about Social-Democratic tyranny forbidding the publication of moderate liberal-bourgeois newspapers, the fact remains that *Proletary*,[3] the

[2] *Guchkov, A.I.* (1862-1936)—a monarchist representative of the big commercial and industrial bourgeoisie.

[3] *Proletary* (The Proletarian)—an illegal Bolshevik weekly, Central Organ of the R.S.D.L.P., founded by decision of the Third Party Congress. On April 27 (May 10), 1905, a plenary meeting of the Central Committee of the Party appointed Lenin editor-in-chief of *Proletary*. The weekly appeared in Geneva from May 14 (27) to November 12 (25), 1905. Twenty-six issues were published in all. The weekly continued the line of the old, Leninist *Iskra*, and of the Bolshevik paper *Vperyod*.

Lenin contributed about 90 articles and short items to *Proletary*. His articles determined the political line of the weekly, its ideological content and Bolshevik course. Lenin did a tremendous amount of work as the leader and editor of the weekly. He edited the material to be published, lending it the utmost fidelity to principle, a Party spirit, and precision and clarity in discussing important theoretical problems and elucidating questions of the revolutionary movement.

The editorial board was constantly assisted by V.V. Vorovsky, A.V. Lunacharsky and M.S. Olminsky. N.K. Krupskaya, V.M. Velichkina and V.A. Karpinsky had a big share in the editorial work. The weekly was closely linked with the working-class movement in Russia. It carried articles and other items by workers directly engaged in the revolutionary movement. V.D. Bonch-Bruyevich, S.I. Gusev and A.I. Ulyanova-Yelizarova arranged for the collection of articles in Russia and their dispatch to Geneva. N.K. Krupskaya and L.A. Fotieva were in charge of the weekly's correspondence with Party organisations and readers in Russia.

Proletary was prompt to react to all major events in the Russian and international working-class movement. It fought relentlessly against the Mensheviks and other opportunist, revisionist elements.

The weekly did much to propagate the decisions of the Third Party Congress and played a prominent role in the organisational and ideological unification of the Bolsheviks. It was the only Russian Social-Democratic paper that consistently upheld revolutionary Marxism and dealt with all the principal issues of the revolution developing in Russia. By giving full information on the events of 1905, it roused the broad masses of the working people to fight for the victory of the revolution.

Proletary had great influence over the Social-Democratic organisations in Russia where some of Lenin's articles were reprinted from it by Bolshevik papers and circulated in leaflet form.

Proletary ceased to appear shortly after Lenin had left for Russia early in November 1905. Its last two issues (Nos. 25 and 26) were published under the editorship of V.V. Vorovsky. The several articles Lenin had written for

Central Organ of the Russian Social-Democratic Labour Party, still remains outside the locked doors of *autocratic*, police-ridden Russia.

Be that as it may, the half-way revolution compels all of us to set to work at once organising the whole thing on new lines. Today literature, even that published "legally", can be nine-tenths party literature. It must become party literature in contradistinction to bourgeois customs, to the profit-making, commercialised bourgeois press, to bourgeois literary careerism and individualism, "aristocratic anarchism" and drive for profit, the socialist proletariat must put forward the principle of *party literature*, must develop this principle and put it into practice as fully and completely as possible.

What is this principle of party literature? It is not simply that, for the socialist proletariat, literature cannot be a means of enriching individuals or groups: it cannot, in fact, be an individual undertaking, independent of the common cause of the proletariat. Down with non-partisan writers! Down with literary supermen! Literature must become *part* of the common cause of the proletariat, "a cog and a screw" of one single great Social-Democratic mechanism set in motion by the entire politically-conscious vanguard of the entire working class. Literature must become a component of organised, planned and integrated Social-Democratic Party work.

"All comparisons are lame," says a German proverb. So is my comparison of literature with a cog, of a living movement with a mechanism. And I daresay there will even be hysterical intellectuals to raise a howl about such a comparison, which degrades, deadens, "bureaucratises" the free battle of ideas, freedom of criticism, freedom of literary creation, etc., etc. Such outcries, in point of fact, would be nothing more than an expression of bourgeois-intellectual individualism. There is no question that literature is least of all subject to· mechanical adjustment or levelling, to the rule of the majority over the minority. There is no question, either, that in this field greater scope must undoubtedly be allowed for personal initiative, individual inclination, thought and fantasy, form and content. All this is undeniable; but all this simply shows that the literary side of the proletarian party cause cannot be mechanically identified with its other sides. This, however, does not in the least refute the proposition, alien and strange to the bourgeoisie and bourgeois democracy, that literature must by all means and necessarily become an element of Social-Democratic Party work, inseparably bound up with the other elements. Newspapers must become the organs of the various party organisations, and their writers

those issues appeared when he had left Geneva.

must by all means become members of these organisations. Publishing and distributing centres, bookshops and reading-rooms, libraries and similar establishments—must all be under party control. The organised socialist proletariat must keep an eye on all this work, supervise it in its entirety, and, from beginning to end, without any exception, infuse into it the life-stream of the living proletarian cause, thereby cutting the ground from under the old, semi-Oblomov,[4] semi-shopkeeper Russian principle: the writer does the writing, the reader does the reading.

We are not suggesting, of course, that this transformation of literary work, which has been defiled by the Asiatic censorship and the European bourgeoisie, can be accomplished all at once. Far be it from us to advocate any kind of standardised system, or a solution by means of a few decrees. Cut-and-dried schemes are least of all applicable here. What is needed is that the whole of our Party, and the entire politically-conscious Social-Democratic proletariat throughout Russia, should become aware of this new problem, specify it clearly and everywhere set about solving it. Emerging from the captivity of the feudal censorship, we have no desire to become, and shall not become, prisoners of bourgeois-shopkeeper literary relations. We want to establish, and we shall establish, a free press, free not simply from the police, but also from capital, from careerism, and what is more, free from bourgeois-anarchist individualism.

These last words may sound paradoxical, or an affront to the reader. What! some intellectual, an ardent champion of liberty, may shout. What, you want to impose collective control on such a delicate, individual matter as literary work! You want workmen to decide questions of science, philosophy, or aesthetics by a majority of votes! You deny the absolute freedom of absolutely individual ideological work!

Calm yourselves, gentlemen! First of all, we are discussing party literature and its subordination to party control. Everyone is free to write and say whatever he likes, without any restrictions. But every voluntary association (including the party) is also free to expel members who use the name of the party to advocate anti-party views. Freedom of speech and the press must be complete. But then freedom of association must be complete too. I am bound to accord you, in the name of free speech, the full right to shout, lie and write to your heart's content. But you are bound to grant me, in the name of freedom of association, the right to enter into, or withdraw from, association with people advocating this or

[4] *Oblomov*—a landlord, the chief character in a novel of the same name by the Russian writer I.A. Goncharov. Oblomov was the personification of routine, stagnation, and incapacity for action.

that view. The party is a voluntary association, which would inevitably break up, first ideologically and then physically, if it did not cleanse itself of people advocating anti-party views. And to define the border-line between party and anti-party there is the party programme, the party's resolutions on tactics and its rules and, lastly, the entire experience of international Social-Democracy, the voluntary international associations of the proletariat, which has constantly brought into its parties individual elements and trends not fully consistent, not completely Marxist and not altogether correct and which, on the other hand, has constantly conducted periodical "cleansings" of its ranks. So it will be with us too, supporters of bourgeois "freedom of criticism", *within* the Party. We are now becoming a mass party all at once, changing abruptly to an open organisation, and it is inevitable that we shall be joined by many who are inconsistent (from the Marxist standpoint), perhaps we shall be joined even by some Christian elements, and even by some mystics. We have sound stomachs and we are rock-like Marxists. We shall digest those inconsistent elements. Freedom of thought and freedom of criticism within the Party will never make us forget about the freedom of organising people into those voluntary associations known as parties.

Secondly, we must say to you bourgeois individualists that your talk about absolute freedom is sheer hypocrisy. There can be no real and effective "freedom" in a society based on the power of money, in a society in which the masses of working people live in poverty and the handful of rich live like parasites. Are you free in relation to your bourgeois publisher, Mr. Writer, in relation to your bourgeois public, which demands that you provide it with pornography in frames[5] and paintings, and prostitution as a "supplement" to "sacred" scenic art? This absolute freedom is a bourgeois or an anarchist phrase (since, as a world outlook, anarchism is bourgeois philosophy turned inside out). One cannot live in society and be free from society. The freedom of the bourgeois writer, artist or actress is simply masked (or hypocritically masked) dependence on the money-bag, on corruption, on prostitution.

And we socialists expose this hypocrisy and rip off the false labels, not in order to arrive at a non-class literature and art (that will be possible only in a socialist extra-class society), but to contrast this hypocritically free literature, which is in reality linked to the bourgeoisie, with a really free one that will be *openly* linked to the proletariat.

It will be a free literature, because the idea of socialism and sympathy

[5] There must be a misprint in the source, which says *ramkakh* (frames), while the context suggests *romanakh* (novels).

with the working people, and not greed or careerism, will bring ever new forces to its ranks. It will be a free literature, because it will serve, not some satiated heroine, not the bored "upper ten thousand" suffering from fatty degeneration, but the millions and tens of millions of working people—the flower of the country, its strength and its future. It will be a free literature, enriching the last word in the revolutionary thought of mankind with the experience and living work of the socialist proletariat, bringing about permanent interaction between the experience of the past (scientific socialism, the completion of the development of socialism from its primitive, utopian forms) and the experience of the present (the present struggle of the worker comrades).

To work, then, comrades! We are faced with a new and difficult task. But it is a noble and grateful one—to organise a broad, multiform and varied literature inseparably linked with the Social-Democratic working-class movement. All Social-Democratic literature must become Party literature. Every newspaper, journal, publishing house, etc., must immediately set about reorganising its work, leading up to a situation in which it will, in one form or another, be integrated into one Party organisation or another. Only then will "Social-Democratic" literature really become worthy of that name, only then will it be able to fulfill its duty and, even within the framework of bourgeois society, break out of bourgeois slavery and merge with the movement of the really advanced and thoroughly revolutionary class.

Part III

Imperialism

THE SOCIALIST REVOLUTION AND THE RIGHT OF NATIONS TO SELF-DETERMINATION (1916)

THESES

1. IMPERIALISM, SOCIALISM AND THE LIBERATION OF OPPRESSED NATIONS

Imperialism is the highest stage in the development of capitalism. In the foremost countries capital has outgrown the bounds of national states, has replaced competition by monopoly and has created all the objective conditions for the achievement of socialism. In Western Europe and in the United States, therefore, the revolutionary struggle of the proletariat for the overthrow of capitalist governments and the expropriation of the bourgeoisie is on the order of the day. Imperialism forces the masses into this struggle by sharpening class contradictions on a tremendous scale, by worsening the conditions of the masses both economically—trusts, high cost of living—and politically—the growth of militarism, more frequent wars, more powerful reaction, the intensification and expansion of national oppression and colonial plunder. Victorious socialism must necessarily establish a full democracy and, consequently, not only introduce full equality of nations but also realise the right of the oppressed nations to self-determination, i.e., the right to free political separation. Socialist parties which did not show by all their activity, both now, during the revolution, and after its victory, that they would liberate the enslaved nations and build up relations with them on the basis of a free union—and free union is a false phrase without the right to secede—these parties would be betraying socialism.

Democracy, of course, is also a form of state which must disappear when the state disappears, but that will only take place in the transition from conclusively victorious and consolidated socialism to full communism.

2. THE SOCIALIST REVOLUTION AND THE STRUGGLE FOR DEMOCRACY

The socialist revolution is not a single act, it is not one battle on one front, but a whole epoch of acute class conflicts, a long series of battles on all fronts, i.e., on all questions of economics and politics, battles that can only end in the expropriation of the bourgeoisie. It would be a radical mistake to think that the struggle for democracy was capable of diverting the proletariat from the socialist revolution or of hiding, overshadowing it, etc. On the contrary, in the same way as there can be no victorious socialism that does not practise full democracy, so the proletariat cannot prepare for its victory over the bourgeoisie without an all-round, consistent and revolutionary struggle for democracy.

It would be no less a mistake to remove one of the points of the democratic programme, for example, the point on the self-determination of nations, on the grounds of it being "impracticable" or "illusory" under imperialism. The contention that the right of nations to self-determination is impracticable within the bounds of capitalism can be understood either in the absolute, economic sense, or in the conditional, political sense.

In the first case it is radically incorrect from the standpoint of theory. First, in that sense, such things as, for example, labour money, or the abolition of crises, etc., are impracticable under capitalism. It is absolutely untrue that the self-determination of nations is *equally* impracticable. Secondly, even the one example of the secession of Norway from Sweden in 1905 is sufficient to refute "impracticability" in that sense. Thirdly, it would be absurd to deny that some slight change in the political and strategic relations of, say, Germany and Britain, might today or tomorrow make the formation of a new Polish, Indian and other similar state fully "practicable". Fourthly, finance capital, in its drive to expand, can "freely" buy or bribe the freest democratic or republican government and the elective officials of any, even an "independent", country. The domination of finance capital and of capital in general is not to be abolished by *any* reforms in the sphere of political democracy; and self-determination belongs wholly and exclusively to this sphere. This domination of finance capital, however, does not in the least nullify the significance of political democracy as a freer, wider and clearer *form* of class oppression and class struggle. Therefore all arguments about the "impracticability", in the economic sense, of one of the demands of political democracy under capitalism are reduced to a theoretically incorrect definition of the general and basic relationships of capitalism and of political democracy as a whole.

In the second case the assertion is incomplete and inaccurate. This is because not only the right of nations to self-determination, but *all* the fundamental demands of political democracy are only partially "practicable" under imperialism, and then in a distorted form and by way of exception (for example, the secession of Norway from Sweden in 1905). The demand for the immediate liberation of the colonies that is put forward by all revolutionary Social-Democrats is also "impracticable" under capitalism without a series of revolutions. But from this it does not by any means follow that Social-Democracy should reject the immediate and most determined struggle for *all* these demands—such a rejection would only play into the hands of the bourgeoisie and reaction—but, on the contrary, it follows that these demands must be formulated and put through in a revolutionary and not a reformist manner, going beyond the bounds of bourgeois legality, breaking them down, going beyond speeches in parliament and verbal protests, and drawing the masses into decisive action, extending and intensifying the struggle for every fundamental democratic demand up to a direct proletarian onslaught on the bourgeoisie, i.e., up to the socialist revolution that expropriates the bourgeoisie. The socialist revolution may flare up not only through some big strike, street demonstration or hunger riot or a military insurrection or colonial revolt, but also as a result of a political crisis such as the Dreyfus case[1] or the Zabern incident,[2] or in connection with a referendum on the secession of an oppressed nation, etc.

Increased national oppression under imperialism does not mean that Social-Democracy should reject what the bourgeoisie call the "utopian" struggle for the freedom of nations to secede but, on the contrary, it should make greater use of the conflicts that arise in this sphere, *too*, as grounds for mass action and for revolutionary attacks on the bourgeoisie.

3. THE SIGNIFICANCE OF THE RIGHT TO SELF-DETERMINATION AND ITS RELATION TO FEDERATION

The right of nations to self-determination implies exclusively the right to independence in the political sense, the right to free political

[1] A frame-up trial instituted in 1894 by reactionary royalist circles among the French militarists against Dreyfus, a Jewish officer of the General Staff, who was falsely accused of espionage and high treason. A court martial sentenced him to life imprisonment. The public movement for a review of the case took the form of a fierce struggle between the republicans and the royalists and led to his eventual release in 1906.

Lenin said the Dreyfus case was "one of the many thousands of fraudulent tricks of the reactionary military caste".

[2] The incident was caused by the brutality of a Prussian officer towards Alsatians in Zabern, Alsace, in November 1913, and resulted in a burst of indignation among the local, mainly French, population against the Prussian militarists (see Lenin's article "Zabern" in *LCW*, Vol. 19, 1977, pp. 513-15).

separation from the oppressor nation. Specifically, this demand for political democracy implies complete freedom to agitate for secession and for a referendum on secession by the seceding nation. This demand, therefore, is not the equivalent of a demand for separation, fragmentation and the formation of small states. It implies only a consistent expression of struggle against all national oppression. The closer a democratic state system is to complete freedom to secede the less frequent and less ardent will the desire for separation be in practice, because big states afford indisputable advantages, both from the standpoint of economic progress and from that of the interests of the masses and, furthermore, these advantages increase with the growth of capitalism. Recognition of self-determination is not synonymous with recognition of federation as a principle. One may be a determined opponent of that principle and a champion of democratic centralism but still prefer federation to national inequality as the only way to full democratic centralism. It was from this standpoint that Marx, who was a centralist, preferred even the federation of Ireland and England to the forcible subordination of Ireland to the English.[3]

The aim of socialism is not only to end the division of mankind into tiny states and the isolation of nations in any form, it is not only to bring the nations closer together but to integrate them. And it is precisely in order to achieve this aim that we must, on the one hand, explain to the masses the reactionary nature of Renner and Otto Bauer's idea of so-called "cultural and national autonomy"[4] and, on the other, demand the liberation of oppressed nations in a clearly and precisely formulated political programme that takes special account of the hypocrisy and cowardice of socialists in the oppressor nations, and not in general nebulous phrases, not in empty declamations and not by way of "relegating" the question until socialism has been achieved. In the same way as mankind can arrive at the abolition of classes only through a transition period of the dictatorship of the oppressed class, it can arrive at the inevitable integration of nations only through a transition period of the complete emancipation of all oppressed nations, i.e., their freedom to secede.

[3] Marx's letters to Engels of November 2 (no English translation available) and November 30, 1867 (Marx and Engels, *Selected Correspondence*, Moscow, 1955, pp. 234-37).

[4] For a critique of Renner and Bauer's reactionary idea of "cultural and national autonomy" see Lenin's "'Cultural-National' Autonomy" (*LCW*, Vol. 19, 1977) and "Critical Remarks on the National Question" (*LCW*, Vol. 20, 1977).

4. THE PROLETARIAN-REVOLUTIONARY PRESENTATION OF THE QUESTION OF THE SELF-DETERMINATION OF NATIONS

The petty bourgeoisie had put forward not only the demand for the self-determination of nations but *all* the points of our democratic minimum programme long *before*, as far back as the seventeenth and eighteenth centuries. They are still putting them *all* forward in a utopian manner because they fail to see the class struggle and its increased intensity under democracy, and because they believe in "peaceful" capitalism. That is the exact nature of the utopia of a peaceful union of equal nations under imperialism which deceives the people and which is defended by Kautsky's followers. The programme of Social-Democracy, as a counter-balance to this petty-bourgeois, opportunist utopia, must postulate the division of nations into oppressor and oppressed as basic, significant and inevitable under imperialism.

The proletariat of the oppressor nation's must not confine themselves to general, stereotyped phrases against annexation and in favour of the equality of nations in general, such as any pacifist bourgeois will repeat. The proletariat cannot remain silent on the question of the *frontiers* of a state founded on national oppression, a question so "unpleasant" for the imperialist bourgeoisie. The proletariat must struggle against the enforced retention of oppressed nations within the bounds of the given state, which means that they must fight for the right to self-determination. The proletariat must demand freedom of political separation for the colonies and nations oppressed by "their own" nation. Otherwise, the internationalism of the proletariat would be nothing but empty words; neither confidence nor class solidarity would be possible between the workers of the oppressed and the oppressor nations, the hypocrisy of the reformists and Kautskyites, who defend self-determination but remain silent about the nations oppressed by "their own" nation and kept in "their own" state by force, would remain unexposed.

On the other hand, the socialists of the oppressed nations must, in particular, defend and implement the full and unconditional unity, including organisational unity, of the workers of the oppressed nation and those of the oppressor nation. Without this it is impossible to defend the independent policy of the proletariat and their class solidarity with the proletariat of other countries in face of all manner of intrigues, treachery and trickery on the part of the bourgeoisie. The bourgeoisie of the oppressed nations persistently utilise the slogans of national liberation to deceive the workers; in their internal policy they use these slogans for reactionary agreements with the bourgeoisie of the dominant nation (for example, the Poles in Austria and Russia who come to terms with reactionaries for the oppression of the Jews and Ukrainians); in their foreign policy they strive to come to terms with one of the rival imperialist powers for the sake of implementing their predatory plans (the policy of the small Balkan states, etc.).

The fact that the struggle for national liberation against one imperialist power may, under certain conditions, be utilised by another "great" power for its own, equally imperialist, aims, is just as unlikely to make the Social-Democrats refuse to recognise the right of nations to self-determination as the numerous cases of bourgeois utilisation of republican slogans for the purpose of political deception and financial plunder (as in the Romance countries, for example) are unlikely to make the Social-Democrats reject their republicanism.[5]

5. MARXISM AND PROUDHONISM ON THE NATIONAL QUESTION

In contrast to the petty-bourgeois democrats, Marx regarded every democratic demand without exception not as an absolute, but as an historical expression of the struggle of the masses of the people, led by the bourgeoisie, against feudalism. There is not one of these demands which could not serve and has not served, under certain circumstances, as an instrument in the hands of the bourgeoisie for deceiving the workers. To single out, in this respect, one of the demands of political democracy, specifically, the self-determination of nations, and to oppose it to the rest, is fundamentally wrong in theory. In practice, the proletariat can retain its independence only by subordinating its struggle for all democratic demands, not excluding the demand for a republic, to its revolutionary struggle for the overthrow of the bourgeoisie.

On the other hand, in contrast to the Proudhonists who "denied" the national problem "in the name of social revolution", Marx, mindful

[5] It would, needless to say, be quite ridiculous to reject the right to self-determination on the grounds that it implies "defence of the fatherland". With equal right, i.e., with equal lack of seriousness the social-chauvinists of 1914-16 refer to any of the demands of democracy (to its republicanism, for example) and to any formulation of the struggle against national oppression in order to justify "defence of the fatherland". Marxism deduces the defence of the fatherland in wars, for example, in the great French Revolution or the wars of Garibaldi, in Europe, and the renunciation of defence of the fatherland in the imperialist war of 1914-16, from an analysis of the concrete historical peculiarities of each individual war and never from any "general principle", or any one point of a programme.—*Au.*

in the first place of the interests of the proletarian class struggle in the advanced countries, put the fundamental principle of internationalism and socialism in the foreground—namely, that no nation can be free if it oppresses other nations.[6] It was from the standpoint of the interests of the German workers' revolutionary movement that Marx in 1848 demanded that victorious democracy in Germany should proclaim and grant freedom to the nations oppressed by the Germans.[7] It was from the standpoint of the revolutionary struggle of the English workers that Marx, in 1869, demanded the separation of Ireland from England, and added: ". . . even if federation should follow upon separation."[8] Only by putting forward this demand was Marx really educating the English workers in the spirit of internationalism. Only in this way could he counterpose the opportunists and bourgeois reformism—which even to this day, half a century later, has not carried out the Irish "reform"—with a revolutionary solution of the given historical task. Only in this way could Marx maintain—in contradiction to the apologists of capital who shout that the freedom of small nations to secede is utopian and impracticable and that not only economic but also political concentration is progressive—that this concentration is progressive when it is *non*-imperialist, and that nations should not be brought together by force, but by a free union of the proletarians of all countries. Only in this way could Marx, in opposition to the merely verbal, and often hypocritical, recognition of the equality and self-determination of nations, advocate the revolutionary action of the masses in the settlement of national questions *as well*. The imperialist war of 1914-16, and the Augean stables of hypocrisy on the part of the opportunists and Kautskyites that it has exposed, have strikingly confirmed the correctness of Marx's policy, which should serve as a model for all advanced countries, for all of them are now oppressing other nations.[9]

[6] Karl Marx, "Konfidentielle Mitteilung", quoted from the manuscript kept in the archives of the Institute of Marxism-Leninism of the C.C. C.P.S.U.

[7] Friedrich Engels, "Der Prager Aufstand", in *Neue Rheinische Zeitung* No. 18, June 18, 1848.

[8] Marx's proposition on the Irish question was stated in his letters to Kugelmann on November 29 and to Engels on December 10, 1869 (Marx and Engels, *Selected Correspondence*, pp. 276-78 and pp. 279-81). Lenin quotes from Marx's letter to Engels on November 2, 1867 (no English translation available).

[9] Reference is often made—e.g., recently by the German chauvinist Lensch in *Die Glocke* [*Die Glocke* (The Bell)—a magazine published in Munich and later in Berlin from 1915 to 1925 by the social-chauvinist Parvus (A.L. Helfand), a member of the German Social-Democratic Party.] Nos. 8 and 9—to the

6. THREE TYPES OF COUNTRIES WITH RESPECT TO THE SELF-DETERMINATION OF NATIONS

In this respect, countries must be divided into three main types. First, the advanced capitalist countries of Western Europe and the United States. In these countries progressive bourgeois national movements came to an end long ago. Every one of these "great" nations oppresses other nations both in the colonies and at home. The tasks of the proletariat of these ruling nations are the same as those of the proletariat in England in the nineteenth century in relation to Ireland.[10]

Secondly, Eastern Europe: Austria, the Balkans and particularly Russia. Here it was the twentieth century that particularly developed the bourgeois-democratic national movements and intensified the national struggle. The tasks of the proletariat in these countries, both in completing their bourgeois-democratic reforms, and rendering assistance to the socialist revolution in other countries, cannot be carried out without championing the right of nations to self-determination. The

---

fact that Marx's objection to the national movement of certain peoples, to that of the Czechs in 1848, for example, refutes the necessity of recognising the self-determination of nations from the Marxist standpoint. But this is incorrect for in 1848 there were historical and political grounds for drawing a distinction between "reactionary" and revolutionary democratic nations. Marx was right to condemn the former and defend the latter. [Friedrich Engels, "Der demokratische Panslawismus". Lenin used *Aus dem literarischen Nachlass von Karl Marx*, Friedrich Engels und Ferdinand Lassalle, hrsg. von Franz Mehring, Stuttgart, 1902, Bd. III, S. 246-64, in which the author of the article is not named.] The right to self-determination is one of the demands of democracy which must naturally be subordinated to its general interests. In 1848 and the following years these general interests consisted primarily in combating tsarism.—*Au.*

[10] In some small states which have kept out of the war of 1914-16—Holland and Switzerland, for example—the bourgeoisie makes extensive use of the "self-determination of nations" slogan to justify participation in the imperialist war. This is a motive inducing the Social-Democrats in such countries to repudiate self-determination. Wrong arguments are being used to defend a correct proletarian policy, the repudiation of "defence of the fatherland" in an *imperialist* war. This results in a distortion of Marxism in theory, and in practice leads to a peculiar small-nation narrow-mindedness, neglect of the *hundreds of millions* of people in nations that are enslaved by the "dominant" nations. Comrade Gorter, in his excellent pamphlet *Imperialism, War and Social-Democracy* wrongly rejects the principle of self-determination of nations, but correctly *applies* it, when he demands the *immediate* granting of "political and national independence" to the Dutch Indies and exposes the Dutch opportunists who refuse to put forward this demand and to fight for it.—*Au.*

most difficult and most important task in this is to unite the class struggle of the workers of the oppressor nations with that of the workers of the oppressed nations.

Thirdly, the semi-colonial countries, such as China, Persia and Turkey, and all the colonies, which have a combined population of 1,000 million. In these countries the bourgeois-democratic movements either have hardly begun, or have still a long way to go. Socialists must not only demand the unconditional and immediate liberation of the colonies without compensation—and this demand in its political expression signifies nothing else than the recognition of the right to self-determination; they must also render determined support to the more revolutionary elements in the bourgeois-democratic movements for national liberation in these countries and assist their uprising—or revolutionary war, in the event of one—*against* the imperialist powers that oppress them.

7. SOCIAL-CHAUVINISM AND THE SELF-DETERMINATION OF NATIONS

The imperialist epoch and the war of 1914-16 has laid special emphasis on the struggle against chauvinism and nationalism in the leading countries. There are two main trends on the self-determination of nations among the social-chauvinists, that is, among the opportunists and Kautskyites, who hide the imperialist, reactionary nature of the war by applying to it the "defence of the fatherland" concept.

On the one hand, we see quite undisguised servants of the bourgeoisie who defend annexation on the plea that imperialism and political concentration are progressive, and who deny what they call the utopian, illusory, petty-bourgeois, etc., right to self-determination. This includes Cunow, Parvus and the extreme opportunists in Germany, some of the Fabians and trade union leaders in England, and the opportunists in Russia: Semkovsky, Liebman, Yurkevich, etc.

On the other hand, we see the Kautskyites, among whom are Vandervelde, Renaudel, many pacifists in Britain and France, and others. They favour unity with the former and in practice are completely identified with them; they defend the right to self-determination hypocritically and by words alone; they consider "excessive" ("*zu viel verlangt*"; Kautsky in *Die Neue Zeit*, May 21, 1915) the demand for free political separation, they do not defend the necessity for revolutionary tactics on the part of the socialists of the oppressor nations in particular but, on the contrary, obscure their revolutionary obligations, justify their opportunism, make easy for them their deception of the people, and avoid the very question of the *frontiers* of a state forcefully retaining under-privileged nations within its bounds, etc.

Both are equally opportunist, they prostitute Marxism, having lost all ability to understand the theoretical significance and practical urgency of the tactics which Marx explained with Ireland as an example.

As for annexations, the question has become particularly urgent in connection with the war. But what is annexation? It is quite easy to see that a protest against annexations either boils down to recognition of the self-determination of nations or is based on the pacifist phrase that defends the *status quo* and is hostile to *any*, even revolutionary, violence. Such a phrase is fundamentally false and incompatible with Marxism.

8. THE CONCRETE TASKS OF THE PROLETARIAT IN THE IMMEDIATE FUTURE

The socialist revolution may begin in the very near future. In this case the proletariat will be faced with the immediate task of winning power, expropriating the banks and effecting other dictatorial measures. The bourgeoisie—and especially the intellectuals of the Fabian and Kautskyite type—will, at such a moment, strive to split and check the revolution by foisting limited, democratic aims on it. Whereas *any* purely democratic demands are in a certain sense liable to act as a hindrance to the revolution, provided the proletarian attack on the pillars of bourgeois power has begun, the necessity to proclaim and grant liberty to *all* oppressed peoples (i.e., their right to self-determination) will be as urgent in the socialist revolution as it was for the victory of the bourgeois-democratic revolution in, say, Germany in 1848, or Russia in 1905.

It is possible, however, that five, ten or more years will elapse before the socialist revolution begins. This will be the time for the revolutionary education of the masses in a spirit that will make it impossible for socialist-chauvinists and opportunists to belong to the working-class party and gain a victory, as was the case in 1914-16. The socialists must explain to the masses that British socialists who do not demand freedom to separate for the colonies and Ireland, German socialists who do not demand freedom to separate for the colonies, the Alsatians, Danes and Poles, and who do not extend their revolutionary propaganda and revolutionary mass activity directly to the sphere of struggle against national oppression, or who do not make use of such incidents as that at Zabern for the broadest illegal propaganda among the proletariat of the oppressor nation, for street demonstrations and revolutionary mass action—Russian socialists who do not demand freedom to separate for Finland, Poland, the Ukraine, etc., etc.—that such socialists act as chauvinists and lackeys of bloodstained and filthy imperialist monarchies and the imperialist bourgeoisie.

9. THE ATTITUDE OF RUSSIAN AND POLISH SOCIAL-DEMOCRATS AND OF THE SECOND INTERNATIONAL TO SELF-DETERMINATION

The differences between the revolutionary Social-Democrats of Russia and the Polish Social-Democrats on the question of self-determination came out into the open as early as 1903, at the Congress which adopted the Programme of the R.S.D.L. Party, and which, despite the protest by the Polish Social-Democrat delegation, inserted Clause 9, recognising the right of nations to self-determination. Since then the Polish Social-Democrats have on no occasion repeated, in the name of their party, the proposal to remove Clause 9 from our Party's Programme, or to replace it by some other formula.

In Russia, where the oppressed nations account for no less than 57 per cent of the population, or over 100 million, where they occupy mostly the border regions, where some of them are more highly cultured than the Great Russians, where the political system is especially barbarous and medieval, where the bourgeois-democratic revolution has not been consummated—there, in Russia, recognition of the right of nations oppressed by tsarism to free secession from Russia is absolutely obligatory for Social-Democrats, for the furtherance of their democratic and socialist aims. Our Party, re-established in January 1912, adopted a resolution in 1913[11] reaffirming the right to self-determination and explaining it in precisely the above concrete sense. The rampage of Great-Russian chauvinism in 1914-16 both among the bourgeoisie and among the opportunist socialists (Rubanovich, Plekhanov, *Nashe Dyelo*, etc.) has given us even more reason to insist on this demand and to regard those who deny it as actual supporters of Great-Russian chauvinism and tsarism. Our Party declares that it most emphatically declines to accept any responsibility for such actions against the right to self-determination.

[11] The resolution was on the national question; it was written by Lenin and adopted by the meeting of the R.S.D.L.P. Central Committee and Party officials, which was held at Poronin, near Cracow, on October 6-14, 1913. For reasons of secrecy it was known as the "Summer" or "August" Meeting. For the text of the resolution, see *LCW*, Vol. 19, 1977, pp. 427-29.

The latest formulation of the position of the Polish Social-Democrats on the national question (the declaration of the Polish Social-Democrats at the Zimmerwald Conference) contains the following ideas:

The declaration condemns the German and other governments that regard the "Polish regions" as a pawn in the forthcoming compensation game, "*depriving the Polish people of the opportunity of deciding their own fate themselves*". "Polish Social-Democrats resolutely and solemnly protest against the *carving up and parcelling out of a whole country*". . . . They flay the socialists who left it to the Hohenzollerns "*to liberate the oppressed peoples*". They express the conviction that only participation in the approaching struggle of the international revolutionary proletariat, the struggle for socialism, "*will break the fetters of national oppression* and destroy *all forms of foreign* rule, will ensure for *the Polish people* the possibility of free all-round development as an *equal* member of a concord of nations". The declaration recognises that "*for the Poles*" the war is "*doubly* fratricidal". (*Bulletin of the International Socialist Committee* No. 2, September 27, 1915, p. 15. Russian translation in the symposium *The International and the War*, p. 97.)

These propositions do not differ in substance from recognition of the right of nations to self-determination, although their political formulations are even vaguer and more indeterminate than those of most programmes and resolutions of the Second International. Any attempt to express these ideas as precise political formulations and to define their applicability to the capitalist system or only to the socialist system will show even more clearly the mistake the Polish Social-Democrats make in denying the self-determination of nations.

The decision of the London International Socialist Congress of 1896, which recognised the self-determination of nations, should be supplemented on the basis of the above theses by specifying: (1) the particular urgency of this demand under imperialism, (2) the political conventionalism and class content of all the demands of political democracy, the one under discussion included, (3) the necessity to distinguish the concrete tasks of the Social-Democrats of the oppressor nations from those of the Social-Democrats of the oppressed nations, (4) the inconsistent, purely verbal recognition of self-determination by the opportunists and the Kautskyites, which is, therefore, hypocritical in its political significance, (5) the actual identity of the chauvinists and those Social-Democrats, especially those of the Great Powers (Great Russians, Anglo-Americans, Germans, French, Italians, Japanese, etc.), who do not uphold the freedom to secede for colonies and nations oppressed by "their own" nations, (6) the necessity to subordinate the struggle for the demand under discussion and for all the basic demands of political democracy directly to the revolutionary mass struggle for the overthrow of the bourgeois governments and for the achievement of socialism.

The introduction into the International of the viewpoint of certain small nations, especially that of the Polish Social-Democrats, who have been led by their struggle against the Polish bourgeoisie, which deceives the people with its nationalist slogans, to the incorrect denial of self-determination, would be a theoretical mistake, a substitution of Proudhonism for Marxism implying in practice involuntary support for the most dangerous chauvinism and opportunism of the Great-Power nations.

Editorial Board of *Sotsial-Demokrat*,
Central Organ of R.S.D.L.P.

Postscript. In *Die Neue Zeit* for March 3, 1916, which has just appeared, Kautsky openly holds out the hand of Christian reconciliation to Austerlitz, a representative of the foulest German chauvinism, rejecting freedom of separation for the oppressed nations of Hapsburg Austria but recognising it for *Russian* Poland, as a menial service to Hindenburg and Wilhelm II. One could not have wished for a better self-exposure of Kautskyism!

IMPERIALISM, THE LAST STAGE OF CAPITALISM (1916)

PREFACE TO THE FRENCH AND GERMAN EDITIONS (1920)

[. . .] It is proved in the pamphlet that the war of 1914-18 was imperialist (that is, an annexationist, predatory, war of plunder) on the part of both sides; it was a war for the division of the world, for the partition and repartition of colonies and spheres of influence of finance capital, etc.[1]

[1] This pamphlet was written in Zurich in January-June 1916.

Lenin began to take note of new developments in capitalism long before the outbreak of the First World War. In several of his writings from 1895 to 1913—"Draft and Explanation of a Programme for the Social-Democratic Party" (1895-96); "The War in China" (1900); "The Lessons of the Crisis" (1901), "Review of Home Affairs" (1901); "Concentration of Production in Russia" (1912); "The Growth of Capitalist Wealth" (1913); "Backward Europe and Advanced Asia" (1913); "The Historical Destiny of the Doctrine of Karl Marx" (1913); "Concerning Certain Speeches by Workers' Deputies" (1912), and others—Lenin pointed out and analysed some characteristic aspects of the imperialist epoch—the concentration of production and the growth of monopoly; the export of capital; the struggle for new markets and spheres of influence; the internationalisation of economic relations; the parasitism and decay of capitalism; the growth of contradictions between labour and capital and the sharpening of the class struggle; and the creation of the material conditions for the transition to socialism. He devoted special attention to exposing predatory colonial policy, the fight for a division and redivision of the world, and the preparation of imperialist wars of aggrandisement. In his article, "Marxism and Revisionism", written in 1908, he came out against the attempts to revise Marxism and undermine it from inside under the pretext of amending and correcting the theory in particular, Marx's theory of crises. Lenin wrote: "The forms, the sequence, the picture of particular crises changed, but crises remained an inevitable component of the capitalist system. While uniting production, the cartels and trusts at the same time and in a way that was obvious to all, aggravated the anarchy of production, the insecurity of existence of the proletariat and the oppression of capital, thereby intensifying class antagonisms to an unprecedented degree. That capitalism is heading for a breakdown—in the sense both of individual political and economic crises and of the complete collapse of the entire capitalist system—has been made particularly clear, and on a particularly large scale, precisely by the new giant trusts" (see *LCW*, Vol. 15, 1977, pp. 35-36).

Lenin kept abreast of all the latest writings on capitalism, as will be seen from his review of Hobson's *The Evolution of Modern Capitalism*. In August

Proof of what was the true social, or rather, the true class character of

1904, Lenin began a translation of Hobson's Imperialism, the manuscript of which has not yet been found.

It was on the outbreak of the First World War that Lenin undertook a comprehensive study of the monopoly stage of capitalist development. This was required by the working-class revolutionary struggle in Russia and other capitalist countries. In order to provide correct leadership for the revolutionary movement and combat the ideology of imperialist reaction and the reformist policy of conciliation with imperialists, it was necessary to see one's way in the key economic question without a study of which there was no understanding of the assessment of modern war or modern politics, namely: "the economic essence of imperialism".

Lenin must have started his close study of the writings on imperialism in mid-1915, when he was in Berne, for his first indexes of literature, plans, extracts, notes and summaries date to that period. The preparatory materials for *Imperialism, the Highest Stage of Capitalism* (*Notebooks on Imperialism*) make up about 800 printed pages. They contain extracts from 148 books (including 106 in German, 23 in French, 17 in English, and 2 translations into Russian), and 232 articles (of them 206 in German, 13 in French, and 3 in English) from 49 periodicals (34 German, 7 French and 8 English).

In early January 1916, Lenin accepted an order for a book on imperialism from the legal *Parus* Publishers, founded in Petrograd in December 1915. Lenin wrote to Maxim Gorky on December 29, 1915 (January 11, 1916): "I am getting down to the writing of a pamphlet on imperialism" (see *LCW*, Vol. 35, 1973). In the early part of February 1916, he left Berne for Zurich, where he continued to collect and work on materials on imperialism. He worked at the Zurich Cantonal Library and ordered books from other towns.

On June 19 (July 2), 1916, Lenin wrote to M.N. Pokrovsky, who was then living in France and editing for Parus a series of pamphlets about West-European countries during the First World War: "Today, I sent you a manuscript by registered mail" (see *LCW*, Vol. 35, 1977). The manuscript, which was mailed with the letter, did not reach Pokrovsky, and another copy had to be sent. Besides, the publishers suggested that the finished manuscript should be shortened from eighty to fifty pages, but Lenin objected because "it is absolutely impossible to cut it down once again and squeeze it into fifty pages" (ibid.).

When the book reached the publishers, Menshevik elements among the management deleted from the book parts sharply criticising Kautsky and Martov, and made corrections in the text which not only distorted Lenin's style but also his ideas. Thus, Lenin's terms *pererastaniye* (capitalism *growing into* imperialism) was altered to *prevrashcheniye* (transformation); *reaktstonny kharakter* (reactionary nature of the theory of ultra-imperialism) to *otstaly kharakter* (backward character), etc. In mid-1917, the book was published under the title *Imperialism, the Latest Stage of Capitalism* (*A Popular Outline*) with a preface by Lenin, dated April 26, 1917.

The preface was first published under the title "Imperialism and Capitalism" in *Communist International* No. 18, dated October, 1921.

the war is naturally to be found, not in the diplomatic history of the war, but in an analysis of the *objective* position of the ruling *classes* in *all* the belligerent countries. In order to depict this objective position one must not take examples or isolated data (in view of the extreme complexity of the phenomena of social life it is always possible to select any number of examples or separate data to prove any proposition), but *all* the data on the *basis* of economic life in *all* the belligerent countries and the *whole* world.

It is precisely irrefutable summarised data of this kind that I quoted in describing the *partition of the world* in 1876 and 1914 (in Chapter VI) and the division of the world's *railways* in 1890 and 1913 (in Chapter VII). Railways are a summation of the basic capitalist industries, coal, iron and steel; a summation and the most striking index of the development of world trade and bourgeois-democratic civilisation. How the railways are linked up with large-scale industry, with monopolies, syndicates, cartels, trusts, banks and the financial oligarchy is shown in the preceding chapters of the book. The uneven distribution of the railways, their uneven development—sums up, as it were, modern monopolist capitalism on a world-wide scale. And this summary proves that imperialist wars are absolutely inevitable under *such* an economic system, *as long as* private property in the means of production exists.

The building of railways seems to be a simple, natural, democratic, cultural and civilising enterprise; that is what it is in the opinion of the bourgeois professors who are paid to depict capitalist slavery in bright colours, and in the opinion of petty-bourgeois philistines. But as a matter of fact the capitalist threads, which in thousands of different intercrossings bind these enterprises with private property in the means of production in general, have converted this railway construction into an instrument for oppressing *a thousand million* people (in the colonies and semi-colonies), that is, more than half the population of the globe that inhabits the dependent countries, as well as the wage-slaves of capital in the "civilised" countries.

Private property based on the labour of the small proprietor, free competition, democracy, all the catchwords with which the capitalists and their press deceive the workers and the peasants—are things of the distant past. Capitalism has grown into a world system of colonial oppression and of the financial strangulation of the overwhelming majority of the population of the world by a handful of "advanced" countries. And this "booty" is shared between two or three powerful world plunderers armed to the teeth (America, Great Britain, Japan), who are drawing the whole world into *their* war over the division of *their* booty.

[. . .]

VII. IMPERIALISM AS A SPECIAL STAGE OF CAPITALISM

We must now try to sum up, to draw together the threads of what has been said above on the subject of imperialism. Imperialism emerged as the development and direct continuation of the fundamental characteristics of capitalism in general. But capitalism only became capitalist imperialism at a definite and very high stage of its development, when certain of its fundamental characteristics began to change into their opposites, when the features of the epoch of transition from capitalism to a higher social and economic system had taken shape and revealed themselves in all spheres. Economically, the main thing in this process is the displacement of capitalist free competition by capitalist monopoly. Free competition is the basic feature of capitalism, and of commodity production generally; monopoly is the exact opposite of free competition, but we have seen the latter being transformed into monopoly before our eyes, creating large-scale industry and forcing out small industry, replacing large-scale by still larger-scale industry, and carrying concentration of production and capital to the point where out of it has grown and is growing monopoly: cartels, syndicates and trusts, and merging with them, the capital of a dozen or so banks, which manipulate thousands of millions. At the same time the monopolies, which have grown out of free competition, do not eliminate the latter, but exist above it and alongside it, and thereby give rise to a number of very acute, intense antagonisms, frictions and conflicts. Monopoly is the transition from capitalism to a higher system.

If it were necessary to give the briefest possible definition of imperialism we should have to say that imperialism is the monopoly stage of capitalism. Such a definition would include what is most important, for, on the one hand, finance capital is the bank capital of a few very big monopolist banks, merged with the capital of the monopolist associations of industrialists; and, on the other hand, the division of the world is the transition from a colonial policy which has extended without hindrance to territories unseized by any capitalist power, to a colonial policy of monopolist possession of the territory of the world, which has been completely divided up.

But very brief definitions, although convenient, for they sum up the main points, are nevertheless inadequate, since we have to deduce from them some especially important features of the phenomenon that has to be defined. And so, without forgetting the conditional and relative value of all definitions in general, which can never embrace all the concatenations of a phenomenon in its full development, we must give a definition of imperialism that will include the following five of its basic features:

(1) the concentration of production and capital has developed to such a high stage that it has created monopolies which play a decisive role in economic life; (2) the merging of bank capital with industrial capital, and the creation, on the basis of this "finance capital", of a financial oligarchy; (3) the export of capital as distinguished from the export of commodities acquires exceptional importance; (4) the formation of international monopolist capitalist associations which share the world among themselves, and (5) the territorial division of the whole world among the biggest capitalist powers is completed. Imperialism is capitalism at that stage of development at which the dominance of monopolies and finance capital is established; in which the export of capital has acquired pronounced importance; in which the division of the world among the international trusts has begun, in which the division of all territories of the globe among the biggest capitalist powers has been completed.

We shall see later that imperialism can and must be defined differently if we bear in mind not only the basic, purely economic concepts—to which the above definition is limited—but also the historical place of this stage of capitalism in relation to capitalism in general, or the relation between imperialism and the two main trends in the working-class movement. The thing to be noted at this point is that imperialism, as interpreted above, undoubtedly represents a special stage in the development of capitalism. To enable the reader to obtain the most well-grounded idea of imperialism, I deliberately tried to quote as extensively as possible *bourgeois* economists who have to admit the particularly incontrovertible facts concerning the latest stage of capitalist economy. With the same object in view, I have quoted detailed statistics which enable one to see to what degree bank capital, etc., has grown, in what precisely the transformation of quantity into quality, of developed capitalism into imperialism, was expressed. Needless to say, of course, all boundaries in nature and in society are conventional and changeable, and it would be absurd to argue, for example, about the particular year or decade in which imperialism "definitely" became established.

[. . .]

"From the purely economic point of view," writes Kautsky, "it is not impossible that capitalism will yet go through a new phase, that of the extension of the policy of the cartels to foreign policy, the phase of ultra-imperialism,"[2] i.e., of a superimperialism, of a union of the imperialisms of the whole world and not struggles among them, a phase when wars shall cease under capitalism, a phase of "the joint exploitation of the world by internationally united finance capital".[3]

We shall have to deal with this "theory of ultra-imperialism" later on in order to show in detail how decisively and completely it breaks with Marxism. At present, in keeping with the general plan of the present work, we must examine the exact economic data on this question. "From the purely economic point of view", is "ultra-imperialism" possible, or is it ultra-nonsense?

If the purely economic point of view is meant to be a "pure" abstraction, then all that can be said reduces itself to the following proposition: development is proceeding towards monopolies, hence, towards a single world monopoly, towards a single world trust. This is indisputable, but it is also as completely meaningless as is the statement that "development is proceeding" towards the manufacture of foodstuffs in laboratories. In this sense the "theory" of ultra-imperialism is no less absurd than a "theory of ultra-agriculture" would be.

If, however, we are discussing the "purely economic" conditions of the epoch of finance capital as a historically concrete epoch which began at the turn of the twentieth century, then the best reply that one can make to the lifeless abstractions of "ultra-imperialism" (which serve exclusively a most reactionary aim: that of diverting attention from the depth of *existing* antagonisms) is to contrast them with the concrete economic realities of the present-day world economy. Kautsky's utterly meaningless talk about ultra-imperialism encourages, among other things, that profoundly mistaken idea which only brings grist to the mill of the apologists of imperialism, i.e., that the rule of finance capital *lessens* the unevenness and contradictions inherent in the world economy, whereas in reality it *increases* them.

R. Calwer, in his little book, *An Introduction to the World Economy*,[4] made an attempt to summarise the main, purely economic, data that enable one to obtain a concrete picture of the internal relations of the world economy at the turn of the twentieth century. He divides the world into five "main economic areas", as follows: (1) Central Europe

[2] *Die Neue Zeit*, 1914, 2 (B. 32), S. 921, Sept. 11, 1914. Cf. 1915. 2, S. 107 et seq.—*Au.*

[3] *Die Neue Zeit*, 1915, 1, S. 144, April 30, 1915.—*Au.*

[4] R. Calwer, *Einführung in die Weltwirtschaft*, Berlin, 1906.—*Au.*

(the whole of Europe with the exception of Russia and Great Britain); (2) Great Britain; (3) Russia; (4) Eastern Asia; (5) America; he includes the colonies in the "areas" of the states to which they belong and "leaves aside" a few countries not distributed according to areas, such as Persia, Afghanistan, and Arabia in Asia, Morocco and Abyssinia in Africa, etc.

[. . .]

We see three areas of highly developed capitalism (high development of means of transport, of trade and of industry): the Central European, the British and the American areas. Among these are three states which dominate the world: Germany, Great Britain, and the United States. Imperialist rivalry and the struggle between these countries have become extremely keen because Germany has only an insignificant area and few colonies; the creation of "Central Europe" is still a matter for the future, it is being born in the midst of a desperate struggle. For the moment the distinctive feature of the whole of Europe is political disunity. In the British and American areas, on the other hand, political concentration is very highly developed, but there is a vast disparity between the immense colonies of the one and the insignificant colonies of the other. In the colonies, however, capitalism is only beginning to develop. The struggle for South America is becoming more and more acute.

There are two areas where capitalism is little developed: Russia and Eastern Asia. In the former, the population is extremely sparse, in the latter it is extremely dense; in the former political concentration is high, in the latter it does not exist. The partitioning of China is only just beginning, and the struggle for it between Japan, the U.S., etc., is continually gaining in intensity.

Compare this reality—the vast diversity of economic and political conditions, the extreme disparity in the rate of development of the various countries, etc., and the violent struggles among the imperialist states—with Kautsky's silly little fable about "peaceful" ultra-imperialism. Is this not the reactionary attempt of a frightened philistine to hide from stern reality? Are not the international cartels which Kautsky imagines are the embryos of "ultra-imperialism" (in the same way as one "can" describe the manufacture of tablets in a laboratory as ultra-agriculture in embryo) an example of the division *and the redivision* of the world, the transition from peaceful division to non-peaceful division and vice versa? Is not American and other finance capital, which divided the whole world peacefully with Germany's participation in, for example, the international rail syndicate, or in the international mercantile shipping trust, now engaged in *redividing* the world on the basis of a new relation of forces that is being changed by methods *anything but* peaceful?

[. . .]

Let us consider India, Indo-China and China. It is known that these three colonial and semi-colonial countries, with a population of 600-700 million, are subjected to the exploitation of the finance capital of several imperialist powers: Great Britain, France, Japan, the U.S.A., etc. Let us assume that these imperialist countries form alliances against one another in order to protect or enlarge their possessions, their interests and their spheres of influence in these Asiatic states; these alliances will be "inter-imperialist", or "ultra-imperialist" alliances. Let us assume that *all* the imperialist countries conclude an alliance for the "peaceful" division of these parts of Asia; this alliance would be an alliance of "internationally united finance capital". There are actual examples of alliances of this kind in the history of the twentieth century—the attitude of the powers to China, for instance. We ask, is it "conceivable", assuming that the capitalist system remains intact—and this is precisely the assumption that Kautsky does make—that such alliances would be more than temporary, that they would eliminate friction, conflicts and struggle in every possible form?

The question has only to be presented clearly for any other than a negative answer to be impossible. This is because the only conceivable basis under capitalism for the division of spheres of influence, interests, colonies, etc., is a calculation of the *strength* of those participating, their general economic, financial, military strength, etc. And the strength of these participants in the division does not change to an equal degree, for the *even* development of different undertakings, trusts, branches of industry, or countries is impossible under capitalism. Half a century ago Germany was a miserable, insignificant country, if her capitalist strength is compared with that of the Britain of that time; Japan compared with Russia in the same way. Is it "conceivable" that in ten or twenty years' time the relative strength of the imperialist powers will have remained *un*changed? It is out of the question.

Therefore, in the realities of the capitalist system, and not in the banal philistine fantasies of English parsons, or of the German "Marxist", Kautsky, "inter-imperialist" or "ultra-imperialist" alliances, no matter what form they may assume, whether of one imperialist coalition against another, or of a general alliance embracing *all* the imperialist powers, are *inevitably* nothing more than a "truce" in periods between wars. Peaceful alliances prepare the ground for wars, and in their turn grow out of wars;

the one conditions the other, producing alternating forms of peaceful and non-peaceful struggle on *one and the same* basis of imperialist connections and relations within world economics and world politics.

[. . .]

X. THE PLACE OF IMPERIALISM IN HISTORY

We have seen that in its economic essence imperialism is monopoly capitalism. This in itself determines its place in history, for monopoly that grows out of the soil of free competition, and precisely out of free competition, is the transition from the capitalist system to a higher socio-economic order. We must take special note of the four principal types of monopoly, or principal manifestations of monopoly capitalism, which are characteristic of the epoch we are examining.

Firstly, monopoly arose out of the concentration of production at a very high stage. This refers to the monopolist capitalist associations, cartels, syndicates and trusts. We have seen the important part these play in present-day economic life. At the beginning of the twentieth century, monopolies had acquired complete supremacy in the advanced countries, and although the first steps towards the formation of the cartels were taken by countries enjoying the protection of high tariffs (Germany, America), Great Britain, with her system of free trade, revealed the same basic phenomenon, only a little later, namely, the birth of monopoly out of the concentration of production.

Secondly, monopolies have stimulated the seizure of the most important sources of raw materials, especially for the basic and most highly cartelised industries in capitalist society: the coal and iron industries. The monopoly of the most important sources of raw materials has enormously increased the power of big capital, and has sharpened the antagonism between cartelised and non-cartelised industry.

Thirdly, monopoly has sprung from the banks. The banks have developed from modest middleman enterprises into the monopolists of finance capital. Some three to five of the biggest banks in each of the foremost capitalist countries have achieved the "personal link-up" between industrial and bank capital, and have concentrated in their hands the control of thousands upon thousands of millions which form the greater part of the capital and income of entire countries. A financial oligarchy, which throws a close network of dependence relationships over all the economic and political institutions of present-day bourgeois society without exception—such is the most striking manifestation of this monopoly.

Fourthly, monopoly has grown out of colonial policy. To the numerous "old" motives of colonial policy, finance capital has added the struggle for the sources of raw materials, for the export of capital, for spheres of influence, i.e., for spheres for profitable deals, concessions, monopoly profits and so on, economic territory in general. When the colonies of the European powers, for instance, comprised only one-tenth of the territory of Africa (as was the case in 1876), colonial policy was able to develop—by methods other than those of monopoly—by the "free grabbing" of territories, so to speak. But when nine-tenths of Africa had been seized (by 1900), when the whole world had been divided up, there was inevitably ushered in the era of monopoly possession of colonies and, consequently, of particularly intense struggle for the division and the redivision of the world.

The extent to which monopolist capital has intensified all the contradictions of capitalism is generally known. It is sufficient to mention the high cost of living and the tyranny of the cartels. This intensification of contradictions constitutes the most powerful driving force of the transitional period of history, which began from the time of the final victory of world finance capital.

Monopolies, oligarchy, the striving for domination and not for freedom, the exploitation of an increasing number of small or weak nations by a handful of the richest or most powerful nations—all these have given birth to those distinctive characteristics of imperialism which compel us to define it as parasitic or decaying capitalism. More and more prominently there emerges, as one of the tendencies of imperialism, the creation of the "rentier state", the usurer state, in which the bourgeoisie to an ever-increasing degree lives on the proceeds of capital exports and by "clipping coupons". It would be a mistake to believe that this tendency to decay precludes the rapid growth of capitalism. It does not. In the epoch of imperialism, certain branches of industry, certain strata of the bourgeoisie and certain countries betray, to a greater or lesser degree, now one and now another of these tendencies. On the whole, capitalism is growing far more rapidly than before; but this growth is not only becoming more and more uneven in general, its unevenness also manifests itself, in particular, in the decay of the countries which are richest in capital (Britain).

In regard to the rapidity of Germany's economic development, Riesser, the author of the book on the big German banks, states: "The progress of the preceding period (1848-70), which had not been exactly slow, compares with the rapidity with which the whole of Germany's national economy, and with it German banking, progressed during this period (1870-1905) in about the same way as the speed of the mail coach in the good old days compares with the speed of the present-day automobile . . . which is whizzing past so fast that it endangers not only innocent pedestrians in its path, but also the occupants of the car." In its turn, this finance capital which has grown with such extraordinary rapidity is not unwilling, precisely because it has grown so quickly, to pass on to a more "tranquil" possession of colonies which have to be seized—and not only by peaceful methods—from richer nations. In the United States, economic development in the last decades has been even more rapid than in Germany, *and for this very reason*, the parasitic features of modern American capitalism have stood out with particular prominence. On the other hand, a comparison of, say, the republican American bourgeoisie with the monarchist Japanese or German bourgeoisie shows that the most pronounced political distinction diminishes to an extreme degree in the epoch of imperialism—not because it is unimportant in general, but because in all these cases we are talking about a bourgeoisie which has definite features of parasitism.

The receipt of high monopoly profits by the capitalists in one of the numerous branches of industry, in one of the numerous countries, etc., makes it economically possible for them to bribe certain sections of the workers, and for a time a fairly considerable minority of them, and win them to the side of the bourgeoisie of a given industry or given nation against all the others. The intensification of antagonisms between imperialist nations for the division of the world increases this urge. And so there is created that bond between imperialism and opportunism, which revealed itself first and most clearly in Great Britain, owing to the fact that certain features of imperialist development were observable there much earlier than in other countries. Some writers, L. Martov, for example, are prone to wave aside the connection between imperialism and opportunism in the working-class movement—a particularly glaring fact at the present time—by resorting to "official optimism" (*à la* Kautsky and Huysmans) like the following: the cause of the opponents of capitalism would be hopeless if it were progressive capitalism that led to the increase of opportunism, or, if it were the best-paid workers who were inclined towards opportunism, etc. We must have no illusions about "optimism" of this kind. It is optimism in respect of opportunism; it is optimism which serves to conceal opportunism. As a matter of fact the extraordinary rapidity and the particularly revolting character of the development of opportunism is by no means a guarantee that its victory will be durable: the rapid growth of a painful abscess on a healthy body can only cause it to burst more quickly and thus relieve the body of it. The most dangerous of all in this respect are those who do not wish to understand that the fight against imperialism is a sham and humbug unless it is inseparably bound up with the fight against opportunism.

From all that has been said in this book on the economic essence of imperialism, it follows that we must define it as capitalism in transition, or, more precisely, as moribund capitalism. It is very instructive in this respect to note that bourgeois economists, in describing modern capitalism, frequently employ catchwords and phrases like "interlocking", "absence of isolation", etc.; "in conformity with their functions and course of development", banks are "not purely private business enterprises; they are more and more outgrowing the sphere of purely private business regulation". And this very Riesser, whose words I have just quoted, declares with all seriousness that the "prophecy" of the Marxists concerning "socialisation" has "not come true"!

What then does this catchword "interlocking" express? It merely expresses the most striking feature of the process going on before our eyes. It shows that the observer counts the separate trees, but cannot see the wood. It slavishly copies the superficial, the fortuitous, the chaotic. It reveals the observer as one who is overwhelmed by the mass of raw material and is utterly incapable of appreciating its meaning and importance. Ownership of shares, the relations between owners of private property "interlock in a haphazard way". But underlying this interlocking, its very base, are the changing social relations of production. When a big enterprise assumes gigantic proportions, and, on the basis of an exact computation of mass data, organises according to plan the supply of primary raw materials to the extent of two-thirds, or three-fourths, of all that is necessary for tens of millions of people; when the raw materials are transported in a systematic and organised manner to the most suitable places of production, sometimes situated hundreds or thousands of miles from each other; when a single centre directs all the consecutive stages of processing the material right up to the manufacture of numerous varieties of finished articles; when these products are distributed according to a single plan among tens and hundreds of millions of consumers (the marketing of oil in America and Germany by the American oil trust)—then it becomes evident that we have socialisation of production, and not mere "interlocking", that private economic and private property relations constitute a shell which no longer fits its contents, a shell which must inevitably decay if its removal is artificially delayed, a shell which may remain in a state of decay for a fairly long period (if, at the worst, the cure of the opportunist abscess is protracted), but which will inevitably be removed.

Part IV

Revolution

LETTERS ON TACTICS
(1917)

FOREWORD[1]

On April 4, 1917, I had occasion to make a report on the subject indicated in the title, first, at a meeting of Bolsheviks in Petrograd. These were delegates to the All-Russia Conference of Soviets of Workers' and Soldiers' Deputies, who had to leave for their homes and therefore could not allow me to postpone it. After the meeting, the chairman, Comrade G. Zinoviev, asked me on behalf of the whole assembly to repeat my report immediately at a joint meeting of Bolshevik and Menshevik delegates, who wished to discuss the question of unifying the Russian Social-Democratic Labour Party.

Difficult though it was for me immediately to repeat my report, I felt that I had no right to refuse once this was demanded of me by *my comrades-in-ideas* as well as by the Mensheviks, who, because of their impending departure, really could not grant me a delay.

In making my report, I read the theses which were published in No. 26 of Pravda, on April 7, 1917.[2]

Both the theses and my report gave rise to differences of opinion among the Bolsheviks themselves and the editors of *Pravda*. After a number of consultations, we unanimously concluded that it would be advisable *openly* to discuss our differences, and thus provide material for the All-Russia Conference of our Party (the Russian Social-Democratic Labour Party, united under the Central Committee) which is to meet in Petrograd on April 20, 1917.

Complying with this decision concerning a discussion, I am publishing the following *letters* in which I do not claim to have made an *exhaustive* study of the question, but wish merely to outline the principal arguments, which are especially essential for the *practical* tasks of the working-class movement.

[1] Lenin's pamphlet *Letters on Tactics. First Letter* was issued in Petrograd in 1917 by the Bolshevik publishing house Priboi in three editions. The April Theses were given as a supplement to all three editions.

[2] I reprint these theses together with the brief comment from the same issue of *Pravda* as an appendix to this letter.—*Au.*

FIRST LETTER

ASSESMENT OF THE PRESENT SITUATION

Marxism requires of us a strictly exact and objectively verifiable analysis of the relations of classes and of the concrete features peculiar to each historical situation. We Bolsheviks have always tried to meet this requirement, which is absolutely essential for giving a scientific foundation to policy.

"Our theory is not a dogma, but a guide to action,"[3] Marx and Engels always said, rightly ridiculing the mere memorising and repetition of "formulas", that at best are capable only of marking out *general* tasks, which are necessarily modifiable by the *concrete* economic and political conditions of each particular *period* of the historical process.

What, then, are the clearly established objective *facts* which the party of the revolutionary proletariat must now be guided by in defining the tasks and forms of its activity?

Both in my first *Letter From Afar* ("The First Stage of the First Revolution") published in *Pravda* Nos. 14 and 15, March 21 and 22, *1917*, and in my theses, I define "the specific feature of the present situation in Russia" as a period of *transition* from the first stage of the revolution to the second. I therefore considered the basic slogan, the "task of the day" at *this* moment to be: "Workers, you have performed miracles of proletarian heroism, the heroism of the people, in the civil war against tsarism. You must perform miracles of organisation, organisation of the proletariat and of the whole people, to prepare the way for your victory in the second stage of the revolution" (*Pravda* No. 15).[4]

What, then, is the first stage?

It is the passing of state power to the bourgeoisie.

Before the February-March revolution of *1917*, state power in Russia was in the hands of one old class, namely, the feudal landed nobility, headed by Nicholas Romanov.

After the revolution, the power is in the hands of a *different* class, a new class, namely, the *bourgeoisie.*

The passing of state power from one *class* to another is the first, the principal, the basic sign of a *revolution,* both in the strictly scientific and in the practical political meaning of that term.

To this extent, the bourgeois, or the bourgeois-democratic, revolution in Russia is *completed.*

[3] See Engels's letter to F.A. Sorge dated November 29, 1886 (Marx and Engels, *Selected Correspondence*, Moscow, 1955, pp. 469-73).

[4] See *LCW*, Vol. 23, 1974, pp. 306-07.

But at this point we hear a clamour of protest from people who readily call themselves "old Bolsheviks". Didn't we always maintain, they say, that the bourgeois-democratic revolution is completed only by the "revolutionary-democratic dictatorship of the proletariat and the peasantry"? Is the agrarian revolution, which is also a bourgeois-democratic revolution, completed? Is it not a fact, on the contrary, that it has *not even* started?

My answer is: The Bolshevik slogans and ideas *on the whole* have been confirmed by history; but *concretely* things have worked out *differently;* they are more original, more peculiar, more variegated than anyone could have expected.

To ignore or overlook this fact would mean taking after those "old Bolsheviks" who more than once already have played so regrettable a role in the history of our Party by reiterating formulas senselessly *learned by rote* instead of *studying* the specific features of the new and living reality.

"The revolutionary-democratic dictatorship of the proletariat and the peasantry" has *already* become a reality[5] in the Russian revolution, for this "formula" envisages only a *relation of classes*, and not a *concrete political institution implementing* this relation, this co-operation. "The Soviet of Workers' and Soldiers' Deputies"—there you have the "revolutionary-democratic dictatorship of the proletariat and the peasantry" already accomplished in reality.

This formula is already antiquated. Events have moved it from the realm of formulas into the realm of reality, clothed it with flesh and bone, concretised it and *thereby* modified it.

A new and different task now faces us: to effect a split *within* this dictatorship between the proletarian elements (the anti-defencist, internationalist, "Communist" elements, who stand for a transition to the commune) and the *small-proprietor* or *petty-bourgeois* elements (Chkheidze, Tsereteli, Steklov, the Socialist-Revolutionaries and the other revolutionary defencists, who are opposed to moving towards the commune and are in favour of "supporting" the bourgeoisie and the bourgeois government).

The person who *now* speaks only of a "revolutionary democratic dictatorship of the proletariat and the peasantry" is behind the times, consequently, he has in effect *gone over* to the petty bourgeoisie against the proletarian class struggle; that person should be consigned to the

[5] In a certain form and to a certain extent.—*Au.*

archive of "Bolshevik" pre-revolutionary antiques (it may be called the archive of "old Bolsheviks").

The revolutionary-democratic dictatorship of the proletariat and the peasantry has already been realised, but in a highly original manner, and with a number of extremely important modifications. I shall deal with them separately in one of my next letters. For the present, it is essential to grasp the incontestable truth that a Marxist must take cognisance of real life, of the true facts of *reality,* and not cling to a theory of yesterday, which, like all theories, at best only outlines the main and the general, only *comes near* to embracing life in all its complexity.

"Theory, my friend, is grey, but green is the eternal tree of life."[6]

To deal with the question of "completion" of the bourgeois revolution *in the old way* is to sacrifice living Marxism to the dead letter.

According to the old way of thinking, the rule of the bourgeoisie could and should be *followed* by the rule of the proletariat and the peasantry, by their dictatorship.

In real life, however, things have *already* turned out *differently;* there has been an extremely original, novel and unprecedented *interlacing of the one with the other.* We have side by side, existing together, simultaneously, *both* the rule of the bourgeoisie (the government of Lvov and Guchkov) and a revolutionary-democratic dictatorship of the proletariat and the peasantry, which is *voluntarily* ceding power to the bourgeoisie, voluntarily making itself an appendage of the bourgeoisie.

For it must not be forgotten that actually, in Petrograd, the power is in the hands of the workers and soldiers; the new government is *not* using and cannot use violence against them, because *there is no* police, *no* army standing apart from the people, *no* officialdom standing all-powerful *above* the people. This is a fact, the kind of fact that is characteristic of a state of the Paris Commune type. This fact does not fit into the old schemes. One must know how to adapt schemes to facts, instead of reiterating the now meaningless words about a "dictatorship of the proletariat and the peasantry" *in general.*

To throw more light on this question let us approach it from another angle.

A Marxist must not abandon the ground of careful analysis of class relations. The bourgeoisie is in power. But is not the mass of the peasants *also* a bourgeoisie, only of a different social stratum, of a different kind, of a different character? Whence does it follow that *this* stratum *cannot*

6 Lenin here quotes the words of Mephistopheles from Goethe's tragedy *Faust.* Erster Teil, Studierzimmer.

come to power, thus "completing" the bourgeois-democratic revolution? Why should this be impossible?

This is how the old Bolsheviks often argue.

My reply is that it is quite possible. But, in assessing a given situation, a Marxist must proceed *not* from what is possible, but from what is real.

And the reality reveals the *fact* that freely elected soldiers' and peasants' deputies are freely joining the second, parallel government, and are freely supplementing, developing and completing it. And, just as freely, they are *surrendering* power to the bourgeoisie—a fact which does not in the least "contravene" the theory of Marxism, for we have always known and repeatedly pointed out that the bourgeoisie maintains itself in power *not* only by force but also by virtue of the lack of class-consciousness and organisation, the routinism and downtrodden state of the masses.

In view of this present-day reality, it is simply ridiculous to turn one's back on the fact and talk about "possibilities".

Possibly the peasantry may seize all the land and all the power. Far from forgetting this possibility, far from confining myself to the present, I definitely and clearly formulate the agrarian programme, taking into account the *new* phenomenon, i.e., the deeper cleavage between the agricultural labourers and the poor peasants on the one hand, and the peasant proprietors on the other.

But there is also another possibility; it is possible that the peasants will take the advice of the petty-bourgeois party of the Socialist-Revolutionaries, which has yielded to the influence of the bourgeoisie, has adopted a defencist stand, and which advises waiting for the Constituent Assembly, although not even the date of its convocation has yet been fixed.[7]

It is possible that the peasants will *maintain* and prolong their deal with the bourgeoisie, a deal which they have now concluded through the Soviets of Workers' and Soldiers' Deputies not only in form, but in fact.

Many things are possible. It would be a great mistake to forget the agrarian movement and the agrarian programme. But it would be no less a mistake to forget the *reality,* which reveals the *fact* that an *agreement,*

[7] Lest my words be misinterpreted, I shall say at once that I am positively in favour of the *Soviets* of Agricultural Labourers and Peasants *immediately* taking over *all* the land, but they should *themselves* observe the strictest order and discipline, not permit the slightest damage to machines, structures, or livestock, and in no case disorganise agriculture and grain production, but rather *develop* them, for the soldiers need *twice* as much bread, and the people must not be allowed to starve.—*Au.*

or—to use a more exact, less legal, but more class-economic term—*class collaboration* exists between the bourgeoisie and the peasantry.

When this fact ceases to be a fact, when the peasantry separates from the bourgeoisie, seizes the land and power despite the bourgeoisie, that will be a new stage in the bourgeois-democratic revolution; and that matter will be dealt with separately.

A Marxist who, in view of the possibility of such a future stage, were to forget his duties in *the present,* when the peasantry is *in agreement* with the bourgeoisie, would turn petty bourgeois. For he would in practice be preaching to the proletariat *confidence* in the petty bourgeoisie ("this petty bourgeoisie, this peasantry, must separate from the bourgeoisie while the bourgeois-democratic revolution is still on"). Because of the "possibility" of so pleasing and sweet a future, in which the peasantry would *not* be the tail of the bourgeoisie, in which the Socialist-Revolutionaries, the Chkheidzes, Tseretelis, and Steklovs would *not* be an appendage of the bourgeois government—because of the "possibility" of so pleasing a future, he would be forgetting *the unpleasant present,* in which the peasantry still forms the tail of the bourgeoisie, and in which the Socialist-Revolutionaries and Social-Democrats have not yet given up their role as an appendage of the bourgeois government, as "His Majesty" Lvov's Opposition.[8]

This hypothetical person would resemble a sweetish Louis Blanc, or a sugary Kautskyite, but certainly not a revolutionary Marxist.

But are we not in danger of falling into subjectivism, of wanting to arrive at the socialist revolution by "skipping" the bourgeois-democratic revolution—which is not yet completed and has not yet exhausted the peasant movement?

I might be incurring this danger if I said: "No Tsar, but a *workers'* government."[9] But I did *not* say that, I said something else. I said that there *can be no* government (barring a bourgeois government) in Russia *other than* that of the Soviets of Workers', Agricultural Labourers',

[8] The expression "*His Majesty's Opposition*" belongs to P.N. Milyukov, the leader of the Cadet Party. In a speech made at a luncheon given by the Lord Mayor of London on June 19 (July 2), 1909, Milyukov said: "So long as there is a legislative chamber in Russia which controls the budget, the Russian Opposition will remain the Opposition of His Majesty, not to His Majesty" (Rech No. 167, June 21 [July 4], 1909).

[9] "*No Tsar, but a workers' government*" was an anti-Bolshevik slogan put forward in 1905 by Parvus and Trotsky. This slogan of a revolution without the peasantry, which became one of the basic postulates of counter-revolutionary Trotskyism, was sharply criticised by Lenin.

Soldiers', and Peasants' Deputies. I said that power in Russia now can pass from Guchkov and Lvov *only* to these Soviets. And in these Soviets, as it happens, it is the peasants, the soldiers, i.e., petty bourgeoisie, who preponderate, to use a scientific, Marxist term, a class characterisation, and not a common, man-in-the-street, professional characterisation.

In my theses, I absolutely ensured myself against skipping over the peasant movement, which has not outlived itself, or the petty-bourgeois movement in general, against any *playing* at "seizure of power" by a workers' government, against any kind of Blanquist adventurism; for I pointedly referred to the experience of the Paris Commune. And this experience, as we know, and as Marx proved at length in 1871 and Engels in 1891,[10] absolutely excludes Blanquism, absolutely ensures the direct, immediate and unquestionable rule of the *majority* and the activity of the masses only to the extent that the majority itself acts *consciously.*

In the theses, I very definitely reduced the question to one of *a struggle for influence within* the Soviets of Workers', Agricultural Labourers', Peasants', and Soldiers' Deputies. To leave no shadow of doubt on this score, I *twice* emphasised in the theses the need for patient and persistent "explanatory" work "adapted to the *practical* needs of the *masses*".

Ignorant persons or renegades from Marxism, like Mr. Plekhanov, may shout about anarchism, Blanquism, and so forth. But those who want to think and learn cannot fail to understand that Blanquism means the seizure of power by a minority, whereas the Soviets are *admittedly* the direct and immediate organisation of the *majority* of the people. Work confined to a struggle for influence *within* these Soviets cannot, simply *cannot,* stray into the swamp of Blanquism. Nor can it stray into the swamp of anarchism, for anarchism denies *the need for a state and state power* in the period of *transition* from the rule of the bourgeoisie to the rule of the proletariat, whereas I, with a precision that precludes any possibility of misinterpretation, *advocate* the need for a state in this period, although, in accordance with Marx and the lessons of the Paris Commune, I advocate not the usual parliamentary bourgeois state, but a state *without* a standing army, *without* a police opposed to the people, *without* an officialdom placed above the people.

When Mr. Plekhanov, in his newspaper *Yedinstvo,* shouts with all his might that this is anarchism, he is merely giving further proof of his break with Marxism. Challenged by me in Pravda (No. 26) to tell us what

[10] See Marx and Engels, *Selected Works*, Vol. I, Moscow, 1962, pp. 516-30, 473-74.

Marx and Engels taught on the subject in 1871, 1872 and 1875,[11] Mr. Plekhanov can only preserve silence on the question at issue and shout out abuse after the manner of the enraged bourgeoisie.

Mr. Plekhanov, the ex-Marxist, has *absolutely* failed to understand the Marxist doctrine of the state. Incidentally, the germs of this lack of understanding are also to he found in his German pamphlet on anarchism.[12]

* * *

Now let us see how Comrade Y. Kamenev, in *Pravda* No. 27, formulates his "disagreements" with my theses and with the views expressed above. This will help us to grasp them more clearly.

> "As for Comrade Lenin's general scheme," writes Comrade Kamenev, "it appears to us unacceptable, inasmuch as it proceeds from the assumption that the bourgeois-democratic revolution is *completed,* and builds on the immediate transformation of this revolution into a socialist revolution."

There are two big mistakes here.

First. The question of "completion" of the bourgeois-democratic revolution is *stated* wrongly. The question is put in an abstract, simple, so to speak one-colour, way, which does *not* correspond to the objective reality. To put the question *this way,* to ask *now* "whether the bourgeois-democratic revolution is completed" and say *no more,* is to prevent oneself from seeing the exceedingly complex reality, which is at least two-coloured. This is in theory. In practice, it means surrendering helplessly to *petty-bourgeois revolutionism.*

Indeed, reality shows us *both* the passing of power into the hands of the bourgeoisie (a "completed" bourgeois-democratic revolution of the usual type) and, side by side with the real government, the existence of a parallel government which represents the "revolutionary-democratic dictatorship of the proletariat and the peasantry". This "second government" has *itself* ceded the power to the bourgeoisie, has chained *itself* to the bourgeois government.

Is this reality covered by Comrade Kamenev's old-Bolshevik formula, which says that "the bourgeois-democratic revolution is not completed"?

[11] See *LCW*, Vol. 24, 1974, p. 26.

[12] Lenin refers to Plekhanov's pamphlet *Anarchism and Socialism*, first published in German in 1894.

It is not. The formula is obsolete. It is no good at all. It is dead. And it is no use trying to revive it.

Second. A practical question. Who knows whether it is still possible at present for a *special* "revolutionary-democratic dictatorship of the proletariat and the peasantry", *detached* from the bourgeois government, to emerge in Russia? Marxist tactics cannot be based on the unknown.

But *if* this is still possible, then there is one, and only one, way towards it, namely, an immediate, resolute, and irrevocable separation of the proletarian Communist elements from the petty-bourgeois elements.

Why?

Because the entire petty bourgeoisie has, not by chance but of necessity, turned towards chauvinism (=defencism), towards "support" of the bourgeoisie, towards dependence on it, towards the *fear* of having to do without it, etc., etc.

How can the petty bourgeoisie be "pushed" into power, if even now it can take the power, but *does not want to?*

This can be done only by separating the proletarian, the Communist, party, by waging a proletarian class struggle *free from* the timidity of those petty bourgeois. Only the consolidation of the proletarians who are free from the influence of the petty bourgeoisie in deed and not only in word can make the ground so hot under the feet of the petty bourgeoisie that it will be *obliged* under certain circumstances to take the power; it is even within the bounds of possibility that Guchkov and Milyukov—again under certain circumstances—will be forgiving full and sole power to Chkheidze, Tsereteli, the S.R.s, and Steklov, since, after all, these are "*defencists*".

To separate the proletarian elements of the Soviets (i.e., the proletarian, Communist, party) from the petty-bourgeois elements right now, immediately and irrevocably, is to give correct expression to the interests of the movement in *either* of two possible events: in the event that Russia will yet experience a special "dictatorship of the proletariat and the peasantry" independent of the bourgeoisie, and in the event that the petty bourgeoisie will not be able to tear itself away from the bourgeoisie and will oscillate eternally (that is, until socialism is established) between us and it.

To be guided in one's activities merely by the simple formula, "the bourgeois-democratic revolution is not completed", is like taking it upon oneself to guarantee that the petty bourgeoisie is definitely capable of being independent of the bourgeoisie. To do so is to throw oneself at the given moment on the mercy of the petty bourgeoisie.

Incidentally, in connection with the "formula" of the dictatorship of the proletariat and the peasantry, it is worth mentioning that, in *Two Tactics* (July 1905), I made a point of emphasising (*Twelve Years*, p. 435[13]) this:

"Like everything else in the world, the revolutionary-democratic dictatorship of the proletariat and the peasantry has a past and a future. Its past is autocracy, serfdom, monarchy, and privilege. . . . Its future is the struggle against private property, the struggle of the wage-worker against the employer, the struggle for socialism. . . ."[14]

Comrade Kamenev's mistake is that even in 1917 he sees only *the past* of the revolutionary-democratic dictatorship of the proletariat and the peasantry. As a matter of fact its *future* has already begun, for the interests and policies of the wage-worker and the petty proprietor have *actually* diverged already, even in such an important question as that of "defencism", that of the attitude towards the imperialist war.

This brings me to the second mistake in Comrade Kamenev's argument quoted above. He criticises me, saying that my scheme "builds" on "the immediate transformation of this [bourgeois-democratic] revolution into a socialist revolution".

This is incorrect. I not only do not "build" on the "immediate transformation" of our revolution into a *socialist* one, but I actually warn against it, when in Thesis No. 8, I state: "It is *not* our *immediate* task to 'introduce' socialism . . .".[15]

Is it not clear that no person who builds on the immediate transformation of our revolution into a socialist revolution could be opposed to the immediate task of introducing socialism?

Moreover, even a "commune state" (i.e., a state organised along the lines of the Paris Commune) *cannot* be introduced in Russia "immediately", because to do that it would be necessary for the *majority* of the deputies in all (or in most) Soviets to clearly recognise all the erroneousness and harm of the tactics and policy pursued by the S.R.s, Chkheidze, Tsereteli, Steklov, etc. As for me, I declared unmistakably that in this respect I "build" only on "patient" explaining (does one have to be patient to bring about a change which can be effected "immediately"?).

[13] Lenin here refers to the volume of his writings published in St. Petersburg at the end of 1907: Vl. Ilyin *Twelve Years. A Collection of Articles. Volume I. Two Trends in Russian Marxism and Russian Social-Democracy.*

[14] See *LCW*, Vol. 9, 1977, pp. 84-85.

[15] See *LCW*, Vol. 24, 1974, p. 24.

Comrade Kamenev has somewhat overreached himself in his eagerness, and has repeated the bourgeois prejudice about the Paris Commune having wanted to introduce socialism "immediately". This is not so. The Commune, unfortunately, was too slow in introducing socialism. The real essence of the Commune is not where the bourgeois usually looks for it, but in the creation of a *state* of a special type. Such a state has *already* arisen in Russia, it is the Soviets of Workers' and Soldiers' Deputies!

Comrade Kamenev has not pondered on the *fact,* the significance, of the *existing* Soviets, their identity, in point of type and socio-political character, with the commune state, and instead of studying the *fact,* he began to talk about something I was supposed to be "building" on for the "immediate" future. The result is, unfortunately, a repetition of the method used by many bourgeois: from the question as to *what are* the Soviets, whether they are of a *higher* type than a parliamentary republic, whether they are *more useful* for the people, *more democratic, more convenient* for the struggle, for combating, for instance, the grain shortage, etc.—from this real, urgent, vital issue, attention is diverted to the empty, would-be scientific, but actually hollow, professorially dead question of "building on an immediate transformation".

An idle question falsely presented. I "build" *only* on this, *exclusively* on this—that the workers, soldiers and peasants will deal better than the officials, better than the police, with the difficult *practical,* problems of producing more grain, distributing it better and keeping the soldiers better supplied, etc., etc.

I am deeply convinced that the Soviets will make the independent activity of the *masses* a reality more quickly and effectively than will a parliamentary republic (I shall compare the two types of state in greater detail in another letter). They will more effectively, more practically and more correctly decide what *steps* can be taken towards socialism and how these steps should be taken. Control over a bank, the merging of all banks into one, is *not yet* socialism, but it is *a step towards* socialism. Today such steps are being taken in Germany by the Junkers and the bourgeoisie against the people. Tomorrow the Soviet will be able to take these steps more effectively for the benefit of the people if the whole state power is in its hands.

What *compels* such steps?

Famine. Economic disorganisation. Imminent collapse. The horrors of war. The horrors of the wounds inflicted on mankind by the war.

Comrade Kamenev concludes his article with the remark that "in a broad discussion he hopes to carry his point of view, which is the only possible one for revolutionary Social-Democracy if it wishes to and should remain to the very end the party of the revolutionary masses of the proletariat and not turn into a group of Communist propagandists".

It seems to me that these words betray a completely erroneous estimate of the situation. Comrade Kamenev contraposes to a "party of the masses" a "group of propagandists". But the "masses" have now succumbed to the craze of "revolutionary" defencism. Is it not more becoming for internationalists at this moment to show that they can resist "mass" intoxication rather than to "wish to remain" with the masses, i.e., to succumb to the general epidemic? Have we not seen how in all the belligerent countries of Europe the chauvinists tried to justify themselves on the grounds that they wished to "remain with the masses"? Must we not be able to remain for a time in the minority against the "mass" intoxication? Is it not the work of the propagandists at the present moment that forms the key point for *disentangling* the proletarian line from the defencist and petty-bourgeois "mass" intoxication? It was this fusion of the masses, proletarian and non-proletarian, regardless of class differences within the masses, that formed one of the conditions for the defencist epidemic. To speak contemptuously of a "group of propagandists" advocating a *proletarian* line does not seem to be very becoming.

STATE AND REVOLUTION
(1917)

CHAPTER 1: CLASS SOCIETY AND THE STATE

1. THE STATE—A PRODUCT OF THE IRRECONCILABILITY OF CLASS ANTAGONISMS

What is now happening to Marx's theory has, in the course of history, happened repeatedly to the theories of revolutionary thinkers and leaders of oppressed classes fighting for emancipation. During the lifetime of great revolutionaries, the oppressing classes constantly hounded them, received their theories with the most savage malice, the most furious hatred and the most unscrupulous campaigns of lies and slander. After their death, attempts are made to convert them into harmless icons, to canonise them, so to say, and to hallow their *names* to a certain extent for the "consolation" of the oppressed classes and with the object of duping the latter, while at the same time robbing the revolutionary theory of its *substance*, blunting its revolutionary edge and vulgarising it. Today, thc bourgcoisic and the opportunists within the labour movement concur in this doctoring of Marxism. They omit, obscure or distort the revolutionary side of this theory, its revolutionary soul. They push to the foreground and extol what is or seems acceptable to the bourgeoisie. All the social-chauvinists are now "Marxists" (don't laugh!). And more and more frequently German bourgeois scholars, only yesterday specialists in the annihilation of Marxism, are speaking of the "national-German" Marx, who, they claim, educated the labour unions which are so splendidly organised for the purpose of waging a predatory war!

In these circumstances, in view of the unprecedentedly widespread distortion of Marxism, our prime task is to *re-establish* what Marx really taught on the subject of the state. This will necessitate a number of long quotations from the works of Marx and Engels themselves. Of course, long quotations will render the text cumbersome and not help at all to make it popular reading, but we cannot possibly dispense with them. All, or at any rate all the most essential passages in the works of Marx and Engels on the subject of the state must by all means be quoted as fully as possible so that the reader may form an independent opinion of the totality of the views of the founders of scientific socialism, and of the evolution of those views, and so that their distortion by the "Kautskyism" now prevailing may be documentarily proved and clearly demonstrated.

Let us begin with the most popular of Engels's works, *The Origin of the Family, Private Property and the State*, the sixth edition of which was published in Stuttgart as far back as 1894. We have to translate the quotations from the German originals, as the Russian translations, while very numerous, are for the most part either incomplete or very unsatisfactory.

Summing up his historical analysis, Engels says:

> "The state is, therefore, by no means a power forced on society from without; just as little is it 'the reality of the ethical idea', 'the image and reality of reason', as Hegel maintains. Rather, it is a product of society at a certain stage of development; it is the admission that this society has become entangled in an insoluble contradiction with itself, that it has split into irreconcilable antagonisms which it is powerless to dispel. But in order that these antagonisms, these classes with conflicting economic interests, might not consume themselves and society in fruitless struggle, it became necessary to have a power, seemingly standing above society, that would alleviate the conflict and keep it within the bounds of 'order'; and this power, arisen out of society but placing itself above it, and alienating itself more and more from it, is the state." (pp. 177-78, sixth German edition.)[1]

This expresses with perfect clarity the basic idea of Marxism with regard to the historical role and the meaning of the state. The state is a product and a manifestation of the *irreconcilability* of class antagonisms. The state arises where, when and insofar as class antagonism objectively *cannot* be reconciled. And, conversely, the existence of the state proves that the class antagonisms are irreconcilable.

It is on this most important and fundamental point that the distortion of Marxism, proceeding along two main lines, begins.

On the one hand, the bourgeois, and particularly the petty-bourgeois, ideologists, compelled under the weight of indisputable historical facts to admit that the state only exists where there are class antagonisms and a class struggle, "correct" Marx in such a way as to make it appear that the state is an organ for the *reconciliation* of classes. According to Marx, the state could neither have arisen nor maintained itself had it been possible to

[1] See Frederick Engels, *The Origin of the Family, Private Property and the State* (Karl Marx and Frederick Engels, *Selected Works*, Vol. 3, Moscow, 1973, pp. 326-27).

reconcile classes. From what the petty-bourgeois and philistine professors and publicists say, with quite frequent and benevolent references to Marx, it appears that the state does reconcile classes. According to Marx, the state is an organ of class *rule*, an organ for the *oppression* of one class by another; it is the creation of "order", which legalises and perpetuates this oppression by moderating the conflict between the classes. In the opinion of the petty-bourgeois politicians, however, order means the reconciliation of classes, and not the oppression of one class by another; to alleviate the conflict means reconciling classes and not depriving the oppressed classes of definite means and methods of struggle to overthrow the oppressors.

For instance, when, in the revolution of 1917, the question of the significance and role of the state arose in all its magnitude as a practical question demanding immediate action, and, moreover, action on a mass scale, all the Social-Revolutionaries and Mensheviks descended at once to the petty-bourgeois theory that the "state" "reconciles" classes. Innumerable resolutions and articles by politicians of both these parties are thoroughly saturated with this petty-bourgeois and philistine "reconciliation" theory. That the state is an organ of the rule of a definite class which *cannot* be reconciled with its antipode (the class opposite to it) is something the petty-bourgeois democrats will never be able to understand. Their attitude to the state is one of the most striking manifestations of the fact that our Socialist-Revolutionaries and Mensheviks are not socialists at all (a point that we Bolsheviks have always maintained), but petty-bourgeois democrats using near-socialist phraseology.

On the other hand, the "Kautskyite" distortion of Marxism is far more subtle. "Theoretically", it is not denied that the state is an organ of class rule, or that class antagonisms are irreconcilable. But what is overlooked or glossed over is this: if the state is the product of the irreconcilability of class antagonisms, if it is a power standing *above* society and "*alienating* itself *more and more* from it", it is clear that the liberation of the oppressed class is impossible not only without a violent revolution, *but also without the destruction* of the apparatus of state power which was created by the ruling class and which is the embodiment of this "alienation". As we shall see later, Marx very explicitly drew this theoretically self-evident conclusion on the strength of a concrete historical analysis of the tasks of the revolution. And—as we shall show in detail further on—it is this conclusion which Kautsky has "forgotten" and distorted.

2. SPECIAL BODIES OF ARMED MEN, PRISONS, ETC.

Engels continues:

> "As distinct from the old gentile [tribal or clan] order,[2] the state, first, divides its subjects *according to territory*. . . ."
>
> This division seems "natural" to us, but it costs a prolonged struggle against the old organisation according to generations or tribes.
>
> "The second distinguishing feature is the establishment of a *public power* which no longer directly coincides with the population organising itself as an armed force. This special, *public power* is necessary because a self-acting armed organisation of the population has become impossible since the split into classes. . . . This public power exists in every state; it consists not merely of armed men but also of material adjuncts, prisons, and institutions of coercion of all kinds, of which gentile [clan] society knew nothing. . . ."

Engels elucidates the concept of the "power" which is called the state, a power which arose from society but places itself above it and alienates itself more and more from it. What does this power mainly consist of? It consists of special bodies of armed men having prisons, etc., at their command.

We are justified in speaking of special bodies of armed men, because the public power which is an attribute of every state "does not directly coincide" with the armed population, with its "self-acting armed organisation".

Like all great revolutionary thinkers, Engels tries to draw the attention of the class-conscious workers to what prevailing philistinism regards as least worthy of attention, as the most habitual thing, hallowed by prejudices that are not only deep-rooted but, one might say, petrified.

[2] *Gentile, or tribal, organisation of society*—the primitive communal system, or the first socio-economic formation in history. The tribal commune was a community of blood relatives linked by economic and social ties. The tribal system went through the matriarchal and the patriarchal periods. The patriarchate culminated in primitive society becoming a class society and in the rise of the state. Relations of production under the primitive communal system were based on social ownership of the means of production and equalitarian distribution of all products. This corresponded in the main to the low level of the productive forces and to their character at the time.

For the primitive communal system, see Karl Marx, *Conspectus of Lewis Morgan's "Ancient Society"*, and Frederick Engels, *The Origin of the Family, Private Property and the State* (Karl Marx and Frederick Engels, Selected Works, Vol. 3, Moscow, 1973, pp. 204-334).

A standing army and police are the chief instruments of state power. But how can it be otherwise?

From the viewpoint of the vast majority of Europeans of the end of the nineteenth century, whom Engels was addressing, and who had not gone through or closely observed a single great revolution, it could not have been otherwise. They could not understand at all what a "self-acting armed organisation of the population" was. When asked why it became necessary to have special bodies of armed men placed above society and alienating themselves from it (police and a standing army), the West-European and Russian philistines are inclined to utter a few phrases borrowed from Spencer or Mikhailovsky, to refer to the growing complexity of social life, the differentiation of functions, and so on.

Such a reference seems "scientific", and effectively lulls the ordinary person to sleep by obscuring the important and basic fact, namely, the split of society into irreconcilable antagonistic classes.

Were it not for this split, the "self-acting armed organisation of the population" would differ from the primitive organisation of a stick-wielding herd of monkeys, or of primitive men, or of men united in clans, by its complexity, its high technical level, and so on. But such an organisation would still be possible.

It is impossible because civilised society is split into antagonistic, and, moreover, irreconcilably antagonistic classes, whose "self-acting" arming would lead to an armed struggle between them. A state arises, a special power is created, special bodies of armed men, and every revolution, by destroying the state apparatus, shows us the naked class struggle, clearly shows us how the ruling class strives to restore the special bodies of armed men which serve *it*, and how the oppressed class strives to create a new organisation of this kind, capable of serving the exploited instead of the exploiters.

In the above argument, Engels raises theoretically the very same question which every great revolution raises before us in practice, palpably and, what is more, on a scale of mass action, namely, the question of the relationship between "special" bodies of armed men and the "self-acting armed organisation of the population". We shall see how this question is specifically illustrated by the experience of the European and Russian revolutions.

But to return to Engels's exposition.

He points out that sometimes—in certain parts of North America, for example—this public power is weak (he has in mind a rare exception in capitalist society, and those parts of North America in its pre-imperialist days where the free colonists predominated), but that, generally speaking, it grows stronger:

> "It [the public power] grows stronger, however, in proportion as class antagonisms within the state become more acute, and as adjacent states become larger and more populous. We have only to look at our present-day Europe, where class struggle and rivalry in conquest have tuned up the public power to such a pitch that it threatens to swallow the whole of society and even the state."

This was written not later than the early nineties of the last century, Engels's last preface being dated June 16, 1891. The turn towards imperialism—meaning the complete domination of the trusts, the omnipotence of the big banks, a grand-scale colonial policy, and so forth—was only just beginning in France, and was even weaker in North America and in Germany. Since then "rivalry in conquest" has taken a gigantic stride, all the more because by the beginning of the second decade of the twentieth century the world had been completely divided up among these "rivals in conquest", i.e., among the predatory Great Powers. Since then, military and naval armaments have grown fantastically and the predatory war of 1914-17 for the domination of the world by Britain or Germany, for the division of the spoils, has brought the "swallowing" of all the forces of society by the rapacious state power close to complete catastrophe.

Engels could, as early as 1891, point to "rivalry in conquest" as one of the most important distinguishing features of the foreign policy of the Great Powers, while the social-chauvinist scoundrels have ever since 1914, when this rivalry, many times intensified, gave rise to an imperialist war, been covering up the defence of the predatory interests of "their own" bourgeoisie with phrases about "defence of the fatherland", "defence of the republic and the revolution", etc.!

3. THE STATE—AN INSTRUMENT FOR THE EXPLOITATION OF THE OPPRESSED CLASS

The maintenance of the special public power standing above society requires taxes and state loans.

> "Having public power and the right to levy taxes," Engels writes, "the officials now stand, as organs of society, *above* society. The free, voluntary respect that was accorded to the organs of the gentile [clan] constitution

> does not satisfy them, even if they could gain it. . . ." Special laws are enacted proclaiming the sanctity and immunity of the officials. "The shabbiest police servant" has more "authority" than the representative of the clan, but even the head of the military power of a civilised state may well envy the elder of a clan the "unrestrained respect" of society.

The question of the privileged position of the officials as organs of state power is raised here. The main point indicated is: what is it that places them *above* society? We shall see how this theoretical question was answered in practice by the Paris Commune in 1871 and how it was obscured from a reactionary standpoint by Kautsky in 1912.

> "Because the state arose from the need to hold class antagonisms in check, but because it arose, at the same time, in the midst of the conflict of these classes, it is, as a rule, the state of the most powerful, economically dominant class, which, through the medium of the state, becomes also the politically dominant class, and thus acquires new means of holding down and exploiting the oppressed class. . . ." The ancient and feudal states were organs for the exploitation of the slaves and serfs; likewise, "the modern representative state is an instrument of exploitation of wage-labour by capital. By way of exception, however, periods occur in which the warring classes balance each other so nearly that the state power as ostensible mediator acquires, for the moment, a certain degree of independence of both. . . ." Such were the absolute monarchies of the seventeenth and eighteenth centuries, the Bonapartism of the First and Second Empires in France, and the Bismarck regime in Germany.

Such, we may add, is the Kerensky government in republican Russia since it began to persecute the revolutionary proletariat, at a moment when, owing to the leadership of the petty-bourgeois democrats, the Soviets have *already* become impotent, while the bourgeoisie are not *yet* strong enough simply to disperse them.

> In a democratic republic, Engels continues, "wealth exercises its power indirectly, but all the more surely", first, by means of the "direct corruption of officials" (America); secondly, by means of an "alliance of the government and the Stock Exchange" (France and America).

At present, imperialism and the domination of the banks have "developed" into an exceptional art both these methods of upholding and giving effect to the omnipotence of wealth in democratic republics of all descriptions. Since, for instance, in the very first months of the Russian democratic republic, one might say during the honeymoon of the "socialist" S.R.s and Mensheviks joined in wedlock to the bourgeoisie, in the coalition government, Mr. Palchinsky obstructed every measure intended for curbing the capitalists and their marauding practices, their plundering of the state by means of war contracts; and since later on Mr. Palchinsky, upon resigning from the Cabinet (and being, of course, replaced by another quite similar Palchinsky), was "rewarded" by the capitalists with a lucrative job with a salary of 120,000 rubles per annum—what would you call that? Direct or indirect bribery? An alliance of the government and the syndicates, or "merely" friendly relations? What role do the Chernovs, Tseretelis, Avksentyevs and Skobelevs play? Are they the "direct" or only the indirect allies of the millionaire treasury-looters?

Another reason why the omnipotence of "wealth" is more *certain* in a democratic republic is that it does not depend on defects in the political machinery or on the faulty political shell of capitalism. A democratic republic is the best possible political shell for capitalism, and, therefore, once capital has gained possession of this very best shell (through the Palchinskys, Chernovs, Tseretelis and Co.), it establishes its power so securely, so firmly, that *no* change of persons, institutions or parties in the bourgeois-democratic republic can shake it.

We must also note that Engels is most explicit in calling universal suffrage as well an instrument of bourgeois rule. Universal suffrage, he says, obviously taking account of the long experience of German Social-Democracy, is

> "the gauge of the maturity of the working class. It cannot and never will be anything more in the present-day state."

The petty-bourgeois democrats, such as our Socialist-Revolutionaries and Mensheviks, and also their twin brothers, all the social-chauvinists and opportunists of Western Europe, expect just this "more" from universal suffrage. They themselves share, and instill into the minds of the people, the false notion that universal suffrage "in the *present-day* state" is really capable of revealing the will of the majority of the working people and of securing its realisation.

Here, we can only indicate this false notion, only point out that Engels's perfectly clear, precise and concrete statement is distorted at every step in the propaganda and agitation of the "official" (i.e., opportunist) socialist parties. A detailed exposure of the utter falsity of this notion which Engels brushes aside here is given in our further account of the views of Marx and Engels on the "*present-day*" state.

Engels gives a general summary of his views in the most popular of his works in the following words:

> "The state, then, has not existed from all eternity. There have been societies that did without it, that had no idea of the state and state power. At a certain stage of economic development, which was necessarily bound up with the split of society into classes, the state became a necessity owing to this split. We are now rapidly approaching a stage in the development of production at which the existence of these classes not only will have ceased to be a necessity, but will become a positive hindrance to production. They will fall as inevitably as they arose at an earlier stage. Along with them the state will inevitably fall. Society, which will reorganise production on the basis of a free and equal association of the producers, will put the whole machinery of state where it will then belong: into a museum of antiquities, by the side of the spinning-wheel and the bronze axe."

We do not often come across this passage in the propaganda and agitation literature of the present-day Social-Democrats. Even when we do come across it, it is mostly quoted in the same manner as one bows before an icon, i.e., it is done to show official respect for Engels, and no attempt is made to gauge the breadth and depth of the revolution that this relegating of "the whole machinery of state to a museum of antiquities" implies. In most cases we do not even find an understanding of what Engels calls the state machine.

4. THE "WITHERING AWAY" OF THE STATE, AND VIOLENT REVOLUTION

Engels's words regarding the "withering away" of the state are so widely known, they are often quoted, and so clearly reveal the essence of the customary adaptation of Marxism to opportunism that we must deal with them in detail. We shall quote the whole argument from which they are taken.

> "*The proletariat seizes state power and turns the means of production into state property to begin with.* But thereby it abolishes itself as the proletariat, abolishes all class distinctions and class antagonisms, and abolishes also the state as state. Society thus far, operating amid class antagonisms,

> needed the state, that is, an organisation of the particular exploiting class, for the maintenance of its external conditions of production, and, therefore, especially, for the purpose of forcibly keeping the exploited class in the conditions of oppression determined by the given mode of production (slavery, serfdom or bondage, wage-labour). The state was the official representative of society as a whole, its concentration in a visible corporation. But it was this only insofar as it was the state of that class which itself represented, for its own time, society as a whole: in ancient times, the state of slave-owning citizens; in the Middle Ages, of the feudal nobility; in our own time, of the bourgeoisie. When at last it becomes the real representative of the whole of society, it renders itself unnecessary. As soon as there is no longer any social class to be held in subjection, as soon as class rule, and the individual struggle for existence based upon the present anarchy in production, with the collisions and excesses arising from this struggle, are removed, nothing more remains to be held in subjection—nothing necessitating a special coercive force, a state. The first act by which the state really comes forward as the representative of the whole of society—the taking possession of the means of production in the name of society—is also its last independent act as a state. State interference in social relations becomes, in one domain after another, superfluous, and then dies down of itself. The government of persons is replaced by the administration of things, and by the conduct of processes of production. The state is not 'abolished'. *It withers away*. This gives the measure of the value of the phrase 'a free people's state', both as to its justifiable use for a long time from an agitational point of view, and as to its ultimate scientific insufficiency; and also of the so-called anarchists' demand that the state be abolished overnight." (*Herr Eugen Dühring's Revolution in Science* [*Anti-Dühring*], pp. 301-03, third German edition.)[3]

It is safe to say that of this argument of Engels's, which is so remarkably rich in ideas, only one point has become an integral part of socialist thought among modern socialist parties, namely, that according to Marx that state "withers away"—as distinct from the anarchist doctrine of the "abolition" of the state. To prune Marxism to such an extent means reducing it to opportunism, for this "interpretation" only leaves a vague notion of a slow, even, gradual change, of absence of leaps and storms, of absence of revolution. The current, widespread, popular, if one may say so, conception of the "withering away" of the state undoubtedly means obscuring, if not repudiating, revolution.

[3] See Frederick Engels, *Anti-Dühring*, Moscow, 1969, pp. 332-33.

Such an "interpretation", however, is the crudest distortion of Marxism, advantageous only to the bourgeoisie. In point of theory, it is based on disregard for the most important circumstances and considerations indicated in, say, Engels's "summary" argument we have just quoted in full.

In the first place, at the very outset of his argument, Engels says that, in seizing state power, the proletariat thereby "abolishes the state as state". It is not done to ponder over the meaning of this. Generally, it is either ignored altogether, or is considered to be something in the nature of "Hegelian weakness" on Engels's part. As a matter of fact, however, these words briefly express the experience of one of the greatest proletarian revolutions, the Paris Commune of 1871, of which we shall speak in greater detail in its proper place. As a matter of fact, Engels speaks here of the proletariat revolution "abolishing" the *bourgeois* state, while the words about the state withering away refer to the remnants of the *proletarian* state *after* the socialist revolution. According to Engels, the bourgeois state does not "wither away", but is "*abolished*" by the proletariat in the course of the revolution. What withers away after this revolution is the proletarian state or semi-state.

Secondly, the state is a "special coercive force". Engels gives this splendid and extremely profound definition here with the utmost lucidity. And from it follows that the "special coercive force" for the suppression of the proletariat by the bourgeoisie, of millions of working people by handfuls of the rich, must be replaced by a "special coercive force" for the suppression of the bourgeoisie by the proletariat (the dictatorship of the proletariat). This is precisely what is meant by "abolition of the state as state". This is precisely the "act" of taking possession of the means of production in the name of society. And it is self-evident that *such* a replacement of one (bourgeois) "special force" by another (proletarian) "special force" cannot possibly take place in the form of "withering away".

Thirdly, in speaking of the state "withering away", and the even more graphic and colourful "dying down of itself", Engels refers quite clearly and definitely to the period *after* "the state has taken possession of the means of production in the name of the whole of society", that is, *after* the socialist revolution. We all know that the political form of the "state" at that time is the most complete democracy. But it never enters the head of any of the opportunists, who shamelessly distort Marxism, that Engels is consequently speaking here of *democracy* "dying down of itself", or "withering away". This seems very strange at first sight. But it is "incomprehensible" only to those who have not thought about democracy *also* being a state and, consequently, also disappearing when the state disappears. Revolution alone can "abolish" the bourgeois state. The state in general, i.e., the most complete democracy, can only "wither away".

Fourthly, after formulating his famous proposition that "the state withers away", Engels at once explains specifically that this proposition is directed against both the opportunists and the anarchists. In doing this, Engels puts in the forefront that conclusion, drawn from the proposition that "the state withers away", which is directed against the opportunists.

One can wager that out of every 10,000 persons who have read or heard about the "withering away" of the state, 9,990 are completely unaware, or do not remember, that Engels directed his conclusions from that proposition not against anarchists *alone*. And of the remaining ten, probably nine do not know the meaning of a "free people's state" or why an attack on this slogan means an attack on opportunists. This is how history is written! This is how a great revolutionary teaching is imperceptibly falsified and adapted to prevailing philistinism. The conclusion directed against the anarchists has been repeated thousands of times; it has been vulgarised, and rammed into people's heads in the shallowest form, and has acquired the strength of a prejudice, whereas the conclusion directed against the opportunists has been obscured and "forgotten"!

The "free people's state" was a programme demand and a catchword current among the German Social-Democrats in the seventies. This catchword is devoid of all political content except that it describes the concept of democracy in a pompous philistine fashion. Insofar as it hinted in a legally permissible manner at a democratic republic, Engels was prepared to "justify" its use "for a time" from an agitational point of view. But it was an opportunist catchword, for it amounted to something more than prettifying bourgeois democracy, and was also failure to understand the socialist criticism of the state in general. We are in favour of a democratic republic as the best form of state for the proletariat under capitalism. But we have no right to forget that wage slavery is the lot of the people even in the most democratic bourgeois republic. Furthermore, every state is a "special force" for the suppression of the oppressed class. Consequently, *every* state is *not* "free" and *not* a "people's state". Marx and Engels explained this repeatedly to their party comrades in the seventies.

Fifthly, the same work of Engels's, whose arguments about the withering away of the state everyone remembers, also contains an argument of the significance of violent revolution. Engels's historical analysis of its role becomes a veritable panegyric on violent revolution.

This, "no one remembers". It is not done in modern socialist parties to talk or even think about the significance of this idea, and it plays no part whatever in their daily propaganda and agitation among the people. And yet it is inseparably bound up with the "withering away" of the state into one harmonious whole.

Here is Engels's argument:

> "... That force, however, plays yet another role [other than that of a diabolical power] in history, a revolutionary role; that, in the words of Marx, it is the midwife of every old society which is pregnant with a new one, that it is the instrument with which social movement forces its way through and shatters the dead, fossilised political forms—of this there is not a word in Herr Dühring. It is only with sighs and groans that he admits the possibility that force will perhaps be necessary for the overthrow of an economy based on exploitation—unfortunately, because all use of force demoralises, he says, the person who uses it. And this in spite of the immense moral and spiritual impetus which has been given by every victorious revolution! And this in Germany, where a violent collision—which may, after all, be forced on the people—would at least have the advantage of wiping out the servility which has penetrated the nation's mentality following the humiliation of the Thirty Years' War.[4] And this person's mode of thought—dull, insipid, and impotent—presumes to impose itself on the most revolutionary party that history has ever known!" (p. 193, third German edition, Part II, end of Chap. IV)

How can this panegyric on violent revolution, which Engels insistently brought to the attention of the German Social-Democrats between 1878 and 1894, i.e., right up to the time of his death, be combined with the

[4] *Thirty Years' War (1618-48)*, the first European war, resulted from an aggravation of the antagonisms between various alignments of European states, and took the form of a struggle between Protestants and Catholics. It began with a revolt in Bohemia against the tyranny of the Hapsburg monarchy and the onslaught of Catholic reaction. The states which then entered the war formed two camps. The Pope, the Spanish and Austrian Hapsburgs and the Catholic princes of Germany, who rallied to the Catholic Church, opposed the Protestant countries—Bohemia, Denmark, Sweden, the Dutch Republic, and a number of German states that had accepted the Reformation. The Protestant countries were backed by the French kings, enemies of the Hapsburgs. Germany became the chief battlefield and object of military plunder and predatory claims. The war ended in 1648 with the signing of the Peace Treaty of Westphalia, which completed the political dismemberment of Germany.

theory of the "withering away" of the state to form a single theory?

Usually the two are combined by means of eclecticism, by an unprincipled or sophistic selection made arbitrarily (or to please the powers that be) of first one, then another argument, and in ninety-nine cases out of a hundred, if not more, it is the idea of the "withering away" that is placed in the forefront. Dialectics are replaced by eclecticism—this is the most usual, the most widespread practice to be met with in present-day official Social-Democratic literature in relation to Marxism. This sort of substitution is, of course, nothing new; it was observed even in the history of classical Greek philosophy. In falsifying Marxism in opportunist fashion, the substitution of eclecticism for dialectics is the easiest way of deceiving the people. It gives an illusory satisfaction; it seems to take into account all sides of the process, all trends of development, all the conflicting influences, and so forth, whereas in reality it provides no integral and revolutionary conception of the process of social development at all.

We have already said above, and shall show more fully later, that the theory of Marx and Engels of the inevitability of a violent revolution refers to the bourgeois state. The latter *cannot* be superseded by the proletarian state (the dictatorship of the proletariat) through the process of "withering away", but, as a general rule, only through a violent revolution. The panegyric Engels sang in its honour, and which fully corresponds to Marx's repeated statements (see the concluding passages of *The Poverty of Philosophy*[5] and the *Communist Manifesto*,[6] with their proud and open proclamation of the inevitability of a violent revolution; see what Marx wrote nearly thirty years later, in criticising the Gotha Programme of 1875, when he mercilessly castigated the opportunist character of that programme[7])—this panegyric is by no means a mere "impulse", a mere declamation or a polemical sally. The necessity of systematically imbuing

[5] See Karl Marx, *The Poverty of Philosophy*, Moscow, 1973, pp. 151-52.

[6] See Karl Marx and Frederick Engels, *Selected Works*, Vol. 1, Moscow, 1973, p. 137.

[7] *Gotha Programme*—the programme adopted by the Socialist Workers' Party of Germany in 1875, at the Gotha Congress, which united two German socialist parties, namely, the Eisenachers—led by August Bebel and Wilhelm Liebknecht and influenced by Marx and Engels—and the Lassalleans. The programme betrayed eclecticism and was opportunist, because the Eisenachers had made concessions to the Lassalleans on major issues and accepted Lassallean formulations. Marx in his *Critique of the Gotha Programme*, and Engels in his letter to Bebel of March 18-28, 1875, devastated the Gotha Programme, which they regarded as a serious step backwards compared with the Eisenach programme of 1869.

the masses with *this* and precisely this view of violent revolution lies at the root of the *entire* theory of Marx and Engels. The betrayal of their theory by the now prevailing social-chauvinist and Kautskyite trends expresses itself strikingly in both these trends ignoring *such* propaganda and agitation.

The supersession of the bourgeois state by the proletarian state is impossible without a violent revolution. The abolition of the proletarian state, i.e., of the state in general, is impossible except through the process of "withering away".

A detailed and concrete elaboration of these views was given by Marx and Engels when they studied each particular revolutionary situation, when they analysed the lessons of the experience of each particular revolution. We shall now pass to this, undoubtedly the most important, part of their theory.

ON COMPROMISES
(1917)

The term compromise in politics implies the surrender of certain demands, the renunciation of part of one's demands, by agreement with another party.

The usual idea the man in the street has about the Bolsheviks, an idea encouraged by a press which slanders them, is that the Bolsheviks will never agree to a compromise with anybody.

The idea is flattering to us as the party of the revolutionary proletariat, for it proves that even our enemies are compelled to admit our loyalty to the fundamental principles of socialism and revolution. Nevertheless, we must say that this idea is wrong. Engels was right when, in his criticism of the Manifesto of the Blanquist Communists[1] (1873), he ridiculed their declaration: "No compromises!"[2] This, he said, was an empty phrase, for compromises are often unavoidably forced upon a fighting party by circumstances, and it is absurd to refuse once and for all to accept "payments on account".[3] The task of a truly revolutionary party is not to declare that it is impossible to renounce all compromises, but to be able, *through all compromises*, when they are unavoidable, to remain true to its principles, to its class, to its revolutionary purpose, to its task of paving the way for revolution and educating the mass of the people for victory in the revolution.

To agree, for instance, to participate in the Third and Fourth Dumas was a compromise, a temporary renunciation of revolutionary demands. But this was a compromise absolutely forced upon us, for the balance of forces made it impossible for us for the time being to conduct a mass

[1] *Blanquists*—supporters of a trend in the French socialist movement, headed by Louis-Auguste Blanqui (1805-1881), the French revolutionary and Utopian communist. The Blanquists expected that "mankind will be emancipated from wage slavery not by the proletarian class struggle, but through a conspiracy of a small minority of intellectuals" (see *LCW*, Vol. 10, 1978, p. 392). Substituting the actions of a small group of conspirators for those of a revolutionary party, they ignored the actual situation necessary for a victorious insurrection, and spurned contact with the masses.

[2] See Frederick Engels, *Flüchtlingsliteratur. II. Programm der blanquistischen Kommuneflüchtlinge*, Marx/Engels, *Werke*, Bd. 18, Berlin, 1962, S. 528-35.

[3] See Karl Marx and Frederick Engels, *Selected Correspondence*, Moscow, 1965, p. 470.

revolutionary struggle, and in order to prepare this struggle over a long period we *had* to be able to work even from *inside* such a "pigsty". History has proved that this approach to the question by the Bolsheviks as a party was perfectly correct.

Now the question is not of a forced, but of a voluntary compromise.

Our Party, like any other political party, is striving after political domination *for itself.* Our aim is the dictatorship of the revolutionary proletariat. Six months of revolution have proved very clearly, forcefully and convincingly that this demand is correct and inevitable in the interests of *this particular* revolution, for otherwise the people will never obtain a democratic peace, land for the peasants, or complete freedom (a fully democratic republic). This has been shown and proved by the course of events during the six months of our revolution, by the struggle of the classes and parties and by the development of the crises of April 20-21, June 9-10 and 18-19, July 3-5 and August 27-31.

The Russian revolution is experiencing so abrupt and original a turn that we, as a party, may offer a voluntary compromise—true, not to our direct and main class enemy, the bourgeoisie, but to our nearest adversaries, the "ruling" petty-bourgeois-democratic parties, the Socialist-Revolutionaries and Mensheviks.

We may offer a compromise to these parties only by way of exception, and only by virtue of the particular situation, which will obviously last only a very short time. And I think we should do so.

The compromise on our part is our return to the pre-July demand of all power to the Soviets and a government of S.R.s and Mensheviks responsible to the Soviets.

Now, and only now, perhaps *during only a few days* or a week or two, such a government could be set up and consolidated in a perfectly peaceful way. In all probability it could secure the peaceful *advance* of the whole Russian revolution, and provide exceptionally good chances for great strides in the world movement towards peace and the victory of socialism.

In my opinion, the Bolsheviks, who are partisans of world revolution and revolutionary methods, may and should consent to this compromise only for the sake of the revolution's peaceful development—an opportunity that is *extremely* rare in history and *extremely* valuable, an opportunity that only occurs once in a while.

The compromise would amount to the following: the Bolsheviks, without making any claim to participate in the government (which is impossible for the internationalists unless a dictatorship of the proletariat and the poor peasants has been realised), would refrain from demanding the immediate transfer of power to the proletariat and the poor peasants and from employing revolutionary methods of fighting for this demand. A condition that is self-evident and not new to the S.R.s and Mensheviks would be complete freedom of propaganda and the convocation of the Constituent Assembly without further delays or even at an earlier date.

The Mensheviks and S.R.s, being the government bloc, would then agree (assuming that the compromise had been reached) to form a government wholly and exclusively responsible to the Soviets, the latter taking over all power locally as well. This would constitute the "new" condition. I think the Bolsheviks would advance no other conditions, trusting that the revolution would proceed peacefully and party strife in the Soviets would be *peacefully overcome* thanks to really complete freedom of propaganda and to the immediate establishment of a new democracy in the composition of the Soviets (new elections) and in their functioning.

Perhaps this is *already* impossible? Perhaps. But if there is even one chance in a hundred, the attempt at realising this opportunity is still worthwhile.

What would both "contracting" parties gain by this "compromise", i.e., the Bolsheviks, on the one hand, and the S.R. and Menshevik bloc, on the other? If *neither* side gains anything, then the compromise must be recognised as impossible, and nothing more is to be said. No matter how difficult this compromise may be at present (after July and August, two months equivalent to two decades in "peaceful", somnolent times), I think it stands a small chance of being realised. This chance has been created by the decision of the S.R.s and Mensheviks not to participate in a government together with the Cadets.

The Bolsheviks would gain the opportunity of quite freely advocating their views and of trying to win influence in the Soviets under a really complete democracy. In words, "everybody" now concedes the Bolsheviks this freedom. In reality, this freedom is *impossible* under a bourgeois government or a government in which the bourgeoisie participate, or under any government, in fact, other than the Soviets. Under a Soviet government, such freedom would be *possible* (we do not say it would be a certainty, but still it would be possible). For the sake of such a possibility at such a difficult time, it would be worth compromising with the present majority in the Soviets. *We* have nothing to fear from real democracy, for reality is on our side, and even the course of development of trends within the S.R. and Menshevik parties, which are hostile to us, proves us right.

The Mensheviks and S.R.s would gain in that they would at once obtain every opportunity to carry out *their* bloc's programme with the support of the obviously overwhelming majority of the people and in that they would secure for themselves the "peaceful" use of their majority in the Soviets.

Of course, there would probably be two voices heard from this bloc, which is heterogeneous both because it is a bloc and because petty-bourgeois democracy is *always* less homogeneous than the bourgeoisie and the proletariat.

One voice would say: we cannot follow the same road as the Bolsheviks and the revolutionary proletariat. It will demand too much anyway and will entice the peasant poor by demagogy. It will demand peace and a break with the Allies. That is impossible. We are better off and safer with the bourgeoisie; after all, we have not parted ways with them but only had a temporary *quarrel*, and only over the Kornilov incident. We have quarrelled, but we shall make it up. Moreover, the Bolsheviks are not "ceding" us anything, for their attempts at insurrection are as doomed to defeat as was the Commune of 1871.

The other voice would say: the allusion to the Commune is very superficial and even foolish. For, in the first place, the Bolsheviks have learnt something since 1871; they would not fail to seize the banks, and would not refuse to advance on Versailles. Under such conditions even the Commune might have been victorious. Furthermore, the Commune could not immediately offer the people what the Bolsheviks will be able to offer if they come to power, namely, land to the peasants, an immediate offer of peace, real control over production, an honest peace with the Ukrainians, Finns, etc. The Bolsheviks, to put it bluntly, hold ten times more "trumps" than the Commune did. In the second place, the Commune, after all, means a strenuous civil war, a set-back to peaceful cultural development for a long time to come, an opportunity for all sorts of MacMahons and Kornilovs to operate and plot with greater ease—and such operations are a menace to our whole bourgeois society. Is it wise to risk a Commune?

Now a Commune is inevitable in Russia if we do not take power into our own hands, if things remain in as grave a state as they were between May 6 and August 31. Every revolutionary worker and soldier will inevitably think about the Commune and believe in it; he will inevitably attempt to bring it about, for he will argue: "The people are perishing; war, famine and ruin are spreading. Only the Commune can save us. So let us all perish, let us die, but let us set up the Commune." Such thoughts are inevitable with the workers, and it will not be as easy to crush the Commune now as it was in 1871. The Russian Commune will have allies throughout the world, allies a hundred times stronger than those the Commune had in 1871. . . . Is it wise for us to risk a Commune? I cannot agree, either, that the Bolsheviks virtually cede us nothing by their compromise. For, in all civilised countries, civilised ministers value highly every agreement with the proletariat in war-time, however small. They value it very, very highly. And these are men of action, real ministers. The Bolsheviks are rapidly becoming stronger, in spite of repression, and the weakness of their press. . . . Is it wise for us to risk a Commune?

We have a safe majority; the peasant poor will not wake up for some time to come; we are safe for our lifetime. I do not believe that in a peasant country the majority will follow the extremists. And against an obvious majority, no insurrection is possible in a really democratic republic. This is what the second voice would say.

There may also be a third voice coming from among the supporters of Martov or Spiridonova, which would say: I am indignant, "comrades", that both of you, speaking about the Commune and its likelihood, unhesitatingly side with its opponents. In one form or another, both of you side with those who suppressed the Commune. I will not undertake to campaign for the Commune and I cannot promise beforehand to fight in its ranks as every Bolshevik will do, but I must say that *if* the Commune does start *in spite* of my efforts, I shall rather help its defenders than its opponents.

The medley of voices in the "bloc" is great and inevitable, for a host of shades is represented among the petty-bourgeois democrats—from the complete bourgeois, perfectly eligible for a post in the government, down to the semi-pauper who is not yet capable of taking up the proletarian position. Nobody knows what will be the result of this medley of voices at any given moment.

* * *

The above lines were written on Friday, September 1, but due to unforeseen circumstances (under Kerensky, as history will tell, not all Bolsheviks were free to choose their domicile) they did not reach the editorial office that day. After reading Saturday's and today's (Sunday's) papers, I say to myself: perhaps it is already too late to offer a compromise. Perhaps the few days in which a peaceful development was *still* possible have passed *too*. Yes, to all appearances, they have already passed.[4] In one way or another, Kerensky will abandon both the S.R. Party and the S.R.s themselves, and will consolidate his position with the aid of the bourgeoisie *without* the S.R.s, and thanks to their inaction. . . . Yes, to all appearances, the days when by chance the path of peaceful development became possible have *already* passed. All that remains is to send these notes to the editor with the request to have them entitled: "Belated Thoughts". Perhaps even belated thoughts are sometimes not without interest.

[4] After the suppression of the Kornilov revolt the question of forming a new provisional cabinet came up for discussion. The new cabinet was expected to include Cadets in addition to Mensheviks and S.R.s. The Mensheviks and S.R.s, fearing that they might completely forfeit popular confidence, announced their refusal to join a cabinet which included Cadets. On September 1 (14), 1917, the Provisional Government decided to form a Directory of five: A.F. Kerensky, A.I. Verkhovsky, D.N. Verderevsky, A.M. Nikitin and M.I. Tereshchenko. Officially no Cadets were included in this cabinet, but its formation was a result of a behind-the-scenes compromise with them. At a joint plenary session of the C.E.C. of Soviets of Workers' and Soldiers' Deputies and the Executive Committee of the Congress of Peasants' Deputies on September 2 (15), the Mensheviks and S.R.s passed a resolution in support of the new cabinet. This meant that although they had declared they would have nothing to do with the Cadets, the Mensheviks and S.R.s again helped the landowners and capitalists to retain power.

MARXISM AND INSURRECTION
(1917)
A Letter to the Central Committee of the R.S.D.L.P.(B.)

One of the most vicious and probably most widespread distortions of Marxism resorted to by the dominant "socialist" parties is the opportunist lie that preparation for insurrection, and generally the treatment of insurrection as an art, is "Blanquism".

Bernstein, the leader of opportunism, has already earned himself unfortunate fame by accusing Marxism of Blanquism, and when our present-day opportunists cry Blanquism they do not improve on or "enrich" the meagre "ideas" of Bernstein one little bit.

Marxists are accused of Blanquism for treating insurrection as an art! Can there be a more flagrant perversion of the truth, when not a single Marxist will deny that it was Marx who expressed himself on this score in the most definite, precise and categorical manner, referring to insurrection specifically as an *art,* saying that it must be treated as an art, that you must win the first success and then proceed from success to success, never ceasing the *offensive* against the enemy, taking advantage of his confusion, etc., etc.?

To be successful, insurrection must rely not upon conspiracy and not upon a party, but upon the advanced class. That is the first point. Insurrection must rely upon a *revolutionary upsurge of the people.* That is the second point. Insurrection must rely upon that *turning-point* in the history of the growing revolution when the activity of the advanced ranks of the people is at its height, and when the *vacillations* in the ranks of the enemy and *in the ranks of the weak, half-hearted and irresolute friends of the revolution* are strongest. That is the third point. And these three conditions for raising the question of insurrection distinguish *Marxism from Blanquism.*

Once these conditions exist, however, to refuse to treat insurrection as an *art* is a betrayal of Marxism and a betrayal of the revolution.

To show that it is precisely the present moment that the Party *must* recognise as the one in which the entire course of events has objectively placed *insurrection* on the order of the day and that insurrection must be treated as an art, it will perhaps be best to use the method of comparison, and to draw a parallel between July 3-4[1] and the September days.

[1] What Lenin has in mind are the mass demonstrations which took place in Petrograd on July 3-4 (16-17), 1917. It was a movement of soldiers, sailors and workers, who were incensed at the Provisional Government for sending troops into a patently hopeless offensive which proved a fiasco. It started on July 3 (16) with a demonstration by the First Machine-Gun Regiment in the Vyborg District, and threatened to develop into an armed revolt against the Provisional Government.

The Bolshevik Party was opposed to insurrection at that time because it believed that the revolutionary crisis had not yet come to a head. The Central Committee, meeting at 4.00 p.m. on July 3 (16), decided to refrain from taking action, and a similar decision was adopted by the Second Petrograd City Conference of Bolsheviks which was just then in session. Its delegates went to the factories and the districts to stop the masses from going into action, but the movement had already got underway and nothing could be done to stop it.

Late that night, the Central Committee, together with the Petrograd Committee and the Military Organisation, took account of the mood of the masses and decided to take part in the demonstration to lend it a peaceful and organised character. Lenin was away on a short holiday after an exhausting stretch of work. Being informed of the events, he returned to Petrograd on the morning of July 4 (17) and assumed leadership.

More than 500,000 persons took part in the demonstration on July 4 (17). The demonstrators carried Bolshevik slogans, such as "All Power to the Soviets", and demanded that the All-Russia Central Executive Committee of the Soviet should take power. But the Socialist-Revolutionary and Menshevik leaders refused to do so. The Provisional Government, with the knowledge and consent of the Central Executive Committee, which was dominated by the Mensheviks and Socialist-Revolutionaries, sent detachments of officer cadets and Cossacks to attack and shoot down the peaceful demonstrators. Counter-revolutionary troops were brought in from the front to disperse the demonstrations.

That night, Lenin presided at a meeting of members of the Central Committee and the Petrograd Committee, which adopted a decision to stop the demonstrations in an organised manner. This was a wise step, for it helped to save the main revolutionary force from defeat. The Mensheviks and Socialist-Revolutionaries acted in a manner which helped the counter-revolutionaries: they joined the bourgeoisie in attacking the Bolshevik Party. The Bolshevik newspapers, *Pravda*, *Soldatskaya Pravda* (Soldiers' Truth) and others were closed down by the Provisional Government, while the Trud Printing House, operated on funds donated by the workers, was destroyed. The workers were disarmed and arrested, and searches and persecution were started. The revolutionary units of the Petrograd garrison were withdrawn from the capital and sent to the front.

On July 3-4 it could have been argued, without violating the truth, that the correct thing to do was to take power, for our enemies would in any case have accused us of insurrection and ruthlessly treated us as rebels. However, to have decided on this account in favour of taking power at that time would have been wrong, because the objective conditions for the victory of the insurrection did not exist.

(1) We still lacked the support of the class which is the vanguard of the revolution.

We still did not have a majority among the workers and soldiers of Petrograd and Moscow. Now we have a majority in both Soviets. It was created *solely* by the history of July and August, by the experience of the "ruthless treatment" meted out to the Bolsheviks, and by the experience of the Kornilov revolt.[2]

(2) There was no country-wide revolutionary upsurge at that time. There is now, after the Kornilov revolt; the situation in the provinces and

---

After the July events, power in the country passed into the hands of the counter-revolutionary Provisional Government, with the Soviet an impotent appendage. The period of dual power was at an end, and so was the revolution's peaceful stage. The Bolsheviks were faced with the task of preparing an armed insurrection to overthrow the Provisional Government.

[2] The counter-revolutionary revolt of the bourgeoisie and the landowners in August 1917, which was headed by the Commander-in-Chief of the Army, the tsarist General Kornilov. The plotters planned to take Petrograd, destroy the Bolshevik Party, disperse the Soviets and set up a military dictatorship with a view to restoring the monarchy. Kerensky, the head of the Provisional Government, took part in the plot, but when the revolt got under way he realised that he would be swept away with Kornilov and washed his hands of the whole business: he declared the revolt was aimed against the Provisional Government.

It broke out on August 25 (September 7), with Kornilov sending the Third Cavalry Corps against Petrograd, where counter-revolutionary organisations were itching to go into action.

The mass struggle against Kornilov was led by the Bolshevik Party, which continued, as Lenin demanded, to expose the Provisional Government and its Socialist-Revolutionary and Menshevik accomplices. The Central Committee of the Bolshevik Party rallied the workers of Petrograd, and the revolutionary soldiers and sailors to struggle against the mutineers. Petrograd workers swiftly organised Red Guard units and revolutionary committees were set up in several places. The advance of the Kornilov troops was stopped and their morale undermined by Bolshevik agitators.

The Kornilov revolt was crushed by the workers and peasants led by the Bolshevik Party. Under the pressure of the masses, the Provisional Government was forced to order the arrest and prosecution of Kornilov and his accomplices on charges of organising the revolt.

assumption of power by the Soviets in many localities prove this.

(3) At that time there was no *vacillation* on any serious political scale among our enemies and among the irresolute petty bourgeoisie. Now the vacillation is enormous. Our main enemy, Allied and world imperialism (for world imperialism is headed by the "Allies"), *has begun to waver* between a war to a victorious finish and a separate peace directed against Russia. Our petty-bourgeois democrats, having clearly lost their majority among the people, have begun to vacillate enormously, and have rejected a bloc, i.e., a coalition, with the Cadets.[3]

(4) Therefore, an insurrection on July 3-4 would have been a mistake; we could not have retained power either physically or politically. We could not have retained it physically even though Petrograd was at times in our hands, because at that time our workers and soldiers would not have *fought and died* for Petrograd. There was not at the time that "savageness", or fierce hatred *both of* the Kerenskys *and* of the Tseretelis and Chernovs. Our people had still not been tempered by the experience of the persecution of the Bolsheviks in which the Socialist-Revolutionaries and Mensheviks participated.

We could not have retained power politically on July 3-4 because, *before the Kornilov revolt*, the army and the provinces could and would have marched against Petrograd.

Now the picture is entirely different.

We have the following of the majority of a *class*, the vanguard of the revolution, the vanguard of the people, which is capable of carrying the masses with it.

We have the following of the *majority* of the people, because

[3] *Cadets* (Constitutional-Democratic Party)—the leading party of the liberal-monarchist bourgeoisie in Russia, set up in October 1905. Its membership was made up of capitalists, landowners serving on local councils and bourgeois intellectuals. Among its more prominent members were P.N. Milyukov, S.A. Muromtsev, V.A. Maklakov, A.I. Shingaryov, and P.B. Struve. The Cadets eventually developed into a party of the imperialist bourgeoisie. During the First World War they actively supported the tsarist government's foreign policy of aggrandisement. During the bourgeois-democratic revolution of February 1917, they tried to save the monarchy; playing a keg part in the bourgeois Provisional Government, they conducted a counter-revolutionary policy opposed to the people's interests.

After the Great October Socialist Revolution they became rabid enemies of Soviet power and took part in all the counter-revolutionary military operations and the campaigns of the interventionists. After the defeat of the interventionists and whiteguards, the Cadets fled abroad to continue their anti-Soviet counter-revolutionary activity.

Chernov's resignation, while by no means the only symptom, is the most striking and obvious symptom that the peasants *will not receive land* from the Socialist-Revolutionaries' bloc (or from the Socialist-Revolutionaries themselves). And that is the chief reason for the popular character of the revolution.

We are in the advantageous position of a party that knows for certain which way to go at a time when *imperialism as a whole* and the Menshevik and Socialist-Revolutionary bloc as a whole are vacillating in an incredible fashion.

Our victory is assured, for the people are close to desperation, and we are showing the entire people a sure way out; we demonstrated to the entire people during the "Kornilov days" the value of our leadership, and then *proposed* to the politicians of the bloc a compromise, *which they rejected,* although there is no let-up in their vacillations.

It would be a great mistake to think that our offer of a compromise had not *yet* been rejected, and that the Democratic Conference may *still* accept it. The compromise was proposed *by a party to parties;* it could not have been proposed in any other way. It was rejected by *parties.* The Democratic Conference is a *conference,* and nothing more. One thing must not be forgotten, namely, that the *majority* of the revolutionary people, the poor, embittered peasants, are not represented in it. It is a conference of a *minority of the people—this* obvious truth must not be forgotten. It would be a big mistake, sheer parliamentary cretinism on our part, if we were to regard the Democratic Conference as a parliament; for even *if it were* to proclaim itself a permanent and sovereign parliament of the revolution, it would nevertheless *decide nothing.* The power of decision lies *outside it* in the working-class quarters of Petrograd and Moscow.

All the objective conditions exist for a successful insurrection. We have the exceptional advantage of a situation in which *only* our victory in the insurrection can put an end to that most painful thing on earth, vacillation, which has worn the people out; in which *only* our victory in the insurrection will give the peasants land immediately; a situation in which only *our* victory in the insurrection can *foil* the game of a separate peace directed against the revolution—foil it by publicly proposing a fuller, juster and earlier peace, a peace that will *benefit* the revolution.

Finally, our Party alone *can*, by a victorious insurrection, save Petrograd; for if our proposal for peace is rejected, if we do not secure even an armistice, then *we* shall become "defencists", we shall place ourselves *at the head of the war parties,* we shall be the *war party par excellence,* and we shall conduct the war in a truly revolutionary manner. We shall take away all the bread and boots from the capitalists. We shall leave them only crusts and dress them in bast shoes. We shall send all the bread and footwear to the front.

And then we shall save Petrograd.

The resources, both material and spiritual, for a truly revolutionary war in Russia are still immense; the chances are a hundred to one that the Germans will grant us at least an armistice. And to secure an armistice now would in itself mean to win the *whole world.*

* * *

Having recognised the absolute necessity for an insurrection of the workers of Petrograd and Moscow in order to save the revolution and to save Russia from a "separate" partition by the imperialists of both groups, we must first adapt our political tactics at the Conference to the conditions of the growing insurrection; secondly, we must show that it is not only in words that we accept Marx's idea that insurrection must be treated as an art.

At the Conference we must immediately cement the Bolshevik group, without striving after numbers, and without fearing to leave the waverers in the waverers' camp. They are more useful to the cause of the revolution *there* than in the camp of the resolute and devoted fighters.

We must draw up a brief declaration from the Bolsheviks, emphasising in no uncertain manner the irrelevance of long speeches and of "speeches" in general, the necessity for immediate action to save the revolution, the absolute necessity for a complete break with the bourgeoisie, for the removal of the present government, in its entirety, for a complete rupture with the Anglo-French imperialists, who are preparing a "separate" partition of Russia, and for the immediate transfer of all power to *revolutionary democrats, headed by the revolutionary proletariat.*

Our declaration must give the briefest and most trenchant formulation of *this* conclusion in connection with the programme proposals of peace for the peoples, land for the peasants, confiscation of scandalous profits, and a check on the scandalous sabotage of production by the capitalists.

The briefer and more trenchant the declaration, the better. Only two other highly important points must be clearly indicated in it, namely, that the people are worn out by the vacillations, that they are fed up with the irresolution of the Socialist-Revolutionaries and Mensheviks; and that we are definitely breaking with these *parties* because they have betrayed the revolution.

And another thing. By immediately proposing a peace without annexations, by immediately breaking with the Allied imperialists and with all imperialists, either we shall at once obtain an armistice, or the entire revolutionary proletariat will rally to the defence of the country, and a really just, really revolutionary war will then be waged by revolutionary democrats under the leadership of the proletariat.

Having read this declaration, and having appealed for *decisions* and not talk, for *action* and not resolution-writing, we must *dispatch* our entire group to the *factories and the barracks.* Their place is there, the pulse of life is there, there is the source of salvation for our revolution, and there is the motive force of the Democratic Conference.

There, in ardent and impassioned speeches, we must explain our programme and put the alternative: either the Conference adopts it *in its entirety,* or else insurrection. There is no middle course. Delay is impossible. The revolution is dying.

By putting the question in this way, by concentrating our entire group in the factories and barracks, *we shall be able to determine the right moment to start the insurrection.*

In order to treat insurrection in a Marxist way, i.e., as an art, we must at the same time, without losing a single moment, organise a *headquarters* of the insurgent detachments, distribute our forces, move the reliable regiments to the most important points, surround the Alexandrinsky Theatre, occupy the Peter and Paul Fortress,[4] arrest the General Staff and the government, and move against the officer cadets and the Savage Division[5] those detachments which would rather die than allow the enemy to approach the strategic points of the city. We must mobilise the armed workers and call them to fight the last desperate fight, occupy the telegraph and the telephone exchange at once, move *our*

[4] *The Alexandrinsky Theatre* in Petrograd was the place where the Democratic Conference was convened.

The Peter and Paul Fortress on the Neva opposite the Winter Palace, served as a state prison for the tsar's political opponents. Now a museum, it had a large arsenal and was strategically situated.

[5] *The Savage Division*—formed during the First World War from volunteer mountaineers of the North Caucasus. General Kornilov tried to use it as a battering ram in his assault on revolutionary Petrograd.

insurrection headquarters to the central telephone exchange and connect it by telephone with all the factories, all the regiments, all the points of armed fighting, etc.

Of course, this is all by way of example, only to *illustrate* the fact that at the present moment it is impossible to remain loyal to Marxism, to remain loyal to the revolution *unless insurrection is treated as an art.*

N. Lenin

CAN THE BOLSHEVIKS RETAIN STATE POWER? (1917)

FOREWORD TO THE SECOND EDITION[1]

The present pamphlet,[2] as is evident from the text, was written at the end of September and was finished on October 1, 1917.

The October 25 Revolution has transferred the question raised in this pamphlet from the sphere of theory to the sphere of practice.

This question must now be answered by deeds, not words. The theoretical arguments advanced against the Bolsheviks taking power were feeble in the extreme. These arguments have been shot to pieces.

The task now is for the advanced class—the proletariat—to prove *in practice* the viability of the workers' and peasants' government. All class-conscious workers, all the active and honest peasants, all working and exploited people, will do everything they can to solve the immense historic question in practice.

[1] First published in 1918 in the pamphlet by N. Lenin, *Can the Bolsheviks Retain State Power?*, "Soldiers' and Peasants' Library" Series, St. Petersburg. Published according to the pamphlet.

[2] Written at Vyborg in late September-October 1 (14), 1917. First published in the magazine *Prosveshcheniye* (Enlightenment) No. 1-2 for October 1917.

Prosveshcheniye, a monthly Bolshevik theoretical journal legally published in Petersburg from December 1911 to June 1914. It had a peak circulation of 5,000.

It was put out on Lenin's suggestion, and contained contributions from Vorovsky, Ulyanova-Yelizarova, Krupskaya, Olminsky and others. Gorky edited the *belle-lettres* section. Lenin directed its policy from Paris and then from Cracow and Poronin; he edited some of the articles and kept up a regular correspondence with members of the editorial board.

The magazine exposed opportunists—liquidators, otzovists and Trotskyites—and also bourgeois nationalists, and reported on the working-class struggle at the time of the new revolutionary upsurge; it popularised Bolshevik slogans in the electoral campaign for the Fourth Duma and opposed revisionism and centrism in the parties of the Second International. It had a great part to play in educating forward-looking workers in Russia in the Marxist international spirit.

On the eve of the First World War, in June 1914 it was closed down by the tsarist government, and resumed publication in the autumn of 1917, but only one double issue was put out.

To work, everybody to work, the cause of the world socialist revolution must and will triumph.

St. Petersburg, November 9, 1917.

N. Lenin

* * *

On what are all trends agreed, from *Rech* to *Novaya Zhizn*[3] inclusively, from the Kornilovite Cadets to the semi-Bolsheviks, *all*, except the Bolsheviks?

They all agree that the Bolsheviks will either never dare take over full state power alone, or, if they do dare, and do take power, they will not be able to retain it even for the shortest while.

If anybody asserts that the question of the Bolsheviks alone taking over full state power is a totally unfeasible political question, that only a swelled-headed "fanatic" of the worst kind can regard it as feasible, we refute this assertion by quoting the exact statements of the most responsible and most influential political parties and trends of various "hues".

But let me begin with a word or two about the first of the questions mentioned—will the Bolsheviks dare take over full state power alone? I have already had occasion, at the All-Russia Congress of Soviets, to answer this question in the affirmative in no uncertain manner by a remark that I shouted from my seat during one of Tsereteli's[4] ministerial speeches. And I have not met in the press, or heard, any statements by Bolsheviks to the effect that we ought not to take power alone. I still maintain that a political party—and the party of the advanced class in particular—would have no right to exist, would be unworthy of the name of party, would be a nonentity in any sense, if it refused to take power when opportunity offers.

[3] *Novaya Zhizn* (New Life)—a Menshevik daily, the organ of a group of Social-Democrats known as the internationalists, among whom were Mensheviks, the followers of Martov and Menshevik minded intellectuals. Published in Petrograd from April 1917 to July 1918.

[4] This happened on June 4 (17), 1917, during a speech of the Menshevik Tsereteli, a Minister of the Provisional Government, who had said that there was no political party in Russia which was prepared to take full power in the country. On behalf of the Bolshevik Party, Lenin interrupted Tsereteli with the remark: "There is!" In his speech from the rostrum later, Lenin declared that the Bolshevik Party "is ready to take over full power at any moment" (see *LCW*, Vol. 25, 1974, p. 20).

We shall now quote statements by the Cadets, Socialist-Revolutionaries and semi-Bolsheviks (I would prefer to say quarter-Bolsheviks) on the question that interests us.

The leading article in *Rech* of September 16:

> "Discord and confusion reigned in the Alexandrinsky Theatre, and the socialist press reflects the same picture. Only the views of the Bolsheviks are definite and straightforward. At the Conference, they are the views of the minority. In the Soviets, they represent a constantly growing trend. But in spite of all their verbal pugnacity, their boastful phrases and display of self-confidence, the Bolsheviks, except for a few fanatics, are brave only in words. They would not attempt to take 'full power' on their own accord. Disorganisers and disrupters *par excellence*, they are really cowards who in their heart of hearts are fully aware of both their own intrinsic ignorance and the ephemeral nature of their present successes. They know as well as we all do that the first day of their ultimate triumph would also be the first day of their precipitous fall. Irresponsible by their very nature, anarchists in method and practice, they should be regarded only as a trend of political thought, or rather, as one of its aberrations. The best way to get rid of Bolshevism for many a year, to banish it, would be to place the country's fate in the hands of its leaders. And if it were not for the awareness that experiments of this kind are impermissible and fatal, one might in desperation decide on even this heroic measure. Happily, we repeat, these dismal heroes of the day are not by any means actually out to seize full power. Not under any circumstances are they capable of constructive work. Thus, all their definite and straightforward views are confined to the political rostrum, to soap-box oratory. For practical purposes their position cannot be taken into consideration from any point of view. In one respect, however, it has some practical consequence: it unites all other shades of 'socialist thought' opposed to it. . . ."

This is the way the Cadets reason. Here, however, is the view of the biggest, "ruling and governing", party in Russia, the Socialist-Revolutionaries, also expressed in an unsigned, i.e., editorial, leading article in their official organ *Dyelo Naroda* of September 21:

> ". . . If the bourgeoisie refuse, pending the convocation of the Constituent Assembly, to work with the democracy on the basis of the platform that was endorsed by the Conference, then the *coalition must arise from within the Conference itself.* This would be a serious sacrifice on the part of the supporters of the coalition, *but even those campaigning for the idea of a 'pure*

> *line' of power will have to agree to it.* We are afraid, however, that agreement may not be reached here. In that case a third and final combination remains, namely: the government *must* be organised by that half of the Conference which on *principle* advocated the idea of a homogeneous government.
>
> "Let us put it definitely: *the Bolsheviks will be obliged to form a Cabinet.* With the greatest energy, they imbued the revolutionary democrats with hatred of the coalition, promising them all sorts of benefits as soon as 'compromise' was abandoned, and attributing to the latter all the country's misfortunes.
>
> "If they were aware of what they were doing by their agitation, if they were *not deceiving the people, it is their duty* to redeem the promissory notes they have been handing out right and left.
>
> "The question is clear.
>
> "Let them not make futile attempts to hide behind hastily concocted theory that it is impossible for them to take power.
>
> "The democracy will not accept these theories.
>
> "At the same time, the advocates of coalition must guarantee them full support. These are the three combinations, the three ways, open to us—there are no others!" (The italics are those of *Dyelo Naroda*.)

This is the way the Socialist-Revolutionaries reason. And here, finally, is the "position" (if attempts to sit between two stools can be called a position) of the *Novaya Zhizn* "quarter-Bolsheviks", taken from the editorial in *Novaya Zhizn* of September 23.

> "If a coalition with Konovalov and Kishkin is formed again, it will mean nothing but a new capitulation by the democracy and the abrogation of the Conference resolution on the formation of a responsible government on the platform of August 14. . . .
>
> "A homogeneous ministry of Mensheviks and Socialist-Revolutionaries will be able to feel its responsibility as little as the responsible socialist ministers felt it in the coalition cabinet. . . . This government would not only be incapable of rallying the 'live forces' of the revolution around itself, but would not even be able to count on any active support from its vanguard—the proletariat.
>
> "But the formation of another type of homogeneous cabinet, a government of the 'proletariat and poor peasants', would be, not a better, but an even worse way out of the situation, in fact it would not be a way out at all, but sheer bankruptcy. True, nobody is advancing such a slogan except in casual, timid and later systematically 'explained away' comments in *Rabochy Put*."

(This glaring untruth is "boldly" written by responsible journalists who have forgotten even the *Dyelo Naroda* editorial of September 21.)

> "Formally, the Bolsheviks have now revived the slogan 'All Power to the Soviets'. It was withdrawn after the July days, when the Soviets, represented by the Central Executive Committee, definitely adopted an active anti-Bolshevik policy. Now, however, not only can the 'Soviet line' be regarded as straightened out, but there is every ground to assume that at the proposed Congress of Soviets the Bolsheviks will have a majority. Under such circumstances the slogan 'All Power to the Soviets', resurrected by the Bolsheviks, is a 'tactical line' for achieving precisely the dictatorship of the proletariat and the 'poor peasants'. True, the Soviets also imply the Soviets of Peasants' Deputies; the Bolshevik slogan therefore implies a power resting on the overwhelmingly greater part of the entire democracy of Russia. In that case, however, the slogan 'All Power to the Soviets' loses all independent significance, for it makes the Soviets almost identical in composition to the Pre-parliament set up by the Conference. . . ."

(*Novaya Zhizn*'s assertion is a brazen lie, equivalent to declaring that spurious and fraudulent democracy is "almost identical" to democracy: the Pre-parliament is a *sham* which passes off the will of the minority of the people, particularly of Kuskova, Berkenheim, Chaikovsky and Co., as the will of the majority. This is the first point. The second point is that at the Conference even the Peasants' Soviets that had been packed by the Avksentyevs and Chaikovskys gave such a high percentage opposed to the coalition that taken together with the Soviets of Workers' and Soldiers' Deputies, they would have brought about the *absolute collapse of the coalition*. And the third point is that "Power to the Soviets" means that the power of the Peasants' Soviets would embrace mainly the rural districts, and in the rural districts the predominance of the *poor* peasants is assured.)

> "If it is one and the same thing, then the Bolshevik slogan should be immediately withdrawn. If, however, 'Power to the Soviets' is only a disguise for the dictatorship of the proletariat, then such a power would mean precisely the failure and collapse of the revolution.
>
> "Does it need proof that the proletariat, isolated not only from the other classes in the country, but also from the real live forces of the democracy, will not be able either technically to lay hold of the state apparatus and set it in motion in an exceptionally complicated situation, or politically to resist all

the pressure by hostile forces that will sweep away not only the proletarian dictatorship, but the entire revolution into the bargain?

"The only power that will answer the requirements of the present situation is a really honest coalition within the democracy."

* * *

We apologise to the reader for quoting these lengthy extracts, but they are absolutely necessary. It is necessary to present a precise picture of the positions taken by the different parties hostile to the Bolsheviks. It is necessary to prove in a definite manner the extremely important fact that *all* these parties have admitted that the question of the Bolsheviks taking full state power alone is not only feasible, but also urgent.

Let us now proceed to examine the arguments which convince "everybody", from the Cadets to the *Novaya Zhizn* people, that the Bolsheviks will not be able to retain power.

The respectable *Rech* advances no arguments whatsoever. It merely pours out upon the Bolsheviks a flood of the choicest and most irate abuse. The extract we quoted shows, among other things, how utterly wrong it would be to say, "Watch out, comrades, for what the enemy advises must certainly be bad", thinking that *Rech* is "provoking" the Bolsheviks to take power. If, instead of weighing up the general and concrete considerations in a practical way, we allow ourselves to be "persuaded" by the plea that the bourgeoisie are "provoking" us to take power, we shall be fooled by the bourgeoisie, for the latter will of course always maliciously prophesy millions of disasters that will result from the Bolsheviks taking power and will always maliciously shout, "It would be better to get rid of the Bolsheviks at one blow and 'for many a year' by allowing them to take power and then crushing them." These cries are also "provocation", if you will, but from a different angle. The Cadets and the bourgeoisie do not by any means "advise", and have never "advised", us to take power; they are only trying to *frighten* us with the allegedly insoluble problems of government.

No. We must not allow ourselves to be frightened by the screams of the frightened bourgeoisie. We must bear firmly in mind that we have never set ourselves "insoluble" social problems, and as for the *perfectly* soluble problem of taking immediate steps towards socialism, which is the only way out of the exceedingly difficult situation, that will be *solved only* by the dictatorship of the proletariat and poor peasants. Victory, and lasting victory, is now more than ever, more than anywhere else, assured for the proletariat in Russia if it takes power.

We shall in a purely practical manner discuss the *concrete* circumstances that make a certain moment unfavourable; but we shall not for a moment allow ourselves to be scared by the savage howls of the bourgeoisie; and we shall not forget that the question of the Bolsheviks taking full power is becoming really *urgent*. Our Party will now be threatened with an immeasurably greater danger if we forget this than if we were to admit that taking power is "premature". In this respect, there can be *nothing* "premature" now: there is every chance in a million, except one or two perhaps, in favour of this.

Concerning the irate abuse poured out by *Rech*, we can, and must, say:

In savage cries of irritation
We hear the voice of approbation,
Not in dulcet sounds of praise.[5]

That the bourgeoisie hate us so passionately is one of the most striking proofs that we are showing the people the *right* ways and means of overthrowing the rule of the bourgeoisie.

* * *

This time, by way of rare exception, *Dyelo Naroda* did not deign to honour us with its abuse nor did it advance a ghost of an argument. It merely tried, by indirect hints, to *frighten* us with the prospect that "the Bolsheviks will be obliged to form a cabinet". I can quite believe that while trying to frighten us, the Socialist-Revolutionaries are themselves sincerely scared to death by the phantom of the frightened liberal. I can equally believe that the Socialist-Revolutionaries do succeed in certain exceptionally high and exceptionally rotten institutions, such as the Central Executive Committee and similar "contact" (i.e., contact with the Cadets, in plain language, hobnobbing with the Cadets) commissions, in scaring some Bolsheviks because, first, the atmosphere in all those Central Executives, pre-parliaments, etc., is abominable, putrid to the point of nausea, and harmful for *any* man to breathe for any length of time; and secondly, sincerity is contagious, and a sincerely frightened philistine is capable of converting even an individual revolutionary into a philistine for a time.

But however much we may, "humanly" speaking, understand the sincere fright of a Socialist-Revolutionary who has had the misfortune

[5] From Nekrasov's poem, *Blessed is the Gentle Poet.*

to be a minister in the company of the Cadets, or who is eligible as a minister in the eyes of the Cadets, we would be committing a political error that might only too easily border on treachery to the proletariat if we allowed ourselves to be scared. Let us have your practical arguments, gentlemen! Cherish no hope that we shall allow ourselves to be scared by your fright!

* * *

This time we find practical arguments only in *Novaya Zhizn*. On this occasion the paper comes out in the role of counsel for the bourgeoisie, a role that suits it far better than that of counsel for the defence of the Bolsheviks, which so obviously "shocks" this lady with many good points.[6]

The counsel has advanced *six* pleas:

(1) the proletariat is "isolated from the other classes in the country";

(2) it is "isolated from the real live forces of the democracy";

(3) it "will not be able technically to lay hold of the state apparatus";

(4) it "will not be able to set this apparatus in motion";

(5) "the situation is exceptionally complicated";

(6) it "will be incapable of resisting all the pressure by hostile forces that will sweep away not only the proletarian dictatorship, but the entire revolution into the bargain".

Novaya Zhizn formulates the first plea in a ridiculously clumsy fashion, for in capitalist and semi capitalist society we know of only three classes: the bourgeoisie, the petty bourgeoisie (which consists mainly of the peasantry), and the proletariat. What sense is there in talking about the proletariat being isolated from the other classes when the point at issue is the proletariat's struggle against the bourgeoisie, revolution against the bourgeoisie?

Evidently, *Novaya Zhizn* wanted to say that the proletariat is isolated from the peasants, for it could not possibly have meant the landowners. It could not, however, say clearly and definitely that the proletariat is now isolated from the peasants, for the utter incorrectness of this assertion would be too obvious.

It is difficult to imagine that in a capitalist country the proletariat should be so little isolated from the petty bourgeoisie—and, mark you, in a revolution *against the bourgeoisie*—as the proletariat now is in Russia. The latest returns of the voting by "curias" *for* and *against* coalition with the bourgeoisie in Tsereteli's "Bulygin Duma", i.e., in the

[6] Reference to a character from Gogol's *Dead Souls*.

notorious "Democratic" Conference, constitute one of the objective and incontrovertible proofs of this. If we take the Soviets' curias we get:

	For Coalition	*Against*
Soviets of Workers' and Soldiers' Deputies	83	192
Soviets of Peasants' Deputies	102	70
All Soviets	185	262

So, the majority as a whole is on the side of the proletarian slogan: *against* coalition with the bourgeoisie. We have seen above that even the Cadets are obliged to admit the growth of Bolshevik influence in the Soviets. And here we have the Conference convened by *yesterday*'s leaders in the Soviets, Socialist-Revolutionaries and Mensheviks, who have an assured majority in the central institutions! Obviously, the *actual* degree to which the Bolsheviks predominate in the Soviets is here *understated.*

Both on the question of coalition with the bourgeoisie and on the question of immediately transferring the landed estates to peasant committees, the Bolsheviks already have a *majority* in the Soviets of Workers', Soldiers' and Peasants' Deputies, a *majority of the people*, a majority of the petty bourgeoisie. *Rabochy Put* No. 19, of September 24 quotes from No. 25 of the organ of the Socialist-Revolutionaries *Znamya Truda*[7] a report on a conference of local Soviets of Peasants' Deputies held in Petrograd on September 18. At this conference the Executive Committees of four Peasants' Soviets (Kostroma, Moscow, Samara and Taurida gubernias) voted for an unrestricted coalition. The Executive Committees of *three* gubernias and *two* armies (Vladimir, Ryazan and the Black Sea gubernias) voted in favour of a coalition without the Cadets. The Executive Committees of *twenty-three* gubernias and *four* armies voted against a coalition.

So, the majority of the peasants are against a coalition!

So much for the "isolation of the proletariat".

We should note, by the way, that the supporters of a coalition were three outlying gubernias, Samara, Taurida and the Black Sea, where there

[7] *Znamya Truda* (The Banner of Labour)—a daily, the organ of the Petrograd Committee of the Socialist-Revolutionary Party published from August 23 (September 5), 1917. From November 1 (14), 1917 (No. 59), the organ of the Petrograd Committee of the Socialist-Revolutionary Party and the group of Left Socialist-Revolutionaries of the Central Executive Committee of the Second All-Russia Congress of Soviets. From December 28, 1917 (January 10, 1918) (No. 105), the paper became the Central Organ of the Party of Left Socialist-Revolutionaries. Closed down in July 1918 during the Left Socialist-Revolutionaries' revolt.

is a relatively very large number of rich peasants and big landowners who employ hired labour, and also four industrial gubernias (Vladimir, Ryazan, Kostroma and Moscow) in which the peasant bourgeoisie are also stronger than in the majority of the gubernias in Russia. It would be interesting to collect more detailed figures on this question and to ascertain whether information is available concerning the *poor* peasants in the gubernias where there are larger numbers of "*rich*" peasants. It is interesting, moreover, that the "non-Russian groups" revealed a considerable predominance of opponents of a coalition, namely, 40 votes against 15. The policy of annexation and open violence pursued by the Bonapartist Kerensky and Co. towards the non-sovereign nations of Russia has borne fruit. Wide sections of the people of the oppressed nations (i.e., including the mass of the petty bourgeoisie) trust the proletariat of Russia more than they do the bourgeoisie, for here history has brought to the fore the struggle for liberation of the oppressed nations against the oppressing nations. The bourgeoisie has despicably betrayed the cause of freedom of the oppressed nations; the proletariat is faithful to the cause of freedom.

At the present time the national and agrarian questions are fundamental questions for the petty-bourgeois sections of the population of Russia. This is indisputable. And on both these questions the proletariat is "*not* isolated"—farther from it than ever. It has the majority of the people behind it. It *alone* is capable of pursuing such a determined, genuinely "revolutionary-democratic" policy on both questions which would immediately ensure the proletarian state power not only the support of the majority of the population, but also a real outburst of revolutionary enthusiasm among the people. This is because, for the first time, the people would not see the ruthless oppression of peasants by landowners and of Ukrainians by Great Russians on the part of the government, as was the case under tsarism, nor the effort to continue the same policy camouflaged in pompous phrases under the republic, nor nagging, insult, chicanery, procrastination, underhand dealing and evasions (all that with which Kerensky rewards the peasants and the oppressed nations), but would receive warm sympathy proved by deeds, immediate and revolutionary measures against the landowners, immediate restitution of *full* freedom for Finland, the Ukraine, Byelorussia, for the Moslems, and so on.

The Socialist-Revolutionary and Menshevik gentlemen know this perfectly well, and are therefore dragging in the semi-Cadet bosses of the co-operative societies to help them pursue their *reactionary*-democratic policy *against* the people. That is why they will never dare canvass popular opinion, take a popular referendum, or at least a vote of all the local Soviets, of all the local organisations, concerning definite points of practical policy, for example, whether all the landed estates should at once be handed over to peasant committees, whether certain demands of the Finns or the Ukrainians should be conceded, etc.

Take the question of peace, the crucial issue of today. The proletariat "is isolated from the other classes".... On this issue the proletariat truly represents the *whole* nation, all live and honest people *in all* classes, the vast majority of the petty bourgeoisie; because only the proletariat, on achieving power, will *immediately* offer a just peace to all the belligerent nations, because only the proletariat will dare take genuinely *revolutionary* measures (publication of the secret treaties, and so forth) to achieve the speediest and most just peace possible.

The proletariat is not isolated. The gentlemen of *Novaya Zhizn* who are shouting about the proletariat being isolated are only betraying their subjective fear of the bourgeoisie. The objective state of affairs in Russia is undoubtedly such that the proletariat, *precisely at the present time*, is not "isolated" from the majority of the petty bourgeoisie. Precisely now, after the sad experience with the "coalition", the proletariat enjoys the sympathy of the *majority* of the people. *This* condition for the retention of power by the Bolsheviks *does exist*.

* * *

The second plea is that the proletariat "is isolated from the real live forces of the democracy". What this means is incomprehensible. It is probably "Greek", as the French say in such cases.

The writers of *Novaya Zhizn* would make good ministers. They would be quite suitable as ministers in a Cadet cabinet because all these ministers need is the ability to spout plausible, polished, but utterly meaningless phrases with which to cover up the dirtiest work and which are therefore sure of winning the applause of the imperialists and social-imperialists. The *Novaya Zhizn* writers are sure to earn the applause of the Cadets, Breshkovskaya, Plekhanov and Co. for asserting that the proletariat is isolated from the real live forces of the democracy, because *indirectly* they imply—or will be understood to imply—that the Cadets, Breshkovskaya, Plekhanov, Kerensky and Co. are the "live forces of democracy".

This is not true. They are dead forces. The history of the coalition has proved this.

Overawed by the bourgeoisie and by their bourgeois intellectual environment, the *Novaya Zhizn* people regard as "live" the Right wing of the Socialist-Revolutionaries and Mensheviks like *Volya Naroda*,[8] *Yedinstvo*, and others who in essentials do not differ from the Cadets. We, however, regard as live only those who are connected with the people and not with the kulaks, only those whom the lessons of the coalition have repelled. The "active live forces" of the petty-bourgeois democracy are represented by the Left wing of the Socialist-Revolutionaries and Mensheviks. That this wing has gained strength, particularly since the July counter-revolution, is one of the surest objective signs that the proletariat is *not* isolated.

This has been made even more strikingly evident by the very recent swing to the left of the Socialist-Revolutionary Centrists, as is proved by Chernov's statement on September 24 that his group cannot support the new coalition with Kishkin and Co. This swing to the left of the Socialist-Revolutionary Centre, which up to now had constituted the overwhelming majority of the members of the Socialist-Revolutionary Party, the leading and dominant party from the point of view of the number of votes it obtained in the urban and particularly in the rural districts, proves that the statements we quoted from *Dyelo Naroda* that the democracy must, under certain circumstances, "guarantee full support" for a purely Bolshevik government are at any rate not mere empty phrases.

Facts like the refusal of the Socialist-Revolutionary Centre to support the new coalition with Kishkin, or the predominance of the *opponents* of the coalition among the *Menshevik-defencists* in the provinces (Jordania in the Caucasus, etc.), are objective proof that a certain section of the *people* which has up to now followed the Mensheviks and Socialist-Revolutionaries *will support* a purely Bolshevik government.

It is precisely from the *live* forces of the democracy that the proletariat of Russia is now not isolated.

* * *

The third plea, that the proletariat "will not be able technically to lay hold of the state apparatus" is, perhaps, the most common and most frequent. It deserves most attention for this reason, and also because it indicates one of the most *serious* and *difficult* tasks that will confront the victorious proletariat. There is no doubt that these tasks will be very

[8] *Volya Naroda* (People's Will)—a daily, the organ of the Right wing of the Socialist-Revolutionary Party. Published in Petrograd from April 29, 1917; closed down in November 1917. Later published under other names. Closed down for good in February 1918.

difficult, but if we, who call ourselves socialists, indicate this difficulty only to *shirk* these tasks, in practice the distinction between us and the lackeys of the bourgeoisie will be reduced to nought. The difficulty of the tasks of the proletarian revolution should prompt the proletariat's supporters to make a closer and more definite study of the means of carrying out these tasks.

The state apparatus is primarily the standing army, the police and the bureaucracy. By saying that the proletariat will not be able technically to lay hold of this apparatus, the writers of *Novaya Zhizn* reveal their utter ignorance and their reluctance to take into account either facts or the arguments long ago cited in Bolshevik literature.

All the *Novaya Zhizn* writers regard themselves, if not as Marxists, then at least as being familiar with Marxism, as educated socialists. But Marx, basing himself on the experience of the Paris Commune, taught that the proletariat cannot simply lay hold of the ready-made state machine and use it for its own purposes, that the proletariat must smash this machine and substitute a new one for it (I deal with this in greater detail in a pamphlet, the first part of which is now finished and will soon appear under the title *The State and Revolution. A Marxist Theory of the State and the Tasks of the Proletariat in the Revolution*[9]). This new type of state machinery was created by the Paris Commune, and the Russian Soviets of Workers', Soldiers' and Peasants' Deputies are a "state apparatus" of the *same type*. I have indicated this many times since April 4, 1917; it is dealt with in the resolutions of Bolshevik conferences and also in Bolshevik literature. *Novaya Zhizn* could, of course, have expressed its utter disagreement with Marx and with the Bolsheviks, but for a paper that has so often, and so haughtily, scolded the Bolsheviks for their allegedly frivolous attitude to difficult problems to evade this question completely is tantamount to issuing itself a certificate of mental poverty.

The proletariat *cannot* "lay hold of" the "state apparatus" and "set it in motion". But it can *smash* everything that is oppressive, routine, incorrigibly bourgeois in the old state apparatus and substitute its *own*, new apparatus. The Soviets of Workers', Soldiers' and Peasants' Deputies are exactly this apparatus.

That *Novaya Zhizn* has completely forgotten about this "state apparatus" can be called nothing but monstrous. Behaving in this way in their theoretical reasoning, the *Novaya Zhizn* people are, in essence, doing in the sphere of political theory what the Cadets are doing in political

[9] See *LCW*, Vol. 25, 1974.

practice. Because, if the proletariat and the revolutionary democrats *do not* in fact *need* a new state apparatus, then the Soviets lose their *raison d'être*, lose their right to existence, and the Kornilovite Cadets are *right* in trying to reduce the Soviets to nought!

This monstrous theoretical blunder and political blindness on the part of *Novaya Zhizn* is all the more monstrous because even the internationalist Mensheviks (with whom *Novaya Zhizn* formed a bloc during the last City Council elections in Petrograd) have on this question shown some proximity to the Bolsheviks. So, in the declaration of the Soviet majority made by Comrade Martov at the Democratic Conference, we read:

> "The Soviets of Workers', Soldiers' and Peasants' Deputies, set up in the first days of the revolution by a mighty burst of creative enthusiasm that stems from the people themselves, constitute the new fabric of the revolutionary state that has replaced the outworn state fabric of the old regime. . . ."

This is a little too flowery; that is to say, rhetoric here covers up lack of clear political thinking. The Soviets have *not yet* replaced the old "fabric", and this old "fabric" is *not* the state fabric of the old regime, but the state fabric of *both* tsarism *and* of the bourgeois republic. But at any rate, Martov here stands head and shoulders above *Novaya Zhizn*.

The Soviets are a new state apparatus which, in the first place, provides an armed force of workers and peasants; and this force is not divorced from the people, as was the old standing army, but is very closely bound up with the people. From the military point of view this force is incomparably more powerful than previous forces; from the revolutionary point of view, it cannot be replaced by anything else. Secondly, this apparatus provides a bond with the people, with the majority of the people, so intimate, so indissoluble, so easily verifiable and renewable, that nothing even remotely like it existed in the previous state apparatus. Thirdly, this apparatus, by virtue of the fact that its personnel is elected and subject to recall at the people's will without any bureaucratic formalities, is far more democratic than any previous apparatus. Fourthly, it provides a close contact with the most varied professions, thereby facilitating the adoption of the most varied and most radical reforms without red tape. Fifthly, it provides an organisational form for the vanguard, i.e., for the most class-conscious, most energetic and most progressive section of the *oppressed* classes, the workers and peasants, and so constitutes an apparatus by means of which the vanguard of the oppressed classes can elevate, train, educate, and lead *the entire vast mass* of these classes, which has up to now stood completely outside of political life and history. Sixthly, it makes it possible to combine the advantages of the parliamentary system with those of immediate and direct democracy, i.e., to vest in the people's elected representatives both legislative *and executive* functions. Compared with the bourgeois parliamentary system, this is an advance in democracy's development which is of world-wide, historic significance.

In 1905, our Soviets existed only in embryo, so to speak, as they lived altogether only a few weeks. Clearly, under the conditions of that time, their comprehensive development was out of the question. It is still out of the question in the 1917 Revolution, for a few months is an extremely short period and—this is most important—the Socialist-Revolutionary and Menshevik leaders have *prostituted* the Soviets, have reduced their role to that of a talking shop, of an accomplice in the compromising policy of the leaders. The Soviets have been rotting and decaying alive under the leadership of the Liebers, Dans, Tseretelis and Chernovs. The Soviets will be able to develop properly, to display their potentialities and capabilities to the full only by taking over *full* state power; for otherwise they have *nothing to do*, otherwise they are either simply embryos (and to remain an embryo too long is fatal), or playthings. "Dual power" means paralysis for the Soviets.

If the creative enthusiasm of the revolutionary classes had not given rise to the Soviets, the proletarian revolution in Russia would have been a hopeless cause, for the proletariat could certainly not retain power with the old state apparatus, and it is impossible to create a new apparatus immediately. The sad history of the prostitution of the Soviets by the Tseretelis and Chernovs, the history of the "coalition", is also the history of the liberation of the Soviets from petty-bourgeois illusions, of their passage through the "purgatory" of the practical experience of the utter abomination and filth of *all* and *sundry* bourgeois coalitions. Let us hope that this "purgatory" has steeled rather than weakened the Soviets.

* * *

The chief difficulty facing the proletarian revolution is the establishment on a country-wide scale of the most precise and most conscientious accounting and control, of *workers' control* of the production and distribution of goods.

When the writers of *Novaya Zhizn* argued that in advancing

the slogan "workers' control" we were slipping into syndicalism, this argument was an example of the stupid schoolboy method of applying "Marxism" without studying it, just *learning it by rote* in the Struve manner. Syndicalism either repudiates the revolutionary dictatorship of the proletariat, or else relegates it, as it does political power in general, to a back seat. We, however, put it in the forefront. If we simply say in unison with the *Novaya Zhizn* writers: *not* workers' control *but* state control, it is simply a bourgeois-reformist phrase, it is, in essence, a purely Cadet formula, because the Cadets have no objection to the workers *participating* in "state" control. The Kornilovite Cadets know perfectly well that such participation offers the bourgeoisie the best way of fooling the workers, the most subtle way of politically *bribing* all the Gvozdyovs, Nikitins, Prokopoviches, Tseretelis and the rest of that gang.

When we say: "workers' control", always *juxtaposing* this slogan to dictatorship of the proletariat, always putting it *immediately after* the latter, we thereby explain what kind of state we mean. The state is the organ of *class* domination. Of which class? If of the bourgeoisie, then it is the Cadet-Kornilov-"Kerensky" state which has been "Kornilovising" and "Kerenskyising" the working people of Russia for more than six months. If it is of the proletariat, if we are speaking of a proletarian state, *that is*, of the proletarian dictatorship, then workers' control *can* become the country-wide, all-embracing, omnipresent, most precise and most conscientious *accounting* of the production and distribution of goods.

This is the chief difficulty, the chief task that faces the proletarian, i.e., socialist, revolution. Without the Soviets, this task would be impracticable, at least in Russia. The Soviets *indicate* to the proletariat the organisational work which *can* solve this historically important problem.

This brings us to another aspect of the question of the state apparatus. In addition to the chiefly "oppressive" apparatus—the standing army, the police and the bureaucracy—the modern state possesses an apparatus which has extremely close connections with the banks and syndicates, an apparatus which performs an enormous amount of accounting and registration work, if it may be expressed this way. This apparatus must not, and should not, be smashed. It must be wrested from the control of the capitalists; the capitalists and the wires they pull must be *cut off, lopped off, chopped away from* this apparatus; it must be *subordinated* to the proletarian Soviets; it must be expanded, made more comprehensive, and nation-wide. And this *can* be done by utilising the achievements already made by large-scale capitalism (in the same way as the proletarian revolution can, in general, reach its goal only by utilising these achievements).

Capitalism has created an accounting *apparatus* in the shape of the banks, syndicates, postal service, consumers' societies, and office employees' unions. *Without big banks socialism would be impossible.*

The big banks *are* the "state apparatus" which we *need* to bring about socialism, and which we *take ready-made* from capitalism; our task here is merely to *lop off* what *capitalistically mutilates* this excellent apparatus, to make it *even bigger*, even more democratic, even more comprehensive. Quantity will be transformed into quality. A single State Bank, the biggest of the big, with branches in every rural district, in every factory, will constitute as much as nine-tenths of the *socialist* apparatus. This will be country wide *book-keeping*, country-wide *accounting* of the production and distribution of goods, this will be, so to speak, something in the nature of the *skeleton* of socialist society.

We can "lay hold of" and "set in motion" this "state apparatus" (which is not fully a state apparatus under capitalism, but which will be so with us, under socialism) at one stroke, by a single decree, because the actual work of book-keeping, control, registering, accounting and counting is performed by *employees*, the majority of whom themselves lead a proletarian or semi-proletarian existence.

By a single decree of the proletarian government these employees can and must be transferred to the status of state employees, in the same way as the watchdogs of capitalism like Briand and other bourgeois ministers, by a single decree, transfer railwaymen on strike to the status of state employees. We shall need many more state employees of this kind, and more *can* be obtained, because capitalism has simplified the work of accounting and control, has reduced it to a comparatively simple system of *book-keeping*, which any literate person can do.

The conversion of the bank, syndicate, commercial, etc., etc., rank-and-file employees into state employees is quite feasible both technically (thanks to the preliminary work performed for us by capitalism, including finance capitalism) and politically, provided the *Soviets* exercise control and supervision.

As for the higher officials, of whom there are very few, but who gravitate towards the capitalists, they will have to be dealt with in the same way as the capitalists, i.e., "severely". Like the capitalists, they will offer *resistance*. This resistance will have to be *broken*, and if the immortally naïve Peshekhonov, as early as June 1917, lisped like the infant that he was in state affairs, that "the resistance of the capitalists has been broken", this childish phrase, this childish boast, this childish swagger, *will be converted by the proletariat into reality.*

We can do this, for it is merely a question of breaking the resistance of an insignificant minority of the population, literally a handful of people, over each of whom the employees' unions, the trade unions, the consumers' societies and the Soviets will institute such *supervision* that every Tit Titych will be *surrounded* as the French were at Sedan.[10] We know these Tit Tityches by name: we only have to consult the lists of directors, board members, large shareholders, etc. There are several hundred, at most several thousand of them in the *whole* of Russia, and the proletarian state, with the apparatus of the Soviets, of the employees' unions, etc., will be able to appoint ten or even a hundred supervisers to each of them, so that instead of "breaking resistance" it may even be possible, by means of *workers' control* (over the capitalists), to make all resistance *impossible.*

The important thing will not be even the confiscation of the capitalists' property, but country-wide, all-embracing workers' control over the capitalists and their possible supporters. Confiscation alone leads nowhere, as it does not contain the element of organisation, of accounting for proper distribution. Instead of confiscation, we could easily impose a *fair* tax (even on the Shingaryov[11] scale, for instance), taking care, of course, to preclude the possibility of anyone evading assessment, concealing the truth, evading the law. And this possibility can be *eliminated only* by the workers' control of the *workers' state.*

Compulsory syndication, i.e., compulsory amalgamation in associations under state control—this is what capitalism has prepared the way for, this is what has been carried out in Germany by the Junkers' state, this is what can be easily carried out in Russia by the Soviets, by the proletarian dictatorship, and this is what will *provide us with a state apparatus* that will be universal, up-to-date, and non-bureaucratic.[12]

[10] *Sedan*—scene of the rout of the French Army by the Prussians on September 1-2, 1870, when more than 100,000 French soldiers, together with their Emperor Napoleon III, were taken prisoner.

[11] *Shingaryov, A.I.* (1869-1918)—Cadet from 1907, member of the Cadet Central Committee. Deputy to the Second, Third and Fourth Dumas. After the bourgeois-democratic revolution of February 1917 was Minister of Agriculture in the First and Minister of Finance in the Second Provisional Government.

[12] For further details of the meaning of compulsory syndication see my pamphlet: The Impending Catastrophe and How to Combat It.—*Au.* (See *LCW*, Vol. 25, 1974, pp. 346-49.)

* * *

The fourth plea of the counsels for the bourgeoisie is that the proletariat will not be able "to set the state apparatus in motion". There is nothing new in this plea compared with the preceding one. We could not, of course, either lay hold of or set in motion the old apparatus. The new apparatus, the Soviets, *has already* been set in motion by "a mighty burst of creative enthusiasm that stems from the people themselves". We only have to free it from the *shackles* put on it by the domination of the Socialist-Revolutionary and Menshevik leaders. This apparatus *is already* in motion; we only have to free it from the monstrous, petty-bourgeois impediments preventing it from going full speed ahead.

Two circumstances must be considered here to supplement what has already been said. In the first place, the new means of control have been created *not* by us, but by capitalism in its military-imperialist stage; and in the second place, it is important to introduce more democracy into the *administration* of a proletarian state.

The grain monopoly and bread rationing were introduced not by us, but by the capitalist state in war-time. It had already introduced universal labour conscription within the framework of capitalism, which is war-time penal servitude for the workers. But here too, as in all its history-making activities, the proletariat takes its weapons from capitalism and does not "invent" or "create them out of nothing".

The grain monopoly, bread rationing and labour conscription in the hands of the proletarian state, in the hands of sovereign Soviets, will be the most powerful means of accounting and control, means which, applied to the capitalists, and to *the rich in general*, applied to them by the *workers*, will provide a force unprecedented in history for "setting the state apparatus in motion", for overcoming the resistance of the capitalists, for subordinating them to the proletarian state. These means of control and of *compelling people to work* will be more potent than the laws of the Convention and its guillotine. The guillotine *only* terrorised, only broke *active* resistance. *For us, this is not enough.*

For us, this is not enough. We must not only "terrorise" the capitalists, i.e., make them feel the omnipotence of the proletarian state and give up all idea of actively resisting it. We must also break *passive* resistance, which is undoubtedly more dangerous and harmful. We must not only break resistance of every kind. We must also *compel the capitalists to work* within the framework of the new state organisation. It is not enough to "remove" the capitalists; we must (after removing the undesirable and incorrigible "resisters") employ them *in the service of the new state*. This applies both to the capitalists and to the upper section of the bourgeois intellectuals, office employees, etc.

And we have the means to do this. The means and instruments for this have been placed in our hands by the capitalist state in the war. These means are the grain monopoly, bread rationing and labour conscription. "He who does not work, neither shall he eat"—this is the fundamental, the first and most important rule the Soviets of Workers' Deputies can and will introduce when they become the ruling power.

Every worker has a work-book. This book does not degrade him, although *at present* it is undoubtedly a document of capitalist wage-slavery, certifying that the workman belongs to some parasite.

The Soviets will introduce work-books *for the rich* and *then* gradually for the whole population (in a peasant country work-books will probably not be needed for a long time for the overwhelming majority of the peasants). The work-book will cease to be the badge of the "common herd", a document of the "lower" orders, a certificate of wage-slavery. It will become a document certifying that in the new society there are no longer any "workmen", nor, on the other hand, are there any longer men *who do not work.*

The rich will be obliged to get a work-book from the workers' or office employees' union with which their occupation is most closely connected, and every week, or other definite fixed period, they will have to get from that union a certificate to the effect that they are performing their work conscientiously; without this they will not be able to receive bread ration cards or provisions in general. The proletarian state will say: we need good organisers of banking and the amalgamation of enterprises (in this matter the capitalists have more experience, and it is easier to work with experienced people), and we need far, far more engineers, agronomists, technicians and scientifically trained specialists of every kind than were needed before. We shall give all these specialists work to which they are accustomed and which they can cope with; in all probability we shall introduce complete wage equality only gradually and shall pay these specialists higher salaries during the transition period. We shall place them, however, under comprehensive workers' control and we shall achieve the complete and absolute operation of the rule "He who does not work, neither shall he eat". We shall not invent the organisational form of the work, but take it ready-made from capitalism—we shall take over the banks, syndicates, the best factories, experimental stations, academies, and so forth; all that we shall have to do is to borrow the best models furnished by the advanced countries.

Of course, we shall not in the least descend to a utopia, we are not deserting the soil of most sober, practical reason when we say that the entire capitalist class will offer the most stubborn resistance, but this resistance will be broken by the organisation of the entire population in Soviets. Those capitalists who are exceptionally stubborn and recalcitrant will, of course, have to be punished by the confiscation of their whole property and by imprisonment. On the other hand, however, the victory of the proletariat will bring about an *increase* in the number of cases of the kind that I read about in today's *Izvestia* for example:

> "On September 26, two engineers came to the Central Council of Factory Committees to report that a group of engineers had decided to form a union of socialist engineers. The Union believes that the present time is actually the beginning of the social revolution and places itself at the disposal of the working people, desiring, in defence of the workers' interests, to work in complete unity with the workers' organisations. The representatives of the Central Council of Factory Committees answered that the Council will gladly set up in its organisation an Engineers' Section which will embody in its programme the main theses of the First Conference of Factory Committees on workers' control over production. A joint meeting of delegates of the Central Council of Factory Committees and of the initiative group of socialist engineers will be held within the next few days." (*Izvestia*, September 27, 1917.)

* * *

The proletariat, we are told, will not be able to set the state apparatus in motion.

Since the 1905 revolution, Russia has been governed by 130,000 landowners, who have perpetrated endless violence against 150,000,000 people, heaped unconstrained abuse upon them, and condemned the vast majority to inhuman toil and semi-starvation.

Yet we are told that the 240,000 members of the Bolshevik Party will not be able to govern Russia, govern her in the interests of the poor and against the rich. These 240,000 are already backed by no less than a million votes of the adult population, for this is precisely the proportion between the number of Party members and the number of votes cast for the Party that has been established by the experience of Europe and the experience of Russia as shown, for example, by the elections to the Petrograd City Council last August. We therefore already have a "state apparatus" of *one million* people devoted to the socialist state for the sake of high ideals and not for the sake of a fat sum received on the 20th of every month.

In addition to that we have a "magic way" to enlarge our state apparatus *tenfold* at once, at one stroke, a way which no capitalist state ever possessed or could possess. This magic way is to draw the working people, to draw the poor, into the daily work of state administration.

To explain how easy it will be to employ this magic way and how faultlessly it will operate, let us take the simplest and most striking example possible.

The state is to forcibly evict a certain family from a flat and move another in. This often happens in the capitalist state, and it will also happen in our proletarian or socialist state.

The capitalist state evicts a working-class family which has lost its breadwinner and cannot pay the rent. The bailiff appears with police, or militia, a whole squad of them. To effect an eviction in a working-class district a whole detachment of Cossacks is required. Why? Because the bailiff and the militiaman refuse to go without a very strong military guard. They know that the scene of an eviction arouses such fury among the neighbours, among thousands and thousands of people who have been driven to the verge of desperation, arouses such hatred towards the capitalists and the capitalist state, that the bailiff and the squad of militiamen run the risk of being torn to pieces at any minute. Large military forces are required, several regiments must be brought into a big city, and the troops must come from some distant, outlying region so that the soldiers will not be familiar with the life of the urban poor, so that the soldiers will not be "infected" with socialism.

The proletarian state has to forcibly move a very poor family into a rich man's flat. Let us suppose that our squad of workers' militia is fifteen strong; two sailors, two soldiers, two class-conscious workers (of whom, let us suppose, only one is a member of our Party, or a sympathiser), one intellectual, and eight from the poor working people, of whom at least five must be women, domestic servants, unskilled labourers, and so forth. The squad arrives at the rich man's flat, inspects it and finds that it consists of five rooms occupied by two men and two women—"You must squeeze up a bit into two rooms this winter, citizens, and prepare two rooms for two families now living in cellars. Until the time, with the aid of engineers (you are an engineer, aren't you?), we have built good dwellings for everybody, you will have to squeeze up a little. Your telephone will serve ten families. This will save a hundred hours of work wasted on shopping, and so forth. Now in your family there are two unemployed persons who can perform light work: a citizeness fifty-five years of age and a citizen fourteen years of age. They will be on duty for three hours a day supervising the proper distribution of provisions for ten families and keeping the necessary account of this. The student citizen in our squad will now write out this state order in two copies and you will be kind enough to give us a signed declaration that you will faithfully carry it out."

This, in my opinion, can illustrate how the distinction between the old bourgeois and the new socialist state apparatus and state administration could be illustrated.

We are not utopians. We know that an unskilled labourer or a cook cannot immediately get on with the job of state administration. In this we agree with the Cadets, with Breshkovskaya, and with Tsereteli. We differ, however, from these citizens in that we demand an immediate break with the prejudiced view that only the rich, or officials chosen from rich families, are capable of *administering* the state, of performing the ordinary, everyday work of administration. We demand that *training* in the work of state administration be conducted by class-conscious workers and soldiers and that this training be begun at once, i.e., that a *beginning* be made at once in training all the working people, all the poor, for this work.

We know that the Cadets are also willing to teach the people democracy. Cadet ladies are willing to deliver lectures to domestic servants on equal rights for women in accordance with the best English and French sources. And also, at the very next concert-meeting, before an audience of thousands, an exchange of kisses will be arranged on the platform: the Cadet lady lecturer will kiss Breshkovskaya, Breshkovskaya will kiss ex-Minister Tsereteli, and the grateful people will therefore receive an object-lesson in republican equality, liberty and fraternity. . . .

Yes, we agree that the Cadets, Breshkovskaya and Tsereteli are in their own way devoted to democracy and are propagating it among the people. But what is to be done if our conception of democracy is somewhat different from theirs?

In our opinion, to ease the incredible burdens and miseries of the war and also to heal the terrible wounds the war has inflicted on the people, *revolutionary* democracy is needed, *revolutionary* measures of the kind described in the example of the distribution of housing accommodation in the interests of the poor. *Exactly the same* procedure must be adopted in both town and country for the distribution of provisions, clothing, footwear, etc., in respect of the land in the rural districts, and so forth.

For the administration of the state in *this* spirit we can *at once set in motion a state* apparatus consisting of ten if not twenty million people, an apparatus such as no capitalist state has ever known. We alone can create such an apparatus, for we are sure of the fullest and devoted sympathy of the vast majority of the population. We alone can create such an apparatus, because we have class-conscious workers disciplined by long capitalist "schooling" (it was not for nothing that we went to learn in the school of capitalism), workers who are *capable* of forming a workers' militia and of *gradually* expanding it (beginning to expand it at once) into a militia *embracing the whole people*. The class-conscious workers must lead, but for the work of administration they can enlist the vast mass of the working and oppressed people.

It goes without saying that this new apparatus is bound to make mistakes in taking its first steps. But did not the peasants make mistakes when they emerged from serfdom and began to manage their own affairs? Is there any way other than practice by which the people can learn to govern themselves and to avoid mistakes? Is there any way other than by proceeding immediately to genuine self-government by the people? The chief thing now is to abandon the prejudiced bourgeois-intellectualist view that only special officials, who by their very social position are entirely dependent upon capital, can administer the state. The chief thing is to put an end to the state of affairs in which bourgeois officials and "socialist" ministers are trying to govern in the old way, but are incapable of doing so and, after seven months, are faced with a peasant revolt in a peasant country! The chief thing is to imbue the oppressed and the working people with confidence in their own strength, to prove to them in practice that they can and must themselves ensure the *proper*, most strictly regulated and organised distribution of bread, all kinds of food, milk, clothing, housing, etc., *in the interests of the poor*. Unless this is done, Russia *cannot* be saved from collapse and ruin. The conscientious, bold, universal move to hand over administrative work to proletarians and semi-proletarians, will, however, rouse such unprecedented revolutionary enthusiasm among the people, will so multiply the people's forces in combating distress, that much that seemed impossible to our narrow, old, bureaucratic forces will become possible for the millions, who will *begin to work for themselves* and not for the capitalists, the gentry, the bureaucrats, and not out of fear of punishment.

* * *

Pertinent to the question of the state apparatus is also the question of centralism raised with unusual vehemence and ineptitude by Comrade Bazarov in *Novaya Zhizn* No. 138, of September 27, in an article entitled: "The Bolsheviks and the Problem of Power".

Comrade Bazarov reasons as follows: "The Soviets are not an apparatus suitable for all spheres of state life", for, he says, seven months' experience has shown, and "scores and hundreds of documents in the possession of the Economic Department of the St. Petersburg Executive Committee" have confirmed, that the Soviets, although actually enjoying "full power" in many places, "have not been able to achieve anything like satisfactory results in combating economic ruin". What is needed is an apparatus "divided up according to branches of production, with strict centralisation within each branch, and subordinated to one, country-wide centre". "It is a matter", if you please, "not of replacing the old apparatus, but merely of reforming it . . . no matter how much the Bolsheviks may jeer at people with a plan. . . ."

All these arguments of Comrade Bazarov's are positively amazing for their helplessness, they echo the arguments of the bourgeoisie and reflect their class point of view.

In fact, to say that the Soviets have anywhere in Russia ever enjoyed "full power" is simply ridiculous (if it is not a repetition of the selfish class lie of the capitalists). Full power means power over all the land, over all the banks, over all the factories; a man who is at all familiar with the facts of history and science on the connection between politics and economics could not have "forgotten" this "trifling" circumstance.

The bourgeoisie's device is to *withhold* power from the Soviets, *sabotage* every important step they take, while at the same time retaining government in their own hands, retaining power over the land, the banks, etc., and then throwing the blame for the ruin upon the Soviets! This is exactly what the whole sad experience of the coalition amounts to.

The Soviets have never had full power, and the measures they have taken could not result in anything but palliatives that added to the confusion.

The effort to prove the necessity for centralism to the Bolsheviks who are centralists by conviction, by their programme and by the entire tactics of their Party, is really like forcing an open door. The writers of *Novaya Zhizn* are wasting their time only because they have totally failed to understand the meaning and significance of our jeers at their "country-wide" point of view. And the *Novaya Zhizn* people have failed to understand this because they merely pay *lip-service* to the doctrine of the class struggle, but do not accept it seriously. Repeating the words about the class struggle they have learned by rote, they are constantly slipping into the "above-class point of view", amusing in theory and reactionary in practice, and are calling this fawning upon the bourgeoisie a "country-wide" plan.

The state, dear people, is a class concept. The state is an organ or instrument of violence exercised by one class against another. So long as it is an instrument of violence exercised by the bourgeoisie against the proletariat, the proletariat can have only one slogan: *destruction* of this state. But when the state will be a proletarian state, when it will be an instrument of violence exercised by the proletariat against the bourgeoisie, we shall be fully and unreservedly in favour of a strong state power and of centralism.

To put it in more popular language, we do not jeer at "plans", but at Bazarov and Co.'s failure to understand that by repudiating "workers' control", by repudiating the "dictatorship of the proletariat" they *are for* the dictatorship of the bourgeoisie. There is no middle course; a middle course is the futile dream of the petty-bourgeois democrat.

Not a single central body, not a single Bolshevik has ever argued against *centralisation* of the Soviets, against their amalgamation. None of us objects to having factory committees in each branch of production, or to their centralisation. Bazarov is *wide of the mark*.

We laugh, have laughed, and will laugh not at "centralism", and not at "plans", but at *reformism*, because, after the experience of the coalition, your reformism is utterly ridiculous. And to say "not replace the apparatus but reform it" means to be a reformist, means to become not a revolutionary but a reformist democrat. Reformism means nothing more than concessions on the part of the ruling class, but *not* its overthrow; it makes concessions, but power remains in *its hands*.

This is precisely what has been tried during six months of the coalition.

This is what we laugh at. Having failed to obtain a thorough grasp of the doctrine of the class struggle, Bazarov allows himself to be caught by the bourgeoisie who sing in chorus "Just so, just so, we are by no means opposed to reform, we are in favour of the workers participating in country-wide control, we fully agree with that", and good Bazarov *objectively* sings the descant for the capitalists.

This has always been and always will be the case with people who in the thick of intense class struggle want to take up a "middle" position. And it is because the writers of *Novaya Zhizn* are incapable of understanding the class struggle that their policy is such a ridiculous and eternal oscillation between the bourgeoisie and the proletariat.

Get busy on "plans", dear citizens, that is not politics, that is not the class struggle; here you may be of use to the people. You have many economists on your paper. Unite with those engineers and others who are willing to work on problems of regulating production and distribution; devote the centre page of your big "apparatus" (your paper) to a practical study of precise facts on the production and distribution of goods in Russia, on banks, syndicates, etc., etc.—that is how you will be of use to the people; that is how your sitting between two stools will not be particularly harmful; such work on "plans" will earn not the ridicule, but the gratitude of the workers.

When the proletariat is victorious it will do the following, it will set economists, engineers, agronomists, and so forth, to work *under the control* of the workers' organisations on drawing up a "plan", on verifying it, on devising labour-saving methods of centralisation, on devising the simplest, cheapest, most convenient and universal measures and methods of control. For this we shall pay the economists, statisticians and technicians good money . . . but we shall not give them anything to eat if they do not perform this work conscientiously and entirely *in the interests of the working people.*

We are in favour of centralism and of a "plan", but of the centralism and plan of the *proletarian* state, of proletarian regulation of production and distribution in the interests of the poor, the working people, the exploited, *against* the exploiters. We can agree to only one meaning of the term "country-wide", namely, that which breaks the resistance of the capitalists, which gives all power to the majority of the people, i.e., the proletarians and semi-proletarians, the workers and the poor peasants.

* * *

The fifth plea is that the Bolsheviks will not be able to retain power because "the situation is exceptionally complicated". . . .

O wise men! They, perhaps, would be willing to reconcile themselves to revolution if only the "situation" were not "exceptionally complicated".

Such revolutions never occur, and sighs for such a revolution amount to nothing more than the reactionary wails of a bourgeois intellectual. Even if a revolution has started in a situation that seemed to be not very complicated, the development of the revolution itself *always* creates an *exceptionally* complicated situation. A revolution, a real, profound, a "people's" revolution, to use Marx's expression,[13] is the

[13] See Marx's letter to L. Kugelmann of April 12, 1871. (Marx and Engels,

incredibly complicated and painful process of the death of the old and birth of the new social order, of the mode of life of tens of millions of people. Revolution is a most intense, furious, desperate class struggle and civil war. Not a single great revolution in history has taken place without civil war. And only a "man in a muffler"[14] can think that civil war is conceivable without an "exceptionally complicated situation".

If the situation were not exceptionally complicated there would be no revolution. If you are afraid of wolves don't go into the forest.

There is nothing to discuss in the fifth plea, because there is no economic, political, or any other meaning whatever in it. It contains only the yearning of people who are distressed and frightened by the revolution. To characterise this yearning I shall take the liberty of mentioning two little things from my personal experience.

I had a conversation with a wealthy engineer shortly before the July days. This engineer had once been a revolutionary, had been in the Social-Democratic movement and even a member of the Bolshevik Party. Now he was full of fear and rage at the turbulent and indomitable workers. "If they were at least like the German workers," he said (he is an educated man and has been abroad), "of course, I understand that the social revolution is, in general, inevitable, but here, when the workers' level has been so reduced by the war . . . it is not a revolution, it is an abyss."

He was willing to accept the social revolution if history were to lead to it in the peaceful, calm, smooth and precise manner of a German express train pulling into a station. A sedate conductor would open the carriage door and announce: "Social Revolution Station! *Alle aussteigen!* (All change!)" In that case he would have no objection to changing his position of engineer under the Tit Tityches to that of engineer under the workers' organisations.

That man has seen strikes. He knows what a storm of passion the most ordinary strike arouses even in the most peaceful times. He, of course, understands how many million times more furious this storm must be when the class struggle has aroused *all* the working people of a vast country, when war and exploitation have driven almost to desperation millions of people who for centuries have been tormented by the landowners, for decades have been robbed and downtrodden by the capitalists and the tsar's officials. He understands all this "theoretically",

Selected Correspondence, Moscow, 1955, p. 318.)

[14] Reference to Chekhov's *The Man in a Muffler*, portraying a timid soul who is afraid of every little innovation.

he only pays *lip-service* to this, he is simply terrified by the "exceptionally complicated situation".

After the July days, thanks to the extremely solicitous attention with which the Kerensky government honoured me, I was obliged to go underground. Of course, it was the workers who sheltered people like us. In a small working-class house in a remote working-class suburb of Petrograd, dinner is being served. The hostess puts bread on the table. The host says: "Look what fine bread. 'They' dare not give us bad bread now. And we had almost given up even thinking that we'd ever get good bread in Petrograd again."

I was amazed at this class appraisal of the July days. My thoughts had been revolving around the political significance of those events, weighing the role they played in the general course of events, analysing the situation that caused this zigzag in history and the situation it would create, and how we ought to change our slogans and alter our Party apparatus to adapt it to the changed situation. As for bread, I, who had not known want, did not give it a thought. I took bread for granted, as a by-product of the writer's work, as it were. The mind approaches the foundation of everything, the class struggle for bread, through political analysis that follows an extremely complicated and devious path.

This member of the oppressed class, however, even though one of the well-paid and quite intelligent workers, takes the bull by the horns with that astonishing simplicity and straightforwardness, with that firm determination and amazing clarity of outlook from which we intellectuals are as remote as the stars in the sky. The whole world is divided into two camps: "us", the working people, and "them", the exploiters. Not a shadow of embarrassment over what had taken place; it was just one of the battles in the long struggle between labour and capital. When you fell trees, chips fly.

"What a painful thing is this 'exceptionally complicated situation' created by the revolution," that's how the bourgeois intellectual thinks and feels.

"We squeezed 'them' a bit; 'they' won't dare to lord it over us as they did before. We'll squeeze again—and chuck them out altogether," that's how the worker thinks and feels.

* * *

The sixth and last plea: the proletariat "will be incapable of resisting all the pressure by hostile forces that will sweep away not only the proletarian dictatorship, but the entire revolution into the bargain".

Don't try to scare us, gentlemen, you won't succeed. We saw these hostile forces and their pressure in Kornilovism (from which the Kerensky regime in no way differs). Everybody saw, and the people remember, how the proletariat and the poor peasants swept away the Kornilov gang, and how pitiful and helpless proved to be the position of the supporters of the bourgeoisie and of the few exceptionally well-to-do local small landowners who were exceptionally "hostile" to the revolution. *Dyelo Naroda* of September 30 urges the workers to "be patient and put up with" Kerensky (i.e., Kornilov) and the fake Tsereteli Bulygin Duma until the convocation of the Constituent Assembly (convened under the protection of "military measures" against insurgent peasants!) and, with great gusto, it repeats precisely *Novaya Zhizn*'s sixth plea and shouts until it is hoarse: "The Kerensky government will under no circumstances submit" (to the rule of the Soviets, the rule of the workers and peasants, which *Dyelo Naroda*, not wishing to lag behind the pogrom-mongers and anti-Semites, monarchists and Cadets, calls the rule of "Trotsky and Lenin": these are the lengths to which the Socialist-Revolutionaries go!).

But neither *Novaya Zhizn* nor *Dyelo Naroda* can scare the class-conscious workers. "The Kerensky government," you say, "will under no circumstances submit", i.e., it will repeat the Kornilov revolt, to put it more simply, bluntly and clearly. And the gentlemen of *Dyelo Naroda* dare to say that this will be "civil war", that this is a "horrible prospect"!

No, gentlemen, you will not fool the workers. It will not be civil war but a hopeless revolt of a handful of Kornilovites. If they want to "refuse to submit" to the people and at all costs provoke a repetition on a wide scale of what happened to the Kornilov men in Vyborg—*if* that is what the Socialist-Revolutionaries *want*, if that is what the member of the Socialist-Revolutionary Party Kerensky wants, he may drive the people to desperation. But you will not scare the workers and soldiers with this, gentlemen.

What boundless insolence. They faked up a new Bulygin Duma; by means of fraud they recruited a crowd of reactionary co-operators and village kulaks to help them, added to these the capitalists and landowners (the so-called property owning classes) and with the aid of this gang of Kornilovites they want *to thwart the will of the people*, the will of the workers and peasants.

They have brought affairs in a peasant country to such a pass that peasant revolt is spreading everywhere like a river in flood! Think of it! In a democratic republic in which 80 per cent of the population are peasants, the peasants have been driven to revolt. . . . This same *Dyelo*

Naroda, Chernov's newspaper, the organ of the "Socialist-Revolutionary" Party, which on September 30 has the effrontery to advise the workers and peasants to "be patient", was obliged to admit in a leading article on September 29:

> "*So far practically nothing* has been done to put an end to those relations of *bondage* that still *prevail* in the villages of central Russia."

This same *Dyelo Naroda*, in the same leading article of September 29, says that "the dead hand of Stolypin is still making itself strongly felt" in the methods employed by the "revolutionary ministers"; in other words, putting it more clearly and simply, it brands Kerensky, Nikitin, Kishkin and Co. as *Stolypins*.

The "Stolypins" Kerensky and Co. have driven the peasants to revolt, are now taking "military measures" against the peasants, are trying to soothe the people with the convocation of the Constituent Assembly (although Kerensky and Tsereteli have already *deceived* the people once by solemnly proclaiming on July 8 that the Constituent Assembly would be convened on the appointed date, September 17; they then *broke their promise* and postponed the Constituent Assembly even against the advice of the *Menshevik Dan*, postponed the Constituent Assembly not to the end of October as the Menshevik Central Executive Committee of that time wished, but to the end of November). The "Stolypins" Kerensky and Co. are trying to soothe the people with the imminent convocation of the Constituent Assembly, as if the people can believe those who have already lied in this matter, as if the people can believe that the Constituent Assembly will be *properly* convened by a government which has taken *military measures* in remote villages, that is to say, is openly *conniving* at the arbitrary arrest of class-conscious peasants and the *rigging* of the elections.

The government has driven the peasants to revolt and now has the effrontery to say to them: "You must 'be patient', you must wait, trust the government which is pacifying insurgent peasants by 'military measures'!"

To bring matters to such a pitch that hundreds of thousands of Russian soldiers perish in the offensive after June 19, the war is being protracted, German sailors have mutinied and are throwing their officers overboard, to bring matters to such a pitch, all the time uttering phrases about peace but *not offering* a just peace to *all* the belligerents, and yet to have the effrontery to tell the workers and peasants, to tell the dying soldiers, "you must be patient", trust the government of the "Stolypin man" Kerensky, trust the Kornilov generals for another month, perhaps in that month they will send several tens of thousands more soldiers to the slaughter. . . . "You must be patient". . . .

Isn't that shameless?

But you won't fool the soldiers, gentlemen of the Socialist-Revolutionaries, Kerensky's fellow party members.

The workers and soldiers will not endure the Kerensky government for a single day, for an *extra* hour, for they know that the *Soviet* Government will *immediately* offer all the belligerents a just peace and therefore will *in all probability* achieve an immediate armistice and a speedy peace.

Not for a single day, not for an *extra* hour will the soldiers of our peasant army allow the Kerensky government—the government which is employing *military measures* to suppress the peasant revolt—to remain in power against the will of the Soviets.

No, gentlemen of the Socialist-Revolutionaries, Kerensky's fellow party members, you won't fool the workers and peasants any more.

* * *

On the question of the pressure by hostile forces which the mortally frightened *Novaya Zhizn* assures us will sweep away the proletarian dictatorship, still another monstrous logical and political mistake is made, which only people who have allowed themselves to be frightened out of their wits can fail to see.

"Pressure by hostile forces will sweep away the proletarian dictatorship," you say. Very well. But you are all economists and educated people, dear fellow-citizens. You all know that to contrast democracy to the bourgeoisie is senseless and a sign of ignorance; it is the same as contrasting pounds to yards, for there is a democratic bourgeoisie and undemocratic groups of the petty bourgeoisie (capable of raising a Vendée).

"Hostile forces" is merely an empty phrase. The class term is *bourgeoisie* (backed by the landowners).

The bourgeoisie and the landowners, the proletariat, and the petty bourgeoisie, the small proprietors, primarily the peasants—these are the three main "forces" into which Russia, like *every* capitalist country, is divided. These are the three main "forces" that have long been revealed in every capitalist country (including Russia) not only by scientific economic analysis, but also by the *political experience* of the modern history of *all* countries, by the experience of *all* European revolutions since the eighteenth century, by the experience of the two Russian revolutions of 1905 and 1917.

So, you threaten the proletariat with the prospect that its rule will be swept away by the pressure of the bourgeoisie? That, and that alone, is what your threat amounts to, it has no other meaning.

Very well. If, for example, the bourgeoisie can sweep away the rule of the workers and poor peasants, then the only alternative is a "coalition", i.e., an alliance, or agreement, between the petty bourgeoisie and the bourgeoisie. Nothing else can be contemplated!

But coalition has been tried for about six months and it has led to bankruptcy, and you yourselves, my dear but dense citizens of *Novaya Zhizn*, have *renounced* coalition.

So what do we get?

You have become so muddled, citizens of *Novaya Zhizn*, you have allowed yourselves to be so scared, that you cannot think straight in the extremely simple matter of *counting even up to three, let alone up to five.*

Either all power to the bourgeoisie—the slogan you have long ceased to advocate, and which the bourgeoisie themselves dare not even hint at, for they know that the people overthrew this power with one hitch of the shoulder at the time of the April 20-21 events, and would overthrow it now with thrice that determination and ruthlessness; or power to the petty bourgeoisie, i.e., a coalition (alliance, agreement) between them and the bourgeoisie, for the petty bourgeoisie do not wish to and *cannot* take power alone and independently, as has been proved by the experience of all revolutions, and as is proved by economics, which explains that in a capitalist country it is possible to stand for capital and it is possible to stand for labour, but it is impossible to stand for long in between. In Russia this coalition has for six months tried scores of ways and failed.

Or, finally, all power to the proletarians and the poor peasants against the bourgeoisie in order to break their resistance. This has not yet been tried, and you, gentlemen of *Novaya Zhizn*, are *dissuading* the people from this, you are trying to frighten them with your own fear of the bourgeoisie.

No fourth way can be invented.

If *Novaya Zhizn*, therefore, is afraid of the proletarian dictatorship and rejects it because, as it claims, the proletarian power may be defeated by the bourgeoisie, it is tantamount to its *surreptitiously reverting* to the position of *compromise* with the capitalists! It is as clear as daylight, that whoever is afraid of resistance, whoever does not believe that it is possible to break this resistance, whoever warns the people: "beware of the resistance of the capitalists, you will not be able to cope with it", is *thereby* again calling for compromise with the capitalists.

Novaya Zhizn is hopelessly and pitifully muddled, as are all the petty-bourgeois democrats who now realise that the coalition is bankrupt, dare not defend it openly and, at the same time, protected by the bourgeoisie, fear the transfer of all power to the proletarians and poor peasants.

* * *

To fear the resistance of the capitalists and yet to call oneself a revolutionary, to wish to be regarded as a socialist—isn't that disgraceful? How low must international socialism, corrupted by opportunism, have fallen ideologically if such voices *could* be raised?

We have already seen the strength of the capitalists' resistance; the entire people have seen it, for the capitalists are more class-conscious than the other classes and at once realised the significance of the Soviets, at once exerted *all their efforts* to the utmost, resorted to everything, went to all lengths, resorted to the most incredible lies and slander, to military plots *in order to frustrate the Soviets*, to reduce them to nought, to prostitute them (with the aid of the Mensheviks and Socialist-Revolutionaries), to transform them into talking-shops, to wear down the peasants and workers by months and months of empty talk and playing at revolution.

We have not yet seen, however, the strength of resistance of the proletarians and poor peasants, for this strength will become fully apparent only when power is in the hands of the proletariat, when tens of millions of people who have been crushed by want and capitalist slavery see from experience and *feel* that state power has passed into the hands of the oppressed classes, that the state is helping the poor to fight the landowners and capitalists, is *breaking* their resistance. *Only* then shall we see what untapped forces of resistance to the capitalists are latent among the people; only then will what Engels called "latent socialism"[15] manifest itself. Only then, for every *ten thousand* overt and concealed enemies of working-class rule, manifesting themselves actively or by passive resistance, there will arise *a million* new fighters who had been politically dormant, writhing in the torments of poverty and despair, having ceased to believe that they were human, that they had the right to live, that they too could be served by the entire might of the modern

[15] See Engels's letter to F.A. Sorge of February 22, 1888.

centralised state, that contingents of the proletarian militia could, with the fullest confidence, also call upon *them* to take a direct, immediate, daily part in state administration.

The capitalists and landowners, with the kind help of Plekhanov, Breshkovskaya, Tsereteli, Chernov and Co., have done *everything* in their power to defile the democratic republic, to defile it by servility to wealth to such a degree that the people are being overcome by apathy, indifference; *it is all the same to them*, because the hungry man cannot see the difference between the republic and the monarchy; the freezing, barefooted, worn-out soldier sacrificing his life for alien interests is not inclined to love the republic.

But when every labourer, every unemployed worker, every cook, every ruined peasant sees, not from the newspapers, but with his own eyes, that the proletarian state is not cringing to wealth but is helping the poor, that this state does not hesitate to adopt revolutionary measures, that it confiscates surplus stocks of provisions from the parasites and distributes them to the hungry, that it forcibly installs the homeless in the houses of the rich, that it compels the rich to pay for milk but does not give them a drop until the children of *all* poor families are sufficiently supplied, that the land is being transferred to the working people and the factories and banks are being placed under the control of the workers, and that immediate and severe punishment is meted out to the millionaires who conceal their wealth—when the poor see and feel this, no capitalist or kulak forces, no forces of world finance capital which manipulates thousands of millions, will vanquish the people's revolution; on the contrary, *the socialist revolution* will triumph all over the world for it is maturing in all countries.

Our revolution will be invincible if it is not afraid of itself, if it transfers all power to the proletariat, for behind us stand the immeasurably larger, more developed, more organised world forces of the proletariat which are temporarily held down by the war but not destroyed; on the contrary, the war has multiplied them.

* * *

How can one be afraid that the Bolshevik government, that is to say, the proletarian government, which is assured of the devoted support of the poor peasants, will be "swept away" by the capitalist gentlemen! What short sightedness! What disgraceful fear of the people! What hypocrisy! Those who show this fear belong to that "high" (by capitalist standards, but actually *rotten*) "society" which utters the word "justice" without believing in it, from habit, as a trite phrase, attaching no meaning to it.

Here is an example.

Mr. Peshekhonov is a well-known semi-Cadet. A more moderate Trudovik, one of the same mind as the Breshkovskayas and Plekhanovs, will not be found. There has never been a minister more servile to the bourgeoisie. The world had never seen a more ardent advocate of "coalition", of compromise with the capitalists.

Here are the admissions this gentleman was *forced* to make in his speech at the "Democratic" (read: Bulygin) Conference as reported by the defencist *Izvestia*:

> "There are two programmes. One is the programme of group claims, class and national claims. This programme is most frankly advocated by the Bolsheviks. It is not easy, however, for the other sections of the democracy to reject this programme. They are the claims of the working people, the claims of the cheated and oppressed nationalities. It is not so easy, therefore, for the democracy to break with the Bolsheviks, to reject these class demands, primarily because in essence these demands are just. But this programme, for which we fought before the revolution, for the sake of which we made the revolution, and which we would all unanimously support under other circumstances, constitutes a very grave danger under present conditions. The danger is all the greater now because these demands have to be presented at a time when it is impossible for the state to comply with them. We must first defend the whole—the state, to save it from doom, and there is only one way to do that, not the satisfaction of demands, however just and cogent they may be, but, on the contrary, restriction and sacrifice, which must be contributed from all quarters." (*Izvestia*, September 17)

Mr. Peshekhonov fails to understand that as long as the capitalists are in power he is defending *not* the whole, but the selfish interests of Russian and "Allied" imperialist capital. Mr. Peshekhonov fails to understand that the war would cease to be an imperialist, predatory war of annexation only after a rupture with the capitalists, with *their* secret treaties, with *their* annexations (seizure of alien territory), with *their* banking and financial swindles. Mr. Peshekhonov fails to understand that only *after* this would the war become—if the enemy rejected the formal offer of a just peace—a defensive war, a just war. Mr. Peshekhonov fails to understand that the defence potential of a country that has thrown off the yoke of capital, that has given the peasants land and has placed the banks and factories under workers' control, would be many times greater than the defence potential of a capitalist country.

The main thing that Mr. Peshekhonov fails to understand is that he surrenders his entire position, the entire position of the entire petty-bourgeois democracy when he is forced to admit the justice of Bolshevism, to admit that its demands are the demands of the "working people", i.e., of the majority of the people.

This is where our strength lies. This is why our government will be invincible; because even our opponents are forced to admit that the Bolshevik programme is that of the "working people" and the "oppressed nationalities".

After all, Mr. Peshekhonov is the political friend of the Cadets, of the *Yedinstvo* and *Dyelo Naroda* people, of the Breshkovskayas and Plekhanovs, he is the representative of the kulaks and of the gentlemen whose wives and sisters would come tomorrow to gouge out with their umbrellas the eyes of wounded Bolsheviks if they were to be defeated by Kornilov's or (which is the same thing) Kerensky's troops.

A gentleman like that is forced to admit the "justice" of the Bolshevik demands.

For him "justice" is merely an empty phrase. For the mass of semi-proletarians, however, and for the majority of the urban and rural petty bourgeoisie who have been ruined, tortured and worn out by the war, it is not an empty phrase, but a most acute, most burning and immense question of death from starvation, of a crust of bread. That is why no policy can be based on a "coalition", on a "compromise" between the interests of the starving and ruined and the interests of the exploiters. That is why the Bolshevik government is assured of the support of the overwhelming majority of these people.

Justice is an empty word, say the intellectuals and those rascals who are inclined to proclaim themselves Marxists on the lofty grounds that they have "contemplated the hind parts" of economic materialism.

Ideas become a power when they grip the people. And precisely at the present time the Bolsheviks, i.e., the representatives of revolutionary proletarian internationalism, have embodied in their policy the idea that is motivating countless working people all over the world.

Justice alone, the mere anger of the people against exploitation, would never have brought them on to the true path of socialism. But now that, thanks to capitalism, the material apparatus of the big banks, syndicates, railways, and so forth, has grown, now that the immense experience of the advanced countries has accumulated a stock of engineering marvels, the employment of which is being *hindered* by capitalism, now that the class-conscious workers have built up a party of a quarter of a million members to systematically lay hold of this apparatus and set it in motion with the support of all the working and exploited people—now that these conditions exist, no power on earth can prevent the Bolsheviks, *if they do not allow themselves to be scared* and if they succeed in taking power, from retaining it until the triumph of the world socialist revolution.

AFTERWORD

The foregoing lines were already written when the leading article in *Novaya Zhizn* of October 1 produced another gem of stupidity which is all the more dangerous because it professes sympathy with the Bolsheviks and offers most sagacious philistine admonitions "not to allow yourselves to be provoked" (not to allow ourselves to be caught in the trap of screams about provocation, the object of which is to frighten the Bolsheviks and cause them to *refrain* from taking power).

Here is this gem:

> "The lessons of movements, like that of July 3-5, on the one hand, and of the Kornilov days, on the other, have shown quite clearly that the democracy, having at its command organs that exercise immense influence among the population, is invincible when it takes a defensive position in civil war, and that it suffers defeat, loses all the middle vacillating groups when it takes the initiative and launches an offensive."

If the Bolsheviks were to yield in any form and in the slightest degree to the philistine stupidity of this argument they would ruin their Party and the revolution.

For the author of this argument, taking it upon himself to talk about civil war (just the subject for a lady with many good points), has distorted *the lessons of history* on this question in an incredibly comical manner.

This is how *these* lessons, the lessons of history on *this* question, were treated by the representative and founder of proletarian revolutionary tactics, Karl Marx:

"Now, insurrection is an art quite as much as war or any other art, and is subject to certain procedural rules which, when neglected, will bring about the downfall of the party neglecting them. These rules, logical deductions from the nature of the parties and the circumstances you have to deal with in such a case, are so plain and simple that the brief experience of 1848 made the Germans fairly well acquainted with them. Firstly, never play with insurrection unless you are fully prepared to go the whole way [literally: face the consequences of your game].[16] Insurrection is an equation with very indefinite magnitudes, the value of which may change every day; the forces opposed to you have all the advantage of organisation, discipline and habitual authority [Marx has in mind the most "difficult" case of insurrection: against the "firmly established" old authority, against the army not yet disintegrated by the influence of the revolution and the vacillation of the government]; unless you bring strong odds against them you are defeated and ruined. Secondly, once you have entered upon the insurrectionary career, act with the greatest determination, and on the offensive. The defensive is the death of every armed rising; it is lost before it measures itself with its enemies. Surprise your antagonists while their forces are scattered, prepare the way for new successes, however small, but prepare daily; keep up the moral superiority which the first successful rising has given to you; rally in this way those vacillating elements to your side which always follow the strongest impulse and which always look out for the safer side; force your enemies to retreat before they can collect their strength against you; in the words of Danton, the greatest master of revolutionary tactics yet known: *de l'audace, de l'audace, encore de l'audace!*" (*Revolution and Counter-revolution in Germany*, German edition, 1907, p. 118.)

We have changed all that, the "would-be Marxists" of *Novaya Zhizn* may say about themselves; instead of triple audacity they have two virtues: "We have two, sir: moderation and accuracy."[17] For "us", the experience of world history, the experience of the Great French Revolution, is nothing. The important thing for "us" is the experience of the two movements in 1917, distorted by Molchalin spectacles.

Let us examine this experience without these charming spectacles.

You compare July 3-5 with "civil war", because you believed Alexinsky, Pereverzev and Co. It is typical of the gentlemen of *Novaya Zhizn* that they believe *such* people (and do absolutely nothing themselves to *collect information* about July 3-5, although they have the huge apparatus of a big daily newspaper at their disposal).

Let us assume for a moment, however, that July 3-5 was not the

[16] Interpolations in square brackets (within passages quoted by Lenin) have been introduced by Lenin unless otherwise indicated.

[17] Reference to the words of Molchalin, a character from Griboyedov's comedy *Wit Works Woe* who became a symbol of sycophancy and toadyism.

rudiment of civil war that was kept within the rudimentary stage by the Bolsheviks, but actual civil war. Let us assume this.

In that case, then, what does this lesson prove?

First, the Bolsheviks did *not* take the offensive, for it is indisputable that on the night of July 3-4, and even on July 4, they would have gained a great deal if they had taken the offensive. Their defensive position was their weakness, if we are to speak of civil war (as *Novaya Zhizn* does, and not of converting a spontaneous outburst into a demonstration of the type of April 20-21, as the *facts* show).

The "lesson" therefore proves that the wise men of *Novaya Zhizn* are *wrong*.

Secondly, if the Bolsheviks did not even set out to start an insurrection on July 3 or 4, if *not a single* Bolshevik *body* even raised such a question, the reason for it lies *beyond* the scope of our controversy with *Novaya Zhizn*. For we are arguing about the *lessons* of "civil war", i.e., of insurrection, and not about the point that obvious lack of a majority to support it restrains the revolutionary party from thinking of insurrection.

Since everybody knows that the Bolsheviks received a majority in the metropolitan Soviets and in the country (over 49 per cent of the Moscow votes) *much later* than July 1917, it again follows that the "lessons" are far, far from what *Novaya Zhizn*, that lady with many good points, would like them to be.

No, no, you had better not meddle with politics, citizens of *Novaya Zhizn*!

If the revolutionary party has no majority in the advanced contingents of the revolutionary classes and in the country, insurrection is out of the question. Moreover, insurrection requires: (1) growth of the revolution on a country-wide scale; (2) the complete moral and political bankruptcy of the old government, for example, the "coalition" government; (3) extreme vacillation in the camp of all middle groups, i.e., those who do *not* fully support the government, although they did fully support it yesterday.

Why did *Novaya Zhizn*, when speaking of the "lessons" of July 3-5, fail even to note this very important lesson? Because a political question was not dealt with by politicians but by a circle of intellectuals who had been terrified by the bourgeoisie.

To proceed. Thirdly, the facts show that it was *after* July 3-4 that the *rot* set in among the Socialist-Revolutionaries and Mensheviks, precisely because the Tseretelis had *exposed* themselves by their *July* policy, precisely because the mass of the *people* realised that the Bolsheviks were *their own* front-rank fighters and that the "social-bloc" advocates were traitors. *Even before* the Kornilov revolt this rot was fully revealed by the Petrograd elections on August 20, which resulted in a victory for the Bolsheviks and the rout of the "social-bloc" advocates (*Dyelo Naroda* recently tried to refute this *by concealing* the returns for *all* parties, but this was both self-deception and deception of its readers; according to the figures published in *Dyen* of August 24, covering only the city, the Cadets' share of the total vote increased from 22 to 23 per cent, but the absolute number of votes cast for the Cadets dropped 40 per cent; the Bolsheviks' share of the total vote increased from 20 to 33 per cent, while the absolute number of votes cast for the Bolsheviks dropped only 10 per cent; the share of all "middle groups" dropped from 58 to 44 per cent, but the absolute number of votes cast for them dropped 60 per cent!).

That a rot had set in among the Socialist-Revolutionaries and Mensheviks after the July days and before the Kornilov days is also proved by the growth of the Left wings in both parties, reaching almost 40 per cent: this is "retribution" for the persecution of the Bolsheviks by the Kerenskys.

In spite of the "loss" of a few hundred members, the proletarian party *gained* enormously from July 3-4, for it was precisely during those stern days that the *people* realised and saw its devotion and the *treachery* of the Socialist-Revolutionaries and Mensheviks. So, the "lesson" is far, very far from being of the *Novaya Zhizn* sort, it is one entirely different, namely: don't desert the seething masses for the "Molchalins of democracy"; and if you launch an insurrection, go over to the offensive while the enemy forces are scattered, catch the enemy unawares.

Is that not so, gentlemen "would-be Marxists" of *Novaya Zhizn*?

Or does "Marxism" mean *not* basing tactics on an exact appraisal of the *objective* situation but senselessly and uncritically lumping together "civil war" and "a Congress of Soviets and the convocation of the Constituent Assembly"?

But this is simply ridiculous, gentlemen, this is a sheer mockery of Marxism and of logic in general!

If there is *nothing* in the *objective* situation that warrants the intensification of the class struggle to the point of "civil war", why did you speak of "civil war" *in connection* with "a Congress of Soviets and the Constituent Assembly"? (For this is the title of the leading article in *Novaya Zhizn* here under discussion.) In that case you should clearly have told the reader and proved to him that there is *no* ground in the objective situation for civil war and that, therefore, peaceful, constitutionally-legal, juridically and parliamentarily "simple" things like a Congress of Soviets and a Constituent Assembly can and should be the cornerstone of tactics. In that case it is *possible* to hold the opinion that such a congress and such an assembly are really capable *of making decisions*.

If, however, the present objective conditions harbour the inevitability or even only the probability of civil war, if you did not "idly" speak about it, but did so clearly seeing, feeling, sensing the existence of a situation of civil war, how could you make a Congress of Soviets or a Constituent Assembly the cornerstone? This is a sheer mockery of the starving and tormented people! Do you think the starving will consent to "wait" two months? Or that the ruin, about the increase of which you yourselves write every day, will consent to "wait" for the Congress of Soviets or for the Constituent Assembly? Or that the German offensive, in the absence of serious steps on our part towards peace (i.e., in the absence of a formal offer of a just peace to all belligerents), will consent to "wait" for the Congress of Soviets or for the Constituent Assembly? Or are you in possession of facts which permit you to conclude that the history of the Russian revolution, which from February 28 to September 30 had proceeded with extraordinary turbulence and unprecedented rapidity, will, from October 1 to November 29,[18] proceed at a super-tranquil, peaceful, legally balanced pace that will preclude upheavals, spurts, military defeats and economic crises? Or will the army at the front, concerning which the *non*-Bolshevik officer Dubasov said officially, in the name of the front, "it will not fight", quietly starve and freeze until the "appointed" date? Or will the peasant revolt cease to be a factor of civil war because you call it "anarchy" and "pogrom", or because Kerensky will send "military" forces *against the peasants*? Or is it possible, *conceivable*, that the government can work calmly, honestly, and *without* deception to convene the Constituent Assembly in a *peasant* country when that same government is *suppressing* the peasant revolt?

[18] Reference to the following: *February 28* (*March 13*)—date of the February revolution, *September 30* (*October 13*)—first tentative date set by the Provisional Government for the convocation of the Constituent Assembly; *November 28* (*December 11*), *1917*—date of the convocation of the Constituent Assembly.

Don't laugh at the "confusion in the Smolny Institute",[19] gentlemen! There is no less confusion in your own ranks. You answer the formidable questions of civil war with confused phrases and pitiful constitutional illusions. That is why I say that if the Bolsheviks were to give in to these moods they would ruin both their Party and their revolution.

October 1, 1917.

N. Lenin

[19] A quotation from N. Sukhanov's article "Another Thunderbolt" carried by the newspaper *Novaya Zhizn* (New Life).

From August 1917, the Smolny Institute was the headquarters of the Bolshevik groups of the All-Russia Central Executive Committee and the Petrograd Soviet of Workers' and Soldiers' Deputies. The Revolutionary Military Committee also had its premises there from October.

"LEFT-WING" COMMUNISM: AN INFANTILE DISORDER (1920)

II. AN ESSENTIAL CONDITION OF THE BOLSHEVIKS' SUCCESS[12]

It is, I think, almost universally realised at present that the Bolsheviks could not have retained power for two and a half months, let alone two and a half years, without the most rigorous and truly iron discipline in our Party, or without the fullest and unreserved support from the entire mass of the working class, that is, from all thinking, honest, devoted and influential elements in it, capable of leading the backward strata or carrying the latter along with them.

[. . .]

Would it not be better if the salutations addressed to the Soviets and the Bolsheviks were *more frequently* accompanied by a *profound analysis* of the reasons *why* the Bolsheviks have been able to build up the discipline needed by the revolutionary proletariat?

As a current of political thought and as a political party, Bolshevism has existed since 1903. Only the history of Bolshevism during the *entire* period of its existence can satisfactorily explain why it has been able to build up and maintain, under most difficult conditions, the iron discipline needed for the victory of the proletariat.

The first questions to arise are: how is the discipline of the proletariat's revolutionary party maintained? How is it tested? How is it reinforced? First, by the class-consciousness of the proletarian vanguard and by its devotion to the revolution, by its tenacity, self-sacrifice and heroism.

[1] Revised translation by Julius Katzer.

[2] *"Left-Wing" Communism—an Infantile Disorder* was written by Lenin in April, and the appendix—on May 12, 1920. It came out on June 8-10, in Russian and almost simultaneously in July in German, English and French. Lenin gave personal attention to the book's type-setting and printing schedule so that it should be published before the opening of the Second Congress of the Communist International, each delegate receiving a copy. Between July and November 1920, the book was re-published in Leipzig, Paris and London, in the German, French and English languages respectively.

The manuscript of the book is subtitled: "An Attempt to Conduct a Popular Discussion on Marxist Strategy and Tactics." This subtitle was deleted in all editions published in Lenin's lifetime. In the fourth (Russian) edition of Lenin's Works, *"Left-Wing" Communism—an Infantile Disorder* is published according to the first edition, the proofs of which were read by Lenin himself.

Second, by its ability to link up, maintain the closest contact, and—if you wish—merge, in certain measure, with the broadest masses of the working people—primarily with the proletariat, *but also with the non-proletarian* masses of working people. Third, by the correctness of the political leadership exercised by this vanguard, by the correctness of its political strategy and tactics, provided the broad masses have seen, *from their own experience*, that they are correct. Without these conditions, discipline in a revolutionary party really capable of being the party of the advanced class, whose mission it is to overthrow the bourgeoisie and transform the whole of society, cannot be achieved. Without these conditions, all attempts to establish discipline inevitably fall flat and end up in phrase-mongering and clowning. On the other hand, these conditions cannot emerge at once. They are created only by prolonged effort and hard-won experience. Their creation is facilitated by a correct revolutionary theory, which, in its turn, is not a dogma, but assumes final shape only in close connection with the practical activity of a truly mass and truly revolutionary movement.

The fact that, in 1917-20, Bolshevism was able, under unprecedentedly difficult conditions, to build up and successfully maintain the strictest centralisation and iron discipline was due simply to a number of historical peculiarities of Russia.

On the one hand, Bolshevism arose in 1903 on a very firm foundation of Marxist theory. The correctness of this revolutionary theory, and of it alone, has been proved, not only by world experience throughout the nineteenth century, but especially by the experience of the seekings and vacillations, the errors and disappointments of revolutionary thought in Russia. For about half a century—approximately from the forties to the nineties of the last century—progressive thought in Russia, oppressed by a most brutal and reactionary tsarism, sought eagerly for a correct revolutionary theory, and followed with the utmost diligence and thoroughness each and every "last word" in this sphere in Europe and America. Russia achieved Marxism—the only correct revolutionary theory—through the *agony* she experienced in the course of half a century of unparalleled torment and sacrifice, of unparalleled revolutionary heroism, incredible energy, devoted searching, study, practical trial, disappointment, verification, and comparison with European experience. Thanks to the political emigration caused by tsarism, revolutionary Russia, in the second half of the nineteenth century, acquired a wealth of international links and excellent information on the forms and theories of the world revolutionary movement, such as no other country possessed.

On the other hand, Bolshevism, which had arisen on this granite foundation of theory, went through 15 years of practical history (1903-17) unequalled anywhere in the world in its wealth of experience. During those fifteen years, no other country knew anything even approximating to that revolutionary experience, that rapid and varied succession of different forms of the movement—legal and illegal, peaceful and stormy, underground and open, local circles and mass movements, and parliamentary and terrorist forms. In no other country has there been concentrated, in so brief a period, such a wealth of forms, shades, and methods of struggle of all classes of modern society, a struggle which, owing to the backwardness of the country and the severity of the tsarist yoke, matured with exceptional rapidity, and assimilated most eagerly and successfully the appropriate "last word" of American and European political experience.

III. THE PRINCIPAL STAGES IN THE HISTORY OF BOLSHEVISM

The years of preparation for revolution (1903-05). The approach of a great storm was sensed everywhere. All classes were in a state of ferment and preparation. Abroad, the press of the political exiles discussed the theoretical aspects of *all* the fundamental problems of the revolution. Representatives of the three main classes, of the three principal political trends—the liberal-bourgeois, the petty-bourgeois-democratic (concealed behind "social-democratic" and "social-revolutionary" labels[3]), and the proletarian-revolutionary—anticipated and prepared the impending open class struggle by waging a most bitter struggle on issues of programme and tactics. *All* the issues on which the masses waged an armed struggle in 1905-07 and 1917-20 can (and should) be studied, in their embryonic form, in the press of the period. Among these three main trends there were, of course, a host of intermediate, transitional or half-hearted forms. It would be more correct to say that those political and ideological trends which were genuinely of a class nature crystallised in the struggle of press organs, parties, factions and groups; the classes were forging the requisite political and ideological weapons for the impending battles.

The years of revolution (1905-07). All classes came out into the open. All programmatical and tactical views were tested by the action of the masses. In its extent and acuteness, the strike struggle had no

[3] The reference is to the Mensheviks (who formed the Right and opportunist wing of Social-Democracy in the R.S.D.L.P.), and to the Socialist-Revolutionaries.

parallel anywhere in the world. The economic strike developed into a political strike, and the latter into insurrection. The relations between the proletariat, as the leader, and the vacillating and unstable peasantry, as the led, were tested in practice. The Soviet form of organisation came into being in the spontaneous development of the struggle. The controversies of that period over the significance of the Soviets anticipated the great struggle of 1917-20. The alternation of parliamentary and non-parliamentary forms of struggle, of the tactics of boycotting parliament and that of participating in parliament, of legal and illegal forms of struggle, and likewise their interrelations and connections—all this was marked by an extraordinary wealth of content. As for teaching the fundamentals of political science to masses and leaders, to classes and parties alike, each month of this period was equivalent to an entire year of "peaceful" and "constitutional" development. Without the "dress rehearsal" of 1905, the victory of the October Revolution in 1917 would have been impossible.

The years of reaction (1907-10). Tsarism was victorious. All the revolutionary and opposition parties were smashed. Depression, demoralisation, splits, discord, defection, and pornography took the place of politics. There was an ever greater drift towards philosophical idealism; mysticism became the garb of counter-revolutionary sentiments. At the same time, however, it was this great defeat that taught the revolutionary parties and the revolutionary class a real and very useful lesson, a lesson in historical dialectics, a lesson in an understanding of the political struggle, and in the art and science of waging that struggle. It is at moments of need that one learns who one's friends are. Defeated armies learn their lesson.

Victorious tsarism was compelled to speed up the destruction of the remnants of the pre-bourgeois, patriarchal mode of life in Russia. The country's development along bourgeois lines proceeded apace. Illusions that stood outside and above class distinctions, illusions concerning the possibility of avoiding capitalism, were scattered to the winds. The class struggle manifested itself in a quite new and more distinct way.

The revolutionary parties had to complete their education. They were learning how to attack. Now they had to realise that such knowledge must be supplemented with the knowledge of how to retreat in good order. They had to realise—and it is from bitter experience that the revolutionary class learns to realise this—that victory is impossible unless one has learned how to attack and retreat properly. Of all the defeated opposition and revolutionary parties, the Bolsheviks effected the most orderly retreat, with the least loss to their "army", with its core best preserved, with the least significant splits (in point of depth and incurability), with the least demoralisation, and in the best condition to resume work on the broadest scale and in the most correct and energetic manner. The Bolsheviks achieved this only because they ruthlessly exposed and expelled the revolutionary phrase-mongers, those who did not wish to understand that one had to retreat, that one had to know how to retreat, and that one had absolutely to learn how to work legally in the most reactionary of parliaments, in the most reactionary of trade unions, co-operative and insurance societies and similar organisations.

The years of revival (1910-14). At first progress was incredibly slow, then, following the Lena events of 1912, it became somewhat more rapid. Overcoming unprecedented difficulties, the Bolsheviks thrust back the Mensheviks, whose role as bourgeois agents in the working-class movement was clearly realised by the entire bourgeoisie after 1905, and whom the bourgeoisie therefore supported in a thousand ways against the Bolsheviks. But the Bolsheviks would never have succeeded in doing this had they not followed the correct tactics of combining illegal work with the utilisation of "legal opportunities", which they made a point of doing. In the elections to the arch-reactionary Duma, the Bolsheviks won thc full support of the worker curia.

The First Imperialist World War (1914-17). Legal parliamentarianism, with an extremely reactionary "parliament", rendered most useful service to the Bolsheviks, the party of the revolutionary proletariat. The Bolshevik deputies were exiled to Siberia.[4] All shades of social-imperialism, social-chauvinism, social-patriotism, inconsistent and consistent internationalism, pacifism, and the revolutionary repudiation of pacifist illusions found full expression in the Russian emigre press. The learned fools and the old women of the Second International, who had

[4] The reference is to the Bolshevik deputies to the Fourth Duma, namely, A.Y. Badayev, M.K. Muranov, G.I. Petrovsky, F.N. Samoilov and N.R. Shagov. At the Duma's session of July 26 (August 8), 1914, at which the representatives of all the bourgeois-landowner Duma groups approved tsarist Russia's entry into the imperialist war, the Bolshevik Duma group declared firm protest: they refused to vote for war credits and launched revolutionary propaganda among the people. In November 1914 the Bolshevik deputies were arrested, in February 1915 they were brought to trial, and exiled for life to Turukhansk Territory in Eastern Siberia. The courageous speeches made by the Bolshevik deputies at their trial, exposing the autocracy, played an important part in anti-war propaganda and in revolutionising the toiling masses.

arrogantly and contemptuously turned up their noses at the abundance of "factions" in the Russian socialist movement and at the bitter struggle they were waging among themselves, were unable—when the war deprived them of their vaunted "legality" in *all* the advanced countries—to organise anything even approximating such a free (illegal) interchange of views and such a free (illegal) evolution of correct views as the Russian revolutionaries did in Switzerland and in a number of other countries. That was why both the avowed social-patriots and the "Kautskyites" of all countries proved to be the worst traitors to the proletariat. One of the principal reasons why Bolshevism was able to achieve victory in 1917-20 was that, since the end of 1914, it has been ruthlessly exposing the baseness and vileness of social-chauvinism and "Kautskyism" (to which Longuetism[5] in France, the views of the Fabians[6] and the leaders of the Independent Labour Party[7] in Britain, of Turati in Italy, etc., correspond),

[5] *Longuetism*—the Centrist trend within the French Socialist Party, headed by Jean Longuet. During the First World War of 1914-18, the Longuetists conducted a policy of conciliation with the social-chauvinists. They rejected the revolutionary struggle and came out for "defence of country" in the imperialist war. Lenin called them petty-bourgeois nationalists. After the victory of the October Socialist Revolution in Russia, the Longuetists called themselves supporters of the proletarian dictatorship, but in fact they remained opposed to it. In December 1920 the Longuetists, together with the avowed reformists, broke away from the Party and joined the so-called Two-and-a-Half International.

[6] *Fabians*—members of the Fabian Society, a British reformist organisation founded in 1884. The membership consisted, in the main, of bourgeois intellectuals. The Fabians denied the necessity of the proletariat's class struggle and the socialist revolution, and contended that the transition from capitalism to socialism was possible only through petty reforms and the gradual reorganisation of society. In 1900 the Fabian Society joined the Labour Party. The Fabians are characterised by Lenin in "British Pacifism and British Dislike of Theory" (see *LCW*, Vol. 21, 1974, pp. 260-65) and elsewhere.

[7] *The Independent Labour Party of Britain* (*I.L.P.*)—a reformist organisation founded in 1893 by leaders of the "new trade unions", in conditions of a revival of the strike struggle and the mounting movement for British working-class independence of the bourgeois parties. The I.L.P. included members of the "new trade unions" and those of a number of the old trade unions, as well as intellectuals and Petty bourgeoisie who were under the influence of the Fabians. The I.L.P. was headed by James Keir Hardie and Ramsay MacDonald. From its very inception, the I.L.P. took a bourgeois-reformist stand, laying particular stress on parliamentary forms of struggle and parliamentary deals with the Liberals. Lenin wrote of the I.L.P. that "in reality it is an opportunist party always dependent on the bourgeoisie".

the masses later becoming more and more convinced, from their own experience, of the correctness of the Bolshevik views.

The second revolution in Russia (February to October 1917). Tsarism's senility and obsoleteness had (with the aid of the blows and hardships of a most agonising war) created an incredibly destructive force directed against it. Within a few days Russia was transformed into a democratic bourgeois republic, freer—in war conditions—than any other country in the world. The leaders of the opposition and revolutionary parties began to set up a government, just as is done in the most "strictly parliamentary" republics; the fact that a man had been a leader of an opposition party in parliament—even in a most reactionary parliament—*facilitated* his subsequent role in the revolution.

[...]

As history would have it, the Soviets came into being in Russia in 1905; from February to October 1917 they were turned to a false use by the Mensheviks, who went bankrupt because of their inability to understand the role and significance of the Soviets, today the idea of Soviet power has emerged *throughout the world* and is spreading among the proletariat of all countries with extraordinary speed. Like our Mensheviks, the old heroes of the Second International are *everywhere* going bankrupt, because they are incapable of understanding the role and significance of the Soviets. Experience has proved that, on certain very important questions of the proletarian revolution, *all* countries will inevitably have to do what Russia has done.

Despite views that are today often to be met with in Europe and America, the Bolsheviks began their victorious struggle against the parliamentary and (in fact) bourgeois republic and against the Mensheviks in a very cautious manner, and the preparations they made for it were by no means simple. At the beginning of the period mentioned, we did *not* call for the overthrow of the government but explained that it was impossible to overthrow it *without* first changing the composition and the temper of the Soviets. We did not proclaim a boycott of the bourgeois parliament, the Constituent Assembly, but said—and following the April (1917) Conference of our Party began to state officially in the name of the Party—that a bourgeois republic with a Constituent Assembly would be better than a bourgeois republic without a Constituent Assembly, but that a "workers' and peasants'" republic, a Soviet republic, would be better than any bourgeois-democratic, parliamentary republic. Without such thorough, circumspect and long preparations, we could not have achieved victory in October 1917, or have consolidated that victory.

[. . .]

X. SEVERAL CONCLUSIONS

[. . .] It is now essential that Communists of every country should quite consciously take into account both the fundamental objectives of the struggle against opportunism and "Left" doctrinairism, and the *concrete features* which this struggle assumes and must inevitably assume in each country, in conformity with the specific character of its economics, politics, culture, and national composition (Ireland, etc.), its colonies, religious divisions, and so on and so forth. Dissatisfaction with the Second International is felt everywhere and is spreading and growing, both because of its opportunism and because of its inability or incapacity to create a really centralised and really leading centre capable of directing the international tactics of the revolutionary proletariat in its struggle for a world Soviet republic. It should be clearly realised that such a leading centre can never be built up on stereotyped, mechanically equated, and identical tactical rules of struggle. As long as national and state distinctions exist among peoples and countries—and these will continue to exist for a very long time to come, even after the dictatorship of the proletariat has been established on a world-wide scale—the unity of the international tactics of the communist working-class movement in all countries demands, not the elimination of variety or the suppression of national distinctions (which is a pipe dream at present), but an application of the *fundamental* principles of communism (Soviet power and the dictatorship of the proletariat), which will *correctly modify* these principles in certain *particulars*, correctly adapt and apply them to national and national-state distinctions.

[. . .]

The proletarian vanguard has been won over ideologically. That is the main thing. Without this, not even the first step towards victory can be made. But that is still quite a long way from victory. Victory cannot be won with a vanguard alone. To throw only the vanguard into the decisive battle, before the entire class, the broad masses, have taken up a position either of direct support for the vanguard, or at least of sympathetic neutrality towards it and of precluded support for the enemy, would be, not merely foolish but criminal. Propaganda and agitation alone are not enough for an entire class, the broad masses of the working people, those oppressed by capital, to take up such a stand. For that, the masses must have their own political experience. Such is the fundamental law of all great revolutions, which has been confirmed with compelling force and vividness, not only in Russia but in Germany as well. To turn resolutely towards communism, it was necessary, not only for the ignorant and often illiterate masses of Russia, but also for the literate and well-educated masses of Germany, to realise from their own bitter experience the absolute impotence and spinelessness, the absolute helplessness and servility to the bourgeoisie, and the utter vileness of the government of the paladins of the Second International; they had to realise that a dictatorship of the extreme reactionaries (Kornilov[8] in Russia; Kapp[9] and Co. in Germany) is inevitably the only alternative to a dictatorship of the proletariat.

[. . .]

History as a whole, and the history of revolutions in particular, is always richer in content, more varied, more multiform, more lively and ingenious than is imagined by even the best parties, the most class-conscious vanguards of the most advanced classes. This can readily be understood, because even the finest of vanguards express the class-consciousness, will, passion and imagination of tens of thousands, whereas at moments of great upsurge and the exertion of all human capacities, revolutions are made by the class-consciousness, will, passion and imagination of tens of millions, spurred on by a most acute struggle of classes. Two very important practical conclusions follow from this:

[8] This refers to the counter-revolutionary mutiny organised in August 1917 by the bourgeoisie and the landowners, under the Supreme Commander-in-Chief, the tsarist General Kornilov. The conspirators hoped to seize Petrograd, smash the Bolshevik Party, break up the Soviets, establish a military dictatorship in the country, and prepare the restoration of the monarchy.

The mutiny began on August 25 (September 7), Kornilov sending the 3rd Cavalry Corps against Petrograd, where Kornilov counter-revolutionary organisations were ready to act.

The Kornilov mutiny was crushed by the workers and peasants led by the Bolshevik Party. Under pressure from the masses, the Provisional Government was forced to order that Kornilov and his accomplices be arrested and brought to trial.

[9] The reference is to the military-monarchist coup d'état, the so-called Kapp *putsch* organised by the German reactionary militarists. It was headed by the monarchist landowner Kapp and Generals Ludendorff, Seeckt and Lüttwitz. The conspirators prepared the coup with the connivance of the Social-Democratic government. On March 13, 1920, the mutinous generals moved troops against Berlin and, meeting with no resistance from the government, proclaimed a military dictatorship. The German workers replied with a general strike. Under pressure from the proletariat, the Kapp government was overthrown on March 17, and the Social-Democrats again took power.

first, that in order to accomplish its task the revolutionary class must be able to master *all* forms or aspects of social activity without exception (completing after the capture of political power—sometimes at great risk and with very great danger—what it did not complete before the capture of power); second, that the revolutionary class must be prepared for the most rapid and brusque replacement of one form by another.

One will readily agree that any army which does not train to use all the weapons, all the means and methods of warfare that the enemy possesses, or may possess, is behaving in an unwise or even criminal manner. This applies to politics even more than it does to the art of war. In politics it is even harder to know in advance which methods of struggle will be applicable and to our advantage in certain future conditions. Unless we learn to apply all the methods of struggle, we may suffer grave and sometimes even decisive defeat, if changes beyond our control in the position of the other classes bring to the forefront a form of activity in which we are especially weak. If, however, we learn to use all the methods of struggle, victory will be certain, because we represent the interests of the really foremost and really revolutionary class, even if circumstances do not permit us to make use of weapons that are most dangerous to the enemy, weapons that deal the swiftest mortal blows. Inexperienced revolutionaries often think that legal methods of struggle are opportunist because, in this field, the bourgeoisie has most frequently deceived and duped the workers (particularly in "peaceful" and non-revolutionary times), while illegal methods of struggle are revolutionary. That, however, is wrong. The truth is that those parties and leaders are opportunists and traitors to the working class that are unable or unwilling (do not say, "I can't"; say, "I shan't") to use illegal methods of struggle in conditions such as those which prevailed, for example, during the imperialist war of 1914-18, when the bourgeoisie of the freest democratic countries most brazenly and brutally deceived the workers, and smothered the truth about the predatory character of the war. But revolutionaries who are incapable of combining illegal forms of struggle with *every* form of legal struggle are poor revolutionaries indeed. It is not difficult to be a revolutionary when revolution has already broken out and is in spate, when all people are joining the revolution just because they are carried away, because it is the vogue, and sometimes even from careerist motives. After its victory, the proletariat has to make most strenuous efforts, even the most painful, so as to "liberate" itself from such pseudo-revolutionaries. It is far more difficult—and far more precious—to be a revolutionary when the conditions for direct, open, really mass and really revolutionary struggle *do not yet exist*, to be able to champion the interests of the revolution (by propaganda, agitation and organisation) in non-revolutionary bodies, and quite often in downright reactionary bodies, in a non-revolutionary situation, among the masses who are incapable of immediately appreciating the need for revolutionary methods of action. To be able to seek, find and correctly determine the specific path or the particular turn of events that will *lead* the masses to the real, decisive and final revolutionary struggle—such is the main objective of communism in Western Europe and in America today.

Part V

Socialist Construction

THE IMMEDIATE TASKS OF THE SOVIET GOVERNMENT (1918)

THE INTERNATIONAL POSITION OF THE RUSSIAN SOVIET REPUBLIC AND THE FUNDAMENTAL TASKS OF THE SOCIALIST REVOLUTION

Thanks to the peace which has been achieved—despite its extremely onerous character and extreme instability—the Russian Soviet Republic has gained an opportunity to concentrate its efforts for a while on the most important and most difficult aspect of the socialist revolution, namely, the task of organisation.[1]

This task was clearly and definitely set before all the working and oppressed people in the fourth paragraph (Part 4) of the resolution adopted at the Extraordinary Congress of Soviets in Moscow on March 15, 1918, in that paragraph (or part) which speaks of the self-discipline of the working people and of the ruthless struggle against chaos and disorganisation.[2]

Of course, the peace achieved by the Russian Soviet Republic is unstable not because she is now thinking of resuming military operations; apart from bourgeois counter-revolutionaries and their henchmen (the Mensheviks and others), no sane politician thinks of doing that. The instability of the peace is due to the fact that in the imperialist states bordering on Russia to the West and the East, which command enormous military forces, the military party, tempted by Russia's momentary

[1] In the manuscript, Lenin's work *The Immediate Tasks of the Soviet Government* was headed "Theses on the Tasks of the Soviet Government in the Present Situation". Lenin's theses were discussed at a meeting of the Party Central Committee on April 26, 1918. The Central Committee unanimously approved them and passed a decision to have them published as an article in *Pravda* and *Izvestia*, and also as a separate pamphlet. In 1918 the pamphlet went through more than ten editions, in Moscow, Petrograd, Saratov, Kazan, Tambov and other cities of Russia. It was published in the same year in English in New York, and in French in Geneva; an abridged version in German, edited by F. Platten, appeared in Zurich under the title *Am Tage nach der Revolution*.

The Central Committee instructed Lenin to give a report on the immediate tasks of the Soviet government at a meeting of the All-Russia C.E.C. and to formulate the Theses briefly as a resolution (see *LCW*, Vol. 27, 1974, pp. 314-17).

[2] See *LCW*, Vol. 27, 1974, p. 200.

weakness and egged on by capitalists, who hate socialism and are eager for plunder, may gain the upper hand at any moment.

Under these circumstances the only real, not paper, guarantee of peace we have is the antagonism among the imperialist powers, which has reached extreme limits, and which is apparent on the one hand in the resumption of the imperialist butchery of the peoples in the West, and on the other hand in the extreme intensification of imperialist rivalry between Japan and America for supremacy in the Pacific and on the Pacific coast.

It goes without saying that with such an unreliable guard for protection, our Soviet Socialist Republic is in an extremely unstable and certainly critical international position. All our efforts must be exerted to the very utmost to make use of the respite given us by the combination of circumstances so that we can heal the very severe wounds inflicted by the war upon the entire social organism of Russia and bring about an economic revival, without which a real increase in our country's defence potential is inconceivable.

It also goes without saying that we shall be able to render effective assistance to the socialist revolution in the West which has been delayed for a number of reasons, only to the extent that we are able to fulfill the task of organisation confronting us.

A fundamental condition for the successful accomplishment of the primary task of organisation confronting us is that the people's political leaders, i.e., the members of the Russian Communist Party (Bolsheviks), and following them all the class-conscious representatives of the mass of the working people, shall fully appreciate the radical distinction in this respect between previous bourgeois revolutions and the present socialist revolution.

In bourgeois revolutions, the principal task of the mass of working people was to fulfill the negative or destructive work of abolishing feudalism, monarchy and medievalism. The positive or constructive work of organising the new society was carried out by the property-owning bourgeois minority of the population. And the latter carried out this task with relative ease, despite the resistance of the workers and the poor peasants, not only because the resistance of the people exploited by capital was then extremely weak, since they were scattered and uneducated, but also because the chief organising force of anarchically built capitalist society is the spontaneously growing and expanding national and international market.

In every socialist revolution, however—and consequently in the socialist revolution in Russia which we began on October 25, 1917—the principal task of the proletariat, and of the poor peasants which it leads, is the positive or constructive work of setting up an extremely intricate and delicate system of new organisational relationships extending to the planned production and distribution of the goods required for the existence of tens of millions of people. Such a revolution can be successfully carried out only if the majority of the population, and primarily the majority of the working people, engage in independent creative work as makers of history. Only if the proletariat and the poor peasants display sufficient class-consciousness, devotion to principle, self-sacrifice and perseverance, will the victory of the socialist revolution be assured. By creating a new, Soviet type of state, which gives the working and oppressed people the chance to take an active part in the independent building up of a new society, we solved only a small part of this difficult problem. The principal difficulty lies in the economic sphere, namely, the introduction of the strictest and universal accounting and control of the production and distribution of goods, raising the productivity of labour and *socialising* production *in practice*.

The development of the Bolshevik Party, which today is the governing party in Russia, very strikingly indicates the nature of the turning-point in history we have now reached, which is the peculiar feature of the present political situation, and which calls for a new orientation of Soviet power, i.e., for a new presentation of new tasks.

The first task of every party of the future is to convince the majority of the people that its programme and tactics are correct. This task stood in the forefront both in tsarist times and in the period of the Chernovs' and Tseretelis' policy of compromise with the Kerenskys and Kishkins. This task has now been fulfilled in the main, for, as the recent Congress of Soviets in Moscow incontrovertibly proved, the majority of the workers and peasants of Russia are obviously on the side of the Bolsheviks; but of course, it is far from being completely fulfilled (and it can never be completely fulfilled).

The second task that confronted our Party was to capture political power and to suppress the resistance of the exploiters. This task has not been completely fulfilled either, and it cannot be ignored because the monarchists and Constitutional-Democrats on the one hand, and their henchmen and hangers-on, the Mensheviks and Right Socialist-Revolutionaries, on the other, are continuing their efforts to unite for the purpose of overthrowing Soviet power. In the main, however, the task of suppressing the resistance of the exploiters was fulfilled in the period from October 25, 1917, to (approximately) February 1918, or to the surrender of Bogayevsky.[3]

A third task is now coming to the fore as the immediate task and one which constitutes the peculiar feature of the present situation, namely, the task of organising *administration* of Russia. Of course, we advanced and tackled this task on the very day following October 25, 1917. Up to now, however, since the resistance of the exploiters still took the form of open civil war, up to now the task of administration *could not* become the *main*, the *central* task.

Now it has become the main and central task. We, the Bolshevik Party, have *convinced* Russia. We have *won* Russia from the rich for the poor, from the exploiters for the working people. Now we must *administer* Russia. And the whole peculiarity of the present situation, the whole difficulty, lies in understanding *the specific features of the transition* from the principal task of convincing the people and of suppressing the exploiters by armed force to the principal task of *administration*.

For the first time in human history a socialist party has managed to complete in the main the conquest of power and the suppression of the exploiters, and has managed to *approach directly* the task of *administration*. We must prove worthy executors of this most difficult (and most gratifying) task of the socialist revolution. We must *fully realise* that in order to administer successfully, *besides* being able to convince people, besides being able to win a civil war, we must be able to do *practical organisational work*. This is the most difficult task, because it is a matter of organising in a new way the most deep-rooted, the economic, foundations of life of scores of millions of people. And it is the most gratifying task, because only *after* it has been fulfilled (in the principal and main outlines) will it be possible to say that Russia *has become* not only a Soviet, but also a socialist, republic.

THE GENERAL SLOGAN OF THE MOMENT

The objective situation reviewed above, which has been created by the extremely onerous and unstable peace, the terrible state of ruin, the unemployment and famine we inherited from the war and the rule of the bourgeoisie (represented by Kerensky and the Mensheviks and Right

[3] *Bogayevsky, M.P.* (1881-1918)—counter-revolutionary leader and organiser of the civil war against Soviet power on the Don. He was defeated and surrendered in the spring of 1918.

Socialist-Revolutionaries who supported him), all this has inevitably caused extreme weariness and even exhaustion of wide sections of the working people. These people insistently demand—and cannot but demand—a respite. The task of the day is to restore the productive forces destroyed by the war and by bourgeois rule; to heal the wounds inflicted by the war, by the defeat in the war, by profiteering and the attempts of the bourgeoisie to restore the overthrown rule of the exploiters; to achieve economic revival; to provide reliable protection of elementary order. It may sound paradoxical, but in fact, considering the objective conditions indicated above, it is absolutely certain that at the present moment the Soviet system can secure Russia's transition to socialism only if these very elementary, extremely elementary problems of maintaining public life are practically solved in spite of the resistance of the bourgeoisie, the Mensheviks and the Right Socialist-Revolutionaries. In view of the specific features of the present situation, and in view of the existence of Soviet power with its land socialisation law, workers' control law, etc., the practical solution of these extremely elementary problems and the overcoming of the organisational difficulties of the first stages of progress toward socialism are now two aspects of the same picture.

Keep regular and honest accounts of money, manage economically, do not be lazy, do not steal, observe the strictest labour discipline—it is these slogans, justly scorned by the revolutionary proletariat when the bourgeoisie used them to conceal its rule as an exploiting class, that are now, since the overthrow of the bourgeoisie, becoming the immediate and the principal slogans of the moment. On the one hand, the practical application of these slogans by *the mass* of working people is the *sole* condition for the salvation of a country which has been tortured almost to death by the imperialist war and by the imperialist robbers (headed by Kerensky); on the other hand, the practical application of these slogans by the *Soviet* State, by *its* methods, on the basis of *its* laws, is a necessary and *sufficient* condition for the final victory of socialism. This is precisely what those who contemptuously brush aside the idea of putting such "hackneyed" and "trivial" slogans in the forefront fail to understand. In a small-peasant country, which overthrew tsarism only a year ago, and which liberated itself from the Kerenskys less than six months ago, there has naturally remained not a little of spontaneous anarchy, intensified by the brutality and savagery that accompany every protracted and reactionary war, and there has arisen a good deal of despair and aimless bitterness. And if we add to this the provocative policy of the lackeys of the bourgeoisie (the Mensheviks, the Right Socialist-Revolutionaries, etc.) it will become perfectly clear what prolonged and persistent efforts must be exerted by the best and the most class-conscious workers and peasants in order to bring about a complete change in the mood of the people and to bring them on to the proper path of steady and disciplined labour. Only such a transition brought about by the mass of the poor (the proletarians and semi-proletarians) can consummate the victory over the bourgeoisie and particularly over the peasant bourgeoisie, more stubborn and numerous.

THE NEW PHASE OF THE STRUGGLE AGAINST THE BOURGEOISIE

The bourgeoisie in our country has been conquered, but it has not yet been uprooted, not yet destroyed, and not even utterly broken. That is why we are faced with a new and higher form of struggle against the bourgeoisie, the transition from the very simple task of further expropriating the capitalists to the much more complicated and difficult task of creating conditions in which it will be impossible for the bourgeoisie to exist, or for a new bourgeoisie to arise. Clearly, this task is immeasurably more significant than the previous one; and until it is fulfilled there will be no socialism.

If we measure our revolution by the scale of West-European revolutions we shall find that at the present moment we are approximately at the level reached in 1793 and 1871. We can be legitimately proud of having risen to this level, and of having certainly, in one respect, advanced somewhat further, namely: we have decreed and introduced throughout Russia the highest *type* of state—Soviet power. Under no circumstances, however, can we rest content with what we have achieved, because we have only just started the transition to socialism, we have *not yet* done the decisive thing in *this* respect.

The decisive thing is the organisation of the strictest and country-wide accounting and control of production and distribution of goods. And yet, we have *not yet* introduced accounting and control in those enterprises and in those branches and fields of economy which we have taken away from the bourgeoisie; and without this there can be no thought of achieving the second and equally essential material condition for introducing socialism, namely, raising the productivity of labour on a national scale.

That is why the present task could not be defined by the simple formula: continue the offensive against capital. Although we have certainly not finished off capital and although it is certainly necessary to continue the offensive against this enemy of the working people, such a formula would be inexact, would not be concrete, would not take into account the *peculiarity* of the present situation in which, in order to go on advancing successfully *in the future*, we must "suspend" our offensive *now*.

This can be explained by comparing our position in the war against capital with the position of a victorious army that has captured, say, a half or two-thirds of the enemy's territory and is compelled to halt in order to muster its forces, to replenish its supplies of munitions, repair and reinforce the lines of communication, build new storehouses, bring up new reserves, etc. To suspend the offensive of a victorious army under such conditions is necessary precisely in order to gain the rest of the enemy's territory, i.e., in order to achieve complete victory. Those who have failed to understand that the objective state of affairs at the present moment dictates to us precisely such a "suspension" of the offensive against capital have failed to understand anything at all about the present political situation.

It goes without saying that we can speak about the "suspension" of the offensive against capital only in quotation marks, i.e., only metaphorically. In ordinary war, a general order can be issued to stop the offensive, the advance can actually be stopped. In the war against capital, however, the advance cannot be stopped, and there can be no thought of our abandoning the further expropriation of capital. What we are discussing is the shifting of the *centre of gravity* of our economic and political work. Up to now measures for the direct expropriation of the expropriators were *in the forefront*. Now the organisation of accounting and control in those enterprises in which the capitalists have already been expropriated, and in all other enterprises, advances *to the forefront*.

If we decided to continue to expropriate capital at the same rate at which we have been doing it up to now, we should certainly suffer defeat, because our work of organising proletarian accounting and control has obviously—obviously to every thinking person—*fallen behind* the work of *directly* "expropriating the expropriators". If we now concentrate all our efforts on the organisation of accounting and control, we shall be able to solve this problem, we shall be able to make up for lost time, we shall *completely* win our "campaign" against capital.

But is not the admission that we must make up for lost time tantamount to admission of some kind of an error? Not in the least. Take another military example. If it is possible to defeat and push back the enemy merely with detachments of light cavalry, it should be done. But if this can be done successfully only up to a certain point, then it is quite conceivable that when this point has been reached, it will be necessary to bring up heavy artillery. By admitting that it is now necessary to make up for lost time in bringing up heavy artillery, we do not admit that the successful cavalry attack was a mistake.

Frequently, the lackeys of the bourgeoisie reproached us for having launched a "Red Guard" attack on capital. The reproach is absurd and is worthy only of the lackeys of the money-bags, because *at one time* the "Red Guard" attack on capital was absolutely dictated by circumstances. Firstly, *at that time* capital put up military resistance through the medium of Kerensky and Krasnov, Savinkov and Gotz (Gegechkori is putting up such resistance even now), Dutov and Bogayevsky. Military resistance cannot be broken except by military means, and the Red Guards fought in the noble and supreme historical cause of liberating the working and exploited people from the yoke of the exploiters.

Secondly, we could not at that time put methods of administration in the forefront in place of methods of suppression, because the art of administration is not innate, but is acquired by experience. At that time we lacked this experience; now we have it. Thirdly, at that time we could not have specialists in the various fields of knowledge and technology at our disposal because those specialists were either fighting in the ranks of the Bogayevskys, or were still able to put up systematic and stubborn passive resistance by way of *sabotage*. Now we have broken the sabotage. The "Red Guard" attack on capital was successful, was victorious, because we broke capital's military resistance and its resistance by sabotage.

Does that mean that a "Red Guard" attack on capital is *always* appropriate, under *all* circumstances, that we have no other means of fighting capital? It would be childish to think so. We achieved victory with the aid of light cavalry, but we also have heavy artillery. We achieved victory by methods of suppression; we shall be able to achieve victory also by methods of administration. We must know how to change our methods of fighting the enemy to suit changes in the situation. We shall not for a moment renounce "Red Guard" suppression of the Savinkovs and Gegechkoris and all other landowner and bourgeois counter-revolutionaries. We shall not be so foolish, however, as to put "Red Guard" methods in the forefront at a time when the period in which Red Guard attacks were necessary has, in the main, drawn to a close (and to a victorious close), and when the period of utilising bourgeois specialists by the proletarian state power for the purpose of reploughing the soil in order to prevent the growth of any bourgeoisie whatever is knocking at the door.

This is a peculiar epoch, or rather stage of development, and in order to defeat capital completely, we must be able to adapt the forms of our struggle to the peculiar conditions of this stage.

Without the guidance of experts in the various fields of knowledge, technology and experience, the transition to socialism will be impossible, because socialism calls for a conscious mass advance to greater productivity of labour compared with capitalism, and on the basis achieved by capitalism. Socialism must achieve this advance *in its own way*, by its own methods—or, to put it more concretely, by *Soviet* methods. And the specialists, because of the whole social environment which made them specialists, are, in the main, inevitably bourgeois. Had our proletariat, after capturing power, quickly solved the problem of accounting, control and organisation on a national scale (which was impossible owing to the war and Russia's backwardness), then we, after breaking the sabotage, would also have completely subordinated these bourgeois experts to ourselves by means of universal accounting and control. Owing to the considerable "delay" in introducing accounting and control generally, we, although we have managed to conquer sabotage, have *not yet* created the conditions which would place the bourgeois specialists at our disposal. The mass of saboteurs are "going to work", but the best organisers and the top experts can be utilised by the state either in the old way, in the bourgeois way (i.e., for high salaries), or in the new way, in the proletarian way (i.e., creating the conditions of national accounting and control from below, which would inevitably and of itself subordinate the experts and enlist them for our work).

Now we have to resort to the old bourgeois method and to agree to pay a very high price for the "services" of the top bourgeois experts. All those who are familiar with the subject appreciate this, but not all ponder over the significance of this measure being adopted by the proletarian state. Clearly, this measure is a compromise, a departure from the principles of the Paris Commune and of every proletarian power, which call for the reduction of all salaries to the level of the wages of the average worker, which urge that careerism be fought not merely in words, but in deeds.

Moreover, it is clear that this measure not only implies the cessation—in a certain field and to a certain degree—of the offensive against capital (for capital is not a sum of money, but a definite social relation); it is also *a step backward* on the part of our socialist Soviet state power, which from the very outset proclaimed and pursued the policy of reducing high salaries to the level of the wages of the average worker.[4]

Of course, the lackeys of the bourgeoisie, particularly the small fry, such as the Mensheviks, the *Novaya Zhizn* people and the Right Socialist-Revolutionaries, will giggle over our confession that we are taking a step backward. But we need not mind their giggling. We must study the specific features of the extremely difficult and new path to socialism without concealing our mistakes and weaknesses, and try to be prompt in doing what has been left undone. To conceal from the people the fact that the enlistment of bourgeois experts by means of extremely high salaries is a retreat from the principles of the Paris Commune would be sinking to the level of bourgeois politicians and deceiving the people. Frankly explaining how and why we took this step backward, and then publicly discussing what means are available for making up for lost time, means educating the people and learning from experience, learning together with the people how to build socialism. There is hardly a single victorious military campaign in history in which the victor did not commit certain mistakes, suffer partial reverses, temporarily yield something and in some places retreat. The "campaign" which we have undertaken against capitalism is a million times more difficult than the most difficult military campaign, and it would be silly and disgraceful to give way to despondency because of a particular and partial retreat.

We shall now discuss the question from the practical point of view. Let us assume that the Russian Soviet Republic requires one thousand first-class scientists and experts in various fields of knowledge, technology and practical experience to direct the labour of the people towards securing the speediest possible economic revival. Let us assume also that we shall have to pay these "stars of the first magnitude"—of course the majority of those who shout loudest about the corruption of the workers

[4] On November 18 (December 1), 1917, the Council of People's Commissars, acting on a proposal made by Lenin, passed a decision "On the Remuneration of People's Commissars and Senior Government Employees and Officials" (published on November 23 [December 6], 1917, in No. 16 of the *Newspaper of the Provisional Workers' and Peasants' Government*). Drafted by Lenin it fixed the maximum monthly salary of a People's Commissar at 500 rubles with an additional 100 rubles for every member of his family unable to work. This corresponded roughly to the worker's average monthly wage. On January 2 (15), 1918, in answer to an inquiry from the People's Commissar for Labour A.G. Shlyapnikov, the Council of People's Commissars issued a decision written by Lenin explaining that the Decree of November 18 (December 1), 1917, fixed no limit for the payment of experts and thus sanctioned higher remuneration for scientific and technical experts.

are themselves utterly corrupted by bourgeois morals—25,000 rubles per annum each. Let us assume that this sum (25,000,000 rubles) will have to be doubled (assuming that we have to pay bonuses for particularly successful and rapid fulfillment of the most important organisational and technical tasks), or even quadrupled (assuming that we have to enlist several hundred foreign specialists, who are more demanding). The question is, would the annual expenditure of fifty or a hundred million rubles by the Soviet Republic for the purpose of reorganising the labour of the people on modern scientific and technological lines be excessive or too heavy? Of course not. The overwhelming majority of the class-conscious workers and peasants will approve of this expenditure because they know from practical experience that our backwardness causes us to lose thousands of millions, and that we have *not yet* reached that degree of organisation, accounting and control which would induce all the "stars" of the bourgeois intelligentsia to participate voluntarily in *our* work.

It goes without saying that this question has another side to it. The corrupting influence of high salaries—both upon the Soviet authorities (especially since the revolution occurred so rapidly that it was impossible to prevent a certain number of adventurers and rogues from getting into positions of authority, and they, together with a number of inept or dishonest commissars, would not be averse to becoming "star" embezzlers of state funds) and upon the mass of the workers—is indisputable. Every thinking and honest worker and poor peasant, however, will agree with us, will admit, that we cannot immediately rid ourselves of the evil legacy of capitalism, and that we can liberate the Soviet Republic from the duty of paying an annual "tribute" of fifty million or one hundred million rubles (a tribute for our own backwardness in organising *country-wide* accounting and control *from below*) only by organising ourselves, by tightening up discipline in our own ranks, by purging our ranks of all those who are "preserving the legacy of capitalism", who "follow the traditions of capitalism", i.e., of idlers, parasites and embezzlers of state funds (now all the land, all the factories and all the railways are the "state funds" of the Soviet Republic). If the class-conscious advanced workers and poor peasants manage with the aid of the Soviet institutions to organise, become disciplined, pull themselves together, create powerful labour discipline in the course of one year, then in a year's time we shall throw off this "tribute", which can be reduced even before that . . . in exact proportion to the successes we achieve in our workers' and peasants' labour discipline and organisation. The sooner we ourselves, workers and peasants, learn the best labour discipline and the most modern technique of labour, using the bourgeois experts to teach us, the sooner we shall liberate ourselves from any "tribute" to these specialists.

Our work of organising country-wide accounting and control of production and distribution under the supervision of the proletariat has lagged very much behind our work of directly expropriating the expropriators. This proposition is of fundamental importance for understanding the specific features of the present situation and the tasks of the Soviet government that follow from it. The centre of gravity of our struggle against the bourgeoisie is shifting to the organisation of such accounting and control. Only with this as our starting-point will it be possible to determine correctly the immediate tasks of economic and financial policy in the sphere of nationalisation of the banks, monopolisation of foreign trade, the state control of money circulation, the introduction of a property and income tax satisfactory from the proletarian point of view, and the introduction of compulsory labour service.

We have been lagging very far behind in introducing socialist reforms in these spheres (very, very important spheres), and this is because accounting and control are insufficiently organised in general. It goes without saying that this is one of the most difficult tasks, and in view of the ruin caused by the war, it can be fulfilled only over a long period of time; but we must not forget that it is precisely here that the bourgeoisie—and particularly the numerous petty and peasant bourgeoisie—are putting up the most serious fight, disrupting the control that is already being organised, disrupting the grain monopoly, for example, and gaining positions for profiteering and speculative trade. We have far from adequately carried out the things we have decreed, and the principal task of the moment is to concentrate all efforts on the businesslike, practical *realisation* of the principles of the reforms which have already become law (but not yet reality).

In order to proceed with the nationalisation of the banks and to go on steadfastly towards transforming the banks into nodal points of public accounting under socialism, we must first of all, and above all, achieve real success in increasing the number of branches of the People's Bank, in attracting deposits, in simplifying the paying in and withdrawal of deposits by the public, in abolishing queues, in catching and *shooting* bribe-takers and rogues, etc. At first we must really carry out the simplest things, properly organise what is available, and then prepare for the more intricate things.

Consolidate and improve the state monopolies (in grain, leather, etc.) which have already been introduced, and by doing so prepare for the state monopoly of foreign trade. Without this monopoly we shall not be able to "free ourselves" from foreign capital by paying "tribute".[5] And the possibility of building up socialism depends entirely upon whether we shall be able, by paying a certain tribute to foreign capital during a certain transitional period, to safeguard our internal economic independence.

We are also lagging very far behind in regard to the collection of taxes generally, and of the property and income tax in particular. The imposing of indemnities upon the bourgeoisie—a measure which in principle is absolutely permissible and deserves proletarian approval—shows that in this respect we are still nearer to the methods of warfare (to win Russia from the rich for the poor) than to the methods of administration. In order to become stronger, however, and in order to be able to stand firmer on our feet, we must adopt the latter methods, we must substitute for the indemnities imposed upon the bourgeoisie the constant and regular collection of a property and income tax, which will bring a *greater* return to the proletarian state, and which calls for better organisation on our part and better accounting and control.[6]

[5] Control over foreign trade was initiated in the early days of Soviet power. At first this was handled by the Petrograd Revolutionary Military Committee, which considered applications for the import and export of goods and supervised the work of the customs. By a decree of the Council of People's Commissars of December 29, 1917 (January 11, 1918) foreign trade was placed under the control of the People's Commissariat for Trade and Industry. This kind of control and customs inspection, however, was not enough to protect the Soviet economy from foreign capital. Lenin emphasised later that the working class of Soviet Russia "would be totally unable to build up its own industry and make Russia an industrial country without the protection, not of tariffs, but of the monopoly of foreign trade" (see V.I. Lenin, *On the Foreign Policy of the Soviet State*, Moscow, p. 424). In December 1917 Lenin proposed introducing a state monopoly on foreign trade, a decree on which was passed by the Council of People's Commissars on April 22, 1918 (see *Decrees of the Soviet Government*, Russ. ed., Vol. 2, 1959, pp. 158-60).

[6] In the first months of Soviet power indemnities and special taxes were one of the principal sources of revenue, particularly in the provinces. When Soviet power became more firmly established the question arose of how to devise a regular system of taxation based primarily on a progressive income tax and a property tax, which would make it possible to place the main burden of taxation on the well-to-do sections of the population. At the First All-Russia Congress of Representatives of the Financial Departments of the Soviets, Lenin pointed out: "We have many plans in this sphere and have cleared the ground on which to build the foundation, but the actual foundation of that building has not yet been built. The time for this has now come" (see

The fact that we are late in introducing compulsory labour service also shows that the work that is coming to the fore at the present time is precisely the preparatory organisational work that, on the one hand, will finally consolidate our gains and that, on the other, is necessary in order to prepare for the operation of "surrounding" capital and compelling it to "surrender". We ought to begin introducing compulsory labour service immediately, but we must do so very gradually and circumspectly, testing every step by practical experience, and, of course, taking the first step by introducing compulsory labour service *for the rich.* The introduction of work and consumers' budget books for every bourgeois, including every rural bourgeois, would be an important step towards completely "surrounding" the enemy and towards the creation of a truly popular accounting and control of the production and distribution of goods.

THE SIGNIFICANCE OF THE STRUGGLE FOR COUNTRY-WIDE ACCOUNTING AND CONTROL

The state, which for centuries has been an organ for oppression and robbery of the people, has left us a legacy of the people's supreme hatred and suspicion of everything that is connected with the state. It is very difficult to overcome this, and only a Soviet government can do it. Even a Soviet government, however, will require plenty of time and enormous perseverance to accomplish it. This "legacy" is especially apparent in the problem of accounting and control—the fundamental problem facing the socialist revolution on the morrow of the overthrow of the bourgeoisie. A certain amount of time will inevitably pass before the people, who feel free for the first time now that the landowners and the bourgeoisie have been overthrown, will understand—not from books, but from their own, *Soviet* experience—will understand and feel that without comprehensive state accounting and control of the production and distribution of goods, the power of the working people, the freedom of the working people, *cannot* be maintained, and that a return to the yoke of capitalism is *inevitable.*

All the habits and traditions of the bourgeoisie, and of the petty

---

LCW, Vol. 27, 1974, pp. 384-85). The Congress accepted Lenin's proposal on the need to introduce an income tax and property tax and elected a special commission to draw up the requisite Statute on the basis of Lenin's theses.

On June 17, 1918, the Council of People's Commissars approved the Decree on the Amendment of the Decree of November 24, 1917, on the Levying of Direct Taxes, which laid down a strict system of income and property taxation (see *Decrees of the Soviet Government*, Russ. ed., Vol. 2, 1959, pp. 441-43).

bourgeoisie in particular, also oppose *state* control, and uphold the inviolability of "sacred private property", of "sacred" private enterprise. It is now particularly clear to us how correct is the Marxist thesis that anarchism and anarcho-syndicalism are *bourgeois* trends, how irreconcilably opposed they are to socialism, proletarian dictatorship and communism. The fight to instill into the people's minds the idea of *Soviet* state control and accounting, and to carry out this idea in practice; the fight to break with the rotten past, which taught the people to regard the procurement of bread and clothes as a "private" affair, and buying and selling as a transaction "which concerns only myself"—is a great fight of world-historic significance, a fight between socialist consciousness and bourgeois-anarchist spontaneity.

We have introduced workers' control as a law, but this law is only just beginning to operate and is only just beginning to penetrate the minds of broad sections of the proletariat. In our agitation we do not sufficiently explain that lack of accounting and control in the production and distribution of goods means the death of the rudiments of socialism, means the embezzlement of state funds (for all property belongs to the state and the state is the Soviet state in which power belongs to the majority of the working people). We do not sufficiently explain that carelessness in accounting and control is downright aiding and abetting the German and the Russian Kornilovs, who can overthrow the power of the working people *only* if we fail to cope with the task of accounting and control, and who, with the aid of the whole of the rural bourgeoisie, with the aid of the Constitutional-Democrats, the Mensheviks and the Right Socialist-Revolutionaries, are "watching" us and waiting for an opportune moment to attack us. And the advanced workers and peasants do not think and speak about this sufficiently. Until workers' control has become a fact, until the advanced workers have organised and carried out a victorious and ruthless crusade against the violators of this control, or against those who are careless in matters of control, it will be impossible to pass from the first step (from workers' control) to the second step towards socialism, i.e., to pass on to workers' regulation of production.

The socialist state can arise only as a network of producers' and consumers' communes, which conscientiously keep account of their production and consumption, economise on labour, and steadily raise the productivity of labour, thus making it possible to reduce the working day to seven, six and even fewer hours. Nothing will be achieved unless the strictest, country-wide, comprehensive accounting and control of *grain* and the *production of grain* (and later of all other essential goods) are set going. Capitalism left us a legacy of mass organisations which can facilitate our transition to the mass accounting and control of the distribution of goods, namely, the consumers' co-operative societies. In Russia these societies are not so well developed as in the advanced countries, nevertheless, they have over ten million members. The Decree on Consumers' Co-operative Societies,[7] issued the other day, is an extremely significant phenomenon, which strikingly illustrates the peculiar position and the specific tasks of the Soviet Socialist Republic at the present moment.

The decree is an agreement with the bourgeois co-operative societies and the workers' co-operative societies which still adhere to the bourgeois point of view. It is an agreement, or compromise, firstly because the representatives of the above-mentioned institutions not only took part in discussing the decree, but actually had a decisive say in the matter, for the parts of the decree which were strongly opposed by these institutions were dropped. Secondly, the essence of the compromise is that the Soviet government has abandoned the principle of admission of new members to co-operative societies without entrance fees (which is the only consistently proletarian principle); it has also abandoned the idea of uniting the whole population of a given locality in a *single* co-operative society. Contrary to this principle, which is the only socialist principle and which corresponds to the task of abolishing classes, the "working-class co-operative societies" (which in this case call themselves "class" societies only because they subordinate themselves to the class interests of the bourgeoisie) were given the right to continue to exist. Finally, the

[7] *Decree on Consumers' Co-operative Societies* was passed by the Council of People's Commissars on April 10, 1918, approved at a meeting of the All-Russia C.E.C. on April 11, and published over Lenin's signature in *Pravda* No. 71 of April 13 and *Izvestia VTsIK* No. 75 of April 16.

The first draft of the decree, written by Lenin, was worked out in detail by the People's Commissariat for Food and published on January 19 (February 1) in *Izvestia TsIK* No. 14. The draft decree was bitterly opposed by bourgeois co-operators, who insisted that co-operative societies should be independent of the organs of Soviet power. In order to use the existing co-operative apparatus for accounting and control of the distribution of foodstuffs the Council of People's Commissars made several concessions during its negotiations with bourgeois co-operators (March to the beginning of April 1918). On April 9 and 10 the C.P.C. discussed the draft decree proposed by the co-operators. Lenin revised the draft considerably (he rewrote points 11, 12 and 13), and the decree with his amendments was passed by the Council of People's Commissars, and then by the All-Russia C.E.C.

Soviet government's proposal to expel the bourgeoisie entirely from the boards of the co-operative societies was also considerably modified, and only owners of private capitalist trading and industrial enterprises were forbidden to serve on the boards.

Had the proletariat, acting through the Soviet government, managed to organise accounting and control on a national scale, or at least laid the foundation for such control, it would not have been necessary to make such compromises. Through the food departments of the Soviets, through the supply organisations under the Soviets we should have organised the population into a single co-operative society under proletarian management. We should have done this without the assistance of the bourgeois co-operative societies, without making any concession to the purely bourgeois principle which prompts the workers' co-operative societies to remain workers' societies *side by side* with bourgeois societies, *instead of* subordinating these bourgeois co-operative societies entirely to themselves, merging the two together and taking the *entire* management of the society and the supervision of the consumption of the rich *in their own* hands.

In concluding such an agreement with the bourgeois co-operative societies, the Soviet government concretely defined its tactical aims and its peculiar methods of action in the present stage of development as follows: by directing the bourgeois elements, utilising them, making certain partial concessions to them, we create the conditions for further progress that will be slower than we at first anticipated, but surer, with the base and lines of communication better secured and with the positions which have been won better consolidated. The Soviets can (*and should*) now gauge their successes in the field of socialist construction, among other things, by extremely clear, simple and practical standards, namely, in how many communities (communes or villages, or blocks of houses, etc.) co-operative societies have been organised, and to what extent their development has reached the point of embracing the whole population.

RAISING THE PRODUCTIVITY OF LABOUR

In every socialist revolution, after the proletariat has solved the problem of capturing power, and to the extent that the task of expropriating the expropriators and suppressing their resistance has been carried out in the main, there necessarily comes to the forefront the fundamental task of creating a social system superior to capitalism, namely, raising the productivity of labour, and in this connection (and for this purpose) securing better organisation of labour. Our Soviet state is precisely in the position where, thanks to the victories over the exploiters—from Kerensky to Kornilov—it is able to approach this task directly, to tackle it in earnest. And here it becomes immediately clear that while it is possible to take over the central government in a few days, while it is possible to suppress the military resistance (and sabotage) of the exploiters even in different parts of a great country in a few weeks, the capital solution of the problem of raising the productivity of labour requires, at all events (particularly after a most terrible and devastating war), several years. The protracted nature of the work is certainly dictated by objective circumstances.

The raising of the productivity of labour first of all requires that the material basis of large-scale industry shall be assured, namely, the development of the production of fuel, iron, the engineering and chemical industries. The Russian Soviet Republic enjoys the favourable position of having at its command, even after the Brest peace, enormous reserves of ore (in the Urals), fuel in Western Siberia (coal), in the Caucasus and the South-East (oil), in Central Russia (peat), enormous timber reserves, water power, raw materials for the chemical industry (Karabugaz), etc. The development of these natural resources by methods of modern technology will provide the basis for the unprecedented progress of the productive forces.

Another condition for raising the productivity of labour is, firstly, the raising of the educational and cultural level of the mass of the population. This is now taking place extremely rapidly, a fact which those who are blinded by bourgeois routine are unable to see; they are unable to understand what an urge towards enlightenment and initiative is now developing among the "lower ranks" of the people thanks to the Soviet form of organisation. Secondly, a condition for economic revival is the raising of the working people's discipline, their skill, the effectiveness, the intensity of labour and its better organisation.

In this respect the situation is particularly bad and even hopeless if we are to believe those who have allowed themselves to be intimidated by the bourgeoisie or by those who are serving the bourgeoisie for their own ends. These people do not understand that there has not been, nor could there be, a revolution in which the supporters of the old system did not raise a howl about chaos, anarchy, etc. naturally, among the people who have only just thrown off an unprecedentedly savage yoke there is deep and widespread seething and ferment; the working out of new principles of labour discipline by the people is a very protracted process, and this process could not even start until complete victory had been achieved over the landowners and the bourgeoisie.

We, however, without in the least yielding to the despair (it is often false despair) which is spread by the bourgeoisie and the bourgeois intellectuals (who have despaired of retaining their old privileges), must under no circumstances conceal an obvious evil. On the contrary, we shall expose it and intensify the Soviet methods of combating it, because the victory of socialism is inconceivable without the victory of proletarian conscious discipline over spontaneous petty-bourgeois anarchy, this real guarantee of a possible restoration of Kerenskyism and Kornilovism.

The more class-conscious vanguard of the Russian proletariat has already set itself the task of raising labour discipline. For example, both the Central Committee of the Metalworkers' Union and the Central Council of Trade Unions have begun to draft the necessary measures and decrees.[8] This work must be supported and pushed ahead with all

[8] The organisation of social production on socialist principles made it necessary to draw up new internal regulations for the nationalised enterprises, and new regulations on labour discipline and on enrolling all able-bodied persons for socially useful work. These questions acquired special importance in the period of the peaceful breathing-space in the spring of 1918.

The first regulations concerning labour discipline were worked out by the Soviet trade unions in conjunction with managerial bodies. They were discussed at a number of meetings of the Presidium of the Supreme Economic Council with representatives of the central organs of the trade unions taking part. On March 27 the Presidium of the Supreme Economic Council after a debate in which Lenin participated passed a decision charging the All-Russia Central Council of Trade Unions with the task of drawing up a general statute on labour discipline. On April 1, with Lenin taking part, the Presidium examined the draft resolution on labour discipline drawn up by the A.C.C.T.U. and proposed that it should be re-worded as a decree, taking into account Lenin's remarks and suggestions. The re-worded Statute on Labour Discipline passed by the A.C.C.T.U. on April 3 was published in the magazine *Narodnoye Khozyaistvo* No. 2, for April 1918. In this statute the A.C.C.T.U. stated that strict regulations regarding internal management should be introduced at all state-owned enterprises, that output quotas and account of labour productivity should be established, that piece-work and a system of bonuses for exceeding output quotas should be introduced, and that stern action should be taken against those who violated labour discipline. On the basis of the Statute specific internal regulations were drawn up at factories and these played an important part in the organisation of socialist industry.

The Central Committee of the Metalworkers' Union was one of the first to carry out Lenin's instructions on raising labour productivity by

speed. We must raise the question of piece-work[9] and apply and test it in practice; we must raise the question of applying much of what is scientific and progressive in the Taylor system; we must make wages correspond to the total amount of goods turned out, or to the amount of work done by the railways, the water transport system, etc., etc.

The Russian is a bad worker compared with people in advanced countries. It could not be otherwise under the tsarist regime and in view of the persistence of the hangover from serfdom. The task that the Soviet government must set the people in all its scope is—learn to work. The Taylor system, the last word of capitalism in this respect, like all capitalist progress, is a combination of the refined brutality of bourgeois exploitation and a number of the greatest scientific achievements in the field of analysing mechanical motions during work, the elimination of superfluous and awkward motions, the elaboration of correct methods of work, the introduction of the best system of accounting and control, etc. The Soviet Republic must at all costs adopt all that is valuable in the achievements of science and technology in this field. The possibility of building socialism depends exactly upon our success in combining the Soviet power and the Soviet organisation of administration with the up-to-date achievements of capitalism. We must organise in Russia the study and teaching of the Taylor system and systematically try it out and adapt it to our own ends. At the same time, in working to raise the productivity of labour, we must take into account the specific features of the transition period from capitalism to socialism, which, on the one hand, require that

introducing a system of piece-work and bonuses. When the question of improving labour discipline was discussed by the A.C.C.T.U. representatives of the Central Committee of the Metalworkers' Union got the thesis on the need for piece rates included in the resolution submitted on April 1 for consideration by the Presidium of the Supreme Economic Council. In April, on the basis of the decisions taken by the A.C.C.T.U. the Central Committee of the Metalworkers' Union instructed all the lower organisations of the union to adopt piece-work and the bonus system in the metal industry.

[9] After the October Revolution piece-work was almost everywhere superseded by a time system of payment, which had an adverse effect on labour productivity and labour discipline.

The introduction of piece-work, which came closest to the socialist principle of "to each according to his work", began at the first nationalised enterprises. During the period of respite, piece-work was widely adopted in industry. By July 1918, for instance, a quarter of the workers of Petrograd went over to piece-work. The principle of payment according to the piece was finally endorsed by the publication in December 1918 of the Soviet Labour Code.

the foundations be laid of the socialist organisation of competition, and, on the other hand, require the use of compulsion, so that the slogan of the dictatorship of the proletariat shall not be desecrated by the practice of a lily-livered proletarian government.

THE ORGANISATION OF COMPETITION

Among the absurdities which the bourgeoisie are fond of spreading about socialism is the allegation that socialists deny the importance of competition. In fact, it is only socialism which, by abolishing classes, and, consequently, by abolishing the enslavement of the people, for the first time opens the way for competition on a really mass scale. And it is precisely the Soviet form of organisation, by ensuring transition from the formal democracy of the bourgeois republic to real participation of the mass of working people in *administration*, that for the first time puts competition on a broad basis. It is much easier to organise this in the political field than in the economic field; but for the success of socialism, it is the economic field that matters.

Take, for example, a means of organising competition such as publicity. The bourgeois republic ensures publicity only formally; in practice, it subordinates the press to capital, entertains the "mob" with sensationalist political trash and conceals what takes place in the workshops, in commercial transactions, contracts, etc., behind a veil of "trade secrets", which protect "the sacred right of property". The Soviet government has abolished trade secrets[10]; it has taken a new path; but we have done hardly anything to utilise publicity for the purpose of encouraging economic competition. While ruthlessly suppressing the thoroughly mendacious and insolently slanderous bourgeois press, we

[10] This refers to the right protected by bourgeois law to keep secret all production, trade and financial operations and also all the relevant documents at private capitalist enterprises.

In his work *The Impending Catastrophe and How to Combat It* Lenin showed that commercial secrecy in the hands of the bourgeoisie was "an instrument for concealing financial swindles and the fantastically high profits of big capital" (see *LCW*, Vol. 25, 1974, p. 339), and showed why commercial secrecy should be abolished. The resolution of the Sixth Congress of the R.S.D.L.P.(B.) "On the Economic Situation" demanded the abolition of commercial secrecy as an essential measure for making workers' control effective (see *The C.P.S.U. in the Resolutions and Decisions of Congresses, Conferences and Plenums of the Central Committee*, Part 1, Russ. ed., 1954, p. 378). After the October Revolution commercial secrecy was abolished by the Statute on Workers' Control passed by the All-Russia C.E.C. and the Council of People's Commissars on November 14 (27), 1917.

must set to work systematically to create a press that will not entertain and fool the people with political sensation and trivialities, but which will submit the questions of everyday economic life to the people's judgement and assist in the serious study of these questions. Every factory, every village is a producers' and consumers' commune, whose right and duty it is to apply the general Soviet laws in their own way ("in their own way", not in the sense of violating them, but in the sense that they can apply them in various forms) and in their own way to solve the problem of accounting in the production and distribution of goods. Under capitalism, this was the "private affair" of the individual capitalist, landowner or kulak. Under the Soviet system, it is not a private affair, but a most important affair of state.

We have scarcely yet started on the enormous, difficult but rewarding task of organising competition between communes, of introducing accounting and publicity in the process of the production of grain, clothes and other things, of transforming dry, dead, bureaucratic accounts into living examples, some repulsive, others attractive. Under the capitalist mode of production, the significance of individual example, say the example of a co-operative workshop, was inevitably very much restricted, and only those imbued with petty-bourgeois illusions could dream of "correcting" capitalism through the example of virtuous institutions. After political power has passed to the proletariat, after the expropriators have been expropriated, the situation radically changes and—as prominent socialists have repeatedly pointed out—force of example for the first time is able to influence the people. Model communes must and will serve as educators, teachers, helping to raise the backward communes. The press must serve as an instrument of socialist construction, give publicity to the successes achieved by the model communes in all their details, must study the causes of these successes, the methods of management these communes employ, and, on the other hand, must put on the "black list" those communes which persist in the "traditions of capitalism", i.e., anarchy, laziness, disorder and profiteering. In capitalist society, statistics were entirely a matter for "government servants", or for narrow specialists; we must carry statistics to the people and make them popular so that the working people themselves may gradually learn to understand and see how long and in what way it is necessary to work, how much time and in what way one may rest, so that *the comparison of the business results* of the various communes may become a matter of general interest and study, and that the most outstanding communes may be rewarded immediately (by reducing the working day, raising remuneration, placing a larger amount of cultural or aesthetic facilities or values at their disposal, etc.).

When a new class comes on to the historical scene as the leader and guide of society, a period of violent "rocking", shocks, struggle and storm, on the one hand, and a period of uncertain steps, experiments, wavering, hesitation in regard to the selection of new methods corresponding to new objective circumstances, on the other, are inevitable. The moribund feudal nobility avenged themselves on the bourgeoisie which vanquished them and took their place, not only by conspiracies and attempts at rebellion and restoration, but also by pouring ridicule over the lack of skill, the clumsiness and the mistakes of the "upstarts" and the "insolent" who dared to take over the "sacred helm" of state without the centuries of training which the princes, barons, nobles and dignitaries had had; in exactly the same way the Kornilovs and Kerenskys, the Gotzes and Martovs, the whole of that fraternity of heroes of bourgeois swindling or bourgeois scepticism, avenge themselves on the working class of Russia for having had the "audacity" to take power.

Of course, not weeks, but long months and years are required for a new social class, especially a class which up to now has been oppressed and crushed by poverty and ignorance, to get used to its new position, look around, organise its work and promote its *own* organisers. It is understandable that the Party which leads the revolutionary proletariat has not been able to acquire the experience and habits of large organisational undertakings embracing millions and tens of millions of citizens; the remoulding of the old, almost exclusively agitators' habits is a very lengthy process. But there is nothing impossible in this, and as soon as the necessity for a change is clearly appreciated, as soon as there is firm determination to effect the change and perseverance in pursuing a great and difficult aim, we shall achieve it. There is an enormous amount of organising talent among the "people", i.e., among the workers and the peasants who do not exploit the labour of others. Capital crushed these talented people in thousands; it killed their talent and threw them on to the scrap-heap. We are not yet able to find them, encourage them, put them on their feet, promote them. But we shall learn to do so if we set about it with all-out revolutionary enthusiasm, without which there can be no victorious revolutions.

No profound and mighty popular movement has ever occurred in history without dirty scum rising to the top, without adventurers and rogues, boasters and ranters attaching themselves to the inexperienced innovators, without absurd muddle and fuss, without individual "leaders" trying to deal with twenty matters at once and not finishing any of them.

Let the lap-dogs of bourgeois society, from Belorussov to Martov, squeal and yelp about every extra chip that is sent flying in cutting down the big, old wood. What else are lap-dogs for if not to yelp at the proletarian elephant? Let them yelp. We shall go our way and try as carefully and as patiently as possible to test and discover real organisers, people with sober and practical minds, people who combine loyalty to socialism with ability without fuss (and in spite of muddle and fuss) to get a large number of people working together steadily and concertedly within the framework of Soviet organisation. *Only* such people, after they have been tested a dozen times, by being transferred from the simplest to the more difficult tasks, should be promoted to the responsible posts of leaders of the people's labour, leaders of administration. We have not yet learned to do this, but we shall learn.

"HARMONIOUS ORGANISATION" AND DICTATORSHIP

The resolution adopted by the recent Moscow Congress of Soviets advanced as the primary task of the moment the establishment of a "harmonious organisation", and the tightening of discipline.[11] Everyone now readily "votes for" and "subscribes to" resolutions of this kind; but usually people do not think over the fact that the application of such resolutions calls for coercion—coercion precisely in the form of dictatorship. And yet it would be extremely stupid and absurdly utopian to assume that the transition from capitalism to socialism is possible without coercion and without dictatorship. Marx's theory very definitely opposed this petty-bourgeois-democratic and anarchist absurdity long ago. And Russia of 1917-18 confirms the correctness of Marx's theory in this respect so strikingly, palpably and imposingly that only those who are hopelessly dull or who have obstinately decided to turn their backs on the truth can be under any misapprehension concerning this. Either the dictatorship of Kornilov (if we take him as the Russian type of bourgeois Cavaignac), or the dictatorship of the proletariat—any other choice is *out of the question* for a country which is developing at an extremely rapid rate with extremely sharp turns and amidst desperate ruin created by one of the most horrible wars in history. Every solution that offers a middle path is either a deception of the people by the bourgeoisie—for the bourgeoisie dare not tell the truth, dare not say that they need Kornilov—or an expression of the dull-wittedness of the petty-bourgeois democrats, of the Chernovs, Tseretelis and Martovs, who chatter about the unity of democracy, the dictatorship of democracy, the general democratic front,

[11] See *LCW*, Vol. 27, 1974, p. 200.

and similar nonsense. Those whom even the progress of the Russian Revolution of 1917-18 has not taught that a middle course is impossible, must be given up for lost.

On the other hand, it is not difficult to see that during every transition from capitalism to socialism, dictatorship is necessary for two main reasons, or along two main channels. Firstly, capitalism cannot be defeated and eradicated without the ruthless suppression of the resistance of the exploiters, who cannot at once be deprived of their wealth, of their advantages of organisation and knowledge, and consequently for a fairly long period will inevitably try to overthrow the hated rule of the poor; secondly, every great revolution, and a socialist revolution in particular, even if there is no external war, is inconceivable without internal war, i.e., civil war, which is even more devastating than external war, and involves thousands and millions of cases of wavering and desertion from one side to another, implies a state of extreme indefiniteness, lack of equilibrium and chaos. And of course, all the elements of disintegration of the old society, which are inevitably very numerous and connected mainly with the petty bourgeoisie (because it is the petty bourgeoisie that every war and every crisis ruins and destroys first), are bound to "reveal themselves" during such a profound revolution. And these elements of disintegration *cannot* "reveal themselves" otherwise than in an increase of crime, hooliganism, corruption, profiteering and outrages of every kind. To put these down requires time and *requires an iron hand.*

There has not been a single great revolution in history in which the people did not instinctively realise this and did not show salutary firmness by shooting thieves on the spot. The misfortune of previous revolutions was that the revolutionary enthusiasm of the people, which sustained them in their state of tension and gave them the strength to suppress ruthlessly the elements of disintegration, did not last long. The social, i.e., the class, reason for this instability of the revolutionary enthusiasm of the people was the weakness of the proletariat, which *alone* is able (if it is sufficiently numerous, class-conscious and disciplined) to win over to its side *the majority* of the working and exploited people (the majority of the poor, to speak more simply and popularly) and retain power sufficiently long to suppress completely all the exploiters as well as all the elements of disintegration.

It was this historical experience of all revolutions, it was this world-historic—economic and political—lesson that Marx summed up when he gave his short, sharp, concise and expressive formula: dictatorship of the proletariat. And the fact that the Russian revolution has been correct in its approach to this world-historic task *has been proved* by the victorious progress of the Soviet form of organisation among all the peoples and tongues of Russia. For Soviet power is nothing but an organisational form of the dictatorship of the proletariat, the dictatorship of the advanced class, which raises to a new democracy and to independent participation in the administration of the state tens upon tens of millions of working and exploited peoples who by their own experience learn to regard the disciplined and class-conscious vanguard of the proletariat as their most reliable leader.

Dictatorship, however, is a big word, and big words should not be thrown about carelessly. Dictatorship is iron rule, government that is revolutionarily bold, swift and ruthless in suppressing both exploiters and hooligans. But our government is excessively mild, very often it resembles jelly more than iron. We must not forget for a moment that the bourgeois and petty-bourgeois element is fighting against the Soviet system in two ways; on the one hand, it is operating from without, by the methods of the Savinkovs, Gotzes, Gegechkoris and Kornilovs, by conspiracies and rebellions, and by their filthy "ideological" reflection, the flood of lies and slander in the Constitutional-Democratic, Right Socialist-Revolutionary and Menshevik press; on the other hand, this element operates from within and takes advantage of every manifestation of disintegration, of every weakness, in order to bribe, to increase indiscipline, laxity and chaos. The nearer we approach the complete military suppression of the bourgeoisie, the more dangerous does the element of petty-bourgeois anarchy become. And the fight against this element cannot be waged solely with the aid of propaganda and agitation, solely by organising competition and by selecting organisers. The struggle must also be waged by means of coercion.

As the fundamental task of the government becomes, not military suppression, but administration, the typical manifestation of suppression and compulsion will be, not shooting on the spot, but trial by court. In this respect also the revolutionary people after October 25, 1917, took the right path and demonstrated the viability of the revolution by setting up their own workers' and peasants' courts, even before the decrees dissolving the bourgeois bureaucratic judiciary were passed. But our revolutionary and people's courts are extremely, incredibly weak. One feels that we have not yet done away with the people's attitude towards the courts as towards something official and alien, an attitude inherited from the yoke of the landowners and of the bourgeoisie. It is not yet sufficiently realised that the courts are an organ which enlists precisely the poor, every one of them, in the work of state administration (for the work of the courts is one of the functions of state administration), that the courts are an *organ of the power* of the proletariat and of the poor peasants, that the courts are an instrument *for inculcating discipline.* There is not yet sufficient appreciation of the simple and obvious fact that if the principal misfortunes of Russia at the present time are hunger and unemployment, these misfortunes cannot be overcome by spurts, but only by comprehensive, all-embracing, country-wide organisation and discipline in order to increase the output of bread for the people and bread for industry (fuel), to transport these in good time to the places where they are required, and to distribute them properly; and it is not fully appreciated that, consequently, it is *those* who violate labour discipline at any factory, in any undertaking, in any matter, who are *responsible* for the sufferings caused by the famine and unemployment, that we must know how to find the guilty ones, to bring them to trial and ruthlessly punish them. Where the petty-bourgeois anarchy against which we must now wage a most persistent struggle makes itself felt is in the failure to appreciate the economic and political connection between famine and unemployment, on the one hand, and general laxity in matters of organisation and discipline, on the other—in the tenacity of the *small-proprietor* outlook, namely, I'll grab all I can for myself; the rest can go hang.

In the rail transport service, which perhaps most strikingly embodies the economic ties of an organism created by large-scale capitalism, the struggle between the element of petty-bourgeois laxity and proletarian organisation is particularly evident. The "administrative" elements provide a host of saboteurs and bribe-takers; the best part of the proletarian elements fight for discipline; but among both elements there are, of course, many waverers and "weak" characters who are unable to withstand the "temptation" of profiteering, bribery, personal gain obtained by spoiling the whole apparatus, upon the proper working of which the victory over famine and unemployment depends.

The struggle that has been developing around the recent decree on the management of the railways, the decree which grants individual executives dictatorial powers (or "unlimited" powers),[12] is characteristic.

[12] The reference is to the decree of the Council of People's Commissars "On Centralisation of Management, Protection of Roads and the Improvement of Their Carrying Capacity" (see *Decrees of the Soviet Government*, Vol. 2, Russ. ed., 1959, pp. 18-20). Having considered on March 18, 1918, the draft decree proposed by the People's Commissariat for Ways of Communication on non-interference by various institutions in the affairs of the Railway Department,

The conscious (and to a large extent, probably, unconscious) representatives of petty-bourgeois laxity would like to see in this granting of "unlimited" (i.e., dictatorial) powers to individuals a departure from the collegiate principle, from democracy and from the principles of Soviet government. Here and there, among Left Socialist-Revolutionaries, a positively hooligan agitation, i.e., agitation appealing to the base instincts and to the small proprietor's urge to "grab all he can", has been developed against the dictatorship decree. The question has become one of really enormous significance. Firstly, the question of principle, namely, is the appointment of individuals, dictators with unlimited powers, in general compatible with the fundamental principles of Soviet government? Secondly, what relation has this case—this precedent, if you will—to the special tasks of government in the present concrete situation? We must deal very thoroughly with both these questions.

That in the history of revolutionary movements the dictatorship of individuals was very often the expression, the vehicle, the channel of the dictatorship of the revolutionary classes has been shown by the irrefutable experience of history. Undoubtedly, the dictatorship of

---

the Council of People's Commissars instructed a special commission to revise the decree on the basis of the following theses put forward by Lenin: (1) Considerable centralisation. (2) Appointment of responsible executives at every local centre as elected by the railway organisations. (3) Unquestioning obedience to their orders. (4) Dictatorial rights to be given to the military detachments for maintaining order. (5) Steps to be taken immediately to take account of rolling stock and its whereabouts. (6) Steps to be taken to set up a technical department. (7) Fuel.

Lenin made several important amendments to the draft, which was submitted by the commission and considered at a meeting of the Council of People's Commissars on March 21, before being approved by the government. In view of the hostility with which the decree was greeted by the All-Russia Executive Committee of Railwaymen (Vikzhedor), which was strongly influenced by the Mensheviks and the Left Socialist-Revolutionaries, the People's Commissariat for Ways of Communication on March 23 proposed amending the decree at a meeting of the Council of People's Commissars. The representatives of Vikzhedor who attended the meeting attacked the decree on the grounds that it meant the "destruction of the role of Vikzhedor and its replacement by the individual authority of a Commissar". Arguing against the opponents of the decree, Lenin explained the need for taking the very firmest measures to eliminate sabotage and inefficiency on the railways and introduced amendments making the decree even more categorical. With these amendments the decree was finally approved by the government on March 23 and published over Lenin's signature on March 26 in No. 57 of *Izvestia VTsIK.*

individuals was compatible with bourgeois democracy. On this point, however, the bourgeois denigrators of the Soviet system, as well as their petty-bourgeois henchmen, always display sleight of hand: on the one hand, they declare the Soviet system to be something absurd, anarchistic and savage, and carefully pass over in silence all our historical examples and theoretical arguments which prove that the Soviets are a higher form of democracy, and what is more, the beginning of a *socialist* form of democracy; on the other hand, they demand of us a higher democracy than bourgeois democracy and say: personal dictatorship is absolutely incompatible with your, Bolshevik (i.e., not bourgeois, but *socialist*), Soviet democracy.

These are exceedingly poor arguments. If we are not anarchists, we must admit that the state, *that is, coercion*, is necessary for the transition from capitalism to socialism. The form of coercion is determined by the degree of development of the given revolutionary class, and also by special circumstances, such as, for example, the legacy of a long and reactionary war and the forms of resistance put up by the bourgeoisie and the petty bourgeoisie. There is, therefore, absolutely *no* contradiction in principle between Soviet (*that is*, socialist) democracy and the exercise of dictatorial powers by individuals. The difference between proletarian dictatorship and bourgeois dictatorship is that the former strikes at the exploiting minority in the interests of the exploited majority, and that it is exercised—*also through individuals*—not only by the working and exploited people, but also by organisations which are built in such a way as to rouse these people to history-making activity. (The Soviet organisations are organisations of this kind.)

In regard to the second question, concerning the significance of individual dictatorial powers from the point of view of the specific tasks of the present moment, it must be said that large-scale machine industry—which is precisely the material source, the productive source, the foundation of socialism—calls for absolute and strict *unity of will*, which directs the joint labours of hundreds, thousands and tens of thousands of people. The technical, economic and historical necessity of this is obvious, and all those who have thought about socialism have always regarded it as one of the conditions of socialism. But how can strict unity of will be ensured? By thousands subordinating their will to the will of one.

Given ideal class-consciousness and discipline on the part of those participating in the common work, this subordination would be something like the mild leadership of a conductor of an orchestra. It may assume the sharp forms of a dictatorship if ideal discipline and class-consciousness are lacking. But be that as it may, *unquestioning subordination* to a single will is absolutely necessary for the success of processes organised on the pattern of large-scale machine industry. On the railways it is twice and three times as necessary. In this transition from one political task to another, which *on the surface* is totally dissimilar to the first, lies the whole originality of the present situation. The revolution has only just smashed the oldest, strongest and heaviest of fetters, to which the people submitted under duress. That was yesterday. Today, however, the same revolution demands—precisely in the interests of its development and consolidation, precisely in the interests of socialism—that the people *unquestioningly obey the single will* of the leaders of labour. Of course, such a transition cannot be made at one step. Clearly, it can be achieved only as a result of tremendous jolts, shocks, reversions to old ways, the enormous exertion of effort on the part of the proletarian vanguard, which is leading the people to the new ways. Those who drop into the philistine hysterics of *Novaya Zhizn* or *Vperyod*,[13] *Dyelo Naroda* or *Nash Vek*[14] do not stop to think about this.

Take the psychology of the average, ordinary representative of the toiling and exploited masses, compare it with the objective, material conditions of his life in society. Before the October Revolution he did *not* see a single instance of the propertied, exploiting classes making any real sacrifice for him, giving up anything for his benefit. He did *not* see them giving him the land and liberty that had been repeatedly promised him, giving him peace, sacrificing "Great Power" interests and the interests of Great Power secret treaties, sacrificing capital and profits. He saw this only *after* October 25, 1917, when he took it himself by force, and had

[13] *Vperyod* (Forward)—a Menshevik daily newspaper, which began to appear in March 1917 in Moscow as the organ of the Moscow organisation of Mensheviks, and subsequently as the organ of the committees of the R.S.D.L.P. (Mensheviks) of the Moscow organisation and the Central Region. On April 2, 1918, the newspaper became the organ of the Mensheviks' Central Committee as well, and L. Martov, F.I. Dan and A.S. Martynov joined its editorial board. It was banned for its counter-revolutionary activities in February 1919 by decision of the All-Russia C.E.C.

[14] *Nash Vek* (Our Age)—one of the names of the newspaper *Rech*, the central organ of the counter-revolutionary party of the Constitutional-Democrats. After it had been banned by a decision of the Petrograd Revolutionary Military Committee of October 26 (November 8), 1917, the newspaper continued to appear until August 1918 under various names: *Nasha Rech* (Our Speech), *Svobodnaya Rech* (Free Speech), *Vek* (Age), *Novaya Rech* (New Speech) and *Nash Vek*.

to defend by force what he had taken, against the Kerenskys, Gotzes, Gegechkoris, Dutovs and Kornilovs. Naturally, for a certain time, all his attention, all his thoughts, all his spiritual strength, were concentrated on taking a breath, on unbending his back, on straightening his shoulders, on taking the blessings of life that were there for the taking, and that had always been denied him by the now overthrown exploiters. Of course, a certain amount of time is required to enable the ordinary working man not only to see for himself, not only to become convinced, but also to feel that he cannot simply "take", snatch, grab things, that this leads to increased disruption, to ruin, to the return of the Kornilovs. The corresponding change in the conditions of life (and consequently in the psychology) of the ordinary working men is only just beginning. And our whole task, the task of the Communist Party (Bolsheviks), which is the class-conscious spokesman for the strivings of the exploited for emancipation, is to appreciate this change, to understand that it is necessary, to stand at the head of the exhausted people who are wearily seeking a way out and lead them along the true path, along the path of labour discipline, along the path of co-ordinating the task of arguing at mass meetings *about* the conditions of work with the task of unquestioningly obeying the will of the Soviet leader, of the dictator, *during* the work.

The "mania for meetings" is an object of the ridicule, and still more often of the spiteful hissing of the bourgeoisie, the Mensheviks, the *Novaya Zhizn* people, who see only the chaos, the confusion and the outbursts of small-proprietor egoism. But without the discussions at public meetings the mass of the oppressed could never have changed from the discipline forced upon them by the exploiters to conscious, voluntary discipline. The airing of questions at public meetings is the genuine democracy of the working people, their way of unbending their backs, their awakening to a new life, their first steps along the road which they themselves have cleared of vipers (the exploiters, the imperialists, the landowners and capitalists) and which they want to learn to build themselves, in their own way, for themselves, on the principles of their own *Soviet*, and not alien, not aristocratic, not bourgeois rule. It required precisely the October victory of the working people over the exploiters, it required a whole historical period in which the working people themselves could first of all discuss the new conditions of life and the new tasks, in order to make possible the durable transition to superior forms of labour discipline, to the conscious appreciation of the necessity for the dictatorship of the proletariat, to unquestioning obedience to the orders of individual representatives of the Soviet government during the work.

This transition has now begun.

We have successfully fulfilled the first task of the revolution; we have seen how the mass of working people evolved in themselves the fundamental condition for its success: they united their efforts against the exploiters in order to overthrow them. Stages like that of October 1905, February and October 1917 are of world-historic significance.

We have successfully fulfilled the second task of the revolution: to awaken, to raise those very "lower ranks" of society whom the exploiters had pushed down, and who only after October 25, 1917, obtained complete freedom to overthrow the exploiters and to begin to take stock of things and arrange life in their own way. The airing of questions at public meetings by the most oppressed and downtrodden, by the least educated mass of working people, their coming over to the side of the Bolsheviks, their setting up everywhere of their own Soviet organisations—this was the second great stage of the revolution.

The third stage is now beginning. We must consolidate what we ourselves have won, what we ourselves have decreed, made law, discussed, planned—consolidate all this in stable forms of *everyday labour discipline*. This is the most difficult, but the most gratifying task, because only its fulfillment will give us a socialist system. We must learn to combine the "public meeting" democracy of the working people—turbulent, surging, overflowing its banks like a spring flood—with *iron* discipline while at work, with *unquestioning obedience* to the will of a single person, the Soviet leader, while at work.

We have not yet learned to do this.

We shall learn it.

Yesterday we were menaced by the restoration of bourgeois exploitation, personified by the Kornilovs, Gotzes, Dutovs, Gegechkoris and Bogayevskys. We conquered them. This restoration, this very same restoration menaces us today in another form, in the form of the element of petty-bourgeois laxity and anarchism, or small-proprietor "it's not my business" psychology, in the form of the daily, petty, but numerous sorties and attacks of this element against proletarian discipline. We must, and we shall, vanquish this element of petty-bourgeois anarchy.

THE DEVELOPMENT OF SOVIET ORGANISATION

The socialist character of Soviet, i.e., *proletarian*, democracy, as concretely applied today, lies first in the fact that the electors are the working and exploited people; the bourgeoisie is excluded. Secondly, it lies in the fact that all bureaucratic formalities and restrictions of elections are abolished; the people themselves determine the order and time of elections, and are completely free to recall any elected person. Thirdly, it lies in the creation of the best mass organisation of the vanguard of the working people, i.e., the proletariat engaged in large-scale industry, which enables it to lead the vast mass of the exploited, to draw them into independent political life, to educate them politically by their own experience; therefore for the first time a start is made by the *entire* population in learning the art of administration, and in beginning to administer.

These are the principal distinguishing features of the democracy now applied in Russia, which is a higher *type* of democracy, a break with the bourgeois distortion of democracy, transition to socialist democracy and to the conditions in which the state can begin to wither away.

It goes without saying that the element of petty-bourgeois disorganisation (which must *inevitably* be apparent to some extent in *every* proletarian revolution, and which is especially apparent in our revolution, owing to the petty-bourgeois character of our country, its backwardness and the consequences of a reactionary war) cannot but leave its impress upon the Soviets as well.

We must work unremittingly to develop the organisation of the Soviets and of the Soviet government. There is a petty-bourgeois tendency to transform the members of the Soviets into "parliamentarians", or else into bureaucrats. We must combat this by drawing *all* the members of the Soviets into the practical work of administration. In many places the departments of the Soviets are gradually merging with the Commissariats. Our aim is to draw *the whole of the poor* into the practical work of administration, and all steps that are taken in this direction—the more varied they are, the better—should be carefully recorded, studied, systematised, tested by wider experience and embodied in law. Our aim is to ensure that *every* toiler, having finished his eight hours' "task" in productive labour, shall perform state duties *without pay*; the transition to this is particularly difficult, but this transition alone can guarantee the final consolidation of socialism. Naturally, the novelty and difficulty of the change lead to an abundance of steps being taken, as it were, gropingly, to an abundance of mistakes, vacillation—without this, any marked progress is impossible. The reason why the present position seems peculiar to many of those who would like to be regarded as socialists is that they have been accustomed to contrasting capitalism with socialism abstractly, and that they profoundly put between the two the word "leap" (some of them; recalling fragments of what they have read of Engels's writings, still more profoundly add the phrase "leap from the realm of necessity into the realm of freedom"[15]). The majority of these so-called socialists, who have "read in books" about socialism but who have never seriously thought over the matter, are unable to consider that by "leap" the teachers of socialism meant turning-points on a world-historical scale, and that leaps of this kind extend over decades and even longer periods. Naturally, in such times, the notorious "intelligentsia" provides an infinite number of mourners of the dead. Some mourn over the Constituent Assembly, others mourn over bourgeois discipline, others again mourn over the capitalist system, still others mourn over the cultured landowner, and still others again mourn over imperialist Great Power policy, etc., etc.

The real interest of the epoch of great leaps lies in the fact that the abundance of fragments of the old, which sometimes accumulate more rapidly than the rudiments (not always immediately discernible) of the new, calls for the ability to discern what is most important in the line or chain of development. History knows moments when the most important thing for the success of the revolution is to heap up as large a quantity of the fragments as possible, i.e., to blow up as many of the old institutions as possible; moments arise when enough has been blown up and the next task is to perform the "prosaic" (for the petty-bourgeois revolutionary, the "boring") task of clearing away the fragments; and moments arise when the careful nursing of the rudiments of the new system, which are growing amidst the wreckage on a soil which as yet has been badly cleared of rubble, is the most important thing.

It is not enough to be a revolutionary and an adherent of socialism or a Communist in general. You must be able at each particular moment to find the particular link in the chain which you must grasp with all your might in order to hold the whole chain and to prepare firmly for the transition to the next link; the order of the links, their form, the manner in which they are linked together, the way they differ from each other in the historical chain of events, are not as simple and not as meaningless as those in an ordinary chain made by a smith.

The fight against the bureaucratic distortion of the Soviet form of organisation is assured by the firmness of the connection between the Soviets and the "people", meaning by that the working and exploited people, and by the flexibility and elasticity of this connection. Even in

[15] Lenin is referring to and quoting from *Anti-Dühring* by F. Engels, Section Three. Socialism. Chapter II. Theoretical.

the most democratic capitalist republics in the world, the poor never regard the bourgeois parliament as "their" institution. But the Soviets are "theirs" and not alien institutions to the mass of workers and peasants. The modern "Social-Democrats" of the Scheidemann or, what is almost the same thing, of the Martov type are repelled by the Soviets, and they are drawn towards the respectable bourgeois parliament, or to the Constituent Assembly, in the same way as Turgenev, sixty years ago, was drawn towards a moderate monarchist and noblemen's Constitution and was repelled by the peasant democracy of Dobrolyubov and Chernyshevsky.[16]

It is the closeness of the Soviets to the "people", to the working people, that creates the special forms of recall and other means of control from below which must be most zealously developed now. For example, the Councils of Public Education, as periodical conferences of Soviet electors and their delegates called to discuss and control the activities of the Soviet authorities in this field, deserve full sympathy and support. Nothing could be sillier than to transform the Soviets into something congealed and self-contained. The more resolutely we now have to stand for a ruthlessly firm government, for the dictatorship of individuals *in definite processes of work*, in definite aspects of *purely executive* functions, the more varied must be the forms and methods of control from below in order to counteract every shadow of a possibility of distorting the principles of Soviet government, in order repeatedly and tirelessly to weed out bureaucracy.

CONCLUSION

An extraordinarily difficult, complex and dangerous situation in international affairs; the necessity of manoeuvring and retreating; a period of waiting for new outbreaks of the revolution which is maturing in the West at a painfully slow pace; within the country a period of slow construction and ruthless "tightening up", of prolonged and persistent struggle waged by stern, proletarian discipline against the menacing element of petty-bourgeois laxity and anarchy—these in brief are the distinguishing features of the special stage of the socialist revolution in which we are now living. This is the link in the historical chain of events

[16] Chernyshevsky describes Turgenev's attitude to Dobrolyubov and himself in an account of a conversation he had with Turgenev in the early sixties of the last century (see the article "An Expression of Gratitude" in *Complete Collected Works* by N.G. Chernyshevsky, Vol. 10, Russ. ed., Moscow, 1951, pp. 122-23).

which we must at present grasp with all our might in order to prove equal to the tasks that confront us before passing to the next link to which we are drawn by a special brightness, the brightness of the victories of the international proletarian revolution.

Try to compare with the ordinary everyday concept "revolutionary" the slogans that follow from the specific conditions of the present stage, namely, manoeuvre, retreat, wait, build slowly, ruthlessly tighten up, rigorously discipline, smash laxity. . . . Is it surprising that when certain "revolutionaries" hear this they are seized with noble indignation and begin to "thunder" abuse at us for forgetting the traditions of the October Revolution, for compromising with the bourgeois experts, for compromising with the bourgeoisie, for being petty bourgeois, reformists, and so on and so forth?

The misfortune of these sorry "revolutionaries" is that even those of them who are prompted by the best motives in the world and are absolutely loyal to the cause of socialism fail to understand the particular, and particularly "unpleasant", condition that a backward country, which has been lacerated by a reactionary and disastrous war and which began the socialist revolution long before the more advanced countries, inevitably has to pass through; they lack stamina in the difficult moments of a difficult transition. Naturally, it is the "Left Socialist-Revolutionaries" who are acting as an "official" opposition of *this* kind against our Party. Of course, there are and always will be individual exceptions from group and class types. But social types remain. In the land in which the small-proprietor population greatly predominates over the purely proletarian population, the difference between the proletarian revolutionary and petty-bourgeois revolutionary will inevitably make itself felt, and from time to time will make itself felt very sharply. The petty-bourgeois revolutionary wavers and vacillates at every turn of events; he is an ardent revolutionary in March 1917 and praises "coalition" in May, hates the Bolsheviks (or laments over their "adventurism") in July and apprehensively turns away from them at the end of October, supports them in December, and, finally, in March and April 1918 such types, more often than not, turn up their noses contemptuously and say: "I am not one of those who sing hymns to 'organic' work, to practicalness and gradualism."

The social origin of such types is the small proprietor, who has been driven to frenzy by the horrors of war, by sudden ruin, by unprecedented torments of famine and devastation, who hysterically rushes about seeking a way out, seeking salvation, places his confidence in the proletariat and supports it one moment and the next gives way to fits of despair. We must clearly understand and firmly remember the fact that socialism cannot be built on such a social basis. The only class that can lead the working and exploited people is the class that unswervingly follows its path without losing courage and without giving way to despair even at the most difficult, arduous and dangerous stages. Hysterical impulses are of no use to us. What we need is the steady advance of the iron battalions of the proletariat.

LETTER TO AMERICAN WORKERS (1918)

Comrades! A Russian Bolshevik who took part in the 1905 Revolution, and who lived in your country for many years afterwards, has offered to convey my letter to you.[1] I have accepted his proposal all the more gladly because just at the present time the American revolutionary workers have to play an exceptionally important role as uncompromising enemies of American imperialism—the freshest, strongest and latest in joining in the world-wide slaughter of nations for the division of capitalist profits. At this very moment, the American multimillionaires, these modern slaveowners have turned an exceptionally tragic page in the bloody history of bloody imperialism by giving their approval—whether direct or indirect, open or hypocritically concealed, makes no difference—to the armed expedition launched by the brutal Anglo-

[1] The dispatch of the letter to America was organised by the Bolshevik M.M. Borodin, who had recently been there. With the foreign military intervention and the blockade of Soviet Russia this involved considerable difficulties. The letter was delivered to the United States by P.I. Travin (Sletov). Along with the letter he brought the Constitution of the R.S.F.S.R. and the Soviet Government's Note to President Wilson containing the demand to stop the intervention. The well-known American socialist and journalist John Reed secured the publication of all these documents in the American press.

In December 1918 a slightly abridged version of the letter appeared in the New York magazine *The Class Struggle* and the Boston weekly *The Revolutionary Age*, both organs of the Left wing of the American Socialist Party. *The Revolutionary Age* was brought out by John Reed and Sen Katayama. The letter evoked keen interest among readers and it was published as a reprint from *The Class Struggle* in a large number of copies. Subsequently it was published many times in the bourgeois and socialist press of the U.S.A. and Western Europe, in the French socialist magazine *Demain* No. 28-29, 1918, in No. 138 of The *Call*, organ of the British Socialist Party, the Berlin magazine *Die Aktion* No. 51-52, 1918, and elsewhere. In 1934 the letter was brought out in New York in the form of a pamphlet, which contained the passages omitted in earlier publications.

The letter was widely used by the American Left Socialists and was instrumental in aiding the development of the labour and communist movement in the U.S. and Europe. It helped advanced workers to appreciate the nature of imperialism and the great revolutionary changes effected by the Soviet government. Lenin's letter aroused a mounting protest in the U.S. against the armed intervention.

Japanese imperialists for the purpose of throttling the first socialist republic.

The history of modern, civilised America opened with one of those great, really liberating, really revolutionary wars of which there have been so few compared to the vast number of wars of conquest which, like the present imperialist war, were caused by squabbles among kings, landowners or capitalists over the division of usurped lands or ill-gotten gains. That was the war the American people waged against the British robbers who oppressed America and held her in colonial slavery, in the same way as these "civilised" bloodsuckers are still oppressing and holding in colonial slavery hundreds of millions of people in India, Egypt, and all parts of the world.

About 150 years have passed since then. Bourgeois civilisation has borne all its luxurious fruits. America has taken first place among the free and educated nations in level of development of the productive forces of collective human endeavour, in the utilisation of machinery and of all the wonders of modern engineering. At the same time, America has become one of the foremost countries in regard to the depth of the abyss which lies between the handful of arrogant multimillionaires who wallow in filth and luxury, and the millions of working people who constantly live on the verge of pauperism. The American people, who set the world an example in waging a revolutionary war against feudal slavery, now find themselves in the latest, capitalist stage of wage-slavery to a handful of multimillionaires, and find themselves playing the role of hired thugs who, for the benefit of wealthy scoundrels, throttled the Philippines in 1898 on the pretext of "liberating" them, and are throttling the Russian Socialist Republic in 1918 on the pretext of "protecting" it from the Germans.

The four years of the imperialist slaughter of nations, however, have not passed in vain. The deception of the people by the scoundrels of both robber groups, the British and the German, has been utterly exposed by indisputable and obvious facts. The results of the four years of war have revealed the general law of capitalism as applied to war between robbers for the division of spoils: the richest and strongest profited and grabbed most, while the weakest were utterly robbed, tormented, crushed and strangled.

The British imperialist robbers were the strongest in number of "colonial slaves". The British capitalists have not lost an inch of "their" territory (i.e., territory they have grabbed over the centuries), but they have grabbed all the German colonies in Africa, they have grabbed

Mesopotamia and Palestine, they have throttled Greece, and have begun to plunder Russia.

The German imperialist robbers were the strongest in organisation and discipline of "their" armies, but weaker in regard to colonies. They have lost all their colonies, but plundered half of Europe and throttled the largest number of small countries and weak nations. What a great war of "liberation" on both sides! How well the robbers of both groups, the Anglo-French and the German capitalists, together with their lackeys, the social-chauvinists, i.e., the socialists who went over to the side of "*their own*" bourgeoisie, have "defended their country"!

The American multimillionaires were, perhaps, richest of all, and geographically the most secure. They have profited more than all the rest. They have converted all, even the richest, countries into their tributaries. They have grabbed hundreds of billions of dollars. And every dollar is sullied with filth: the filth of the secret treaties between Britain and her "allies", between Germany and her vassals, treaties for the division of the spoils, treaties of mutual "aid" for oppressing the workers and persecuting the internationalist socialists. Every dollar is sullied with the filth of "profitable" war contracts, which in every country made the rich richer and the poor poorer. And every dollar is stained with blood—from that ocean of blood that has been shed by the ten million killed and twenty million maimed in the great, noble, liberating and holy war to decide whether the British or the German robbers are to get most of the spoils, whether the British or the German thugs are to be *foremost* in throttling the weak nations all over the world.

While the German robbers broke all records in war atrocities, the British have broken all records not only in the number of colonies they have grabbed, but also in the subtlety of their disgusting hypocrisy. This very day, the Anglo-French and American bourgeois newspapers are spreading, in millions and millions of copies, lies and slander about Russia, and are hypocritically justifying their predatory expedition against her on the plea that they want to "protect" Russia from the Germans!

It does not require many words to refute this despicable and hideous lie; it is sufficient to point to one well-known fact. In October 1917, after the Russian workers had overthrown their imperialist government, the Soviet government, the government of the revolutionary workers and peasants, openly proposed a just peace, a peace without annexations or indemnities, a peace that fully guaranteed equal rights to all nations—and it proposed such a peace to *all* the belligerent countries.

It was the Anglo-French and the American bourgeoisie who refused to accept our proposal; it was they who even refused to talk to us about a general peace! It was *they* who betrayed the interests of all nations; it was they who prolonged the imperialist slaughter!

It was they who, banking on the possibility of dragging Russia back into the imperialist war, refused to take part in the peace negotiations and thereby gave a free hand to the no less predatory German capitalists who imposed the annexationist and harsh Brest Peace upon Russia!

It is difficult to imagine anything more disgusting than the hypocrisy with which the Anglo-French and American bourgeoisie are now "blaming" us *for* the Brest Peace Treaty. The very capitalists of those countries which could have turned the Brest negotiations into general negotiations for a general peace are now our "accusers"! The Anglo-French imperialist vultures, who have profited from the plunder of colonies and the slaughter of nations, have prolonged the war for nearly a whole year after Brest, and yet they "accuse" *us*, the Bolsheviks, who proposed a just peace to all countries, they accuse *us*, who tore up, published and exposed to public disgrace the secret, criminal treaties concluded between the ex-tsar and the Anglo-French capitalists.

The workers of the whole world, no matter in what country they live, greet us, sympathise with us, applaud us for breaking the iron ring of imperialist tics, of sordid imperialist treaties, of imperialist chains—for breaking through to freedom, and making the heaviest sacrifices in doing so—for, as a socialist republic, although torn and plundered by the imperialists, keeping *out* of the imperialist war and raising the banner of peace, the banner of socialism for the whole world to see.

Small wonder that the international imperialist gang hates us for this, that it "accuses" us, that all the lackeys of the imperialists, including our Right Socialist-Revolutionaries and Mensheviks, also "accuse" us. The hatred these watchdogs of imperialism express for the Bolsheviks, and the sympathy of the class-conscious workers of the world, convince us more than ever of the justice of our cause.

A real socialist would not fail to understand that for the sake of achieving victory over the bourgeoisie, for the sake of power passing to the workers, for the sake of *starting* the world proletarian revolution, we *cannot* and must *not* hesitate to make the heaviest sacrifices, including the sacrifice of part of our territory, the sacrifice of heavy defeats at the hands of imperialism. A real socialist would have proved by *deeds* his willingness for "his" country to make the greatest sacrifice to give a real push forward to the cause of the socialist revolution.

For the sake of "their" cause, that is, for the sake of winning world hegemony, the imperialists of Britain and Germany have not hesitated to utterly ruin and throttle a whole number of countries, from Belgium and Serbia to Palestine and Mesopotamia. But must socialists wait with "their" cause, the cause of liberating the working people of the whole world from the yoke of capital, of winning universal and lasting peace, until a path without sacrifice is found? Must they fear to open the battle until an easy victory is "guaranteed"? Must they place the integrity and security of "their" bourgeois-created "fatherland" above the interests of the world socialist revolution? The scoundrels in the international socialist movement who think this way, those lackeys who grovel to bourgeois morality, thrice stand condemned.

The Anglo-French and American imperialist vultures "accuse" us of concluding an "agreement" with German imperialism. What hypocrites, what scoundrels they are to slander the workers' government while trembling because of the sympathy displayed towards us by the workers of "their own" countries! But their hypocrisy will be exposed. They pretend not to see the difference between an agreement entered into by "socialists" with the bourgeoisie (their own or foreign) *against the workers*, against the working people, and an agreement entered into *for the protection* of the workers who have defeated their bourgeoisie, with the bourgeoisie of one national colour *against the bourgeoisie* of another colour in order that the proletariat may take advantage of the antagonisms between the different groups of bourgeoisie.

In actual fact, every European sees this difference very well, and, as I shall show in a moment, the American people have had a particularly striking "illustration" of it in their own history. There are agreements and agreements, there are *fagots et fagots*, as the French say.

When in February 1918 the German imperialist vultures hurled their forces against unarmed, demobilised Russia, who had relied on the international solidarity of the proletariat before the world revolution had fully matured, I did not hesitate for a moment to enter into an "agreement" with the French monarchists. Captain Sadoul, a French army officer who, in words, sympathised with the Bolsheviks, but was in deeds a loyal and faithful servant of French imperialism, brought the French officer de Lubersac to see me. "I am a monarchist. My only aim is to secure the defeat of Germany," de Lubersac declared to me. "That goes without saying (*cela va sans dire*)," I replied. But this did not in the least prevent me from entering into an "agreement" with de Lubersac concerning certain services that French army officers, experts in explosives, were ready to render us by blowing up railway lines in order to hinder the

German invasion. This is an example of an "agreement" of which every class-conscious worker will approve, an agreement in the interests of socialism. The French monarchist and I shook hands, although we knew that each of us would willingly hang his "partner". But for a time our interests coincided. Against the advancing rapacious Germans, *we*, in the interests of the Russian and the world socialist revolution, utilised the equally rapacious counter-interests of *other* imperialists. In this way we served the interests of the working class of Russia and of other countries, we strengthened the proletariat and weakened the bourgeoisie of the whole world, we resorted to the methods, most legitimate and essential in *every* war, of manoeuvre, stratagem, retreat, in anticipation of the moment when the rapidly maturing proletarian revolution in a number of advanced countries *completely matured.*

However much the Anglo-French and American imperialist sharks fume with rage, however much they slander us, no matter how many millions they spend on bribing the Right Socialist-Revolutionary, Menshevik and other social-patriotic newspapers, *I shall not hesitate one second* to enter into a *similar* "agreement" with the German imperialist vultures if an attack upon Russia by Anglo-French troops calls for it. And I know perfectly well that my tactics will be approved by the class-conscious proletariat of Russia, Germany, France, Britain, America—in short, of the whole civilised world. Such tactics will ease the task of the socialist revolution, will hasten it, will weaken the international bourgeoisie, will strengthen the position of the working class which is defeating the bourgeoisie.

The American people resorted to these tactics long ago to the advantage of their revolution. When they waged their great war of liberation against the British oppressors, they had also against them the French and the Spanish oppressors who owned a part of what is now the United States of North America. In their arduous war for freedom, the American people also entered into "agreements" with some oppressors against others for the purpose of weakening the oppressors and strengthening those who were fighting in a revolutionary manner against oppression, for the purpose of serving the interests of the oppressed *people.* The American people took advantage of the strife between the French, the Spanish and the British; sometimes they even fought side by side with the forces of the French and Spanish oppressors against the British oppressors; first they defeated the British and then freed themselves (partly by ransom) from the French and the Spanish.

Historical action is not the pavement of Nevsky Prospekt, said the great Russian revolutionary Chernyshevsky.[2] A revolutionary would not "agree" to a proletarian revolution only "on the condition" that it proceeds easily and smoothly, that there is, from the outset, combined action on the part of the proletarians of different countries, that there are guarantees against defeats, that the road of the revolution is broad, free and straight, that it will not be necessary during the march to victory to sustain the heaviest casualties, to "bide one's time in a besieged fortress", or to make one's way along extremely narrow, impassable, winding and dangerous mountain tracks. Such a person is no revolutionary, he has not freed himself from the pedantry of the bourgeois intellectuals; such a person will be found constantly slipping into the camp of the counter-revolutionary bourgeoisie, like our Right Socialist-Revolutionaries, Mensheviks and even (although more rarely) Left Socialist-Revolutionaries.

Echoing the bourgeoisie, these gentlemen like to blame us for the "chaos" of the revolution, for the "destruction" of industry, for the unemployment and the food shortage. How hypocritical these accusations are, coming from those who welcomed and supported the imperialist war, or who entered into an "agreement" with Kerensky who continued this war! It is this imperialist war that is the cause of all these misfortunes. The revolution engendered by the war cannot avoid the terrible difficulties and suffering bequeathed it by the prolonged, ruinous, reactionary slaughter of the nations. To blame us for the "destruction" of industry, or for the "terror", is either hypocrisy or dull-witted pedantry; it reveals an inability to understand the basic conditions of the fierce class struggle, raised to the highest degree of intensity that is called revolution.

Even when "accusers" of this type do "recognise" the class struggle, they limit themselves to verbal recognition; actually, they constantly slip into the philistine utopia of class "agreement" and "collaboration"; for in revolutionary epochs the class struggle has always, inevitably, and in every country, assumed the form of *civil war*, and civil war is inconceivable without the severest destruction, terror and the restriction of formal democracy in the interests of this war. Only unctuous parsons—whether Christian or "secular" in the persons of parlour, parliamentary socialists—cannot see, understand and feel this necessity. Only a lifeless

[2] Lenin quotes from Chernyshevsky's review of the book by the American economist H. Ch. Carey, *Letters to the President on the Foreign and Domestic Policy of the Union, and its Effects.* Chernyshevsky wrote: "The path of history is not paved like Nevsky Prospekt; it runs across fields, either dusty or muddy, and cuts through swamps or forest thickets. Anyone who fears being covered with dust or muddying his boots, should not engage in social activity."

"man in the muffler" can shun the revolution for this reason instead of plunging into battle with the utmost ardour and determination at a time when history demands that the greatest problems of humanity be solved by struggle and war.

The American people have a revolutionary tradition which has been adopted by the best representatives of the American proletariat, who have repeatedly expressed their complete solidarity with us Bolsheviks. That tradition is the war of liberation against the British in the eighteenth century and the Civil War in the nineteenth century. In some respects, if we only take into consideration the "destruction" of some branches of industry and of the national economy, America in 1870 was *behind* 1860. But what a pedant, what an idiot would anyone be to deny on *these* grounds the immense, world-historic, progressive and revolutionary significance of the American Civil War of 1863-65!

The representatives of the bourgeoisie understand that for the sake of overthrowing Negro slavery, of overthrowing the rule of the slaveowners, it was worth letting the country go through long years of civil war, through the abysmal ruin, destruction and terror that accompany every war. But now, when we are confronted with the vastly greater task of overthrowing capitalist *wage*-slavery, of overthrowing the rule of the bourgeoisie—now, the representatives and defenders of the bourgeoisie, and also the reformist socialists who have been frightened by the bourgeoisie and are shunning the revolution, cannot and do not want to understand that civil war is necessary and legitimate.

The American workers will not follow the bourgeoisie. They will be with us, for civil war against the bourgeoisie. The whole history of the world and of the American labour movement strengthens my conviction that this is so. I also recall the words of one of the most beloved leaders of the American proletariat, Eugene Debs, who wrote in the *Appeal to Reason*,[3] I believe towards the end of 1915, in the article "What Shall I Fight For" (I quoted this article at the beginning of 1916 at a public meeting of workers in Berne, Switzerland)[4]—that he, Debs, would rather be shot than vote credits for the present criminal and reactionary war; that he, Debs, knows of only one holy and, from the proletarian

[3] *Appeal to Reason*—American socialist newspaper, founded in Girard, Kansas, in 1895. The newspaper propagated socialist ideas and was immensely popular among the workers. During the First World War it pursued an internationalist policy.

Debs's article appeared in the paper on September 11, 1915. Its title, which Lenin most probably quoted from memory, was "When I Shall Fight".

[4] See *LCW*, Vol. 22, 1974, p. 123.

standpoint, legitimate war, namely: the war against the capitalists, the war to liberate mankind from wage-slavery.

I am not surprised that Wilson, the head of the American multimillionaires and servant of the capitalist sharks, has thrown Debs into prison. Let the bourgeoisie be brutal to the true internationalists, to the true representatives of the revolutionary proletariat! The more fierce and brutal they are, the nearer the day of the victorious proletarian revolution.

We are blamed for the destruction caused by our revolution. . . . Who are the accusers? The hangers-on of the bourgeoisie, of that very bourgeoisie who, during the four years of the imperialist war, have destroyed almost the whole of European culture and have reduced Europe to barbarism, brutality and starvation. These bourgeoisie now demand we should not make a revolution on these ruins, amidst this wreckage of culture, amidst the wreckage and ruins created by the war, nor with the people who have been brutalised by the war. How humane and righteous the bourgeoisie are!

Their servants accuse us of resorting to terror. . . . The British bourgeoisie have forgotten their 1649, the French bourgeoisie have forgotten their 1793. Terror was just and legitimate when the bourgeoisie resorted to it for their own benefit against feudalism. Terror became monstrous and criminal when the workers and poor peasants dared to use it against the bourgeoisie! Terror was just and legitimate when used for the purpose of substituting one exploiting minority for another exploiting minority. Terror became monstrous and criminal when it began to be used for the purpose of overthrowing *every* exploiting minority, to be used in the interests of the vast actual majority, in the interests of the proletariat and semi-proletariat, the working class and the poor peasants!

The international imperialist bourgeoisie have slaughtered ten million men and maimed twenty million in "their" war, the war to decide whether the British or the German vultures are to rule the world.

If *our* war, the war of the oppressed and exploited against the oppressors and the exploiters, results in half a million or a million casualties in all countries, the bourgeoisie will say that the former casualties are justified, while the latter are criminal.

The proletariat will have something entirely different to say.

Now, amidst the horrors of the imperialist war, the proletariat is receiving a most vivid and striking illustration of the great truth taught by all revolutions and bequeathed to the workers by their best teachers, the founders of modern socialism. This truth is that no revolution can be successful unless *the resistance of the exploiters is crushed.* When we, the workers and toiling peasants, captured state power, it became our duty to crush the resistance of the exploiters. We are proud we have been doing this. We regret we are not doing it with sufficient firmness and determination.

We know that fierce resistance to the socialist revolution on the part of the bourgeoisie is inevitable in all countries, and that this resistance will *grow* with the growth of this revolution. The proletariat will crush this resistance; during the struggle against the resisting bourgeoisie it will finally mature for victory and for power.

Let the corrupt bourgeois press shout to the whole world about every mistake our revolution makes. We are not daunted by our mistakes. People have not become saints because the revolution has begun. The toiling classes who for centuries have been oppressed, downtrodden and forcibly held in the vice of poverty, brutality and ignorance cannot avoid mistakes when making a revolution. And, as I pointed out once before, the corpse of bourgeois society cannot be nailed in a coffin and buried.[5] The corpse of capitalism is decaying and disintegrating in our midst, polluting the air and poisoning our lives, enmeshing that which is new, fresh, young and virile in thousands of threads and bonds of that which is old, moribund and decaying.

For every hundred mistakes we commit, and which the bourgeoisie and their lackeys (including our own Mensheviks and Right Socialist-Revolutionaries) shout about to the whole world, 10,000 great and heroic deeds are performed, greater and more heroic because they are simple and inconspicuous amidst the everyday life of a factory district or a remote village, performed by people who are not accustomed (and have no opportunity) to shout to the whole world about their successes.

But even if the contrary were true—although I know such an assumption is wrong—even if we committed 10,000 mistake for every 100 correct actions we performed, even in that case our revolution would be great and invincible, and *so it will be in the eyes of world history*, because, *for the first time*, not the minority, not the rich alone, not the educated alone, but the real people, the vast majority of the working people, are *themselves* building a new life, are *by their own experience* solving the most difficult problems of socialist organisation.

Every mistake committed in the course of such work, in the course of this most conscientious and earnest work of tens of millions of simple workers and peasants in reorganising their whole life, every such mistake

[5] See *LCW*, Vol. 27, 1974, p. 434.

is worth thousands and millions of "lawless" successes achieved by the exploiting minority—successes in swindling and duping the working people. For only *through* such mistakes will the workers and peasants *learn* to build the new life, learn to do *without* capitalists; only in this way will they hack a path for themselves—through thousands of obstacles—to victorious socialism.

Mistakes are being committed in the course of their revolutionary work by our peasants, who at one stroke, in one night, October 25-26 (old style), 1917, entirely abolished the private ownership of land, and are now, month after month, overcoming tremendous difficulties and correcting their mistakes themselves, solving in a practical way the most difficult tasks of organising new conditions of economic life, of fighting the kulaks, providing land for the *working people* (and not for the rich), and of changing to *communist* large-scale agriculture.

Mistakes are being committed in the course of their revolutionary work by our workers, who have already, after a few months, nationalised almost all the biggest factories and plants, and are learning by hard, everyday work the new task of managing whole branches of industry, are setting the nationalised enterprises going, overcoming the powerful resistance of inertia, petty-bourgeois mentality and selfishness, and, brick by brick, are laying the foundation of *new* social ties, of a *new* labour discipline, of a *new* influence of the workers' trade unions over their members.

Mistakes are committed in the course of their revolutionary work by our Soviets, which were created as far back as 1905 by a mighty upsurge of the people. The Soviets of Workers and Peasants are a new *type* of state, a new and higher *type* of democracy, a form of the proletarian dictatorship, a means of administering the state *without* the bourgeoisie and *against* the bourgeoisie. For the first time democracy is here serving the people, the working people, and has ceased to be democracy for the rich as it still is in all bourgeois republics, even the most democratic. For the first time, the people are grappling, on a scale involving one hundred million, with the problem of implementing the dictatorship of the proletariat and semi-proletariat—a problem which, if not solved, makes socialism *out of the question.*

Let the pedants, or the people whose minds are incurably stuffed with bourgeois-democratic or parliamentary prejudices, shake their heads in perplexity about our Soviets, about the absence of direct elections, for example. These people have forgotten nothing and have learned nothing during the period of the great upheavals of 1914-18.

The combination of the proletarian dictatorship with the new democracy for the working people—of civil war with the widest participation of the people in politics—such a combination cannot be brought about at one stroke, nor does it fit in with the outworn modes of routine parliamentary democracy. The contours of a new world, the world of socialism, are rising before us in the shape of the Soviet Republic. It is not surprising that this world does not come into being ready-made, does not spring forth like Minerva from the head of Jupiter.

The old bourgeois-democratic constitutions waxed eloquent about formal equality and right of assembly; but our proletarian and peasant Soviet Constitution casts aside the hypocrisy of formal equality. When the bourgeois republicans overturned thrones they did not worry about formal equality between monarchists and republicans. When it is a matter of overthrowing the bourgeoisie, only traitors or idiots can demand formal equality of rights for the bourgeoisie. "Freedom of assembly" for workers and peasants is not worth a farthing when the best buildings belong to the bourgeoisie. Our Soviets have *confiscated* all the good buildings in town and country from the rich and have *transferred all* of them to the workers and peasants for *their* unions and meetings. This is *our freedom* of assembly—for the working people! This is the meaning and content of our Soviet, our socialist Constitution!

That is why we are all so firmly convinced that no matter what misfortunes may still be in store for it, our Republic of Soviets is *invincible.*

It is invincible because every blow struck by frenzied imperialism, every defeat the international bourgeoisie inflict on us, rouses more and more sections of the workers and peasants to the struggle, teaches them at the cost of enormous sacrifice, steels them and engenders new heroism on a mass scale.

We know that help from you will probably not come soon, comrade American workers, for the revolution is developing in different countries in different forms and at different tempos (and it cannot be otherwise). We know that although the European proletarian revolution has been maturing very rapidly lately, it may, after all, not flare up within the next few weeks. We are banking on the inevitability of the world revolution, but this does not mean that we are such fools as to bank on the revolution inevitably coming on a *definite* and early date. We have seen two great revolutions in our country, 1905 and 1917, and we know revolutions are not made to order, or by agreement. We know that circumstances brought *our* Russian detachment of the socialist proletariat to the fore not because of our merits, but because of the exceptional backwardness of Russia, and that *before* the world revolution breaks out a number of separate revolutions may be defeated.

In spite of this, we are firmly convinced that we are invincible, because the spirit of mankind will not be broken by the imperialist slaughter. Mankind will vanquish it. And the first country to *break* the convict chains of the imperialist war was *our* country. We sustained enormously heavy casualties in the struggle to break these chains, but we *broke* them. We are *free from* imperialist dependence, we have raised the banner of struggle for the complete overthrow of imperialism for the whole world to see.

We are now, as it were, in a besieged fortress, waiting for the other detachments of the world socialist revolution to come to our relief. These detachments *exist*, they are *more numerous* than ours, they are maturing, growing, gaining more strength the longer the brutalities of imperialism continue. The workers are breaking away from their social-traitors—the Gomperses, Hendersons, Renaudels, Scheidemanns and Renners. Slowly but surely the workers are adopting communist, Bolshevik tactics and are marching towards the proletarian revolution, which alone is capable of saving dying culture and dying mankind.

In short, we are invincible, because the world proletarian revolution is invincible.

N. Lenin

August 20, 1918

THE TASKS OF THE WORKING WOMEN'S MOVEMENT IN THE SOVIET REPUBLIC (1919)

Comrades, it gives me pleasure to greet a conference of working women. I will allow myself to pass over those subjects and questions that, of course, at the moment are the cause of the greatest concern to every working woman and to every politically-conscious individual from among the working people; these are the most urgent questions—that of bread and that of the war situation. I know from the newspaper reports of your meetings that these questions have been dealt with exhaustively by Comrade Trotsky as far as war questions are concerned and by Comrades Yakovleva and Svidersky as far as the bread question is concerned; please, therefore, allow me to pass over those questions.

I should like to say a few words about the general tasks facing the working women's movement in the Soviet Republic, those that are, in general, connected with the transition to socialism, and those that are of particular urgency at the present time. Comrades, the question of the position of women was raised by Soviet power from the very beginning. It seems to me that any workers' state in the course of transition to socialism is faced with a double task. The first part of that task is relatively simple and easy. It concerns those old laws that kept women in a position of inequality as compared to men.

Participants in all emancipation movements in Western Europe have long since, not for decades but for centuries, put forward the demand that obsolete laws be annulled and women and men be made equal by law, but none of the democratic European states, none of the most advanced republics have succeeded in putting it into effect, because wherever there is capitalism, wherever there is private property in land and factories, wherever the power of capital is preserved, the men retain their privileges. It was possible to put it into effect in Russia only because the power of the workers has been established here since October 25, 1917. From its very inception Soviet power set out to be the power of the working people, hostile to all forms of exploitation. It set itself the task of doing away with the possibility of the exploitation of the working people by the landowners and capitalists, of doing away with the rule of capital. Soviet power has been trying to make it possible for the working people to organise their lives without private property in land, without privately-owned factories, without that private property that everywhere, throughout the world, even where there is complete political liberty, even in the most democratic republics, keeps the working people in a state of what is actually poverty and wage-slavery, and women in a state of double slavery.

Soviet power, the power of the working people, in the first months of its existence effected a very definite revolution in legislation that concerns women. Nothing whatever is left in the Soviet Republic of those laws that put women in a subordinate position. I am speaking specifically of those laws that took advantage of the weaker position of women and put them in a position of inequality and often, even, in a humiliating position, i.e., the laws on divorce and on children born out of wedlock and on the right of a woman to summon the father of a child for maintenance.

It is particularly in this sphere that bourgeois legislation, even, it must be said, in the most advanced countries, takes advantage of the weaker position of women to humiliate them and give them a status of inequality. It is particularly in this sphere that Soviet power has left nothing whatever of the old, unjust laws that were intolerable for working people. We may now say proudly and without any exaggeration that apart from Soviet Russia there is not a country in the world where women enjoy full equality and where women are not placed in the humiliating position felt particularly in day-to-day family life. This was one of our first and most important tasks.

If you have occasion to come into contact with parties that are hostile to the Bolsheviks, if there should come into your hands newspapers published in Russian in the regions occupied by Kolchak or Denikin, or if you happen to talk to people who share the views of those newspapers, you may often hear from them the accusation that Soviet power has violated democracy.

We, the representatives of Soviet power, Bolshevik Communists and supporters of Soviet power are often accused of violating democracy and proof of this is given by citing the fact that Soviet power dispersed the Constituent Assembly. We usually answer this accusation as follows: that democracy and that Constituent Assembly which came into being when private property still existed on earth, when there was no equality between people, when the one who possessed his own capital was the boss and the others worked for him and were his wage-slaves—that was a democracy on which we place no value. Such democracy concealed slavery even in the most advanced countries. We socialists are supporters of democracy only insofar as it eases the position of the working and oppressed people. Throughout the world socialism has set itself the task of combating every kind of exploitation of man by man. That democracy has real value for us which serves the exploited, the underprivileged. If those who do not work are disfranchised that would be real equality between people. Those who do not work should not eat.

In reply to these accusations we say that the question must be presented in this way—how is democracy implemented in various countries? We see that equality is proclaimed in all democratic republics but in the civil laws and in laws on the rights of women—those that concern their position in the family and divorce—we see inequality and the humiliation of women at every step, and we say that this is a violation of democracy specifically in respect of the oppressed. Soviet power has implemented democracy to a greater degree than any of the other, most advanced countries because it has not left in its laws any trace of the inequality of women. Again I say that no other state and no other legislation has ever done for women a half of what Soviet power did in the first months of its existence.

Laws alone, of course, are not enough, and we are by no means content with mere decrees. In the sphere of legislation, however, we have done everything required of us to put women in a position of equality and we have every right to be proud of it. The position of women in Soviet Russia is now ideal as compared with their position in the most advanced states. We tell ourselves, however, that this is, of course, only the beginning.

Owing to her work in the house, the woman is still in a difficult position. To effect her complete emancipation and make her the equal of the man it is necessary for the national economy to be socialised and for women to participate in common productive labour. Then women will occupy the same position as men.

Here we are not, of course, speaking of making women the equal of men as far as productivity of labour, the quantity of labour, the length of the working day, labour conditions, etc., are concerned; we mean that the woman should not, unlike the man, be oppressed because of her position in the family. You all know that even when women have full rights, they still remain factually downtrodden because all housework is left to them. In most cases housework is the most unproductive, the most barbarous and the most arduous work a woman can do. It is exceptionally petty and does not include anything that would in any way promote the development of the woman.

In pursuance of the socialist ideal we want to struggle for the full implementation of socialism, and here an extensive field of labour opens up before women. We are now making serious preparations to clear the ground for the building of socialism, but the building of socialism will begin only when we have achieved the complete equality of women and when we undertake the new work together with women who have been emancipated from that petty, stultifying, unproductive work. This is a job that will take us many, many years.

This work cannot show any rapid results and will not produce a scintillating effect.

We are setting up model institutions, dining-rooms and nurseries, that will emancipate women from housework. And the work of organising all these institutions will fall mainly to women. It has to be admitted that in Russia today there are very few institutions that would help woman out of her state of household slavery. There is an insignificant number of them, and the conditions now obtaining in the Soviet Republic—the war and food situation about which comrades have already given you the details—hinder us in this work. Still, it must be said that these institutions that liberate women from their position as household slaves are springing up wherever it is in any way possible.

We say that the emancipation of the workers must be effected by the workers themselves, and in exactly the same way the emancipation of working women is a matter for the working women themselves. The working women must themselves see to it that such institutions are developed, and this activity will bring about a complete change in their position as compared with what it was under the old, capitalist society.

In order to be active in politics under the old, capitalist regime special training was required, so that women played an insignificant part in politics, even in the most advanced and free capitalist countries. Our task is to make politics available to every working woman. Ever since private property in land and factories has been abolished and the power of the landowners and capitalists overthrown, the tasks of politics have become simple, clear and comprehensible to the working people as a whole, including working women. In capitalist society the woman's position is marked by such inequality that the extent of her participation in politics is only an insignificant fraction of that of the man. The power of the working people is necessary for a change to be wrought in this situation, for then the main tasks of politics will consist of matters directly affecting the fate of the working people themselves.

Here, too, the participation of working women is essential—not only of party members and politically-conscious women, but also of the non-party women and those who are least politically conscious. Here Soviet power opens up a wide field of activity to working women.

We have had a difficult time in the struggle against the forces hostile to Soviet Russia that have attacked her. It was difficult for us to fight on the battlefield against the forces who went to war against the power of the working people and in the field of food supplies against the profiteers, because of the too small number of people, working people, who came whole-heartedly to our aid with their own labour. Here, too, there is nothing Soviet power can appreciate as much as the help given by masses of non-party working women. They may know that in the old, bourgeois society, perhaps, a comprehensive training was necessary for participation in politics and that this was not available to women. The political activity of the Soviet Republic is mainly the struggle against the landowners and capitalists, the struggle for the elimination of exploitation; political activity, therefore, is made available to the working woman in the Soviet Republic and it will consist in the working woman using her organisational ability to help the working man.

What we need is not only organisational work on a scale involving millions; we need organisational work on the smallest scale and this makes it possible for women to work as well. Women can work under war conditions when it is a question of helping the army or carrying on agitation in the army. Women should take an active part in all this so that the Red Army sees that it is being looked after, that solicitude is being displayed. Women can also work in the sphere of food distribution, on the improvement of public catering and everywhere opening dining-rooms like those that are so numerous in Petrograd.

It is in these fields that the activities of working women acquire the greatest organisational significance. The participation of working women is also essential in the organisation and running of big experimental farms and should not take place only in isolated cases. This is something that cannot be carried out without the participation of a large number of working women. Working women will be very useful in this field in supervising the distribution of food and in making food products more easily obtainable. This work can well be done by non-party working women and its accomplishment will do more than anything else to strengthen socialist society.

We have abolished private property in land and almost completely abolished the private ownership of factories; Soviet power is now trying to ensure that all working people, non-party as well as Party members, women as well as men, should take part in this economic development.

The work that Soviet power has begun can only make progress when, instead of a few hundreds, millions and millions of women throughout Russia take part in it. We are sure that the cause of socialist development will then become sound. Then the working people will show that they can live and run their country without the aid of the landowners and capitalists. Then socialist construction will be so soundly based in Russia that no external enemies in other countries and none inside Russia will be any danger to the Soviet Republic.

FIRST ALL-RUSSIA CONGRESS ON ADULT EDUCATION (1919)

1
SPEECH OF GREETING
MAY 6

Comrades, it gives me pleasure to greet the Congress on adult education. You do not, of course, expect me to deliver a speech that goes deeply into this subject, like that delivered by the preceding speaker, Comrade Lunacharsky, who is well-informed on the matter and has made a special study of it. Permit me to confine myself to a few words of greeting and to the observations I have made and thoughts that have occurred to me in the Council of People's Commissars when dealing more or less closely with your work. I am sure that there is not another sphere of Soviet activity in which such enormous progress has been made during the past eighteen months as in the sphere of adult education. Undoubtedly, it has been easier for us and for you to work in this sphere than in others. Here we had to cast aside the old obstacles and the old hindrances. Here it was much easier to do something to meet the tremendous demand for knowledge, for free education and free development, which was felt most among the masses of the workers and peasants; for while the mighty pressure of the masses made it easy for us to remove the external obstacles that stood in their path, to break up the historical bourgeois institutions which bound us to imperialist war and doomed Russia to bear the enormous burden that resulted from this war, we nevertheless felt acutely how heavy the task of re-educating the masses was, the task of organisation and instruction, spreading knowledge, combating that heritage of ignorance, primitiveness, barbarism and savagery that we took over. In this field the struggle had to be waged by entirely different methods; we could count only on the prolonged success and the persistent and systematic influence of the leading sections of the population, an influence which the masses willingly submit to, but often we are guilty of doing less than we could do. I think that in taking these first steps to spread adult education, education, free from the old limits and conventionalities, which the adult population welcomes so much, we had at first to contend with two obstacles. Both these obstacles we inherited from the old capitalist society, which is clinging to us to this day, is dragging us down by thousands and millions of threads, ropes and chains.

The first was the plethora of bourgeois intellectuals, who very often regarded the new type of workers' and peasants' educational institution as the most convenient field for testing their individual theories in philosophy and culture, and in which, very often, the most absurd ideas were hailed as something new, and the supernatural and incongruous were offered as purely proletarian art and proletarian culture.[1] (*Applause.*) This was natural and, perhaps, pardonable in the early days, and the broad movement cannot be blamed for it. I hope that, in the long run, we shall try to get rid of all this and shall succeed.

The second was also inherited from capitalism. The broad masses of the petty-bourgeois working people who were thirsting for knowledge, broke down the old system, but could not propose anything of an organising or organised nature. I had opportunities to observe this in the Council of People's Commissars when the mobilisation of literate persons and the Library Department were discussed, and from these brief observations I realised the seriousness of the situation in this field. True, it is not quite customary to refer to something bad in a speech of greeting. I hope that you are free from these conventionalities, and will not be offended with me for telling you of my somewhat sad observations. When we raised the question of mobilising literate persons, the most striking thing was the brilliant victory achieved by our revolution without immediately emerging from the limits of the bourgeois revolution. It

[1] This refers to the anti-Marxist views of A. Bogdanov and others that had been implanted in the Proletcult (Proletarian Culture) literary and art organisations. Bogdanov and his supporters propagandised reactionary bourgeois philosophical views (Machism) in the guise of "proletarian culture", denied the leading role of the

Party and the Soviet state in cultural development, separated the development of Soviet culture from the general tasks of socialist construction and denied the need to make use of cultural achievements of the past. They tried to give the Proletcult organisations a position that made them independent of the Party and of Soviet power. Lenin spoke resolutely against attempts to implant anti-Marxist, bourgeois theories in the Proletcult organisations. The Central Committee of the R.C.P.(B.) and the Communist group at the First All-Russia Congress of Proletcult Organisations in October 1920 took a decision to subordinate Proletcult organisations to the People's Commissariat of Education, making them departments of that Commissariat. The Central Committee of the R.C.P.(B.) condemned the anti-Marxist, bourgeois tendencies in the Proletcult organisations in a letter headed "On the Proletcult Organisations". The organisations began to decline in 1922.

gave freedom for development to the available forces, but these available forces were petty bourgeois and their watchword was the old one—each for himself and God for all—the very same accursed capitalist slogan which can never lead to anything but Kolchak and bourgeois restoration. If we review what we are doing to educate the illiterate, I think we shall have to draw the conclusion that we have done very little, and that our duty in this field is to realise that the organisation of proletarian elements is essential. It is not the ridiculous phrases which remain on paper that matter, but the introduction of measures which the people need urgently and which would compel every literate person to regard it his duty to instruct several illiterate persons. This is what our decree says[2]; but in this field hardly anything has been done.

When another question was dealt with in the Council of People's Commissars, that of the libraries, I said that the complaints we are constantly hearing about our industrial backwardness being to blame, about our having few books and being unable to produce enough—these complaints, I told myself, are justified. We have no fuel, of course, our factories are idle, we have little paper and we cannot produce books. All this is true, but it is also true that we cannot get at the books that are available. Here we continue to suffer from peasant simplicity and peasant helplessness; when the peasant ransacks the squire's library he runs home in the fear that somebody will take the books away from him, because he cannot conceive of just distribution, of state property that is not something hateful, but is the common property of the workers and of the working people generally. The ignorant masses of peasants are not to blame for this, and as far as the development of the revolution is concerned it is quite legitimate, it is an inevitable stage, and when the peasant took the library and kept it hidden, he could not do otherwise, for he did not know that all the libraries in Russia could be amalgamated and that there would be enough books to satisfy those who can read and to teach those who cannot. At present we must combat the survivals of disorganisation, chaos, and ridiculous departmental wrangling. This must be our main task. We must take up the simple and urgent matter of mobilising the literate to combat illiteracy. We must utilise the books that are available and set to work to organise a network of libraries which will help the people to gain access to every available book; there must be no parallel organisations, but a single, uniform planned organisation. This

[2] This was a decree on "*The Mobilisation of the Literate and the Organisation of Propaganda of the Soviet System*" issued by the Council of People's Commissars on December 10, 1918.

small matter reflects one of the fundamental tasks of our revolution. If it fails to carry out this task, if it fails to set about creating a really systematic and uniform organisation in place of our Russian chaos and inefficiency, then this revolution will remain a bourgeois revolution because the major specific feature of the proletarian revolution which is marching towards communism is this organisation—for all the bourgeoisie wanted was to break up the old system and allow freedom for the development of peasant farming, which revived the same capitalism as in all earlier revolutions.

Since we call ourselves the Communist Party, we must understand that only now that we have removed the external obstacles and have broken down the old institutions have we come face to face with the primary task of a genuine proletarian revolution in all its magnitude, namely, that of organising tens and hundreds of millions of people. After the eighteen months' experience that we all have acquired in this field, we must at last take the right road that will lead to victory over the lack of culture, and over the ignorance and barbarism from which we have suffered all this time. (*Stormy applause.*)

2
DECEPTION OF THE PEOPLE WITH SLOGANS OF FREEDOM AND EQUALITY
MAY 19

Comrades, instead of an appraisal of the current situation, which I think some of you expect today, permit me to answer the most important political questions—not only theoretical, of course, but also practical—which now loom before us, characterise the entire stage of the Soviet revolution and give rise to most controversy; they give rise to most of attacks by people who think they are socialists, and they cause most confusion in the minds of people who think they are democrats and who are particularly fond of accusing us of violating democracy. It seems to me that these general political questions are too often, even constantly, to be found in all present-day propaganda and agitation, and in all anti-Bolshevik literature—when, of course, this literature rises slightly above the level of the downright lying, slander and vituperation of all organs of the bourgeois press. If we take the literature of a slightly higher level I think we shall find that the fundamental questions are the relations between democracy and dictatorship, the tasks of the revolutionary class in a revolutionary period, the tasks of the transition to socialism in general, and the relations between the working class and the peasantry;

I think that these questions serve as the main basis for all present-day political controversies, and although it may sometimes seem to you that it is something of a digression from the immediate topics of the day, the explanation of these issues should be our chief duty. I cannot, of course, undertake to cover all these questions in a short lecture. I have chosen some, which I should like to talk to you about.

I

The first point I have chosen is that of the difficulties of every revolution, of every transition to a new system. If you examine the attacks that are made against the Bolsheviks by people who think that they are socialists and democrats—and as examples of such I can quote the groups of writers in *Vsegda Vperyod!* and *Dyelo Naroda*, newspapers which in my opinion have quite rightly been suppressed in the interests of the revolution, and the representatives of which most often resort to theoretical criticism in attacks of the type natural for organs which our authorities regard as counter-revolutionary—if you examine the attacks on Bolshevism made by this camp, you will find that a constant accusation is the following: "The Bolsheviks promised you, the working people, bread, peace and freedom; but they have not given you bread, or peace, or freedom, they have deceived you, and they have deceived you by abandoning democracy." I shall deal with the departure from democracy separately. At present I will take the other side of this accusation—"The Bolsheviks promised bread, peace and freedom, but the Bolsheviks gave you a continuation of the war, an exceptionally fierce and stubborn struggle, a war of all the imperialists, of the capitalists of all the Entente countries—which means of the most civilised and advanced countries—against tormented, tortured, backward and weary Russia." And these accusations, I repeat, you will find in both the newspapers I have mentioned; you will hear them made in conversation with every bourgeois intellectual who, of course, thinks that he is not bourgeois; you will constantly hear them in conversation with every philistine. And so I ask you to give some thought to this sort of accusation.

Yes, the Bolsheviks did set out to make a revolution against the bourgeoisie, to overthrow the bourgeois government violently, to break away from all the traditional customs, promises and commandments of bourgeois democracy; they did set out to wage a most desperate and violent struggle and war to crush the propertied classes; they did this to extricate Russia, and then the whole of mankind, from the imperialist slaughter and to put an end to all war. Yes, the Bolsheviks did set out to make a revolution in order to achieve all this, and, of course, they have never thought of abandoning this fundamental and main object. Nor is there any doubt that the attempts to emerge from this imperialist slaughter, to smash the rule of the bourgeoisie, prompted all the civilised countries to attack Russia; for such is the political programme of France, Britain and America, no matter how much they insist that they have abandoned the idea of intervention. No matter how much the Lloyd Georges, Wilsons and Clemenceaus may assure us that they have abandoned the idea of intervention, we know that they are lying. We know that the Allied warships which left, and were compelled to leave, Odessa and Sevastopol, are now blockading the Black Sea coast, and are even giving artillery cover to that part of the Crimean Peninsula, near Kerch, where the volunteers[3] are concentrated. They say: "We cannot surrender this to you. Even if the volunteers fail to cope with you, we cannot surrender this part of the Crimean Peninsula, because, if we did, you would be masters of the Azov Sea, you will cut us off from Denikin and prevent us from sending supplies to our friends." Or take the offensive now developing against Petrograd. Yesterday one of our destroyers fought against four enemy destroyers. Is it not clear that this is intervention? Is not the British navy taking part in it? Is not the same thing happening in Archangel and Siberia? The fact is that the whole civilised world is now fighting against Russia.

The question is, did we contradict ourselves when we called upon the working people to make a revolution, promising them peace, and brought things to the pitch that the whole civilised world is now attacking weak, weary, backward and ruined Russia? Or are those who have the presumption to hurl such a reproach at us acting in contradiction to the elementary concepts of democracy and socialism? That is the question. To present this question in its theoretical, general form, I shall draw an analogy. We talk about the revolutionary class, the revolutionary policy of the people, but I suggest you take an individual revolutionary. Take, for example, Chernyshevsky, and appraise his activities. What would be the appraisal of an absolutely ignorant man? Probably he would say: "Well, the man wrecked his own life, found himself in Siberia, and achieved nothing." This is a sample. If we were to hear an argument like this from some unknown person we would say: "At best it comes from a man who is hopelessly ignorant and who is, perhaps, not to blame for being so ignorant that he cannot understand the importance of the activities of an individual revolutionary in the general chain of revolutionary events; or

[3] This refers to whiteguard units of officer volunteers.

else it comes from a scoundrel, a supporter of reaction, who is deliberately trying to frighten the working people away from the revolution." I took the example of Chernyshevsky because, no matter which trend the people who call themselves socialists may belong to, there cannot be any serious disagreement in their appraisal of this individual revolutionary. Everybody will agree that if an individual revolutionary is appraised from the point of view of the outwardly useless and often fruitless sacrifices he has made and the nature of his activities and their connection with the activities of preceding and succeeding revolutionaries is ignored—if the importance of his activities is appraised from this point of view, it is due either to complete ignorance, or to a vicious and hypocritical defence of the interests of reaction, oppression, exploitation and class tyranny. On this point there can be no disagreement.

Now I ask you to carry your thoughts from the individual revolutionary to the revolution of a whole nation, of a whole country. Has any Bolshevik ever denied that the revolution can be finally victorious only when it embraces all, or at all events, some of the most important advanced countries? We have always said that. Did we ever say that it was possible to emerge from the imperialist war simply by the men sticking their bayonets into the ground? I deliberately use this expression which, in the Kerensky period, I personally, and all our comrades, constantly used in resolutions, speeches and newspaper articles. We said: The war cannot be brought to a close by the men sticking their bayonets into the ground. If there are Tolstoyans who think otherwise, they must be pitied as people who have taken leave of their senses, and you can expect nothing better from them.

We said that emergence from this war may involve us in a revolutionary war. We said this from 1915 onwards, and then later, in the Kerensky period. Of course, revolutionary war is also war, just as arduous, sanguinary and painful. And when the revolution develops on a world scale it inevitably arouses resistance on the same world scale. The situation now being such that all the civilised countries in the world are fighting against Russia, we must not be surprised that extremely ignorant peasants are accusing us of failing to keep our promises. Nothing else is to be expected from them. In view of their absolute ignorance, we cannot blame them. Indeed, how can you expect a very ignorant peasant to understand that there are different kinds of wars, that there are just and unjust wars, progressive and reactionary wars, wars waged by advanced classes and wars waged by backward classes, wars waged for the purpose of perpetuating class oppression and wars waged for the purpose of eliminating oppression? To understand this one must be familiar with the class struggle, with the principles of socialism, and at least a little bit familiar with the history of revolution. You cannot expect this from an ignorant peasant.

But when a man who calls himself a democrat, or a socialist, gets up on a platform to make a public statement—irrespective of what he calls himself, Menshevik, Social-Democrat, Socialist-Revolutionary, true socialist, adherent of the Berne International, there are lots of titles of this sort, titles are cheap—when such an individual gets up and charges us with having promised peace and called forth war, what answer should be made to him? Are we to assume that he is as ignorant as the ignorant peasant who cannot distinguish one kind of war from another? Are we to assume that he does not see the difference between the imperialist war, which was a predatory war, and which has now been utterly exposed as such—since the Treaty of Versailles only those who are totally incapable of reasoning and thinking, or who are totally blind, can fail to see that it was a predatory war on both sides—are we to assume that there is even one literate person who fails to see the difference between that predatory war and the war we are waging and which is assuming world-wide dimensions, because the world bourgeoisie have realised that they must fight their last decisive battle? We cannot assume any of this. And that is why we say that anybody who claims to be a democrat, or a socialist, of whatever shade, is a supporter of the bourgeoisie if he in one way or another, directly or indirectly, spreads among the people the accusation that the Bolsheviks are dragging out the Civil War, which is an arduous and painful war, whereas they promised peace; and this is how we shall answer him, and we shall take our stand against him just as we do against Kolchak. Such is our answer. Such is the entire issue.

The gentlemen of *Dyelo Naroda* express astonishment and say: "But we are opposed to Kolchak; what terrible injustice to persecute us!"

It is a great pity, gentlemen, that you refuse to be logical and do not wish to understand the simple ABC of politics from which certain definite deductions must be made. You say that you are opposed to Kolchak. I take up the newspapers *Vsegda Vperyod!* and *Dyelo Naroda* and read the philistine arguments of this type, these moods that are so numerous and that prevail among the intelligentsia. I say that every one of you who spreads such accusations among the people is supporting Kolchak, because he does not understand the elementary, fundamental difference, which every literate person sees, between the imperialist war which we smashed, and the Civil War in which we have become involved. We never concealed from the people the fact that we were taking this risk. We are straining every nerve to defeat the bourgeoisie in this Civil War and to prevent all possibility of class oppression. There has never been, nor can there ever be, a revolution that was guaranteed against a long and arduous struggle, and perhaps filled with the most desperate sacrifices. Those who are unable to distinguish between the sacrifices made in the course of a revolutionary struggle for the sake of its victory, when all the propertied, all the counter-revolutionary classes are fighting against the revolution, those who cannot distinguish between these sacrifices and the sacrifices involved in a predatory war waged by the exploiters, are either abysmally ignorant—and such people ought to be made to learn their ABC, before giving them adult education they ought to be given the most elementary education—or they are out-and-out Kolchak-supporting hypocrites, whatever they may call themselves, or under whichever title they may try to disguise themselves. And these accusations against the Bolsheviks are the most common and widespread. They are really linked up with the broad masses of the working people, because the ignorant peasants find it difficult to understand; they suffer from all war, no matter what the war is about. I am not surprised when I hear an ignorant peasant say: "We had to fight for the tsar, we fought for the Mensheviks, and now we have to fight for the Bolsheviks." This does not surprise me. Indeed, war is war, and entails endless heavy sacrifices. "The tsar said that it was a war for freedom and liberation from a yoke; the Mensheviks said that it was a war for freedom and liberation from a yoke. And now the Bolsheviks say the same thing. They all say the same thing; how can we sort this all out?"

Indeed, how can an ignorant peasant sort it all out? Such a man still has to learn elementary politics. But what can we say about a man who uses such words as "revolution", "democracy", and "socialism", and claims that these words should be used with understanding. He cannot juggle with such words unless he wants to be a political faker, for the difference between a war between two groups of robbers and a war waged by an oppressed class which has risen in revolt against all robbery is an elementary, radical and fundamental difference. The issue is not one of a certain party, class or government justifying war—the real point at issue is the nature of the war, its class content, which class is waging it, and what policy is embodied in it.

II

I shall now leave the question of appraising the arduous and difficult period we are now passing through, and which is inevitably connected with the revolution, for another political issue, which also comes up in all debates, and also gives rise to confusion. This is the question of a bloc with the imperialists, of an alliance, an agreement with the imperialists.

Probably you have read in the newspapers the names of the Socialist-Revolutionaries Volsky and, I believe, Svyatitsky, who recently wrote in *Izvestia*, and issued their manifesto. They regard themselves as Socialist-Revolutionaries who cannot possibly be accused of having supported Kolchak. They left Kolchak, they suffered at the hands of Kolchak, and on coming over to us they rendered us a service against Kolchak. That is true. But examine the arguments these citizens advance. See how they appraise the question of a bloc with the imperialists, of an alliance, or agreement, with the imperialists. I had occasion to read their arguments when the authorities combating counter-revolution confiscated their writings, and when I had to examine their papers to be able to judge correctly the extent of their association with Kolchak. These are undoubtedly the best of the Socialist-Revolutionaries. In their writings I found the following argument, "What do you mean? You want us to repent; you are waiting for us to repent. Never! We have nothing to repent of! You accuse us of having entered into a bloc, an agreement with the Entente, with the imperialists. But did you Bolsheviks not enter into an agreement with the German imperialists? What is the Brest peace? Is not the Brest peace an agreement with imperialism? You entered into an agreement with German imperialism at Brest; we entered into an agreement with French imperialism; we are quits, we have nothing to repent of!"

This argument, which I found in the writings of the persons I have mentioned and of their colleagues, is one that I also find when I call to mind the newspapers I mentioned and when I try to sum up my impressions of philistine conversations. We constantly hear arguments of this kind, it is one of the chief political arguments we have to deal with. I therefore ask you to examine and analyse this argument, and to study it theoretically. What does it amount to? Are those right who say: "We democrats and socialists were in a bloc with the Entente; you were in a bloc with Wilhelm, you concluded the Brest peace. We have no grounds for mutual reproach. We are quits"? Or are we right when we say that those who not merely in words but in deeds are in agreement with the Entente against the Bolshevik revolution are supporters of Kolchak? Although they may deny it a thousand times, although they have personally deserted Kolchak and have proclaimed to the whole people that they are opposed to him, their very roots, the whole nature and significance of their arguments and their deeds make them Kolchak supporters. Who is right? This is the fundamental question of the revolution; and some thought must be given to this.

To explain this point, permit me to draw another analogy, this time, however, not with an individual revolutionary, but with an individual man in the street. Let us suppose that you were riding in an automobile and suddenly your car is surrounded by bandits who point a revolver at your head. Let us suppose that after this you surrender your money and weapons to the bandits, and even let them take the car and ride off. Well? You have given the bandits weapons and money. That is a fact. Now let us suppose that another citizen gave these bandits weapons and money so as to take part in their attacks on peaceful citizens.

In both cases an agreement is reached, whether written or verbal makes no difference. We can picture to ourselves a man giving up his revolver, his weapons and his money, without uttering a word. The nature of the agreement is clear: "I give you my revolver, my weapons and money, and you give me the opportunity to rid myself of your pleasant company." (*Laughter.*) The agreement is a fact. It is also possible for a tacit agreement to be concluded by the man who gives the bandits weapons and money to enable them to rob other people and afterwards give him part of the loot. This, too, is a tacit agreement.

Now I ask you, could any literate person fail to distinguish between these two agreements? You will say that if a man is unable to distinguish between these two agreements and says, "You gave the bandits money and weapons and so don't accuse other people of banditism; what right have you to accuse other people of banditism?"—such a man must be a cretin. If you were to meet such a literate person you would have to admit, or at least 999 out of 1,000 would admit, that he had taken leave of his senses, and that it is useless to discuss political, or even criminal, subjects with such a man.

I now ask you to carry your thoughts from this example to the comparison between the Brest peace and the agreement with the Entente. What was the Brest peace? Was it not an act of violence on the part of bandits who had attacked us when we were honestly proposing peace and were calling upon all nations to overthrow *their own* bourgeoisie? It would have been ridiculous had we started by trying to overthrow the German bourgeoisie! We denounced this treaty before the whole world as a most predatory, plundering treaty, we condemned it and at first even refused to sign it, as we counted on the assistance of the German workers. But when the robbers put a revolver to our heads we said, take the weapons and the money, we will settle accounts with you later on by other means. We know that German imperialism has another enemy, whom blind people have not noticed, namely, the German workers. Can this agreement with imperialism be put on a par with the agreement entered into by democrats, socialists and Socialist-Revolutionaries—don't laugh, the more radical the title the more resonant it sounds—with the agreement they entered into with the Entente to fight against the workers of their own country? But that is what they did, and are doing to this day. The most influential Mensheviks and Socialist-Revolutionaries, those with European reputations, are living abroad even today, and they are in alliance with the Entente. I do not know whether this is a written agreement; probably not, clever people do such things on the quiet. But it is obvious that such an agreement exists, since they are being made such a fuss of, are given passports, and wireless messages are being sent all over the world stating that Axelrod delivered a speech today, that Savinkov, or Avksentyev, will deliver a speech tomorrow, and that Breshkovskaya will speak the day after tomorrow. Is this not an agreement, even if a tacit one? But is it the same kind of agreement with the imperialists as we concluded? Outwardly it resembles ours as much as the act of a man who gives weapons and money to bandits resembles any act of this nature, irrespective of its object and character, at all events, irrespective of the object for which I give the bandits money and weapons: whether it is to get rid of them when they attack me and I find myself in a position where if I do not give them my revolver they will kill me; or I give the bandits money and weapons for the purpose of robbery, of which I am aware, and in the proceeds of which I am to share.

"I, of course, call this liberating Russia from the dictatorship of tyrants. I, of course, am a democrat, because I support the famous Siberian or Archangel democracy, and am fighting, of course, for a Constituent Assembly. Don't dare to suspect that I am pursuing some evil object. And even if I am rendering assistance to those bandits, the British, French and American imperialists, I am doing so only in the interests of democracy, of the Constituent Assembly, of government by the people, of the unity of the working classes of the population, and in order to overthrow those tyrants and usurpers, the Bolsheviks!"

Noble aims, no doubt. But has not everybody who engages in politics heard that politics are not judged by bare statements but by real class content? Which class do you serve? If you are in agreement with the imperialists, are you participating in imperialist banditism or not?

In my "Letter to American Workers", I spoke, among other things, about the American revolutionary people fighting to liberate themselves from England in the eighteenth century, when they were waging one of the first and greatest wars for real liberation in human history, one of the few really revolutionary wars in human history—and this great revolutionary American people, in fighting for their liberation, entered into agreements with the bandits of Spanish and French imperialism, who at that time had colonies in neighbouring parts of America. In alliance with these bandits, the American people fought the English and liberated themselves from them. Have you ever met any literate person anywhere in the world, have you seen any socialists, Socialist-Revolutionaries, representatives of democracy, or whatever it is they call themselves—even the Mensheviks—have you ever heard that any of these have the temerity publicly to blame the American people for this, to say that they violated the principle of democracy, freedom, and so forth? Such a crank has not yet been born. But today, we get people here who call themselves by these titles, and even claim a right to belong to the same International that we belong to, and say that it is merely a piece of Bolshevik mischievousness—and everybody knows that the Bolsheviks are mischievous—to organise their own International and refuse to join the good, old, common to all, united, Berne International!

And there are people who say: "We have nothing to repent of. You entered into an agreement with Wilhelm, we entered into an agreement with the Entente, we are quits!"

I say that if these people have even an elementary knowledge of politics they are Kolchak supporters, no matter how much they personally may have denied this, no matter how much they personally are sick and tired of Kolchak, no matter how much they have suffered at his hands and in spite of their having come over to our side. They are Kolchak supporters because it is impossible to imagine that they do not see the difference between an agreement one is compelled to make in the course of the struggle against the exploiters—and which the exploited classes have been compelled to make over and over again throughout the history of the revolution—and the conduct of our most influential alleged democrats, representatives of our "socialist" intelligentsia, some of whom yesterday and some today entered into agreements with the bandits and robbers of international imperialism against a *section*—as they say—a section of the working classes of their own country. These are Kolchak people, and the only relations possible with them are those between conscious revolutionaries and Kolchak supporters.

III

I now come to the next question, that of our attitude towards democracy in general.

I have already said that the democrats and socialists plead democracy as the most common justification, the most common defence of the political stand taken against us. The most emphatic supporter of this point of view in European literature is, as you, of course, know, Kautsky, the ideological leader of the Second International, and to this day a member of the Berne International. "The Bolsheviks have chosen a method which violates democracy; the Bolsheviks have chosen the method of dictatorship. Hence, their cause is unjust," he says. This argument has been repeated a thousand and a million times, it occurs constantly in all periodicals, including the newspapers I have mentioned. It is being constantly repeated by all intellectuals, and sometimes the ordinary man in the street sub-consciously repeats it in his arguments. "Democracy means freedom, it means equality, it means settling questions by a majority. What can be higher than freedom, equality, and majority decisions? Since you Bolsheviks have departed from this, and even have the presumption to say publicly that you stand above freedom, equality and majority decisions, you must not be surprised, nor must you complain, when we call you usurpers and tyrants!"

We are not in the least surprised at this, for what we desire most of all is clarity; and the only thing we rely on is that the advanced section of the working people should really be conscious of its position. Yes, we said, and say it all the time in our programme, in the programme of our Party, that we shall not allow ourselves to be deceived by such high-sounding slogans as freedom, equality and the will of the majority, and that we shall treat as aiders and abettors of Kolchak those who call themselves democrats, adherents of pure democracy, adherents of consistent democracy and who, directly or indirectly, oppose it to the dictatorship of the proletariat.

Get this clear—you must get it clear. Are the pure democrats guilty of merely preaching pure democracy, defending it from the usurpers, or are they guilty of being on the side of the propertied classes, on the side of Kolchak?

We shall begin our examination with the question of freedom. Needless to say, for every revolution, socialist or democratic, freedom is a very, very important slogan. But our programme says that if freedom runs counter to the emancipation of labour from the yoke of capital, it is a deception. And every one of you who has read Marx—and, I think, even every one who has read at least one popular exposition of Marx's theories—knows that Marx devoted the greater part of his life, the greater part of his literary work, and the greater part of his scientific studies to ridiculing freedom, equality, the will of the majority, and all the Benthams who wrote so beautifully about these things, and to proving that these phrases were merely a screen to cover up the freedom of the commodity owners, the freedom of capital, which these owners use to oppress the masses of the working people.

At the present time, when things have reached the stage of overthrowing the rule of capital all over the world, or at all events in one country; in this historical epoch, when the struggle of the oppressed working people for the complete overthrow of capital and the abolition of commodity production stands in the forefront, we say that all those who in such a political situation talk about "freedom in general", who in the name of this freedom oppose the dictatorship of the proletariat are doing nothing more nor less than aiding and abetting the exploiters, for unless freedom promotes the emancipation of labour from the yoke of capital, it is a deception, as we openly say in our Party programme. Perhaps this is superfluous from the point of view of the outward structure of the programme, but it is most fundamental from the point of view of our propaganda and agitation, from the point of view of the principle of the proletarian struggle and proletarian power. We know perfectly well that we have to contend against world capital; we know perfectly well that at one time it was the task of world capital to create freedom, that it overthrew feudal slavery, that it created bourgeois freedom. We know perfectly well that this was epoch-making progress. And yet we say that we are opposing capitalism in general, republican capitalism, democratic capitalism, free capitalism; and, of course, we know that it will raise the standard of liberty against us. But to this we have our answer, and we deemed it necessary to give this answer in our programme—all freedom is deception if it runs counter to the emancipation of labour from the yoke of capital.

But, perhaps, this is not the case? Perhaps there is no contradiction between freedom and the emancipation of labour from the yoke of capital? Take the West-European countries that you have visited, or at least have read about. Every book you read describes their system as the freest system. And now, these civilised countries of Western Europe—France and Britain—and America have raised this standard, are marching against the Bolsheviks "in the name of freedom". Only the other day—we now get French newspapers but rarely because we are completely surrounded, but we do get wireless information, because, after all, they cannot blockade the air, and we intercept foreign wireless messages—the other day I had the opportunity of reading a wireless message that was sent out by the predatory government of France to the effect that in fighting the Bolsheviks and supporting their opponents, France was remaining true to her "lofty ideals of freedom". We hear this sort of thing at every step, it is the general tone of their polemics against us.

But what do they mean by freedom? By freedom these civilised Frenchmen, Englishmen and Americans mean, say, freedom of assembly. The constitution should contain the clause: "Freedom of assembly for all citizens." "This," they say, "is the substance, this is the principal manifestation of freedom. But you Bolsheviks have violated freedom of assembly."

To this we answer indeed, the freedom that you British, French and American gentlemen preach is a deception if it runs counter to the emancipation of labour from the yoke of capital. You have forgotten a detail, you civilised gentlemen. You have forgotten that your freedom is inscribed in a constitution which *sanctions private property*. That is the whole point.

In your constitution you have freedom side by side with private property. The fact that you recognise freedom of assembly, of course, marks vast progress compared with the feudal system, with medievalism, with serfdom. All socialists admitted this when they took advantage of the freedom of bourgeois society to teach the proletariat how to throw off the yoke of capitalism.

But your freedom is only freedom on paper, but not in fact. By that I mean that the large halls that are to be found in big cities—like this hall, for example—belong to the capitalists and landowners, and are sometimes called "Assembly Rooms for the Gentry". You may freely assemble in these halls, citizens of the Russian Democratic Republic, but remember that they are private property and, pardon me for saying so, you must respect private property, otherwise you will be Bolsheviks, criminals, murderers, robbers and mischief-makers. But we say: "We shall change all this. We shall first convert these Assembly Rooms into premises for workers' organisations and then begin to talk about freedom of assembly." You accuse us of violating freedom. But we say that all freedom is deception if it is not subordinated to the task of emancipating labour from the yoke of capital. The freedom of assembly inscribed in the constitutions of all bourgeois republics is a deception because in order to assemble in a civilised country, which after all has not abolished winter, has not changed its climate, it is necessary to have premises in which to assemble, and the best of these premises are private property. First, we shall confiscate the best premises and then begin to talk about freedom.

We say that to grant freedom of assembly to the capitalists would be a heinous crime against the working people; it would mean freedom of assembly for counter-revolutionaries. We say to the bourgeois intellectual gentlemen, to the gentlemen who advocate democracy—you lie when you throw in our face the accusation of violating freedom. When your great bourgeois revolutionaries made a revolution in England in 1649, and in France in 1792-93, they did not grant freedom of assembly to the royalists. The French revolution is called great because it did not suffer from the flabbiness, half-heartedness and phrase mongering which distinguished many of the revolutions of 1848, but was an effective revolution which, after overthrowing the royalists, completely crushed them. And we shall do the same thing with the capitalist gentlemen; for we know that in order to emancipate the working people from the yoke of capital we must deprive the capitalists of freedom of assembly; their "freedom" must be abolished, or curtailed. This will help to emancipate labour from the yoke of capital; it will help the cause of that true freedom under which there will be no buildings inhabited by single families, and which belong to private individuals, such as landowners, capitalists, or to joint-stock companies. When that time comes, when people have forgotten that it was possible for public buildings to be somebody's property, we shall be in favour of complete "freedom". When the world is inhabited only by those who work, and when people have forgotten that it was possible for idlers to have been members of society—this will not be very soon, and the bourgeois and bourgeois intellectual gentlemen are to blame for the delay—we shall then be in favour of freedom of assembly for all. At the present time, however, freedom of assembly would mean freedom of assembly for the capitalists, for counter-revolutionaries. We are fighting against them, we are resisting them, and we say that we deprive them of this freedom.

We are marching into battle—this is the meaning of the dictatorship of the proletariat. Gone is the time of naïve, utopian, fantastic, mechanical and intellectual socialism, when people imagined that it was sufficient to convince the majority, that it was sufficient to paint a beautiful picture of socialist society to persuade the majority to adopt socialism. Gone, too, is the time when it was possible to entertain oneself and others with these children's fairy-tales. Marxism, which recognises the necessity for the class struggle, asserts that mankind can reach the goal of socialism only through the dictatorship of the proletariat. The word dictatorship is a cruel, stern, bloody and painful one; it is not a word to play with. Socialists advance this slogan because they know that the exploiters will surrender only after a desperate and relentless struggle, and that they will try to cover up their own rule by means of all sorts of high-sounding words.

Freedom of assembly—what can be loftier, what can be finer than this term? Is the development of the working people and of their mentality conceivable without freedom of assembly? Are the principles of humanity conceivable without freedom of assembly? But we say that the freedom of assembly inscribed in the constitution of Great Britain and the United States of America is a deception because it ties the hands of the masses of the working people during the whole period of their transition to socialism; it is a deception because we know perfectly well that the bourgeoisie will do all in their power to overthrow this new government, which is so unusual, and which seems so "monstrous" at first. Those who have thought about the class struggle and have anything like a clear and definite idea of the relations between the workers in revolt and the bourgeoisie, who have been overthrown in one country, but have not yet been overthrown in all countries, and who, because they have not been overthrown everywhere, are rushing into the struggle with greater ferocity than ever, will agree that it cannot be otherwise.

It is precisely after the bourgeoisie is overthrown that the class struggle assumes its acutest forms. And we have no use for those democrats and socialists who deceive themselves and deceive others by saying: "The bourgeoisie have been overthrown, the struggle is all over." The struggle is not over, it has only just started, because, to this day, the bourgeoisie have not reconciled themselves to the idea that they have been overthrown. On the eve of the October Revolution they were very nice and polite, and Milyukov, Chernov and the *Novaya Zhizn* people said jestingly: "Now, please, Bolshevik gentlemen, form a Cabinet, take power yourselves for a few weeks, that would be a great help to us!" This is exactly what Chernov wrote on behalf of the Socialist-Revolutionaries, what Milyukov wrote in *Rech*, and what the semi-Menshevik *Novaya Zhizn* wrote. They spoke in jest because they did not take matters seriously. But now they see that matters are serious, and the British, French and Swiss bourgeoisie, who thought that their "democratic republics" were armour which protected them, see and realise that matters have become serious, and now they are all arming. If only you could see what is going on in free Switzerland, how, literally, every bourgeois is arming, how they are forming a White Guard, because they know that it is now a matter of preserving the privileges which enable them to keep millions of people in a state of wage-slavery. The struggle has now assumed world-wide dimensions, and therefore, anybody who opposes us with such catchwords as "democracy", and "freedom", takes the side of the propertied classes, deceives the people, for he fails to understand that up to now freedom and democracy have meant freedom and democracy *for the propertied classes* and only crumbs from their table for the propertyless.

What is freedom of assembly when the working people are crushed by slavery to capital and by toil for the benefit of capital? It is a deception; and in order to achieve freedom for the working people it is first of all necessary to overcome the resistance of the exploiters, and since I am faced with the resistance of a whole class, it is obvious that I cannot promise this class either freedom, equality, or majority decisions.

IV

I shall now pass from freedom to equality. This is a much more profound subject. This brings us to a still more serious, a more painful question, one that gives rise to considerable disagreement.

The revolution in its course sweeps away one exploiting class after another. First, it swept away the monarchy, and by equality implied an elected government, a republic. Proceeding further it swept away the landowners; and you know that the keynote of the entire struggle against the medieval system, against feudalism, was the slogan "equality". All are equal irrespective of social-estate; all are equal, millionaires and paupers alike. This is what the great revolutionaries of the period that has gone into history as the period of the great French Revolution said, thought and sincerely believed. The slogan of the revolution against the landowners was equality, and by equality was meant that the millionaires and the workers should have equal rights. The revolution developed. It said that "equality"—we did not specify this in our programme, for one cannot go on repeating the same thing endlessly; it is as clear as what we said about freedom—that equality is a deception if it runs counter to the emancipation of labour from the yoke of capital. That is what we say, and it is absolutely true. We say that a democratic republic with present-day equality is a fraud, a deception; here there is no equality, nor can there be. It is prevented by the private ownership of the means of production and money, capital. It is possible, at one stroke, to confiscate privately-owned mansions and fine buildings, it is possible in a relatively short period to confiscate capital and the means of production. But try to abolish the private ownership of money.

Money is congealed social wealth, congealed social labour. Money is a token which enables its owner to take tribute from all the working people. Money is a survival of yesterday's exploitation. That is what money is. Can it be abolished at one stroke? No. Even before the socialist revolution the socialists wrote that it is impossible to abolish money at one stroke, and our experience corroborates this. There must be very considerable technical and, what is much more difficult and much more important, organisational achievement before we can abolish money; and until then we must put up with equality in words, in the constitution; we must put up with a situation in which everybody who possesses money practically has the right to exploit. We could not abolish money at one stroke. We say that for the time being money will remain, and remain for a fairly long time in the transition period from the old capitalist system to the new socialist system. Equality is a deception if it runs counter to the emancipation of labour from the yoke of capital.

Engels was a thousand times right when he said that the concept of equality is a most absurd and stupid prejudice *if it does not imply* the abolition of classes.[4] Bourgeois professors attempted to use the concept equality as grounds for accusing us of wanting all men to be alike. They themselves invented this absurdity and wanted to ascribe it to the socialists. But in their ignorance they did not know that the socialists—and precisely the founders of modern scientific socialism, Marx and Engels—had said: equality is an empty phrase if it does not imply the abolition of classes. We want to abolish classes, and in this sense we are for equality. But the claim that we want all men to be alike is just nonsense, the silly invention of an intellectual who sometimes conscientiously strikes a pose, juggles with words, but says nothing—I don't care whether he calls himself a writer, a scholar, or anything else.

But we say that our goal is equality, and by that we mean the abolition of classes. Then the class distinction between workers and peasants should be abolished. That is exactly our object. A society in which the class distinction between workers and peasants still exists is neither a communist society nor a socialist society. True, if the word socialism is interpreted in a certain sense, it might be called a socialist society, but that would be mere sophistry, an argument about words. Socialism is the first stage of communism; but it is not worthwhile arguing about words.

[4] Frederick Engels, *Anti-Dühring*, Moscow, 1959, pp. 147-48.

One thing is clear, and that is, that as long as the class distinction between workers and peasants exists, it is no use talking about equality, unless we want to bring grist to the mill of the bourgeoisie. The peasantry constitute a class of the patriarchal era, a class which has been reared by decades and centuries of slavery; and throughout all these decades the peasants existed as *small proprietors*, first, under the heel of other classes, and later, formally free and equal, but as *property-owners and the owners of food products.*

This brings us to the question which most of all rouses the ire of our enemies, which most of all creates doubt in the minds of inexperienced and thoughtless people, and which separates us most of all from those would-be democrats and socialists who are offended because we do not recognise them as such, but call them supporters of the capitalists, perhaps due to their ignorance, but supporters of the capitalists all the same.

Their social conditions, production, living and economic conditions make the peasant half worker and half huckster.

This is a fact. And you cannot get away from this fact until you have abolished money, until you have abolished exchange. And for this years and years of the stable rule by the proletariat is needed; for only the proletariat is capable of vanquishing the bourgeoisie. We are told: "You are violators of equality, you have violated equality not only with the exploiters—'with this I am inclined to agree', some Socialist-Revolutionary or Menshevik who does not know what he is talking about may say—but you have violated equality between the workers and the peasants, you have violated the equality of 'labour democracy', you are criminals!" In answer to this we say: "Yes, we have violated equality between the workers and peasants, and we assert that you who stand for this equality are supporters of Kolchak." Recently I read a splendid article by Comrade Germanov, in *Pravda*, in which he deals with the theses drawn up by Citizen Sher, one of the most "socialistic" of the Menshevik Social-Democrats. These theses were submitted to one of our co-operative organisations, and they are of such a nature that they deserve to be engraved on a tablet and hung up in every volost executive committee with an inscription underneath stating: "This is Kolchak's man."

I know perfectly well that Citizen Sher and his friends will call me a slanderer for this, and perhaps something worse. Nevertheless, I invite those people who have learned the ABC of political economy and of politics to make a very careful study to see who is right and who is wrong. Citizen Sher says that the Soviet government's food policy, and its economic policy in general, is all wrong; that it is necessary, gradually at first, and then to an increasing degree, to grant freedom to trade in food products, and to safeguard private property.

I say that this is Kolchak's economic programme, his economic basis. I assert that anybody who has read Marx, especially the first chapter of *Capital*, anybody who has read at least Kautsky's popular outline of Marx's theories entitled *The Economic Theories of Karl Marx*, must come to the conclusion that in the midst of a proletarian revolution against the bourgeoisie, at a time when landowner and capitalist property is being abolished, when the country that has been ruined by four years of imperialist war is starving, freedom to trade in grain would mean freedom for the capitalists, freedom to restore the rule of capital. This is Kolchak's economic programme, for Kolchak does not rest on air.

It is rather silly to denounce Kolchak only because of the atrocities he committed against the workers, or even because he flogged schoolmistresses for sympathising with the Bolsheviks. This is a vulgar defence of democracy, a silly accusation against Kolchak. Kolchak operates with the means he has at hand. But what is his economic basis? His basis is freedom of trade. This is what he stands for; and *this is why* all the capitalists support him. But you say: "I have left Kolchak, I do not support him." This stands to your credit, of course; but it does not prove that you have a head on your shoulders and are able to think. This is the answer we give to these people, without casting any slur on the honour of the Socialist-Revolutionaries and the Mensheviks who deserted Kolchak when they realised that he is a tyrant. But if such people, in a country which is fighting a desperate struggle against Kolchak, continue to fight for the "equality of labour democracy", for freedom to trade in grain, they are still supporting Kolchak, the only trouble being that they do not understand this and cannot reason logically.

Kolchak—it does not matter whether his name is Kolchak or Denikin, their uniforms may be different, but their natures are the same—is able to hold out because, having captured a region rich in grain, he grants freedom to trade in grain and permits the *free restoration of capitalism*. This was the case in all revolutions, and this will be the case in this country if we abandon the dictatorship of the proletariat for the sake of the "freedom" and "equality" of the democratic, Socialist-Revolutionary, Left-Menshevik and other gentlemen, sometimes including the anarchists—the number of titles is infinite. In the Ukraine at the present time, every gang chooses a political title, each more free and democratic than the other, and there is a gang to every uyezd.

The "advocates of the interests of the working peasantry", mainly the Socialist-Revolutionaries, propose equality between the workers and the peasants. Others, like Citizen Sher, have studied Marxism, but they still do not understand that there can be no equality between the workers and the peasants in the period of transition from capitalism to socialism, and that those who promise this should be regarded as advocating Kolchak's programme, even if they do so unwittingly. I assert that anybody who gives some thought to the actual conditions prevailing in this completely ruined country will understand this.

The "socialists" who assert that in this country we are in the period of the bourgeois revolution, constantly accuse us of having introduced "consumers'" communism. Some of them say it is communism for soldiers, and imagine that they are superior to this, imagine that they have risen above this "base" form of communism. But these are simply people who juggle with words. They have seen books, studied books, repeat what is in books, but they understand nothing about what the books say. There are scholars, and even very learned scholars, like that. They have read in books that socialism represents the highest development of production. Kautsky does nothing else but repeat this sort of thing even now. The other day I read in a German newspaper, which got here by accident, a report of the last Congress of Workers' Councils in Germany. Kautsky was one of the *rapporteurs* at this Congress, and in his report he emphasised—not he personally, but his wife; he was sick, and so his wife read the report—in this report he emphasised that socialism represents the highest development of production, that without production neither capitalism nor socialism was possible, and that this the German workers did not understand.

Poor German workers. They are fighting Scheidemann and Noske, fighting against the butchers, striving to overthrow the power of Scheidemann and Noske, the butchers who continue to call themselves Social-Democrats, and they think civil war is going on! Liebknecht was murdered, and so was Rosa Luxemburg. All the Russian bourgeois say—and this was stated in an Ekaterinodar newspaper: "This is what ought to be done to our Bolsheviks!" This is exactly what this paper stated. Those who understand what is going on know perfectly well that this is the opinion of the entire world bourgeoisie. We must defend ourselves. Scheidemann and Noske are waging civil war against the proletariat. War is war. The German workers think that they are in a state of civil war and all other questions are of minor importance. The first task is to feed the workers. Kautsky thinks that this is "soldiers'" or "consumers'" communism, and that it is necessary to develop production! . . .

Oh, how clever you are, gentlemen! But how can production be developed in a country that is being plundered and ruined by the imperialists, and which lacks coal, raw materials and machinery? "Develop production!" There is not a meeting of the Council of People's Commissars, or of the Council of Defence that does not share out the last millions of *poods* of coal or oil, and find ourselves in a terrible fix when the commissars take the last scraps and even then no one has enough, and we have to decide which factory to close down, in which place to leave the workers without work—a painful question, but one we are compelled to decide because we have no coal. The coal is in the Donets Basin; the coal has been destroyed by the German invaders. This is a typical state of affairs. Take Belgium or Poland. The same thing is happening everywhere as a consequence of the imperialist war. Hence, unemployment and starvation are likely to last many years, for some flooded mines take many years to restore. And yet we are told that socialism means increasing output. You have read books, good, kind gentlemen, you have written books, but you don't understand a scrap of what is in the books. (*Applause.*)

Of course, if it were a case of capitalist society in peacetime, peacefully developing into socialism, there would be no more urgent task before us than that of increasing output. But the little word "if" makes all the difference. *If* only socialism had come into being peacefully, in the way the capitalist gentlemen did not want to see it born. But there was a slight hitch. Even if there had been no war, the capitalist gentlemen would have done all in their power to prevent such a peaceful evolution. Great revolutions, even when they commence peacefully, as was the case with the great French Revolution, end in furious wars which are instigated by the counter-revolutionary bourgeoisie. Nor can it be otherwise, if we look at it from the point of view of the class struggle and not from the point of view of philistine phrase-mongering about liberty, equality, labour democracy and the will of the majority, of all the dull-witted, philistine phrase-mongering to which the Mensheviks, Socialist-Revolutionaries and all these "democrats" treat us. There can be no peaceful evolution towards socialism. In the present period, after the imperialist war, it is ridiculous to expect peaceful evolution, especially in a ruined country. Take France. France is one of the victors, and yet the production of grain there has dropped to half. In Britain they are saying that they are now paupers—I read this in an English bourgeois newspaper. And yet the

Communists in a ruined country are blamed because industry is at a standstill! Whoever says this is either an utter idiot—even if he thrice calls himself a leader of the Berne International—or else a traitor to the workers.

The primary task in a ruined country is to save the working people. The primary productive force of human society as a whole, is the workers, the working people. If they survive, we shall save and restore *everything.*

We shall have to put up with many years of poverty, retrogression to barbarism. The imperialist war has thrown us back to barbarism; but if we save the working people, if we save the primary productive force of human society—the workers—we shall recover everything, but if we fail to save them, we shall perish, so that those who are now shouting about "consumers'", or "soldiers'", communism, who look down upon others with contempt and imagine that they are superior to these Bolshevik Communists, are, I repeat, absolutely ignorant of political economy, and pick out passages from books like a scholar whose head is a card index box filled with quotations from books, which he picks out as he needs them; but if a new situation arises which is not described in any book, he becomes confused and grabs the wrong quotation from the box.

At the present time, when the country is ruined, our main and fundamental task is to save the lives of the workers, *to save the workers*, for the workers are dying because the factories are at a standstill, and the factories are at a standstill because there is no fuel, and because our production is all artificial, industry is isolated from raw material sources. It is the same thing all over the world. Raw materials for the Russian cotton mills must be transported from Egypt, America, or the nearer Turkestan. Try to obtain these when the counter-revolutionary gangs and the British forces have captured Ashkhabad and Krasnovodsk. Try to obtain them from Egypt or America when the railways lie in ruins, when they are at a standstill because there is no coal.

We must save the workers even if they are unable to work. If we keep them alive for the next few years we shall save the country, save society and socialism. If we don't, we shall slip back into wage-slavery. This is how things stand with the socialism that springs not from the imagination of a peaceful simpleton who calls himself a Social-Democrat, but from actual reality, from the fierce, desperately fierce class struggle. This is a fact. We must sacrifice everything to save the lives of the workers. And in the light of this, when people come to us and say they are in favour of the equality of labour democracy, whereas the Communists do not even allow equality between the workers and peasants, our answer is: the workers and peasants are equal as working people, but the well-fed grain profiteer is not the equal of the hungry worker. This is the only reason why our Constitution says that the workers and peasants are not equal.

Do you say that they ought to be equal? Let us weigh and count it up. Take sixty peasants and ten workers. The sixty peasants possess surplus stocks of grain. They are clothed in rags, but they have bread. Take the ten workers. After the imperialist war they, too, are in rags, but they are also exhausted, they have no bread, fuel or raw materials. The factories are idle. Well, are they equal? Should the sixty peasants have the right to decide and the ten workers be obliged to obey? The great principle of equality, unity of labour democracy and deciding by a majority vote!

That is what they tell us. And we tell them that they are mere clowns who confuse the hunger problem and obscure it with their high-sounding phrases.

We ask you whether the workers in a ruined country where the factories are idle ought to submit to the decision of the majority of peasants when the latter refuse to deliver their surplus stocks of grain. Have they the right to take these surplus stocks, by force, if necessary, if there is no other way? Give us a straightforward answer! But when we get right down to brass tacks they begin to twist and wriggle.

Industry is ruined in all countries, and it will remain in that state for several years, because it is easy to set fire to factories or to flood mines, it is easy to blow up railway wagons and to wreck locomotives—any fool can do that, even if he calls himself a German or French officer, and is very efficient, especially when he has good instruments for causing explosions, good fire-arms, and so forth. But it is a very difficult matter to restore it all. That will take years.

The peasantry constitute a special class. As working people they are hostile to capitalist exploitation; but at the same time they are property-owners. For centuries the peasant has been brought up to believe that the grain is his and he is at liberty to sell it. "This is my right," each one thinks, "because it is the fruit of my labour, my sweat and blood." This mentality cannot be changed overnight. It can be changed only as a result of a long and stern struggle. Whoever imagines that socialism can be achieved by one person convincing another, and that one a third, is at best an infant, or else a political hypocrite; and, of course, the majority of those who speak on political platforms belong to the latter category.

The whole point is that the peasants are accustomed to having the right to trade in grain. After we had abolished the capitalist institutions we found that there was still another force which kept capitalism going—

the force of habit. And the more resolutely we abolished the institutions on which capitalism was based, the more strongly we felt the effects of this other force on which capitalism was based—the force of habit. Under favourable circumstances, institutions can be smashed at one stroke; but habit, never, no matter how favourable circumstances may be. Although we have given all the land to the peasants, have liberated them from landed proprietorship, and have swept away everything that held them in bondage, they nevertheless continue to think that "freedom" means freedom to trade in grain; and they regard as tyranny the compulsory surrendering of surplus stocks of grain at fixed prices. Why, what do you mean by "surrender"? they ask indignantly, especially since our grain supply apparatus is still defective because the entire bourgeois intelligentsia is on the side of Sukharevka.[5] Naturally, this machinery has to rely on people who are only just learning, at best—if they are conscientious and devoted to their task—will learn their business in a few years, and until that time the machinery will be defective, and sometimes all sorts of rascals who call themselves Communists will find their way into it. This danger threatens every ruling party, the victorious proletariat of every country, for it is impossible either to break the resistance of the bourgeoisie or to build up efficient machinery overnight. We know perfectly well that the machinery of the Commissariat of Food is still bad. Recently a scientific statistical investigation was made into the food conditions of the workers in the non-agricultural *gubernias*. The investigation showed that the workers obtain half their food from the Commissariat of Food and the other half from the profiteers; for the first half they pay one-tenth of their total expenditure on food, and for the other half they pay nine-tenths.

The first half of the food supplies, collected and delivered by the Commissariat of Food, is badly collected, of course, but it is collected on socialist and not on capitalist lines. It is collected by defeating the profiteers, and not by compromising with them; it is collected by sacrificing all other interests in the world, including the interests of the formal "equality" which the Mensheviks, Socialist-Revolutionaries and Co. make so much fuss about, to the interests of the starving workers. You keep your "equality", gentlemen, and we shall keep our hungry workers we have saved from starvation. No matter how much the Mensheviks may accuse us of violating "equality", the fact is that we have solved half

[5] *Sukharevka*—the name of a market that once existed in Moscow. During the Civil War it was here that profiteers sold their goods. The word "Sukharevka" is used in the broader sense of "freedom to trade in food".

our food problem in spite of unprecedented and incredible difficulties. And we say that if sixty peasants have surplus stocks of grain and ten workers are starving, we must not talk about "equality" in general, or about "the equality of working people", but say that it is the bounden duty of the sixty peasants to submit to the decisions of the ten workers and to give them, or at least to loan them, their surplus stocks of grain.

The science of political economy, if anybody has learned anything from it, the history of revolution, the history of political evolution throughout the whole of the nineteenth century show that the peasants follow the lead of either the workers or the bourgeoisie. Nor can they do otherwise. Some democrats may, of course, take exception to this, others may think that, being a malicious Marxist, I am slandering the peasants. They say the peasants constitute the majority, they are working people, and yet cannot follow their own road. Why?

If you don't know why, I would say to such citizens, read the elements of Marx's political economy in Kautsky's popular exposition, think about the evolution of any of the great revolutions of the eighteenth and nineteenth centuries, about the political history of any country in the nineteenth century, and you will learn why. The economics of capitalist society are such that the ruling power can be only capital or the proletariat which has overthrown capital.

There are no other forces in the economics of this society.

A peasant is half worker and half huckster. He is a worker because he earns his bread by the sweat of his brow and is exploited by the landowners, capitalists and merchants. He is a huckster because he sells grain, an article of necessity, an article for which a man will give up all his possessions if there is a shortage of it. Hunger is no man's friend. People will pay a thousand rubles, any sum of money, will give up all their property, for bread.

The peasant cannot be blamed for this; he is living under a commodity economy and has been for scores and hundreds of years, and is accustomed to exchange grain for money. You cannot change a habit or abolish money overnight. To abolish money you must organise the distribution of products for hundreds of millions of people, and this is something that must take many years. And so, as long as the commodity system exists, as long as there are starving workers side by side with well-fed peasants who are concealing their surplus stocks of grain, the antagonism of workers' and peasants' interests will persist. And whoever attempts to use phrases like "freedom", "equality" and "labour democracy" to brush aside this real antagonism created by the actual state of affairs, is at best a mere phrase-monger, and at worst a hypocritical champion of capitalism. If capitalism defeats the revolution it will do so by taking advantage of the ignorance of the peasants, by bribing them and luring them with the prospect of a return to freedom of trade. Actually, the Mensheviks and Socialist-Revolutionaries side with capitalism against socialism.

The economic programme of Kolchak, Denikin and all the Russian whiteguards is freedom to trade. They understand this, and it is not their fault that Citizen Sher does not. The economic facts of life do not change because a certain party does not understand them. The slogan of the bourgeoisie is freedom to trade. Efforts are made to beguile the peasants by asking them whether it would not be better to live in the good old way. Whether it would not be better to live freely by the free sale of the fruits of farm labour. What could be fairer? This is what those who consciously support Kolchak say, and they are right from the point of view of the interests of capital. To restore the power of capital in Russia it is necessary to rely on tradition—on the prejudices of the peasants as against their common sense, on their old habits of trading on the open market, and it is necessary forcibly to crush the resistance of the workers. There is no other way. The Kolchaks are right from the point of view of capital; their economic and political programme ties up neatly, there are no loose ends; they know there is a connection between freedom for peasants to trade and shooting down the workers. They are connected even though Citizen Sher is unaware of it. Freedom to trade in grain is the economic programme of Kolchak; the shooting of tens of thousands of workers—as occurred in Finland—is a necessary means of realising this programme, because the workers will not voluntarily surrender their gains. The connection cannot be broken, yet the Mensheviks and Social-Revolutionaries, who are totally ignorant of economic science and politics, who, being terrified philistines, have forgotten the ABC of socialism, are trying to make us forget this connection by talking about "equality" and "freedom", by shouting about our violating the principle of equality of "labour democracy" and saying that our Constitution is "unfair".

The vote of one worker is equal to several peasant votes. Is that unfair?

No, in the period when it is necessary to overthrow capital it is quite fair. I know where you have borrowed your conception of fairness from; you have borrowed it from yesterday's capitalist era. The equality, the freedom of commodity owners—that is your conception of fairness. A petty-bourgeois survival of petty-bourgeois prejudices—that is what your fairness, your equality, your labour democracy amount to. We, however, subordinate fairness to the interests of defeating capital. And capital can be defeated only by the united efforts of the proletariat.

Can tens of millions of peasants be firmly united against capital, against freedom of trade, overnight? No, economic conditions would prevent it even if the peasants were quite free and much more cultured. It cannot be done because different economic conditions and long years of preparation are needed for this. And who will make these preparations? Either the proletariat or the bourgeoisie.

Owing to their economic status in bourgeois society the peasants must follow either the workers or the bourgeoisie. *There is no middle way*. They may waver, become confused, conjure up all sorts of things; they may blame, swear, curse the "bigoted" representatives of the proletariat and the "bigoted" representatives of the bourgeoisie and say that they are the minority. You may curse them, talk loud about the majority, about the broad universal character of your labour democracy, about pure democracy. There is no end to the number of words you can string together, but they will only serve to obscure the fact that if the peasants do not follow the lead of the workers they will follow the lead of the bourgeoisie. There is not, nor can there be, a middle course. And those people who in this most difficult period of transition in history, when the workers are hungry and their industry is at a standstill, *do not help the workers* to take grain at a fairer *but not a "free" price*, not at a capitalist, hucksters' price, are carrying out the Kolchak programme no matter how much they may deny this to themselves, and no matter how sincerely they may be convinced that they are carrying out their own programme conscientiously.

V

I will now deal with the last question on my list, that of the defeat and victory of the revolution. Kautsky, whom I mentioned to you as the chief representative of the old, decayed socialism, does not understand the tasks of the dictatorship of the proletariat. He reproached us, saying that a decision taken by a majority might have ensured a peaceful issue. A decision by a dictatorship is a decision taken by military means. Hence, if you do not win by force of arms you will be vanquished and annihilated, because in civil war no prisoners are taken, it is a war of extermination. This is how terrified Kautsky tried to "terrify" us.

Quite right. What you say is true. We confirm the correctness of your observation and there is nothing more to be said. Civil war is more stern and cruel than any other war. This has been the case throughout history since the time of the civil wars in ancient Rome; wars between nations always ended in a deal between the propertied classes, and only during civil war does the oppressed class exert efforts to exterminate the oppressing class, to eliminate the economic conditions of this class' existence.

I ask you, what is the "revolutionary" worth who tries to scare those who have started the revolution with the prospect that it might suffer defeat? There has never been, there is none, there will not be, nor can there be a revolution which did not stand some risk of defeat. A revolution is a desperate struggle of classes that has reached the peak of ferocity. The class struggle is inevitable. One must either reject revolution altogether or accept the fact that the struggle against the propertied classes will be sterner than all other revolutions. Among socialists who are at all intelligent there was never any difference of opinion on this point. A year ago, when I analysed the apostasy that lay behind Kautsky's statements I wrote the following. Even if—this was in September last year—even if the imperialists were to overthrow the Bolshevik government tomorrow we would not for a moment repent that we had taken power. And not a single class-conscious worker who represents the interests of the masses of the working people would repent, or have any doubt that, in spite of it all, our revolution had triumphed; the revolution triumphs if it brings to the forefront the advanced class which strikes effectively at exploitation. Under such circumstances, the revolution triumphs even if it suffered defeat. This may sound like juggling with words; but to prove the truth of it, let us take a concrete example from history.

Take the great French Revolution. It is with good reason that it is called a great revolution. It did so much for the class that it served, for the bourgeoisie, that it left its imprint on the entire nineteenth century, the century which gave civilisation and culture to the whole of mankind. The great French revolutionaries served the interests of the bourgeoisie although they did not realise it for their vision was obscured by the words "liberty, equality and fraternity"; in the nineteenth century, however, what they had begun was continued, carried out piecemeal and finished in all parts of the world.

In a matter of eighteen months our revolution has done ever so much more for our class, the class we serve, the proletariat, than the great French revolutionaries did.

They held out in their own country for two years, and then perished under the blows of united European reaction, under the blows of the united hordes of the whole world, who crushed the French revolutionaries, reinstated the legitimate monarch in France, the Romanov of the period, reinstated the landowners, and for many decades later crushed every revolutionary movement in France. Nevertheless, the great French Revolution triumphed.

Everybody who studies history seriously will admit that although it was crushed, the French Revolution was nevertheless triumphant, because it laid down for the whole world such firm foundations of bourgeois democracy, of bourgeois freedom, that they could never be uprooted.

In a matter of eighteen months our revolution has done ever so much more for the proletariat, for the class which we serve, for the goal towards which we are striving—the overthrow of the rule of capital—than the French Revolution did for its class. And that is why we say that even if we take the hypothetically possible worst contingency, even if tomorrow some lucky Kolchak were to exterminate the Bolsheviks to the last man, the revolution would still be invincible. And what we say is proved by the fact that the new type of state organisation produced by this revolution has achieved a moral victory among the working class all over the world and is already receiving its support. When the prominent French bourgeois revolutionaries perished in the struggle they were isolated, they were not supported in other countries. All the European states turned against them, chief among them England, although it was an advanced country. After only eighteen months of Bolshevik rule, our revolution succeeded in making the new state organisation which it created, the Soviet organisation, comprehensible, familiar and popular to the workers all over the world, in making them regard it as their own.

I have shown you that the dictatorship of the proletariat is an inevitable, essential and absolutely indispensable means of emerging from the capitalist system. Dictatorship does not mean only force, although it is impossible without force, but also a form of the organisation of labour superior to the preceding form. That is why in my brief speech of greeting at the opening of the Congress I emphasised this fundamental, elementary and extremely simple task *of organisation*; and that is why I am so strongly opposed to all these intellectual fads and "proletarian cultures". As opposed to these fads I advocate the ABC of organisation. Distribute grain and coal in such a way as to take care of every *pood*—this is the object of proletarian discipline. Proletarian discipline is not discipline maintained by the lash, as it was under the rule of the serf-owners, or discipline maintained by starvation, as it is under the rule of the capitalists, but comradely discipline, the discipline of the labour unions. If you solve this elementary and extremely simple problem of organisation, we shall win, for then the peasants—who vacillate between the workers and the capitalists, who cannot make up their minds whether to side with the people of whom they are still suspicious, but cannot deny that these people are creating a more just organisation of production under which there will be no exploitation, and under which "freedom" of trade in grain will be a crime against the state, who cannot make up their minds whether to side with these people or with those who, as in the good old days, promise freedom to trade which is alleged to mean also freedom to work in any way one pleased—the peasants, I say, will whole-heartedly side with us. When the peasants see that the proletariat is organising its state power in such a way as to maintain order—and the peasants want this and demand it, and they are right in doing so, although this desire for order is connected with much that is confused and reactionary, and with many prejudices—they, in the long run, after considerable vacillation, will follow the lead of the workers. The peasants cannot simply and easily pass from the old society to the new overnight. They are aware that the old society ensured "order" by ruining the working people and making slaves of them. But they are not sure that the proletariat can guarantee order. More cannot be expected of these downtrodden, ignorant and disunited peasants. They will not believe words and programmes. And they are quite right not to believe words, for otherwise there would be no end to frauds of every kind. They will believe only deeds, practical experience. Prove to them that you, the united proletariat, the proletarian state, the proletarian dictatorship, are able to distribute grain and coal in such a way as to husband every *pood*, that you are able to arrange matters so that every *pood* of surplus grain and coal is distributed not by the profiteers, shall not profit the heroes of Sukharevka, but shall be fairly distributed, supplied to starving workers, even to sustain them during periods of unemployment when the factories and workshops are idle. Prove that you can do this. This is the fundamental task of proletarian culture, of proletarian organisation. Force can be used even if those who resort to it have no economic roots, but in that case, history will doom it to failure. But force can be applied with the backing of the advanced class, relying on the loftier principles of the socialist system, order and organisation. *In that case, it may suffer temporary failure, but in the long run it is invincible.*

If the proletarian organisation proves to the peasants that it can maintain proper order, that labour and bread are fairly distributed and that care is being taken to husband every *pood* of grain and coal, that we workers are able to do this with the aid of our comradely, trade union discipline, that we resort to force in our struggle only to protect the interests of labour, that we take grain from profiteers and not from working people, that we want to reach an understanding with the middle peasants, the working peasants, and that we are ready to provide them with all we can at present—when the peasants see all this, their alliance with the working class, their alliance with the proletariat, will be indestructible. And this is what we aim at.

But I have digressed somewhat from my subject and must return to it. Today, in all countries, the word "Bolshevik" and the word "Soviet" have ceased to be regarded as queer terms, as they were only recently, like the word "Boxer", which we repeated without understanding what it meant. The word "Bolshevik" and the word "Soviet" are now being repeated in all the languages of the world. Every day the class-conscious workers see that the bourgeoisie of all countries release a flood of lies about Soviet power in the millions of copies of their newspapers, but they learn from this vituperation. Recently I read some American newspapers. I read the speech of a certain American parson who said that the Bolsheviks were immoral, that they had nationalised women, that they are robbers and plunderers. And I also read the reply of the American Socialists. They are distributing at five cents a copy the Constitution of the Soviet Republic of Russia, of this "dictatorship", which does not provide "equality of labour democracy". They reply by quoting a clause of the Constitution of these "usurpers", "robbers" and "tyrants" who disrupt the unity of labour democracy. Incidentally, in welcoming Breshkovskaya on the day she arrived in America, the leading capitalist newspaper in New York carried a headline in letters a yard long stating: "Welcome, Granny!" The American Socialists reprinted this and wrote: "She is in favour of political democracy—is there anything surprising, American workers, in the fact that the capitalists praise her?" She stands for political democracy. Why should they praise her? Because she is opposed to the Soviet Constitution. "Well," said the American Socialists, "here is a clause from the Constitution of these robbers." And they always quote the same clause which says that those who exploit the labour of others shall not have the right to elect or be elected. This clause from our Constitution is known all over the world. And it is because Soviet power frankly states that all must be subordinated to the dictatorship of the proletariat, that it is a new type of state organisation—it is precisely for this reason that it has won the sympathies of the workers all over the world. This new state organisation is being born in travail because it is far more difficult, a million times more difficult, to overcome our disruptive, petty-bourgeois laxity than to suppress the tyrannical landowners or the tyrannical capitalists, but the effort bears a million times more fruit in creating the new organisation which knows no exploitation. When proletarian organisation solves this problem, socialism will triumph completely. And it is to this that you must devote all your activities both in the schools and in the field of adult education. Notwithstanding the extremely difficult conditions that prevail, and the fact that the first socialist revolution in history is taking place in a country with a very low level of culture, notwithstanding this, Soviet power has already won the recognition of the workers of other countries. The phrase "dictatorship of the proletariat" is a Latin phrase, and the working people who heard it for the first time did not know what it meant, and did not know how it could be instituted. Now this Latin phrase has been translated into the modern languages and we have shown that the dictatorship or the proletariat is Soviet power, the government under which the workers organise themselves and say that their organisation is superior to every other. No idler, no exploiter can belong to this organisation. This organisation has but one object, and that is, to overthrow capitalism. No false slogans, no fetishes like "freedom", and "equality", will deceive us. We recognise no freedom, no equality, no labour democracy if it conflicts with the cause of emancipating labour from the yoke of capital. This is what we incorporated in the Soviet Constitution, and we have already won for it the sympathies of the workers of all countries. They know that in spite of the difficulty with which the new order is being born, and in spite of the severe trials and even defeats which may fall to the lot of some of the Soviet republics, no power on earth can compel mankind to turn back. (*Stormy applause.*)

PRELIMINARY DRAFT THESES ON THE AGRARIAN QUESTION (1920)

For the Second Congress of the Communist International

In his article,[1] Comrade Marchlewski gave an excellent explanation of the reasons why the Second International, which has now become the yellow International, failed, not only to define the revolutionary proletariat's tactics on the agrarian question, but even to pose that question properly. Comrade Marchlewski then went on to set forth the theoretical fundamentals of the Third International's communist agrarian programme.

These fundamentals can (and, I think, should) serve as the basis of the general resolution on the agrarian question for the Communist International Congress, which will meet on July 15, 1920.

The following is a preliminary draft of that resolution:

1) Only the urban and industrial proletariat, led by the Communist Party, can liberate the working masses of the countryside from the yoke of capital and landed proprietorship, from ruin and the imperialist wars which will inevitably break out again and again if the capitalist system remains. There is no salvation for the working masses of the countryside except in alliance with the communist proletariat, and unless they give the latter devoted support in its revolutionary struggle to throw off the yoke of the landowners (the big landed proprietors) and the bourgeoisie.

On the other hand, the industrial workers cannot accomplish their epoch-making mission of emancipating mankind from the yoke of capital and from wars if they confine themselves to their narrow craft, or trade interests, and smugly restrict themselves to attaining an improvement in their own conditions, which may sometimes be tolerable in the petty-bourgeois sense. This is exactly what happens to the "labour aristocracy" of many advanced countries, who constitute the core of the so-called socialist parties of the Second International; they are actually the bitter enemies and betrayers of socialism, petty-bourgeois chauvinists and agents of the bourgeoisie within the working-class movement. The proletariat is a really revolutionary class and acts in a

[1] Lenin is referring to the article by J. Marchlewski "The Agrarian Question and World Revolution" published in the journal *The Communist International* No. 12, July 20, 1920. Lenin read the article before the issue appeared.

really socialist manner only when it comes out and acts as the vanguard of all the working and exploited people, as their leader in the struggle for the overthrow of the exploiters; this, however, cannot be achieved unless the class struggle is carried into the countryside, unless the rural working masses are united about the Communist Party of the urban proletariat, and unless they are trained by the proletariat.

2) The working and exploited people of the countryside, whom the urban proletariat must lead into the struggle or, at all events, win over, are represented in all capitalist countries by the following classes:

first, the agricultural proletariat, wage-labourers (by the year, season, or day), who obtain their livelihood by working for hire at capitalist agricultural enterprises. The organisation of this class (political, military, trade union, co-operative, cultural, educational, etc.) independently and separately from other groups of the rural population, the conduct of intensive propaganda and agitation among this class, and the winning of its support for the Soviets and the dictatorship of the proletariat constitute the *fundamental* tasks of the Communist parties in all countries;

second, the semi-proletarians or peasants who till tiny plots of land, i.e., those who obtain their livelihood partly as wage-labourers at agricultural and industrial capitalist enterprises and partly by working their own or rented plots of land, which provide their families only with part of their means of subsistence. This group of the rural working population is very numerous in all capitalist countries; its existence and special position are played down by the representatives of the bourgeoisie and by the yellow "socialists" belonging to the Second International, partly by deliberately deceiving the workers and partly by blindly submitting to the routine of petty-bourgeois views and lumping together this group with the mass of the "peasantry". This bourgeois method of duping the workers is to be seen mostly in Germany and in France, but also in America and other countries. If the work of the Communist Party is properly organised, this group will become its assured supporter, for the lot of these semi-proletarians is a very hard one and they stand to gain enormously and immediately from Soviet government and the dictatorship of the proletariat:

third, the small peasantry, i.e., the small-scale tillers who, either as owners or as tenants, hold small plots of land which enable them to satisfy the needs of their families and their farms, and do not hire outside labour. This stratum, as such, undoubtedly stands to gain by the victory of the proletariat, which will fully and immediately bring it: (a) deliverance from the necessity of paying the big landowners rent or a share of the crop (for example, the *métayers* in France, also in Italy and other countries); (b) deliverance from mortgages; (c) deliverance from the numerous forms of oppression by and dependence on the big landowners (forest lands and their use, etc.); (d) immediate aid for their farms from the proletarian state (the use of the agricultural implements and part of the buildings on the big capitalist farms confiscated by the proletariat and the immediate conversion, by the proletarian state, of the rural co-operative societies and agricultural associations from organisations which under capitalism served above all the rich and middle peasants, into organisations that will primarily assist the poor, i.e., proletarians, semi-proletarians, small peasants, etc.), and many other things.

At the same time the Communist Party must clearly realise that during the transitional period from capitalism to communism, i.e., during the dictatorship of the proletariat, this stratum, or at all events part of it, will inevitably vacillate towards unrestricted freedom of trade and the free enjoyment of the rights of private property. That is because this stratum, which, if only in a small way, is a seller of articles of consumption, has been corrupted by profiteering and by proprietary habits. However, if a firm proletarian policy is pursued, and if the victorious proletariat deals very resolutely with the big landowners and the big peasants, this stratum's vacillation cannot be considerable and cannot alter the fact that, on the whole, it will side with the proletarian revolution.

3) Taken together, the three groups enumerated above constitute the majority of the rural population in all capitalist countries. That is why the success of the proletarian revolution is fully assured, not only in the cities but in the countryside as well. The reverse view is widespread; however, it persists only, first, because of the deception systematically practised by bourgeois science and statistics, which do everything to gloss over both the gulf that separates the above-mentioned classes in the countryside from the exploiters, the landowners and capitalists, and that which separates the semi-proletarians and small peasants from the big peasants; second, it persists because of the inability and unwillingness of the heroes of the yellow Second International and of the "labour aristocracy" in the advanced countries, which has been corrupted by imperialist privileges, to conduct genuinely proletarian revolutionary work of propaganda, agitation and organisation among the rural poor; the attention of the opportunists has always been and still is wholly concentrated on inventing theoretical and practical compromises with the bourgeoisie, including the big and middle peasants (who are dealt with below), and not on the revolutionary overthrow of the bourgeois government and the

bourgeoisie by the proletariat; it persists, third, because of the obstinate refusal to understand—so obstinate as to be equivalent to a prejudice (connected with all the other bourgeois-democratic and parliamentary prejudices)—a truth which has been fully proved by Marxist theory and fully corroborated by the experience of the proletarian revolution in Russia, namely, that although the three enumerated categories of the rural population—who are incredibly downtrodden, disunited, crushed, and doomed to semi-barbarous conditions of existence in all countries, even the most advanced—are economically, socially, and culturally interested in the victory of socialism, they are capable of giving resolute support to the revolutionary proletariat only *after* the latter has won political power, only *after* it has resolutely dealt with the big landowners and capitalists, and only *after* these downtrodden people see *in practice* that they have an organised leader and champion, strong and firm enough to assist and lead them and to show them the right path.

4) In the economic sense, one should understand by "middle peasants" those small farmers who, (1) either as owners or tenants, hold plots of land that are also small but, under capitalism, are sufficient not only to provide, as a general rule, a meagre subsistence for the family and the bare minimum needed to maintain the farm, but also produce a certain surplus which may, in good years at least, be converted into capital; (2) quite frequently (for example, one farm out of two or three) resort to the employment of hired labour. A concrete example of the middle peasants in an advanced capitalist country is provided by the group of farms of five to ten hectares in Germany, in which, according to the census of 1907, the number of farms employing hired labourers is about one-third of the total number of farms in this group.[2] In France, where the cultivation of special crops is more developed—for example, grape-growing, which requires a very large amount of labour—this group probably employs outside hired labour to a somewhat greater extent.

The revolutionary proletariat cannot set itself the task—at least not in the immediate future or in the initial period of the dictatorship of the proletariat—of winning over this stratum, but must confine itself to the

[2] Here are the exact figures: the number of farms of five to ten hectares—652,798 (out of a total of 5,736,082), these employed 487,704 hired labourers of various kinds, while members of the farmers' families (*Familienangehörige*) working on the farms numbered 2,003,633. In Austria, according to the census of 1902, this group comprised 383,331 farms, of which 126,136 employed hired labour; the hired labourers working on these farms numbered 146,044 and the working members of the farmers' families 1,265,969. The total number of farms in Austria was 2,856,349.—*Au.*

task of neutralising it, i.e., rendering it neutral in the struggle between the proletariat and the bourgeoisie. This stratum inevitably vacillates between these two forces; in the beginning of the new epoch and in the developed capitalist countries, it will, in the main, incline towards the bourgeoisie. That is because the world outlook and the sentiments of the property-owners are prevalent among this stratum, which has a direct interest in profiteering, in "freedom" of trade and in property, and stands in direct antagonism to the wage-workers. By abolishing rent and mortgages, the victorious proletariat will immediately improve the position of this stratum. In most capitalist countries, however, the proletarian state should not at once completely abolish private property; at all events, it guarantees both the small and the middle peasantry, not only the preservation of their plots of land but also their enlargement to cover the total area they usually rented (the abolition of rent).

A combination of such measures with a ruthless struggle against the bourgeoisie fully guarantees the success of the policy of neutralisation. The proletarian state must effect the transition to collective farming with extreme caution and only very gradually, by the force of example, without any coercion of the middle peasant.

5) The big peasants (*Grossbauern*) are capitalist *entrepreneurs* in agriculture, who as a rule employ several hired labourers and are connected with the "peasantry" only in their low cultural level, habits of life, and the manual labour they themselves perform on their farms. These constitute the biggest of the bourgeois strata who are open and determined enemies of the revolutionary proletariat. In all their work in the countryside, the Communist parties must concentrate their attention mainly on the struggle against this stratum, on liberating the toiling and exploited majority of the rural population from the ideological and political influence of these exploiters, etc.

Following the victory of the proletariat in the cities, all sorts of manifestations of resistance and sabotage, as well as direct armed action of a counter-revolutionary character on the part of this stratum, are absolutely inevitable. The revolutionary proletariat must therefore immediately begin the ideological and organisational preparation of the forces necessary to completely disarm this stratum and, simultaneously with the overthrow of the capitalists in industry, to deal this stratum a most determined, ruthless and smashing blow at the very first signs of resistance; for this purpose, the rural proletariat must be armed and village Soviets organised, in which the exploiters must have no place, and in which proletarians and semi-proletarians must be ensured predominance.

However, the expropriation even of the big peasants can in no way be made an immediate task of the victorious proletariat, because the material and especially the technical conditions, as well as the social conditions, for the socialisation of such farms are still lacking. In individual and probably exceptional cases, those parts of their land which they rent out in small plots or which are particularly needed by the surrounding small-peasant population will be confiscated; the small peasants should also be guaranteed, on certain terms, the free use of part of the agricultural machinery belonging to the big peasants, etc. As a general rule, however, the proletarian state must allow the big peasants to retain their land, confiscating it only if they resist the power of the working and exploited people. The experience of the Russian proletarian revolution, in which the struggle against the big peasantry was complicated and protracted by a number of special conditions, showed nevertheless that, when taught a severe lesson for the slightest attempt at resistance, this stratum is capable of loyally fulfilling the tasks set by the proletarian state, and even begins to be imbued although very slowly with respect for the government which protects all who work and is ruthless towards the idle rich.

The special conditions which, in Russia, complicated and retarded the struggle of the proletariat against the big peasants after it had defeated the bourgeoisie were, in the main, the following: after October 25 (November 7), 1917, the Russian revolution passed through the stage of the "general democratic"—that is, basically the bourgeois-democratic—struggle of the peasantry as a whole against the landowners; the cultural and numerical weakness of the urban proletariat; and, lastly, the enormous distances and extremely poor means of communication. Inasmuch as these retarding conditions do not exist in the advanced countries, the revolutionary proletariat of Europe and America should prepare far more energetically, and achieve far more rapidly, resolutely, and successfully, complete victory over the resistance of the big peasantry, completely depriving it of the slightest possibility of offering resistance. This is imperative because, until such a complete and absolute victory is achieved, the masses of the rural proletarians, semi-proletarians, and small peasants cannot be brought to accept the proletarian state as a fully stable one.

6) The revolutionary proletariat must immediately and unreservedly confiscate all landed estates, those of the big landowners, who, in capitalist

countries—directly or through their tenant farmers—systematically exploit wage-labour and the neighbouring small (and, not infrequently, part of the middle) peasantry, do not themselves engage in manual labour, and are in the main descended from the feudal lords (the nobles in Russia, Germany, and Hungary, the restored seigneurs in France, the lords in Britain, and the former slave-owners in America), or are rich financial magnates, or else a mixture of both these categories of exploiters and parasites.

Under no circumstances is it permissible for Communist parties to advocate or practise compensating the big landowners for the confiscated lands, for under present day conditions in Europe and America this would be tantamount to a betrayal of socialism and the imposition of new tribute upon the masses of working and exploited people, to whom the war has meant the greatest hardships, while it has increased the number of millionaires and enriched them.

As to the mode of cultivation of the land that the victorious proletariat confiscates from the big landowners, the distribution of that land among the peasantry for their use has been predominant in Russia, owing to her economic backwardness; it is only in relatively rare and exceptional cases that state farms have been organised on the former estates which the proletarian state runs at its own expense, converting the former wage-labourers into workers for the state and members of the Soviets, which administer the state. The Communist International is of the opinion that in the case of the advanced capitalist countries it would be correct to keep *most* of the big agricultural enterprises intact and to conduct them on the lines of the "state farms" in Russia.

It would, however, be grossly erroneous to exaggerate or to stereotype this rule and never to permit the free grant of *part* of the land that belonged to the expropriated expropriators to the neighbouring small and sometimes middle peasants.

First, the objection usually raised to this, namely, that large-scale farming is technically superior, often amounts to an indisputable theoretical truth being replaced by the worst kind of opportunism and betrayal of the revolution. To achieve the success of this revolution, the proletariat should not shrink from a temporary decline in production, any more than the bourgeois opponents of slavery in North America shrank from a temporary decline in cotton production as a consequence of the Civil War of 1863-65. What is most important to the bourgeois is production for the sake of production; what is most important to the working and exploited population is the overthrow of the exploiters and the creation of conditions that will permit the working people to work for themselves, and not for the capitalists. It is the primary and fundamental task of the proletariat to ensure the proletarian victory and its stability. There can, however, be no stable proletarian government unless the middle peasantry is neutralised and the support is secured of a very considerable section of the small peasantry, if not all of them.

Second, not merely an increase but even the preservation of large-scale production in agriculture presupposes the existence of a fully developed and revolutionarily conscious rural proletariat with considerable experience of trade union and political organisation behind it. Where this condition does not yet exist, or where this work cannot expediently be entrusted to class-conscious and competent industrial workers, hasty attempts to set up large state-conducted farms can only discredit the proletarian government. Under such conditions, the utmost caution must be exercised and the most thorough preparations made when state farms are set up.

Third, in all capitalist countries, even the most advanced, there still exist survivals of medieval, semi-feudal exploitation of the neighbouring small peasants by the big landowners as in the case of the *Instleute*[3] in Germany, the *métayers* in France, and the sharecroppers in the United States (not only Negroes, who, in the Southern States, are mostly exploited in this way, but sometimes whites too). In such cases it is incumbent on the proletarian state to grant the small peasants free use of the lands they formerly rented, since no other economic or technical basis exists, and it cannot be created at one stroke.

The implements and stock of the big farms must be confiscated without fail and converted into state property, with the absolute condition that, *after* the requirements of the big state farms have been met, the neighbouring small peasants may have the use of these implements gratis, in compliance with conditions drawn up by the proletarian state.

In the period immediately following the proletarian revolution, it is absolutely necessary, not only to confiscate the estates of the big landowners at once, but also to deport or to intern them all as leaders of counter-revolution and ruthless oppressors of the entire rural population. However, with the consolidation of the proletarian power in the countryside as well as in the cities, systematic efforts should be made to employ (under the special control of highly reliable communist workers) those forces within this class that possess valuable experience, know how, and organising skill, to build large-scale socialist agriculture.

[3] Tenant farmers.

7) The victory of socialism over capitalism and the consolidation of socialism may be regarded as ensured only when the proletarian state power, having completely suppressed all resistance by the exploiters and assured itself complete subordination and stability, has reorganised the whole of industry on the lines of large-scale collective production and on a modern technical basis (founded on the electrification of the entire economy). This alone will enable the cities to render such radical assistance, technical and social, to the backward and scattered rural population as will create the material basis necessary to boost the productivity of agricultural and of farm labour in general, thereby encouraging the small farmers by the force of example and in their own interests to adopt large-scale, collective and mechanised agriculture. Although nominally recognised by all socialists, this indisputable theoretical truth is in fact distorted by the opportunism prevalent in the yellow Second International and among the leaders of the German and the British "Independents", the French Longuetists, etc. This distortion consists in attention being directed towards the relatively remote, beautiful, and rosy future; attention is deflected from the immediate tasks of the difficult practical transition and approach to that future. In practice, it consists in preaching a compromise with the bourgeoisie and a "class truce", i.e., complete betrayal of the proletariat, which is now waging a struggle amidst the unprecedented ruin and impoverishment created everywhere by the war, and amidst the unprecedented enrichment and arrogance of a handful of millionaires resulting from that war.

It is in the countryside that a genuine possibility of a successful struggle for socialism demands, first, that all Communist parties should inculcate in the industrial proletariat a realisation of the need to make sacrifices, and be prepared to make sacrifices so as to overthrow the bourgeoisie and consolidate proletarian power—since the dictatorship of the proletariat implies both the ability of the proletariat to organise and lead all the working and exploited people, and the vanguard's ability to make the utmost sacrifices and to display the utmost heroism to that end; second, success demands that, as a result of the workers' victory, the labouring and most exploited masses in the countryside achieve an immediate and considerable improvement in their conditions at the expense of the exploiters—for without that the industrial proletariat cannot get the support of the rural areas and, in particular, will be unable to ensure the supply of food for the cities.

8) The enormous difficulty of organising and training for the revolutionary struggle the masses of rural working people, whom

capitalism has reduced to a state of great wretchedness, disunity and frequently semi-medieval dependence, makes it necessary for the Communist parties to devote special attention to the strike struggle in the rural districts, give greater support to mass strikes by the agricultural proletarians and semi-proletarians, and help develop the strike movement in every way. The experience of the Russian revolutions of 1905 and of 1917, now confirmed and extended by the experience of Germany and other advanced countries, shows that the growing mass strike struggle (into which, under certain conditions, the small peasants can and should also be drawn) is alone capable of rousing the countryside from its lethargy, awakening the class-consciousness of the exploited masses in the countryside, making them realise the need for class organisation, and revealing to them in a vivid and practical manner the importance of their alliance with the urban workers.

This Congress of the Communist International brands as traitors and renegades those socialists—to be found, unfortunately, not only in the yellow Second International, but also in the three very important European parties which have withdrawn from that International—who are not only capable of remaining indifferent to the strike struggle in the countryside, but even (like Karl Kautsky) of opposing it on the grounds that it threatens to reduce the output of articles of consumption. Neither programmes nor the most solemn declarations are of any value whatever unless it is proved in practice, in deed, that the Communists and workers' leaders are able to place above everything else in the world the development and the victory of the proletarian revolution, and to make the greatest sacrifices for it, for otherwise there is no way out, no salvation from starvation, ruin, and new imperialist wars.

In particular, it should be pointed out that the leaders of the old socialist movement and representatives of the "labour aristocracy"—who now often make verbal concessions to communism and even nominally side with it in order to preserve their prestige among the worker masses, which are rapidly becoming revolutionary—should be tested for their loyalty to the cause of the proletariat and their suitability for responsible positions in those spheres of work where the development of revolutionary consciousness and the revolutionary struggle is most marked, the resistance of the landowners and the bourgeoisie (the big peasants, the kulaks) most fierce, and the difference between the socialist compromiser and the communist revolutionary most striking.

9) The Communist parties must exert every effort to begin, as speedily as possible, to set up Soviets of Deputies in the countryside, and

in the first place Soviets of hired labourers and semi-proletarians. Only if they are linked up with the mass strike struggle and with the most oppressed class can the Soviets perform their functions, and become consolidated enough to influence (and later to incorporate) the small peasants. If, however, the strike struggle has not yet developed, and the agricultural proletariat is as yet incapable of strong organisation owing both to the severe oppression by the landowners and the big peasants and to lack of support from the industrial workers and their unions, then the formation of Soviets of Deputies in the rural areas will require lengthy preparation by means of the organisation of communist cells, even if only small ones, intensified agitation—in which the demands of communism are enunciated in the simplest manner and illustrated by the most glaring examples of exploitation and oppression—and the arrangement of systematic visits of industrial workers to the rural districts, and so on.

THE TASKS OF THE YOUTH LEAGUES
(1920)
Speech Delivered at the Third All-Russia Congress of the Russian Young Communist League

(*The Congress greets Lenin with a tremendous ovation.*) Comrades, today I would like to talk on the fundamental tasks of the Young Communist League and, in this connection, on what the youth organisations in a socialist republic should be like in general.[1,2]

It is all the more necessary to dwell on this question because in a certain sense it may be said that it is the youth that will be faced with the actual task of creating a communist society. For it is clear that the generation of working people brought up in capitalist society can, at best, accomplish the task of destroying the foundations of the old, the capitalist way of life, which was built on exploitation. At best it will be able to accomplish the tasks of creating a social system that will help the proletariat and the working classes retain power and lay a firm foundation, which can be built on only by a generation that is starting to work under the new conditions, in a situation in which relations based on the exploitation of man by man no longer exist.

And so, in dealing from this angle with the tasks confronting the youth, I must say that the tasks of the youth in general, and of the Young Communist Leagues and all other organisations in particular, might be summed up in a single word: learn.

Of course, this is only a "single word". It does not reply to the principal and most essential questions: what to learn, and how to learn? And the whole point here is that, with the transformation of the old, capitalist society, the upbringing, training and education of the new generations that will create the communist society cannot be conducted on the old lines. The teaching, training and education of the youth must proceed from the material that has been left to us by the old society. We can build communism only on the basis of the totality of knowledge, organisations and institutions, only by using the stock of human forces and means

1 Revised translation by Julius Katzer.

2 The Third All-Russia Congress of the Russian Young Communist League took place in Moscow between October 2 and 10, and was attended by some 600 delegates. Lenin addressed the Congress at the first session in the evening of October 2.

that have been left to us by the old society. Only by radically remoulding the teaching, organisation and training of the youth shall we be able to ensure that the efforts of the younger generation will result in the creation of a society that will be unlike the old society, i.e., in the creation of a communist society. That is why we must deal in detail with the question of what we should teach the youth and how the youth should learn if it really wants to justify the name of communist youth, and how it should be trained so as to be able to complete and consummate what we have started.

I must say that the first and most natural reply would seem to be that the Youth League, and the youth in general, who want to advance to communism, should learn communism.

But this reply—"learn communism"—is too general. What do we need in order to learn communism? What must be singled out from the sum of general knowledge so as to acquire a knowledge of communism? Here a number of dangers arise, which very often manifest themselves whenever the task of learning communism is presented incorrectly, or when it is interpreted in too one-sided a manner.

Naturally, the first thought that enters one's mind is that learning communism means assimilating the sum of knowledge that is contained in communist manuals, pamphlets and books. But such a definition of the study of communism would be too crude and inadequate. If the study of communism consisted solely in assimilating what is contained in communist books and pamphlets, we might all too easily obtain communist text jugglers or braggarts, and this would very often do us harm, because such people, after learning by rote what is set forth in communist books and pamphlets, would prove incapable of combining the various branches of knowledge, and would be unable to act in the way communism really demands.

One of the greatest evils and misfortunes left to us by the old, capitalist society is the complete rift between books and practical life; we have had books explaining everything in the best possible manner, yet in most cases these books contained the most pernicious and hypocritical lies, a false description of capitalist society.

That is why it would be most mistaken merely to assimilate book knowledge about communism. No longer do our speeches and articles merely reiterate what used to be said about communism, because our speeches and articles are connected with our daily work in all fields. Without work and without struggle, book knowledge of communism obtained from communist pamphlets and works is absolutely worthless, for it would continue the old separation of theory and practice, the old rift which was the most pernicious feature of the old, bourgeois society.

It would be still more dangerous to set about assimilating only communist slogans. Had we not realised this danger in time, and had we not directed all our efforts to averting this danger, the half million or million young men and women who would have called themselves Communists after studying communism in this way would only greatly prejudice the cause of communism.

The question arises: how is all this to be blended for the study of communism? What must we take from the old schools, from the old kind of science? It was the declared aim of the old type of school to produce men with an all-round education, to teach the sciences in general. We know that this was utterly false, since the whole of society was based and maintained on the division of people into classes, into exploiters and oppressed. Since they were thoroughly imbued with the class spirit, the old schools naturally gave knowledge only to the children of the bourgeoisie. Every word was falsified in the interests of the bourgeoisie. In these schools the younger generation of workers and peasants were not so much educated as drilled in the interests of that bourgeoisie. They were trained in such a way as to be useful servants of the bourgeoisie, able to create profits for it without disturbing its peace and leisure. That is why, while rejecting the old type of schools, we have made it our task to take from it only what we require for genuine communist education.

This brings me to the reproaches and accusations which we constantly hear levelled at the old schools, and which often lead to wholly wrong conclusions. It is said that the old school was a school of purely book knowledge, of ceaseless drilling and grinding. That is true, but we must distinguish between what was bad in the old schools and what is useful to us, and we must be able to select from it what is necessary for communism.

The old schools provided purely book knowledge; they compelled their pupils to assimilate a mass of useless, superfluous and barren knowledge, which cluttered up the brain and turned the younger generation into bureaucrats regimented according to a single pattern. But it would mean falling into a grave error for you to try to draw the conclusion that one can become a Communist without assimilating the wealth of knowledge amassed by mankind. It would be mistaken to think it sufficient to learn communist slogans and the conclusions of communist science, without acquiring that sum of knowledge of which communism itself is a result. Marxism is an example which shows how communism arose out of the sum of human knowledge.

You have read and heard that communist theory—the science of communism created in the main by Marx, this doctrine of Marxism—has ceased to be the work of a single socialist of the nineteenth century, even though he was a genius, and that it has become the doctrine of millions and tens of millions of proletarians all over the world, who are applying it in their struggle against capitalism. If you were to ask why the teachings of Marx have been able to win the hearts and minds of millions and tens of millions of the most revolutionary class, you would receive only one answer: it was because Marx based his work on the firm foundation of the human knowledge acquired under capitalism. After making a study of the laws governing the development of human society, Marx realised the inevitability of capitalism developing towards communism. What is most important is that he proved this on the sole basis of a most precise, detailed and profound study of this capitalist society, by fully assimilating all that earlier science had produced. He critically reshaped everything that had been created by human society, without ignoring a single detail. He reconsidered, subjected to criticism, and verified on the working-class movement everything that human thinking had created, and therefrom formulated conclusions which people hemmed in by bourgeois limitations or bound by bourgeois prejudices could not draw.

We must bear this in mind when, for example, we talk about proletarian culture.[3] We shall be unable to solve this problem unless we clearly realise that only a precise knowledge and transformation of the culture created by the entire development of mankind will enable us to create a proletarian culture. The latter is not clutched out of thin air; it is not an invention of those who call themselves experts in proletarian

[3] Lenin is referring to *Proletcult*, a cultural and educational organisation which arose in September 1917 as an independent workers' organisation. After the October Revolution Proletcult, whose leadership fell into the hands of Bogdanov and his supporters, continued to insist on independence, thus setting itself in opposition to the proletarian state. This led to the infiltration of bourgeois intellectuals, who began to exert a decisive influence on Proletcult. Its members actually denied the cultural legacy of the past, neglected cultural and educational work among the masses, isolated themselves from life and aimed at setting up a special "proletarian culture". Bogdanov, the chief Proletcult ideologist, paid lip service to Marxism, but actually preached subjective idealism, Machism. Besides bourgeois intellectuals who held leading positions in many organisations, Proletcult also included young workers who sincerely wished to promote cultural development in the Soviet state. Proletcult organisations had their heyday in 1919. In the early 1920s they began to decline, ceasing to exist in 1932.

culture. That is all nonsense. Proletarian culture must be the logical development of the store of knowledge mankind has accumulated under the yoke of capitalist, landowner and bureaucratic society. All these roads have been leading, and will continue to lead up to proletarian culture, in the same way as political economy, as reshaped by Marx, has shown us what human society must arrive at, shown us the passage to the class struggle, to the beginning of the proletarian revolution.

When we so often hear representatives of the youth, as well as certain advocates of a new system of education, attacking the old schools, claiming that they used the system of cramming, we say to them that we must take what was good in the old schools. We must not borrow the system of encumbering young people's minds with an immense amount of knowledge, nine-tenths of which was useless and one-tenth distorted. This, however, does not mean that we can restrict ourselves to communist conclusions and learn only communist slogans. You will not create communism that way. You can become a Communist only when you enrich your mind with a knowledge of all the treasures created by mankind.

We have no need of cramming, but we do need to develop and perfect the mind of every student with a knowledge of fundamental facts. Communism will become an empty word, a mere signboard, and a Communist a mere boaster, if all the knowledge he has acquired is not digested in his mind. You should not merely assimilate this knowledge, but assimilate it critically, so as not to cram your mind with useless lumber, but enrich it with all those facts that are indispensable to the well-educated man of today. If a Communist took it into his head to boast about his communism because of the cut-and-dried conclusions he had acquired, without putting in a great deal of serious and hard work and without understanding facts he should examine critically, he would be a deplorable Communist indeed. Such superficiality would be decidedly fatal. If I know that I know little, I shall strive to learn more; but if a man says that he is a Communist and that he need not know anything thoroughly, he will never become anything like a Communist.

The old schools produced servants needed by the capitalists; the old schools turned men of science into men who had to write and say whatever pleased the capitalists. We must therefore abolish them. But does the fact that we must abolish them, destroy them, mean that we should not take from them everything mankind has accumulated that is essential to man? Does it mean that we do not have to distinguish between what was necessary to capitalism and what is necessary to communism?

We are replacing the old drill-sergeant methods practised in bourgeois society, against the will of the majority, with the class-conscious discipline of the workers and peasants, who combine hatred of the old society with a determination, ability and readiness to unite and organise their forces for this struggle so as to forge the wills of millions and hundreds of millions of people—disunited, and scattered over the territory of a huge country—into a single will, without which defeat is inevitable. Without this solidarity, without this conscious discipline of the workers and peasants, our cause is hopeless. Without this, we shall be unable to vanquish the capitalists and landowners of the whole world. We shall not even consolidate the foundation, let alone build a new, communist society on that foundation. Likewise, while condemning the old schools, while harbouring an absolutely justified and necessary hatred for the old schools, and appreciating the readiness to destroy them, we must realise that we must replace the old system of instruction, the old cramming and the old drill, with an ability to acquire the sum total of human knowledge, and to acquire it in such a way that communism shall not be something to be learned by rote, but something that you yourselves have thought over, something that will embody conclusions inevitable from the standpoint of present-day education.

That is the way the main tasks should be presented when we speak of the aim: learn communism.

I shall take a practical example to make this clear to you, and to demonstrate the approach to the problem of how you must learn. You all know that, following the military problems, those of defending the republic, we are now confronted with economic tasks. Communist society, as we know, cannot be built unless we restore industry and agriculture, and that, not in the old way. They must be re-established on a modern basis, in accordance with the last word in science. You know that electricity is that basis, and that only after electrification of the entire country, of all branches of industry and agriculture, only when you have achieved that aim, will you be able to build for yourselves the communist society which the older generation will not be able to build. Confronting you is the task of economically reviving the whole country, of reorganising and restoring both agriculture and industry on modern technical lines, based on modern science and technology, on electricity. You realise perfectly well that illiterate people cannot tackle electrification, and that elementary literacy is not enough either. It is insufficient to understand what electricity is; what is needed is the knowledge of how to apply it technically in industry and agriculture, and in the individual branches of industry and agriculture. This has to be learnt for oneself, and it must be taught to the entire rising generation of working people. That is the task confronting every class-conscious Communist, every young person who regards himself a Communist and who clearly understands that, by joining the Young Communist League, he has pledged himself to help the Party build communism and to help the whole younger generation create a communist society. He must realise that he can create it only on the basis of modern education, and if he does not acquire this education communism will remain merely a pious wish.

It was the task of the older generation to overthrow the bourgeoisie. The main task then was to criticise the bourgeoisie, arouse hatred of the bourgeoisie among the masses, and foster class-consciousness and the ability to unite their forces. The new generation is confronted with a far more complex task. Your duty does not lie only in assembling your forces so as to uphold the workers' and peasants' government against an invasion instigated by the capitalists. Of course, you must do that; that is something you clearly realise, and is distinctly seen by the Communist. However, that is not enough. You have to build up a communist society. In many respects half of the work has been done. The old order has been destroyed, just as it deserved, it has been turned into a heap of ruins, just as it deserved. The ground has been cleared, and on this ground the younger communist generation must build a communist society. You are faced with the task of construction, and you can accomplish that task only by assimilating all modern knowledge, only if you arc ablc to transform communism from cut-and-dried and memorised formulas, counsels, recipes, prescriptions and programmes into that living reality which gives unity to your immediate work, and only if you are able to make communism a guide in all your practical work.

That is the task you should pursue in educating, training and rousing the entire younger generation. You must be foremost among the millions of builders of a communist society in whose ranks every young man and young woman should be. You will not build a communist society unless you enlist the mass of young workers and peasants in the work of building communism.

This naturally brings me to the question of how we should teach communism and what the specific features of our methods should be.

I first of all shall deal here with the question of communist ethics.

You must train yourselves to be Communists. It is the task of the Youth League to organise its practical activities in such a way that, by learning, organising, uniting and fighting, its members shall train both themselves and all those who look to it for leadership; it should train Communists. The entire purpose of training, educating and teaching the youth of today should be to imbue them with communist ethics.

But is there such a thing as communist ethics? Is there such a thing as communist morality? Of course, there is. It is often suggested that we have no ethics of our own; very often the bourgeoisie accuse us Communists of rejecting all morality. This is a method of confusing the issue, of throwing dust in the eyes of the workers and peasants.

In what sense do we reject ethics, reject morality?

In the sense given to it by the bourgeoisie, who based ethics on God's commandments. On this point we, of course, say that we do not believe in God, and that we know perfectly well that the clergy, the landowners and the bourgeoisie invoked the name of God so as to further their own interests as exploiters. Or, instead of basing ethics on the commandments of morality, on the commandments of God, they based it on idealist or semi-idealist phrases, which always amounted to something very similar to God's commandments.

We reject any morality based on extra-human and extra-class concepts. We say that this is deception, dupery, stultification of the workers and peasants in the interests of the landowners and capitalists.

We say that our morality is entirely subordinated to the interests of the proletariat's class struggle. Our morality stems from the interests of the class struggle of the proletariat.

The old society was based on the oppression of all the workers and peasants by the landowners and capitalists. We had to destroy all that, and overthrow them but to do that we had to create unity. That is something that God cannot create.

This unity could be provided only by the factories, only by a proletariat trained and roused from its long slumber. Only when that class was formed did a mass movement arise which has led to what we have now—the victory of the proletarian revolution in one of the weakest of countries, which for three years has been repelling the onslaught of the bourgeoisie of the whole world. We can see how the proletarian revolution is developing all over the world. On the basis of experience, we now say that only the proletariat could have created the solid force which the disunited and scattered peasantry are following and which has withstood all onslaughts by the exploiters. Only this class can help the working masses unite, rally their ranks and conclusively defend, conclusively consolidate and conclusively build up a communist society.

That is why we say that to us there is no such thing as a morality that stands outside human society; that is a fraud. To us morality is subordinated to the interests of the proletariat's class struggle.

What does that class struggle consist in? It consists in overthrowing the tsar, overthrowing the capitalists, and abolishing the capitalist class.

What are classes in general? Classes are that which permits one section of society to appropriate the labour of another section. If one section of society appropriates all the land, we have a landowner class and a peasant class. If one section of society owns the factories, shares and capital, while another section works in these factories, we have a capitalist class and a proletarian class.

It was not difficult to drive out the tsar—that required only a few days. It was not very difficult to drive out the landowners—that was done in a few months. Nor was it very difficult to drive out the capitalists. But it is incomparably more difficult to abolish classes; we still have the division into workers and peasants. If the peasant is installed on his plot of land and appropriates his surplus grain, that is, grain that he does not need for himself or for his cattle, while the rest of the people have to go without bread, then the peasant becomes an exploiter. The more grain he clings to, the more profitable he finds it; as for the rest, let them starve: "The more they starve, the dearer I can sell this grain." All should work according to a single common plan, on common land, in common factories and in accordance with a common system. Is that easy to attain? You see that it is not as easy as driving out the tsar, the landowners and the capitalists. What is required is that the proletariat re-educate a section of the peasantry; it must win over the working peasants in order to crush the resistance of those peasants who are rich and are profiting from the poverty and want of the rest. Hence the task of the proletarian struggle is not quite completed after we have overthrown the tsar and driven out the landowners and capitalists; to accomplish that is the task of the system we call the dictatorship of the proletariat.

The class struggle is continuing; it has merely changed its forms. It is the class struggle of the proletariat to prevent the return of the old exploiters, to unite in a single union the scattered masses of unenlightened peasants. The class struggle is continuing and it is our task to subordinate all interests to that struggle. Our communist morality is also subordinated to that task. We say: morality is what serves to destroy the old exploiting society and to unite all the working people around the proletariat, which is building up a new, a communist society.

Communist morality is that which serves this struggle and unites the working people against all exploitation, against all petty private property;

for petty property puts into the hands of one person that which has been created by the labour of the whole of society. In our country the land is common property.

But suppose I take a piece of this common property and grow on it twice as much grain as I need, and profiteer on the surplus? Suppose I argue that the more starving people there are, the more they will pay? Would I then be behaving like a Communist? No, I would be behaving like an exploiter, like a proprietor. That must be combated. If that is allowed to go on, things will revert to the rule of the capitalists, to the rule of the bourgeoisie, as has more than once happened in previous revolutions. To prevent the restoration of the rule of the capitalists and the bourgeoisie, we must not allow profiteering; we must not allow individuals to enrich themselves at the expense of the rest; the working people must unite with the proletariat and form a communist society. This is the principal feature of the fundamental task of the League and the organisation of the communist youth.

The old society was based on the principle: rob or be robbed; work for others or make others work for you; be a slave-owner or a slave. Naturally, people brought up in such a society assimilate with their mother's milk, one might say, the psychology, the habit, the concept which says: you are either a slave-owner or a slave, or else, a small owner, a petty employee, a petty official, or an intellectual—in short, a man who is concerned only with himself, and does not care a rap for anybody else.

If I work this plot of land, I do not care a rap for anybody else; if others starve, all the better, I shall get the more for my grain. If I have a job as a doctor, engineer, teacher, or clerk, I do not care a rap for anybody else. If I toady to and please the powers that be, I may be able to keep my job, and even get on in life and become a bourgeois. A Communist cannot harbour such a psychology and such sentiments. When the workers and peasants proved that they were able, by their own efforts, to defend themselves and create a new society—that was the beginning of the new and communist education, education in the struggle against the exploiters, education in alliance with the proletariat against the self-seekers and petty proprietors, against the psychology and habits which say: I seek my own profit and don't care a rap for anything else.

That is the reply to the question of how the young and rising generation should learn communism.

It can learn communism only by linking up every step in its studies, training and education with the continuous struggle the proletarians and the working people are waging against the old society of exploiters. When people tell us about morality, we say: to a Communist all morality lies in this united discipline and conscious mass struggle against the exploiters. We do not believe in an eternal morality, and we expose the falseness of all the fables about morality. Morality serves the purpose of helping human society rise to a higher level and rid itself of the exploitation of labour.

To achieve this we need that generation of young people who began to reach political maturity in the midst of a disciplined and desperate struggle against the bourgeoisie. In this struggle that generation is training genuine Communists; it must subordinate to this struggle, and link up with it, each step in its studies, education and training. The education of the communist youth must consist, not in giving them suave talks and moral precepts. This is not what education consists in. When people have seen the way in which their fathers and mothers lived under the yoke of the landowners and capitalists; when they have themselves experienced the sufferings of those who began the struggle against the exploiters; when they have seen the sacrifices made to keep what has been won, and seen what deadly enemies the landowners and capitalists are—they are taught by these conditions to become Communists. Communist morality is based on the struggle for the consolidation and completion of communism. That is also the basis of communist training, education, and teaching. That is the reply to the question of how communism should be learnt.

We could not believe in teaching, training and education if they were restricted only to the schoolroom and divorced from the ferment of life. As long as the workers and peasants are oppressed by the landowners and capitalists, and as long as the schools are controlled by the landowners and capitalists, the young generation will remain blind and ignorant. Our schools must provide the youth with the fundamentals of knowledge, the ability to evolve communist views independently; they must make educated people of the youth. While they are attending school, they must learn to become participants in the struggle for emancipation from the exploiters. The Young Communist League will justify its name as the League of the young communist generation only when every step in its teaching, training and education is linked up with participation in the common struggle of all working people against the exploiters. You are well aware that, as long as Russia remains the only workers' republic and the old, bourgeois system exists in the rest of the world, we shall be weaker than they are, and be constantly threatened with a new attack; and that only if we learn to be solidly united shall we win in the further struggle and—having gained strength—become really invincible. Thus, to be a Communist means that you must organise and unite the entire young generation and set an example of training and discipline in this struggle. Then you will be able to start building the edifice of communist society and bring it to completion.

To make this clearer to you, I shall quote an example. We call ourselves Communists. What is a Communist? Communist is a Latin word. *Communis* is the Latin for "common". Communist society is a society in which all things—the land, the factories—are owned in common and the people work in common. That is communism.

Is it possible to work in common if each one works separately on his own plot of land? Work in common cannot be brought about all at once. That is impossible. It does not drop from the skies. It comes through toil and suffering; it is created in the course of struggle. The old books are of no use here; no one will believe them. One's own experience of life is needed. When Kolchak and Denikin were advancing from Siberia and the South, the peasants were on their side. They did not like Bolshevism because the Bolsheviks took their grain at a fixed price. But when the peasants in Siberia and the Ukraine experienced the rule of Kolchak and Denikin, they realised that they had only one alternative: either to go to the capitalists, who would at once hand them over into slavery under the landowners; or to follow the workers, who, it is true, did not promise a land flowing with milk and honey, and demanded iron discipline and firmness in an arduous struggle, but would lead them out of enslavement by the capitalists and landowners. When even the ignorant peasants saw and realised this from their own experience, they became conscious adherents of communism, who had gone through a severe school. It is such experience that must form the basis of all the activities of the Young Communist League.

I have replied to the questions of what we must learn, what we must take from the old schools and from the old science. I shall now try to answer the question of how this must be learnt. The answer is: only by inseparably linking each step in the activities of the schools, each step in training, education and teaching, with the struggle of all the working people against the exploiters.

I shall quote a few examples from the experience of the work of some of the youth organisations so as to illustrate how this training in communism should proceed. Everybody is talking about abolishing illiteracy. You know that a communist society cannot be built in an illiterate country. It is not enough for the Soviet government to issue an order, or for the Party to issue a particular slogan, or to assign a certain number of the best workers to this task. The young generation itself must take up this work. Communism means that the youth, the young men and women who belong to the Youth League, should say: this is our job; we shall unite and go into the rural districts to abolish illiteracy, so that there shall be no illiterates among our young people. We are trying to get the rising generation to devote their activities to this work. You know that we cannot rapidly transform an ignorant and illiterate Russia into a literate country. But if the Youth League sets to work on the job, and if all young people work for the benefit of all, the League, with a membership of 400,000 young men and women, will be entitled to call itself a Young Communist League. It is also a task of the League, not only to acquire knowledge itself, but to help those young people who are unable to extricate themselves by their own efforts from the toils of illiteracy. Being a member of the Youth League means devoting one's labour and efforts to the common cause. That is what a communist education means. Only in the course of such work do young men and women become real Communists. Only if they achieve practical results in this work will they become Communists.

Take, for example, work in the suburban vegetable gardens. Is that not a real job of work? It is one of the tasks of the Young Communist League. People are starving; there is hunger in the factories. To save ourselves from starvation, vegetable gardens must be developed. But farming is being carried on in the old way. Therefore, more class-conscious elements should engage in this work, and then you will find that the number of vegetable gardens will increase, their acreage will grow, and the results will improve. The Young Communist League must take an active part in this work. Every League and League branch should regard this as its duty.

The Young Communist League must be a shock force, helping in every job and displaying initiative and enterprise. The League should be an organisation enabling any worker to see that it consists of people whose teachings he perhaps does not understand, and whose teachings he may not immediately believe, but from whose practical work and activity he can see that they are really people who are showing him the right road.

If the Young Communist League fails to organise its work in this way in all fields, it will mean that it is reverting to the old bourgeois path. We must combine our education with the struggle of the working people against the exploiters, so as to help the former accomplish the tasks set by the teachings of communism.

The members of the League should use every spare hour to improve the vegetable gardens, or to organise the education of young people at some factory, and so on. We want to transform Russia from a poverty-stricken and wretched country into one that is wealthy. The Young Communist League must combine its education, learning and training with the labour of the workers and peasants, so as not to confine itself to schools or to reading communist books and pamphlets. Only by working side by side with the workers and peasants can one become a genuine Communist. It has to be generally realised that all members of the Youth League are literate people and at the same time are keen at their jobs. When everyone sees that we have ousted the old drill-ground methods from the old schools and have replaced them with conscious discipline, that all young men and women take part in subbotniks, and utilise every suburban farm to help the population—people will cease to regard labour in the old way.

It is the task of the Young Communist League to organise assistance everywhere, in village or city block, in such matters as—and I shall take a small example—public hygiene or the distribution of food. How was this done in the old, capitalist society? Everybody worked only for himself and nobody cared a straw for the aged and the sick, or whether housework was the concern only of the women, who, in consequence, were in a condition of oppression and servitude. Whose business is it to combat this? It is the business of the Youth Leagues, which must say: we shall change all this; we shall organise detachments of young people who will help to assure public hygiene or distribute food, who will conduct systematic house-to-house inspections, and work in an organised way for the benefit of the whole of society, distributing their forces properly and demonstrating that labour must be organised.

The generation of people who are now at the age of fifty cannot expect to see a communist society. This generation will be gone before then. But the generation of those who are now fifteen will see a communist society, and will itself build this society. This generation should know that the entire purpose of their lives is to build a communist society. In the old society, each family worked separately and labour was not organised by anybody except the landowners and capitalists, who oppressed the masses of the people. We must organise all labour, no matter how toilsome or messy it may be, in such a way that every worker and peasant will be able to say: I am part of the great army of free labour, and shall be able to build up my life without the landowners and capitalists, able to help establish a communist system. The Young Communist League should teach all young people to engage in conscious and disciplined labour from an early age. In this way we can be confident that the problems now confronting us will be solved. We must assume that no less than ten years will be required for the electrification of the country, so that our impoverished land may profit from the latest achievements of technology. And so, the generation of those who are now fifteen years old, and will be living in a communist society in ten or twenty years' time, should tackle all its educational tasks in such a way that every day, in every village and city, the young people shall engage in the practical solution of some problem of labour in common, even though the smallest or the simplest. The success of communist construction will be assured when this is done in every village, as communist emulation develops, and the youth prove that they can unite their labour. Only by regarding your every step from the standpoint of the success of that construction, and only by asking ourselves whether we have done all we can to be united and politically-conscious working people will the Young Communist League succeed in uniting its half a million members into a single army of labour and win universal respect. (*Stormy applause.*)

SPEECH DELIVERED AT AN ALL-RUSSIA CONFERENCE OF POLITICAL EDUCATION WORKERS OF GUBERNIA AND UYEZD EDUCATION DEPARTMENTS (1920[1])

Comrades, allow me to speak on several ideas, some of which were dealt with by the Central Committee of the Communist Party and by the Council of People's Commissars in connection with the formation of the Chief Committee for Political Education, while others came to me in connection with the draft submitted to the Council of People's Commissars. This draft was adopted yesterday as a basis; its details have still to be discussed.

I shall permit myself only to say, for my part, that at first I was highly averse to any change in the name of your institution. In my opinion, the function of the People's Commissariat of Education is to help people learn and teach others. My Soviet experience has taught me to regard titles as childish jokes; after all, any title is a joke in its way. Another name has now been endorsed: the Chief Committee for Political Education.

As this matter has already been decided, you must take this as nothing more than a personal remark. If the matter is not limited merely to a change of label, it is only to be welcomed.

If we succeed in drawing new people into cultural and educational work, it will not be just a change of title, and then we can reconcile ourselves to the "Soviet" weakness of sticking a label on every new undertaking and every new institution. If we succeed, we shall have achieved something more than ever before.

The link between education and our policy should be the chief

[1] The Conference met in Moscow from November 2 to 8, 1920, with 283 delegates attending. The main question discussed was the establishment of the Chief Committee for Political Education. A.V. Lunacharsky delivered the opening address, in which he dealt with the work done in the sphere of political education. The Conference also heard a report by N.K. Krupskaya on the current plan of work of the Chief Committee for Political Education, and Y.A. Litkens's report on the organisation of local political education departments. Other items on the agenda concerned the food campaign and political education, production propaganda in the light of the rehabilitation of economic activity, and the elimination of illiteracy. Lenin spoke after Krupskaya at the third session of the Conference, on the second day of the proceedings.

inducement in making people join us in our cultural and educational work. A title may express something if there is a need for it, for along the whole line of our educational work we have to abandon the old standpoint that education should be non-political; we cannot conduct educational work in isolation from politics.

That idea has always predominated in bourgeois society. The very term "apolitical" or "non-political" education is a piece of bourgeois hypocrisy, nothing but humbuggery practised on the masses, 99 per cent of whom are humiliated and degraded by the rule of the church, private property and the like. That, in fact, is the way the bourgeoisie, still in the saddle in all bourgeois countries, is deceiving the masses.

The greater the importance of a political apparatus in such countries, the less its independence of capital and its policy.

In all bourgeois states the connection between the political apparatus and education is very strong, although bourgeois society cannot frankly acknowledge it. Nevertheless, this society indoctrinates the masses through the church and the institution of private property.

It is one of our basic tasks to contrapose our own truth to bourgeois "truth", and win its recognition.

The transition from bourgeois society to the policy of the proletariat is a very difficult one, all the more so for the bourgeoisie incessantly slandering us through its entire apparatus of propaganda and agitation. It bends every effort to play down an even more important mission of the dictatorship of the proletariat, its educational mission, which is particularly important in Russia, where the proletariat constitutes a minority of the population. Yet in Russia this mission must be given priority, for we must prepare the masses to build up socialism. The dictatorship of the proletariat would have been out of the question if, in the struggle against the bourgeoisie, the proletariat had not developed a keen class-consciousness, strict discipline and profound devotion, in other words, all the qualities required to assure the proletariat's complete victory over its old enemy.

We do not hold the utopian view that the working masses are ready for a socialist society. From precise facts provided by the entire history of working-class socialism we know that this is not the case, and that preparedness for socialism is created only by large-scale industry, by the strike struggle and by political organisation. To win the victory and accomplish the socialist revolution, the proletariat must be capable of concerted action, of overthrowing the exploiters. We now see that it has acquired all the necessary qualities, and that it translated them into action when it won power.

Education workers, and the Communist Party as the vanguard in the struggle, should consider it their fundamental task to help enlighten and instruct the working masses, in order to cast off the old ways and habituated routine we have inherited from the old system, the private property habits the masses are thoroughly imbued with. This fundamental task of the entire socialist revolution should never be neglected during consideration of the particular problems that have demanded so much attention from the Party's Central Committee and the Council of People's Commissars. What kind of structure should the Chief Committee for Political Education have? How should it be linked up with other institutions? How should it be linked up, not only with the centre but with local bodies? These questions will be answered by comrades who are more competent in the matter, have already gained considerable experience, and have made a special study of the matter. I would like merely to stress the main principles involved. We must put the matter frankly and openly affirm, despite all the old untruths, that education cannot but be linked up with politics.

We are living in an historic period of struggle against the world bourgeoisie, which is far stronger than we are. At this stage of the struggle, we have to safeguard the development of the revolution and combat the bourgeoisie in the military sense and still more by means of our ideology through education, so that the habits, usages and convictions acquired by the working class in the course of many decades of struggle for political liberty—the sum total of these habits, usages and ideas—should serve as an instrument for the education of all working people. It is for the proletariat to decide how the latter are to be educated. We must inculcate in the working people the realisation that it is impossible and inexcusable to stand aside in the proletariat's struggle, which is now spreading more and more to all capitalist countries in the world, and to stand aside in international politics. An alliance of all the world's powerful capitalist countries against Soviet Russia—such is the real basis of international politics today. And it must, after all, be realised that on this will depend the fate of hundreds of millions of working people in the capitalist countries. We know that, at the present moment, there is not a corner of the earth which is not under the control of a small group of capitalist countries. Thus the situation is shaping in such a way that one is faced with the alternative of standing aloof from the present struggle and thereby proving one's utter lack of political consciousness, just like those benighted people who have held aloof from the revolution and the war and do not see the bourgeoisie's gross deception of the masses, the deliberate way in which the bourgeoisie is keeping the masses in ignorance; or else of joining the struggle for the dictatorship of the proletariat.

It is with absolute frankness that we speak of this struggle of the proletariat; each man must choose between joining our side or the other side. Any attempt to avoid taking sides in this issue must end in fiasco.

Observation of the many remnants of the Kerensky gang, the Socialist-Revolutionaries and the Social-Democrats, as represented by the Yudeniches, Kolchaks, Petlyuras, Makhnos and others, has shown us such a variety of forms and shades of counter-revolution in various parts of Russia that we have every reason to consider ourselves far more steeled in the struggle than anybody else is. A glance at Western Europe shows the same thing happening there as in our country—a repetition of our own history. Almost everywhere elements similar to the Kerensky gang are to be met alongside the bourgeoisie. They predominate in a number of countries, especially Germany. One can see the same thing everywhere—the impossibility of taking an intermediate position, and a clear realisation that there must be either a whiteguard dictatorship (for which the bourgeoisie of all the countries of Western Europe are preparing by arming against us), or the dictatorship of the proletariat. We have experienced this so acutely and profoundly that there is no need for me to talk at length about the Russian Communists. Hence there can be only a single conclusion, one that should be the corner-stone of all arguments and theories about the Chief Committee for Political Education: the primacy of the Communist Party's policy must be frankly recognised in the work of that body. We know of no other form of guidance, and no other has been evolved in any country. Parties may represent the interests of their class in one degree or another; they may undergo changes or modifications, but we do not yet know of any better form. The entire course of the struggle waged by Soviet Russia, which for three years has withstood the onslaught of world imperialism, is bound up with the fact that the Party has consciously set out to help the proletariat perform its function of educator, organiser and leader, without which the collapse of capitalism is impossible. The working masses, the masses of peasants and workers, must oust the old intellectualist habits and re-educate themselves for the work of building communism. Otherwise the work of construction cannot be undertaken. Our entire experience shows that this is a very serious matter, and we must therefore give prominence to Party primacy and never lose sight of it when discussing our activities and our organisational development. How this is to be done will still have to be discussed at length; it will have to be discussed in the Party's Central Committee and in the Council of People's Commissars. The decree which was endorsed yesterday laid down the fundamentals in respect of the Chief Committee for Political Education, but it has not yet gone through all the stages in the Council of People's Commissars. The decree will be published within the next few days, and you will see that its final form makes no direct mention of relations with the Party.

We must, however, know and remember that, in law and in practice, the Constitution of the Soviet Republic is based on the tenet that the Party rectifies, prescribes and builds according to a single principle—to enable the communist elements linked with the proletariat to imbue the proletariat with their own spirit, win its adherence, and open its eyes to the bourgeois deceit which we have been trying so long to eliminate. The People's Commissariat of Education has gone through a long struggle; for a long time the teachers' organisation resisted the socialist revolution. Bourgeois prejudices have struck very deep root among the teachers. There has been a long struggle in the form of direct sabotage and of tenacious bourgeois prejudices, and we have to fight for the communist positions slowly, step by step and win them. The Chief Committee for Political Education, which is concerned with extra-mural education, the work of educating and enlightening the masses, is faced with the clear task of combining Party leadership with the effort to gain the adherence of, to imbue with its spirit and to animate with its initiative, this half-million strong army of teachers, this vast institution which is now in the service of the workers. Education workers—the teachers—were trained in the spirit of bourgeois prejudices and habits, in a spirit hostile to the proletariat, with which they have had no ties whatever. We must now train a new army of teachers and instructors who must be in close touch with the Party and its ideas, be imbued with its spirit, and attract the masses of workers, instilling the spirit of communism into them and arousing their interest in what is being done by the Communists.

Since the old customs, habits and ideas must be discarded, the Chief Committee for Political Education and its personnel are faced with a most important task, which they must keep uppermost in their minds. Here we indeed have a dilemma: how can we establish a link between the teachers, most of whom are of the old school, with Party members, with the Communists? That is an extremely difficult problem, one that will require a considerable amount of thought.

Let us consider the means of establishing organisational links between people who are so different. In principle, we cannot for a moment doubt the need of the Communist Party's primacy. Consequently, the purpose of political culture, of political instruction, is to train genuine Communists capable of stamping out falsehood and prejudices and helping the working masses to vanquish the old system and build up a state without capitalists, without exploiters, and without landowners. How can that be done? Only by acquiring the sum total of knowledge that the teachers have inherited from the bourgeoisie. Without this the technical achievements of communism will be impossible, and all hopes for those achievements would be pipe dreams. So the question arises: how are we to organise these people, who are not used to bringing politics into their work, especially the politics that is to our advantage, i.e., politics essential to communism? That, as I have said, is a very difficult problem. We have discussed the matter in the Central Committee, and in discussing it have tried to take into account the lessons of experience. We think that a congress like the one I am addressing today, a conference like yours, will be of great value in this respect. Every Party Committee now has to look from a new angle upon every propagandist, who used to be regarded merely as a man belonging to a definite circle, a definite organisation. Each of them belongs to a ruling party which directs the whole state, and the Soviet Russia's world struggle against the bourgeois system. He is a representative of a fighting class and of a party which runs, and must run, an enormous machine of state. Many a Communist who has been through the splendid school of underground work and has been tested and steeled in the struggle is unwilling or unable to understand the full significance of this change, of this transition, which turns the agitator and propagandist into a leader of agitators, a leader in a huge political organisation. The kind of title he is given, even if it is an embarrassing one—such as superintendent of general schools—does not matter much; what is important is that he should be capable of directing the mass of teachers.

It should be said that the hundreds of thousands of teachers constitute a body that must get the work moving, stimulate thought, and combat the prejudices that to this day still persist among the masses. The heritage of capitalist culture, the fact that the mass of the teachers are imbued with its defects, which prevent them from being Communists, should not deter us from admitting these teachers into the ranks of the political education workers, for these teachers possess the knowledge without which we cannot achieve our aim.

We must put hundreds of thousands of useful people to work in the service of communist education. That is a task that was accomplished at the front, in our Red Army, into which tens of thousands of representatives of the old army were incorporated. In the lengthy process of re-education, they became welded with the Red Army, as they ultimately proved by their victories. This is an example that we must follow in our cultural and educational work. True, this work is not so spectacular, but it is even more important. We need every agitator and propagandist; he will be doing his job if he works in a strictly Party spirit but at the same time does not limit himself to Party work, and remembers that it is his duty to direct hundreds of thousands of teachers, whet their interest, overcome their old bourgeois prejudices, enlist them in the work we are doing, and make them realise the immensity of our work. It is only by tackling that job that we can lead this mass of people, whom capitalism suppressed and drew away from us, along the right path.

Such are the aims that every agitator and propagandist working in the sphere of extra-mural education must pursue and constantly keep in sight. A host of practical difficulties will be encountered in the process, and you must help the cause of communism by becoming representatives and leaders, not only of Party study-circles, but of the entire state administration, which is now in the hands of the working *class*.

We must overcome resistance from the capitalists in all its forms, not only in the military and the political spheres, but also ideological resistance, which is the most deep-seated and the strongest. It is the duty of our educational workers to accomplish the re-education of the masses. The interest, the thirst for education and knowledge of communism which are to be seen among them are a guarantee of our victory in this field too, although, perhaps, not as rapid as at the front and only after great difficulties and at times even reverses. However, we shall ultimately win.

Last, I should like to dwell on one more point. Perhaps the title of Chief Committee for Political Education is not properly understood. Inasmuch as it makes mention of the political concept, politics is the main thing here.

But how is politics to be understood? If politics is understood in the old sense, one may fall into a grave and profound error. Politics means a struggle between classes; means the relations of the proletariat in its struggle for its emancipation, against the world bourgeoisie. However, in our struggle two aspects of the matter stand out: on the one hand, there is the task of destroying the heritage of the bourgeois system, of foiling the repeated attempts of the whole bourgeoisie to crush the

Soviet state. This task has absorbed most of our attention hitherto and has prevented us from proceeding to the other task, that of construction. According to the bourgeois world outlook, politics was divorced, as it were, from economics. The bourgeoisie said: peasants, you must work for your livelihood; workers, you must work to secure your means of subsistence on the market; as for economic policy, that is the business of your masters. That, however, is not so; politics should be the business of the people, the business of the proletariat. Here we must emphasise the fact that nine-tenths of our time and our work is devoted to the struggle against the bourgeoisie. The victories over Wrangel, of which we read yesterday, and of which you will read today and probably tomorrow, show that one stage of the struggle is coming to an end and that we have secured peace with a number of Western countries; every victory on the war front leaves our hands freer for the internal struggle, for the politics of state organisation. Every step that brings us closer to victory over the whiteguards gradually shifts the focus of the struggle to economic policy. Propaganda of the old type describes and illustrates what communism is. This kind of propaganda is now useless, for we have to show in practice how socialism is to be built. All our propaganda must be based on the political experience of economic development. That is our principal task; whoever interprets it in the old sense will show himself to be a retrograde, one who is incapable of conducting propaganda work among the masses of the peasants and workers. Our main policy must now be to develop the state economically, so as to gather in more poods of grain and mine more poods of coal, to decide how best to utilise these poods of grain and coal and preclude starvation—that is our policy. All our agitation and propaganda must be focussed on this aim. There must be less fine talk, for you cannot satisfy the working people with fine words. As soon as the war enables us to shift the focus from the struggle against the bourgeoisie, from the struggle against Wrangel and the whiteguards, we shall turn to economic policy. And then agitation and propaganda will play a role of tremendous and ever growing importance.

Every agitator must be a state leader, a leader of all the peasants and workers in the work of economic development. He must tell them what one should know, what pamphlets and books one should read to become a Communist.

That is the way to improve our economic life and make it more secure, more social; that is the way to increase production, improve the food situation and distribution of the goods produced, increase coal output, and restore industry without capitalism and without the capitalist spirit.

What does communism consist in? All propaganda for communism must be conducted in a way that will amount to practical guidance of the state's development. Communism must be made comprehensible to the masses of the workers so that they will regard it as their own cause. That task is being poorly accomplished, and thousands of mistakes are being made. We make no secret of the fact. However, the workers and the peasants must themselves build up and improve our apparatus, with our assistance, feeble and inadequate as it is. To us, that is no longer a programme, a theory, or a task to be accomplished; it has become a matter of actual and practical development. Although we suffered some cruel reverses in our war, we have at least learnt from these reverses and won complete victory. Now, too, we must learn a lesson from every defeat and must remember that the workers and peasants have to be instructed by taking the work already performed as an example. We must point out what is bad, so as to avoid it in future.

By taking constructive work as an example, by repeating it time and again, we shall succeed in turning inefficient communist managers into genuine builders, and, in the first place, into builders of our economic life. We shall achieve our targets and overcome all the obstacles which we have inherited from the old system and cannot be eliminated at a single stroke. We must re-educate the masses; they can be re-educated only by agitation and propaganda. The masses must be brought, in the first place, into the work of building the entire economic life. That must be the principal and basic object in the work of each agitator and propagandist, and when he realises this, the success of his work will be assured. (*Loud applause.*)

November 3, 1920

THE PARTY CRISIS
(1921)

The pre-Congress discussion is in full swing. Minor differences and disagreements have grown into big ones, which always happens when someone persists in a minor mistake and balks at its correction, or when those who are making a big mistake seize on the minor mistake of one or more persons.

That is how disagreements and splits always grow. That is how we "grew up" from minor disagreements to syndicalism, which means a complete break with communism and an inevitable split in the Party if it is not healthy and strong enough to purge itself of the malaise.

We must have the courage to face the bitter truth. The Party is sick. The Party is down with the fever. The whole point is whether the malaise has affected only the "feverish upper ranks", and perhaps only those in Moscow, or the whole organism. And if the latter is the case, is it capable of healing itself completely within the next few weeks, before the Party Congress and at the Party Congress, making a relapse impossible, or will the malaise linger and become dangerous?

What is it that needs to be done for a rapid and certain cure? *All* members of the Party must make a calm and painstaking *study* of 1) the essence of the disagreements and 2) the development of the Party struggle. A study must be made of both, because the essence of the disagreements is revealed, clarified and specified (and very often transformed as well) in the *course of the struggle*, which, passing through its various stages, always shows, at every stage, a *different* line-up and number of combatants, *different* positions in the struggle, etc. A *study* must be made of both, and a demand made for the most exact, printed documents that can be thoroughly verified. Only a hopeless idiot will believe oral statements. If *no* documents are available, there must be an examination of witnesses on *both* or several sides and the grilling must take place in the presence of witnesses.

Let me outline the essence of the disagreements and the successive stages in the struggle, as I see them.

Stage one. The Fifth All-Russia Trade Union Conference November 2-6. The battle is joined. Trotsky and Tomsky are the only Central Committee "combatants". Trotsky lets drop a "catchy phrase" about "shaking up" the trade unions. Tomsky argues very heatedly. The majority of the Central Committee members are on the fence. The serious mistake they (and I above all) made was that we "overlooked" Rudzutak's theses, *The Tasks of the Trade Unions in Production*, adopted by the Fifth Conference. That is the *most* important document in the whole of the controversy.

Stage two. The Central Committee Plenum of November 9. Trotsky submits his "draft theses", *The Trade Unions and Their Future Role*, advocating the "shake-up" policy *camouflaged* or adorned with talk of a "severe crisis" gripping the trade unions, and their new tasks and methods. Tomsky, strongly supported by Lenin, considers that in view of Tsektran's[1] irregularities and bureaucratic excesses it is the "shake-up" that is the crux of the whole controversy. In the course of it, Lenin makes a number of obviously exaggerated and therefore mistaken "attacks", which produces the need for a "buffer group", and this is made up of ten members of the Central Committee (the group includes Bukharin and Zinoviev, but neither Trotsky nor Lenin). It resolves "not to put the disagreements up for broad discussion", and, *cancelling Lenin's report* (to the trade unions), appoints Zinoviev as the rapporteur and instructs him to "present a business-like and non-controversial report".

Trotsky's theses are rejected. Lenin's theses are adopted. In its final form, the resolution is adopted by ten votes to four (Trotsky, Andreyev, Krestinsky and Rykov). And this resolution advocates "sound forms of the militarisation of labour", condemns "the degeneration of centralism and militarised forms of work into bureaucratic practices, petty tyranny, red-tape", etc. Tsektran is instructed to "take a more active part in the

[1] *Tsektran*—the Central Committee of the Joint Trade Union of Rail and Water Transport Workers. In September 1920, the two unions were merged to set up a strong centralised administration capable of tackling the tasks of rapidly rehabilitating transport, whose stoppages tended to paralyse the national economy. Its extraordinary powers and military methods of work, which sprang from the enormity of the tasks before it, bred bureaucratic practices, the appointments system, administration by injunction, etc. It fell into the hands of the Trotskyites, who set the workers against the Party and split their unity. The plenary meetings of the C.C. on November 8 and December 7, 1920, condemned Tsektran's methods and adopted a decision to incorporate it into the general system of the All-Russia Central Council of Trade Unions on a par with other unions. Tsektran was advised to change its methods, develop trade union democracy, make all trade union bodies elective, reduce the appointments system, etc. The First All-Russia Congress of Transport Workers in March 1921 called by the Central Committee of the Party expelled the Trotskyites from the Tsektran leadership and outlined new methods of work.

general work of the All-Russia Central Council of Trade Unions, being incorporated in it on an equal footing with other trade union bodies".

The Central Committee sets up a trade union commission and elects Comrade Trotsky to it. He refuses to work on the commission, magnifying by this step *alone* his original mistake, which subsequently leads to factionalism. Without that step, his mistake (in submitting incorrect theses) remained a very minor one, such as every member of the Central Committee, without exception, has had occasion to make.

Stage three. The conflict between the water transport workers and Tsektran in December. The Central Committee Plenary Meeting of December 7. It is no longer Trotsky and Lenin, but Trotsky and Zinoviev who are the chief "combatants". As chairman of the trade union commission, Zinoviev inquires into the December dispute between the water transport workers and Tsektran. The Central Committee Plenary Meeting of December 7. Zinoviev makes a practical proposal for an immediate change in the composition of Tsektran. This is opposed by a majority of the Central Committee. Rykov goes over to Zinoviev's side. Bukharin's resolution—the substantive part of which is three-quarters in favour of the water transport workers, while the preamble, rejecting the proposal to "reconstruct" the trade unions "from above" (§3), approves of the celebrated "industrial democracy" (§5)—is adopted. Our group of Central Committee members is in the minority, being opposed to Bukharin's resolution chiefly because we consider the "buffer" a paper one; for Trotsky's non-participation in the trade union commission's work actually implies a continuation of the struggle and its transfer outside the Central Committee. We propose that the Party Congress be convened on February 6, 1921. That is adopted. The postponement to March 6 was agreed to later, on the demand of the outlying areas.

Stage four. The Eighth Congress of Soviets. On December 25, Trotsky issues his "platform pamphlet", *The Role and Tasks of the Trade Unions*. From the standpoint of formal democracy, Trotsky had an uncontested right to issue his platform, for on December 24 the Central Committee had permitted free discussion. From the standpoint of revolutionary interest, this was blowing up the mistake out of all proportion and *creating a faction* on a faulty platform. The pamphlet quotes from the Central Committee resolution of December 7 only that part which refers to "industrial democracy" but does *not* quote what was said against "reconstruction from above". The buffer created by Bukharin on December 7 with Trotsky's aid was wrecked by Trotsky on December 25. The pamphlet from beginning to end is shot through with the "shake-up" spirit. Apart from its intellectualist flourishes ("production atmosphere", "industrial democracy"), which are wrong in theory and in practice fall within the concept, ambit and tasks of production propaganda, it *fails* to indicate any "new" "tasks or methods" that were to gild or camouflage or justify the "shake-up".

Stage five. The discussion before thousands of responsible Party workers from all over Russia at the R.C.P. group of the Eighth Congress of Soviets on December 30. The controversy flares up to full blast. Zinoviev and Lenin on one side, Trotsky and Bukharin on the other. Bukharin wants to play the "buffer", but speaks only against Lenin and Zinoviev, and not a word against Trotsky. Bukharin reads out an excerpt from his theses (published on January 16), but only that part which says nothing about the rupture with communism and the switch to syndicalism. Shlyapnikov (on behalf of the Workers' Opposition[2]) reads out the

[2] *The Workers' Opposition*—an anti-Party anarcho-syndicalist group under the leadership of A.G. Shlyapnikov, S.P. Medvedyev, A.M. Kollontai, I.I. Kutuzov, Y.K. Lutovinov, etc. It first came out under its demagogic name at the Ninth All-Russia Conference of the R.C.P.(B.) in September 1920.

In November the group launched a factional struggle undermining the unity of the Party and organised a special discussion at the Moscow Gubernia Conference of the R.C.P.(B.). It took final shape as the Workers' Opposition in 1920-21 during the discussion on the trade unions. Its views constituted an anarcho-syndicalist deviation within the Party and were expounded in full in Kollontai's pamphlet, *The Workers' Opposition*, published on the eve of the Tenth Party Congress, proposing that the national economy should be run by an All-Russia Congress of Producers organised in industrial trade unions. It wanted all economic bodies to be elected by the trade unions, with Party and Soviet organs having no power to reject the candidates nominated by the trade unions. It denied that the Party had the leading role to play in socialist construction and that the dictatorship of the proletariat was the Party's chief instrument. It said it was not the Party but the trade unions that were the highest form of workers' organisation.

The Workers' Opposition had some temporary support among workers swayed by petty-bourgeois influence and tried to use their vacillation to promote its narrow interests. It also had some sympathisers in central and local Party organisations. Thus, its platform won 21 per cent of the vote at the Moscow Gubernia Party Conference in November 1920; 30 per cent at the Communist group meeting of the Second All-Russia Congress of Miners in early 1921, but less than 6 per cent at the Tenth Party Congress. The Congress completely defeated the Workers' Opposition; this was the result of the Party's educational work exposing the Opposition's demagogic anti-Party views. It lost ground among the rank and file and was heavily defeated at the Tenth Congress. Lenin's resolution, "On the Syndicalist and Anarchist Deviation in our Party", stressed that the views of the Workers' Opposition

syndicalist platform, which Trotsky had demolished beforehand (thesis 16 of his platform) and which (partly, perhaps, for that reason) no one is inclined to take seriously.

In my opinion, the climax of the whole discussion of December 30 was the reading of Comrade Rudzutak's theses. Indeed, Comrades Trotsky and Bukharin, far from being able to object to them, even invented the legend that the "best part" of the theses had been drawn up by *members of Tsektran*—Holtzmann, Andreyev and Lyubimov. And that is why Trotsky humorously and amiably twitted Lenin on his unsuccessful "diplomacy", by which, he said, Lenin had wanted to "call off or disrupt" the discussion, and find a "lightning conductor", "accidentally catching hold of Tsektran instead of the lightning conductor".

The legend was exploded that very day, December 30, by Rudzutak, who pointed out that Lyubimov "did not exist" on the All-Russia Central Council of Trade Unions, that in its presidium Holtzmann had voted against these theses, and that they had been drawn up by a commission consisting of Andreyev, Tsiperovich and himself.[3]

were wrong theoretically and "tended to weaken the Communist Party's consistent general line, actually helping the class enemy of the proletarian revolution". See *K.P.S.S. v rezolutsiakh . . .* (The C.P.S.U. in the Resolutions and Decisions of Congresses, Conferences and C.C. Plenary Meetings, Part 1, 1954, p. 532). The Congress decided that the propaganda of the Workers' Opposition ideas was incompatible with membership in the Party. Its resolution on the Party's unity demanded the immediate dissolution of all anti-Party groups, whatever their platforms. Most rank-and-file members of the Opposition broke with the group and gave sincere support to the Party's line. But Shlyapnikov and Medvedyev headed the remnants in an illegal organisation which continued to conduct anti-Party propaganda behind a facade of ultra-revolutionary phrases. In February 1922, they sent to the Executive Committee of the Comintern their "Declaration of 22", a slanderous attack on the Party. The Executive Committee studied the "Declaration", condemned the group, and warned that any further activity on their part would put them outside the Third International. Their organisational defeat was completed by the Party's Eleventh Congress in 1922.

[3] At a joint meeting of the Party groups of the Eighth Congress of Soviets, the All-Russia Central Council of Trade Unions and the Moscow City Council of Trade Unions, an argument took place as to whether Y.E. Rudzutak was the author of the theses, *The Tasks of the Trade Unions in Production*. Lenin asked the Trade Union Central Council for documents on the origin of the theses. He was given an extract from record No. 44 of the minutes of November 1, and a covering note from S.A. Lozovsky. The extract proved that the Presidium had discussed and adopted Rudzutak's theses as a basis

But let us for a moment assume that Comrades Trotsky and Bukharin's legend is true. Nothing so completely defeats them as such an assumption. For what is the conclusion if the "Tsektranites" had inserted their "new" ideas into Rudzutak's resolution, if Rudzutak had accepted them, if all the trade unions had adopted this resolution (November 2-6!), and if Bukharin and Trotsky have nothing to say against it?

It is that all of Trotsky's disagreements are artificial, that *neither* he *nor* the "Tsektranites" *have any* "new tasks or methods", and that everything practical and substantive had been said, adopted and *decided upon* by the trade unions, *even before the question was raised in the Central Committee.*

If anyone ought to be taken thoroughly to task and "shaken up", it is not the All-Russia Central Council of Trade Unions but the Central Committee of the R.C.P., for having "overlooked" Rudzutak's theses, a mistake which allowed an altogether empty discussion to flare up. There is nothing to *cover up* the mistake of the Tsektranites (which is not an excessive one but is, in essence, a very common one, consisting in some exaggeration of bureaucracy). What is more, it needs to be rectified, and not covered up, toned down or justified. That's all there is to it.

I summed up the substance of Rudzutak's theses on December 30 in four points: 1) Ordinary democracy (without any exaggerations, without denying the Central Committee's right of "appointment", etc., but also without any obstinate defence of the mistakes and excesses of certain "appointees", which need to be rectified); 2) Production propaganda (this includes all that is practical in clumsy, ridiculous, theoretically wrong "formulas" like "industrial democracy", "production atmosphere", etc.). We have established a *Soviet institution*, the All-Russia Production Propaganda Bureau. We must do everything to support it and not spoil production work by *producing . . . bad theses*. That's all there is to it; 3)

and had instructed M.P. Tomsky and Rudzutak to put finishing touches to the theses. The note said this was done by Rudzutak alone. The Fifth All-Russia Conference of Trade Unions heard Rudzutak's report, adopted his theses as a basis and elected a commission, consisting of G.V. Tsiperovich, A.A. Andreyev and Rudzutak, to edit them. They worked out several points and amplified the theses.

Lenin sent the documents and Rudzutak's theses to *Pravda* with his covering letter, which said: "I request the Editorial Board to publish Rudzutak's theses, which were adopted by the Fifth All-Russia Trade Union Conference of November 2-6, 1920, and are indispensable to the discussion. I enclose additional material on the disagreements in Party circles concerning the origin of these theses." The documents and Lenin's letter were published in *Pravda* No. 13 on January 21, 1921.

Bonuses in kind and 4) Disciplinary comrades' courts. Without Points 3 and 4, all talk about "the role and tasks in production", etc., is empty, highbrow chatter; and it is these two points that are omitted from Trotsky's "platform pamphlet". But they are in Rudzutak's theses.

While dealing with the December 30 discussion, I must correct another mistake of mine. I said: "Ours is not actually a workers' state but a workers' and peasants' state." Comrade Bukharin immediately exclaimed: "What kind of a state?" In reply I referred him to the Eighth Congress of Soviets, which had just closed. I went back to the report of that discussion and found that I was wrong and Comrade Bukharin was right. What I should have said is: "A workers' state is an abstraction. What we actually have is a workers' state, with this peculiarity, firstly, that it is not the working class but the peasant population that predominates in the country, and, secondly, that it is a workers' state with bureaucratic distortions." Anyone who reads the whole of my speech will see that this correction makes no difference to my reasoning or conclusions.

Stage six. The Petrograd organisation issues an "Appeal to the Party" against Trotsky's platform, and the Moscow Committee issues a counter-statement (*Pravda*, January 13[4]).

This is a transition from the struggle between factions, formed from above, to the intervention of lower organisations. It is a big step towards recovery. Curiously enough, the Moscow Committee noticed the "dangerous" side of the *Petrograd organisation*'s issuing a platform, but refused to notice the *dangerous side* of Comrade Trotsky's forming a

[4] The "Appeal to the Party" was adopted at a discussion meeting of the representatives of Petrograd district Party organisations on January 3, 1921. On January 6, it was approved by a city meeting in People's House which was attended by over 4,000 Party members and candidates. Only 20 votes were cast against it. When it was discussed in the district Party organisations it had the support of 95-98 per cent of the membership.

The Petrograd Bolsheviks supported Lenin and opposed Trotsky on the question of the trade unions' role and tasks. They called the other Party organisations to follow Lenin and stressed the danger of Trotsky's platform, for its realisation would have abolished the trade unions and undermined the dictatorship of the proletariat. *Pravda* No. 7 of January 13 published the Appeal and also the counter-statement of the Moscow Party Committee, which at that time took a "buffer" stand. In a resolution published in the same issue of *Pravda* the Moscow Committee said that it found "it absolutely impossible" to accept the Petrograd proposals; it said the Petrograd Party organisation's stand showed its "extremely dangerous" tendency to become a special centre for preparing the Party Congress; it did not condemn Trotsky's establishment of a faction, thereby giving support to his anti-Party struggle.

faction on December 25! Some wags have said this is "buffer" (one-eyed) blindness.

Stage seven. The trade union commission concludes its work and issues a platform (a pamphlet, entitled *Draft Decision of the Tenth Congress of the R.C.P. on the Role and Tasks of the Trade Unions*,[5] dated January 14 and signed by nine members of the Central Committee—Zinoviev, Stalin, Tomsky, Rudzutak, Kalinin, Kamenev, Petrovsky, Artyom and Lenin, and also by Lozovsky, a member of the trade union commission; Comrades Shlyapnikov and Lutovinov seem to have "fled" to the Workers' Opposition). It was published in *Pravda* on January 18, with the following additional signatures: Schmidt, Tsiperovich and Milyutin.

On January 16, *Pravda* carries the Bukharin platform (signed: "On behalf of a group of comrades, Bukharin, Larin, Preobrazhensky, Serebryakov, Sokolnikov, Yakovleva") and the Sapronov platform (signed: "A group of comrades standing for democratic centralism", Bubnov, Boguslavsky, Kamensky, Maximovsky, Osinsky, Rafail, Sapronov).[6] The

[5] *Draft Decision of the Tenth Congress of the R.C.P. on the Role and Tasks of the Trade Unions* was Lenin's "Platform of 10" tabled before the Central Committee by a group of members of the C.C. and of the Central Committee's Trade Union Commission in opposition to the platforms of the anti-Party groups. It defined the role of the trade unions in the light of the new tasks connected with the end of the Civil War and transition to peaceful socialist construction: the trade unions, being a school of administration, a school of economic management, a school of communism, were chiefly to take part in government, train personnel for government bodies and economic agencies, and help tighten labour discipline. They were to base their work on education, persuasion and democratic practices. The Tenth Congress's resolution on the role and tasks of the trade unions was based on the "Platform of 10", which during the discussion had been supported by a majority of local Party organisations.

[6] An opportunist faction headed by M.S. Boguslavsky, A.Z. Kamensky, V.N. Maximovsky, N. Osinsky, Raphail (P.B. Farbman) and T.V. Sapronov. They first came out against Lenin's line in Party and Soviet organisation at the Eighth Party Congress. At the Ninth Congress, they had their own rapporteurs on economic construction and organisational problems, but failed to find any support among the Bolsheviks. On many questions they had backing only from the Mensheviks.

They denied the Party's leading role in the Soviets and trade unions and demanded freedom of factions and groups, and a merger of the Council of People's Commissars and the Presidium of the All-Russia Central Executive Committee, they opposed the subordination of local to central organs and wanted the Organisation Bureau of the Central Committee deprived of all say in political leadership, which would have split up the C.C.'s political and organisational unity. They opposed one-man management and the personal

enlarged meeting of the Moscow Committee on January 17 was addressed by spokesmen for these platforms, and also by the "Ignatovites"[7] (theses published in Pravda on January 19 and signed by Ignatov, Orekhov, Korzinov, Kuranova, Burovtsev, Maslov).[8]

What we find here is, on the one hand, increased solidarity (for the platform of the nine Central Committee members is in complete accord with the decision of the Fifth All-Russia Conference of Trade Unions); and, on the other, confusion and disintegration, with Bukharin and Co.'s theses being an all-time low in *ideological* disintegration. We have here one of those "turns" which in the old days Marxists used to call "not so much historical as hysterical". Thesis 17 says: "At the present

responsibility of managers in industry. In the Ukraine, they were against the "Poor Peasants' Committees" which were instruments of the proletariat's dictatorship in the countryside.

The group published its platform during the trade union discussion in 1920-21, but at the pre-Congress meetings it won only a handful of votes. At the Tenth Congress they withdrew their platform and allowed their members to vote freely. They continued to fight the Party on questions of organisation, on which V.N. Maximovsky delivered a co-report. After the Tenth Congress, only the leaders continued their anti-Party activity. In 1923, they joined the Trotskyites, and in 1926, formed the "Group of 15" headed by Sapronov and Smirnov, which was expelled from the Party by the Fifteenth Party Congress.

[7] *Ignatovites* or "a group of activists of Moscow city districts" was an anti-Party anarcho-syndicalist group, headed by Y.N. Ignatov, during the trade union discussion of 1920-21. Its activity was limited to the Moscow Party organisation, because it had no influence among the city's workers and rank-and-file Party members. Before the Tenth Party Congress, it came out with two platforms: the current tasks of the trade unions, and Party organisation. The Ignatovites shared the anarcho-syndicalist views of the Workers' Opposition; they set the trade unions in opposition to the Soviet state; denied the Party's leadership in socialist construction: opposed democratic centralism; demanded freedom of discussions, and wanted the Party membership to consist of workers only. They also demanded the handover of the administration of the economy to an organ elected by the All-Russia Trade Union Congress, but in contrast to the Workers' Opposition, they wanted the organ confirmed by the All-Russia Central Executive Committee as well. At the Tenth Congress, Ignatov was the official rapporteur of the Workers' Opposition on problems of Party organisation. After the Congress, the group broke up.

[8] Incidentally, the Party should demand that every "platform" be issued with the full signatures of all the comrades responsible for it. This demand is met by the "Ignatovites" and the "Sapronovites" but not by the "Trotskyites", the "Bukharinites" and the "Shlyapnikovites", who refer to anonymous comrades allegedly responsible for their platforms.—*Au.*

time, these nominations must be made *mandatory*" (that is, the trade unions' nominations to the respective "chief administrations and central boards").

This is a clean break with communism and a transition to syndicalism. It is, in essence, a repetition of Shlyapnikov's "unionise the state" slogan, and means transferring the Supreme Economic Council apparatus piecemeal to the respective trade unions. To say, "I propose *mandatory* nominations", is exactly the same as saying, "I appoint".

Communism says: The Communist Party, the vanguard of the proletariat, leads the non-Party workers' masses, educating, preparing, teaching and training the masses ("school" of communism)—first the workers and then the peasants—to enable them eventually to concentrate in their hands the administration of the whole national economy.

Syndicalism hands over to the mass of non-Party workers, who are compartmentalised in the industries, the management of their industries ("the chief administrations and central boards"), thereby making the Party superfluous, and failing to carry on a sustained campaign either in training the masses or in *actually* concentrating in *their* hands the management *of the whole national economy.*

The Programme of the R.C.P. says: "The trade unions *should eventually arrive*" (which means that they are not yet there or even on the way) "at a *de facto* concentration in their hands" (in *their*, that is, the hands of the trade unions, that is, the hands of the fully organised *masses*; anyone will see how far we have still to go even to the very first approaches to this *de facto* concentration) . . . concentration of what? "of the whole administration of the whole national economy, as a single economic entity" thence, not branches of industry, or even industry as a whole, but industry *plus* agriculture, etc. (Are we anywhere near to actually concentrating the management of agriculture in the hands of the trade unions?). The R.C.P. Programme then speaks of the "ties" between the "central state administration" and the "broad masses of toilers", and of the "*participation* of the trade unions in running the economy".

Why have a Party, if industrial management is to be appointed ("mandatory nomination") by the trade unions nine-tenths of whose members are non-Party workers? Bukharin has talked himself into a logical, theoretical and practical implication of a split in the Party, or, rather, a breakaway of the syndicalists from the Party.

Trotsky, who had been "chief" in the struggle, has now been "outstripped" and entirely "eclipsed" by Bukharin, who has thrown the struggle into an altogether new balance by talking himself into a mistake that is much more serious than all of Trotsky's put together.

How could Bukharin talk himself into a break with communism? We know how soft Comrade Bukharin is; it is one of the qualities which endears him to people, who cannot help liking him. We know that he has been ribbed for being as "soft as wax". It turns out that any "unprincipled" person, any "demagogue" can leave any mark he likes on this "soft wax". The sharp words in quotation marks were used by Comrade Kamenev, during the January 17 discussion, and he had a perfect right to do so. But, of course, neither Kamenev nor anyone else would dream of *attributing* or reducing it all to unprincipled *demagogy*.

On the contrary, there is an objective logic in factional struggles which inevitably leads even the best of men—if they persist in their mistaken attitude—into a state which differs little if at all from unprincipled demagogy. That is the lesson of the entire history of factional wars (for example, the alliance of the Vperyodists and the Mensheviks against the Bolsheviks[9]). That is why we must make a study not only of the nature of the disagreements in the abstract, but also of their concrete development and change at the various stages of the struggle. This development was summed up in the January 17 discussion.[10] Neither the "shake-up" nor the "new production tasks" can any longer be advocated (because all the efficient and sensible ideas went into Rudzutak's theses). The alternative then is to find what Lassalle called "the physical strength of mind" (and character) to admit the mistake, rectify it and turn over this page of the

[9] The reference is to the merger of the anti-Party Vperyod group (which consisted of otzovists, ultimatumists, and god-builders) with Menshevik liquidators and Trotskyites. They united after the Sixth (Prague) All-Russia Conference of the Russian Social-Democratic Labour Party to fight its decisions. They led a malicious campaign against the Bolsheviks in an effort to split the workers' revolutionary movement and weaken the proletarian Party. They formed a bloc demanding the "transformation" of the Party, which, in fact, implied its liquidation. The bloc, which had no principles to hold it together, was unstable and soon fell apart.

[10] The reference is to the trade union discussion at an enlarged session of the Moscow Party Committee together with delegates from Party organisations of Moscow city districts and uyezds on January 17, 1921.

The session debated all the draft theses put forward by various groups during the discussion. In the preliminary voting, Lenin's theses got 76 votes; Trotsky's, 27; Bukharin's, 5; Shlyapnikov's, 4; Sapronov's, 11; Ignatov's, 25; Nogin's, none, and Ryazanov's, none. In the re-vote on the two main platforms, 84 votes were cast for Lenin's theses, and 27, for Trotsky's.

On January 18, the Moscow Party Committee adopted an appeal "To All Party Organisations" asking all Party members to give unanimous support to Lenin's platform.

history of the R.C.P., or—to cling to the remaining allies, no matter who they are, and "ignore" the principles altogether. There remain only the adherents of "democracy" *ad nauseam*. And Bukharin is sliding down towards them and syndicalism.

While we are slowly absorbing what was sound in the "democratic" Workers' Opposition, Bukharin has to cling to what is *unsound*. On January 17, Comrade Bumazhny, a prominent Tsektranite, or Trotskyite, expressed his readiness to accept Bukharin's syndicalist proposals. The "Sapronovites" have gone so far as to insist in the same thesis (3) on a "profound crisis" and a "bureaucratic necrosis" of the trade unions, while proposing, as being "absolutely" necessary, the "extension of the trade unions' *rights* in production" . . . probably because of their "bureaucratic necrosis"? Can this group be taken seriously? They had heard the talk about the *role* of the trade unions in production, and wishing to outshout the others, blurted out: "extension of rights" on the occasion of "bureaucratic necrosis". You need read no more than the first few lines of their "practical" proposals: "The presidium of the Supreme Economic Council shall be nominated by the All-Russia Central Council of Trade Unions and confirmed by the All-Russia Central Executive Committee." And what is their *democratic* position in "principle"? Listen to this (thesis 2): "They [Zinoviev and Trotsky] in fact express two trends within the same group of *ex-militarisers of the economy*."

Taken seriously, this is Menshevism and Socialist-Revolutionarism at their worst. But Sapronov, Osinsky and Co. should not be taken seriously, when, before every Party congress ("every blessed time on this very same spot"), these, I believe, superlative workers have a sort of paroxysmal seizure and try to outshout the others (the "champion shouter" faction) and solemnly make a hash of things. The "Ignatovites" try to keep up with the "Sapronovites". It is, of course, quite permissible (specially before a congress) for various groups to form blocs (and also to go vote chasing). But this should be done within the framework of communism (and not syndicalism) and in such a way as to avoid being ridiculous. Who is the highest bidder? Promisers of more "rights" to non-Party people, unite on the occasion of the congress of the Russian Communist Party! . . .

Our platform up to now has been: Do not defend but rectify the bureaucratic excesses. The fight against bureaucracy is a long and arduous one. Excesses can and must be rectified at once. It is not those who point out harmful excesses and strive to rectify them but those who resist rectification that undermine the prestige of the military workers and appointees. Such were the excesses of certain Tsektranites who, however, will continue to be (and have been) valuable workers. There is no need to harass the trade unions by inventing disagreements with them, when they themselves have decided upon and accepted all that is new, business-like and practical in the tasks of the trade unions in production. On this basis, let us vigorously work together for practical results.

We have now added to our platform the following: We must combat the ideological discord and the unsound elements of the opposition who talk themselves into repudiating all "militarisation of industry", and not only the "appointments method", which has been the prevailing one up to now, but all "appointments", that is, in the last analysis, repudiating the *Party's* leading role in relation to the non-Party masses. We must combat the syndicalist deviation, which will kill the Party unless it is entirely cured of it.

The Entente[11] capitalists will surely try to take advantage of our Party's malaise to mount another invasion, and the Socialist-Revolutionaries, to hatch plots and rebellions. We need have no fear of this because we shall all unite as one man, without being afraid to admit the malaise, but recognising that it demands from all of us a greater discipline, tenacity and firmness at every post. By the time the Tenth Congress of the R.C.P. meets in March, and after the Congress, the Party will not be weaker, but stronger.

January 19, 1921

[11] *Entente* or the "Allies"—Britain, France, the U.S.A., Japan and other countries that took part in the intervention against Soviet Russia. It should not be confused with *Entente cordiale*, the alliance of France and Great Britain and, later, tsarist Russia.—*Tr.*

ON COOPERATION (1923)

I

It seems to me that not enough attention is being paid to the co-operative movement in our country. Not everyone understands that now, since the time of the October revolution and quite apart from NEP (on the contrary, in this connection we must say—because of NEP), our co-operative movement has become one of great significance. There is a lot of fantasy in the dreams of the old co-operators. Often they are ridiculously fantastic. But why are they fantastic? Because people do not understand the fundamental, the rock-bottom significance of the working-class political struggle for the overthrow of the rule of the exploiters. We have overthrown the rule of the exploiters, and much that was fantastic, even romantic, even banal in the dreams of the old co-operators is now becoming unvarnished reality.

Indeed, since political power is in the hands of the working-class, since this political power owns all the means of production, the only task, indeed, that remains for us is to organise the population in co-operative societies. With most of the population organised in co-operatives, the socialism which in the past was legitimately treated with ridicule, scorn and contempt by those who were rightly convinced that it was necessary to wage the class struggle, the struggle for political power, etc., will achieve its aim automatically. But not all comrades realise how vastly, how infinitely important it is now to organise the population of Russia in co-operative societies. By adopting NEP we made a concession to the peasant as a trader, to the principal of private trade; it is precisely for this reason (contrary to what some people think) that the co-operative movement is of such immense importance. All we actually need under NEP is to organise the population of Russia in co-operative societies on a sufficiently large scale, for we have now found that degree of combination of private interest, of private commercial interest, with state supervision and control of this interest, that degree of its subordination to the common interests which was formerly the stumbling-block for very many socialists. Indeed, the power of the state over all large-scale means of production, political power in the hands of the proletariat, the alliance of this proletariat with the many millions of small and very small peasants, the assured proletarian leadership of the peasantry, etc.—is this not all that is necessary to build a complete socialist society out of co-operatives, out of co-operatives alone, which we formerly ridiculed as huckstering and which from a certain aspect we have the right to treat as such now, under NEP? Is this not all that is necessary to build a complete socialist society? It is still not the building of socialist society, but it is all that is necessary and sufficient for it.

It is this very circumstance that is underestimated by many of our practical workers. They look down upon co-operative societies, failing to appreciate their exceptional importance, first, from the standpoint of principle (the means of production are owned by the state), and, second, from the standpoint of transition to the new system by means that are the *simplest, easiest and most acceptable to the peasant.*

But this again is of fundamental importance. It is one thing to draw up fantastic plans for building socialism through all sorts of workers' associations, and quite another to learn to build socialism in practice in such a way that *every* small peasant could take part in it. That is the very stage we have now reached. And there is no doubt that, having reached it, we are taking too little advantage of it.

We went too far when we reintroduced NEP, but not because we attached too much importance to the principle of free enterprise and trade—we went too far because we lost sight of the co-operatives, because we now underrate the co-operatives, because we are already beginning to forget the vast importance of the co-operatives from the above two points of view.

I now propose to discuss with the reader what can and must at once be done practically on the basis of this "co-operative" principle. By what means can we, and must we, start at once to develop this "co-operative" principle so that its socialist meaning may be clear to all?

Co-operation must be politically so organised that it will not only generally and always enjoy certain privileges, but that these privileges should be of a purely material nature (a favourable bank rate, etc.). The co-operatives must be granted state loans that are greater, if only by a little, than the loans we grant to private enterprises, even to heavy industry, etc.

A social system emerges only if it has the financial backing of a definite class. There is no need to mention the hundreds of millions of rubles that the birth of "free" capitalism cost. At present we have to realise that the co-operative system is the social system we must now give more than ordinary assistance, and we must actually give that assistance. But it must be it assistance in the real sense of the word, i.e., it will not be enough to interpret it to mean assistance for any kind of co-operative trade; by assistance we must mean aid to co-operative trade in which *really large classes of the population actually take part.* It is certainly a correct form of assistance to give a bonus to peasants who take part in co-operative trade; but the whole point is to verify the nature of this participation, to verify the awareness behind it, and to verify its quality. Strictly speaking, when a co-operator goes to a village and opens co-operative store, the people take no part in this whatever; but at the same time guided by their own interests they will hasten to try to take part in it.

There is another aspect this question. From the point of view of the "enlightened" (primarily, literate) European there is not much left for us to do to induce absolutely everyone to take not a passive, but an active part in co-operative operations. Strictly speaking, there is *"only"* one thing we have left to do and that is to make our people so "enlightened" that they understand all the advantages of everybody participating in the work of the co-operatives, and organise this participation. *"Only"* that. There are now no other devices needed to advance to socialism. But to achieve this "only", there must be a veritable revolution—the entire people must go through a period of cultural development. Therefore, our rule must be: as little philosophising and as few acrobatics as possible. In this respect NEP is an advance, because it is adjustable to the level of the most ordinary peasant and does not demand anything higher of him. But it will take a whole historical epoch to get the entire population into the work of the co-operatives through NEP. At best we can achieve this in one or two decades. Nevertheless, it will be a distinct historical epoch, and without this historical epoch, without universal literacy, without a proper degree of efficiency, without training the population sufficiently to acquire the habit of book-reading, and without the material basis for this, without a certain sufficiency to safeguard against, say, bad harvests, famine, etc.—without this we shall not achieve our object. The thing now is to learn to combine the wide revolutionary range of action, the revolutionary enthusiasm which we have displayed, and displayed abundantly, and crowned with complete success—to learn to combine this with (I am almost inclined to say) the ability to be an efficient and capable trader, which is quite enough to be a good co-operator. By ability to be a trader I mean the ability to be a cultured trader. Let those Russians, or peasants, who imagine that since they trade they are good traders, get that well into their heads. This does not follow at all. They do trade, but that is far from being cultured traders. They now trade in an Asiatic manner, but to be a good trader one must trade in the European manner. They are a whole epoch behind in that.

In conclusion: a number of economic, financial and banking privileges must be granted to the co-operatives—this is the way our socialist state must promote the new principle on which the population must be organised. But this is only the general outline of the task; it does not define and depict in detail the entire content of the practical task, i.e., we must find what form of "bonus" to give for joining the co-operatives (and the terms on which we should give it), the form of bonus by which we shall assist the co-operatives sufficiently, the form of bonus that will produce the civilised co-operator. And given social ownership of the means of production, given the class victory of the proletariat over the bourgeoisie, the system of civilised co-operators is the system of socialism.

January 4, 1923

II

Whenever I wrote about the New Economic Policy I always quoted the article on state capitalism[1] which I wrote in 1918. This has more than once aroused doubts in the minds of certain young comrades. But their doubts were mainly on abstract political points.

It seemed to them that the term "state capitalism" could not be applied to a system under which the means of production were owned by the working class, a working class that held political power. They did not notice, however, that I used the term "state capitalism", *firstly*, to connect historically our present position with the position adopted in my controversy with the so-called Left Communists; also, I argued at the time that state capitalism would be superior to our existing economy. It was important for me to show the continuity between ordinary state capitalism and the unusual, even very unusual, state capitalism to which I referred in introducing the reader to the New Economic Policy. *Secondly*, the practical purpose was always important to me. And the practical purpose of our New Economic Policy was to lease out concessions. In the prevailing circumstances, concessions in our country would unquestionably have been a pure type of state capitalism. That is how I argued about state capitalism.

[1] Lenin refers to his article "'Left-Wing' Childishness and the Petty-Bourgeois Mentality" (see *LCW*, Vol. 27, 1974, pp. 323-54).

But there is another aspect of the matter for which we may need state capitalism, or at least a comparison with it. It is a question of co-operatives.

In the capitalist state, co-operatives are no doubt collective capitalist institutions. Nor is there any doubt that under our present economic conditions, when we combine private capitalist enterprises—but in no other way than on nationalised land and in no other way than under the control of the working-class state—with enterprises of a consistently socialist type (the means of production, the land on which the enterprises are situated, and the enterprises as a whole belonging to the state), the question arises about a third type of enterprise, the co-operatives, which were not formally regarded as an independent type differing fundamentally from the others. Under private capitalism, co-operative enterprises differ from capitalist enterprises as collective enterprises differ from private enterprises. Under state capitalism, co-operative enterprises differ from state capitalist enterprises, firstly, because they are private enterprises, and, secondly, because they are collective enterprises. Under our present system, co-operative enterprises differ from private capitalist enterprises because they are collective enterprises, but do not differ from socialist enterprises if the land on which they are situated and means of production belong to the state, i.e., the working class.

This circumstance is not considered sufficiently when co-operatives are discussed. It is forgotten that owing to the special features of our political system, our co-operatives acquire an altogether exceptional significance. If we exclude concessions, which, incidentally, have not developed on any considerable scale, co-operation under our conditions nearly always coincides fully with socialism.

Let me explain what I mean. Why were the plans of the old co-operators, from Robert Owen onwards, fantastic? Because they dreamed of peacefully remodelling contemporary society into socialism without taking account of such fundamental questions as the class struggle, the capture of political power by the working class, the overthrow of the rule of the exploiting class. That is why we are right in regarding as entirely fantastic this "co-operative" socialism, and as romantic, and even banal, the dream of transforming class enemies into class collaborators and class war into class peace (so-called class truce) by merely organising the population in co-operative societies.

Undoubtedly we were right from the point of view of the fundamental task of the present day, for socialism cannot be established without a class struggle for the political power in the state.

But see how things have changed now that political power is in the hands of the working class, now that the political power of the exploiters is overthrown and all the means of production (except those which the workers' state voluntarily abandons on specified terms and for a certain time to the exploiters in the form of concessions) are owned by the working class.

Now we are entitled to say that for us the mere growth of co-operation (with the "slight" exception mentioned above) is identical with the growth of socialism, and at the same time we have to admit that there has been a radical modification in our whole outlook on socialism. The radical modification is this; formerly we placed, and had to place, the main emphasis on the political struggle, on revolution, on winning political power, etc. Now the emphasis is changing and shifting to peaceful, organisational, "cultural" work. I should say that emphasis is shifting to educational work, were it not for our international relations, were it not for the fact that we have to fight for our position on a world scale. If we leave that aside, however, and confine ourselves to internal economic relations, the emphasis in our work is certainly shifting to education.

Two main tasks confront us, which constitute the epoch—to reorganise our machinery of state, which is utterly useless, and which we took over in its entirety from the preceding epoch; during the past five years of struggle we did not, and could not, drastically reorganise it. Our second task is educational work among the peasants. And the economic object of this educational work among the peasants is to organise the latter in co-operative societies. If the whole of the peasantry had been organised in co-operatives, we would by now have been standing with both feet on the soil of socialism. But the organisation of the entire peasantry in co-operative societies presupposes a standard of culture among the peasants (precisely among the peasants as the overwhelming mass) that cannot, in fact, be achieved without a cultural revolution.

Our opponents told us repeatedly that we were rash in undertaking to implant socialism in an insufficiently cultured country. But they were misled by our having started from the opposite end to that prescribed by theory (the theory of pedants of all kinds), because in our country the political and social revolution preceded the cultural revolution, that very cultural revolution which nevertheless now confronts us.

This cultural revolution would now suffice to make our country a completely socialist country; but it presents immense difficulties of a purely cultural (for we are illiterate) and material character (for to be cultured we must achieve a certain development of the material means of production, must have a certain material base).

January 6, 1923

BETTER FEWER, BUT BETTER
(1923)

In the matter of improving our state apparatus, the Workers' and Peasants' Inspection should not, in my opinion, either strive after quantity or hurry. We have so far been able to devote so little thought and attention to the efficiency of our state apparatus that it would now be quite legitimate if we took special care to secure its thorough organisation, and concentrated in the Workers' and Peasants' Inspection a staff of workers really abreast of the times, i.e., not inferior to the best West-European standards. For a socialist republic this condition is, of course, too modest. But our experience of the first five years has fairly crammed our heads with mistrust and scepticism. These qualities assert themselves involuntarily when, for example, we hear people dilating at too great length and too flippantly on "proletarian" culture. For a start, we should be satisfied with real bourgeois culture; for a start, we should be glad to dispense with the cruder types of pre-bourgeois culture, i.e., bureaucratic culture or serf culture, etc. In matters of culture, haste and sweeping measures are most harmful. Many of our young writers and Communists should get this well into their heads.

Thus, in the matter of our state apparatus we should now draw the conclusion from our past experience that it would be better to proceed more slowly.

Our state apparatus is so deplorable, not to say wretched, that we must first think very carefully how to combat its defects, bearing in mind that these defects are rooted in the past, which, although it has been overthrown, has not yet been overcome, has not yet reached the stage of a culture that has receded into the distant past. I say culture deliberately, because in these matters we can only regard as achieved what has become part and parcel of our culture, of our social life, our habits. We might say that the good in our social system has not been properly studied, understood, and taken to heart; it has been hastily grasped at; it has not been verified or tested, corroborated by experience, and not made durable, etc. Of course, it could not be otherwise in a revolutionary epoch, when development proceeded at such breakneck speed that in a matter of five years we passed from tsarism to the Soviet system.

It is time we did something about it. We must show sound scepticism for too rapid progress, for boastfulness, etc. We must give thought to testing the steps forward we proclaim every hour, take every minute and then prove every second that they are flimsy, superficial and misunderstood. The most harmful thing here would be haste. The most harmful thing would be to rely on the assumption that we know at least something, or that we have any considerable number of elements necessary for the building of a really new state apparatus, one really worthy to be called socialist, Soviet, etc.

No, we are ridiculously deficient of such an apparatus, and even of the elements of it, and we must remember that we should not stint time on building it, and that it will take many, many years.

What elements have we for building this apparatus? Only two. First, the workers who are absorbed in the struggle for socialism. These elements are not sufficiently educated. They would like to build a better apparatus for us, but they do not know how. They cannot build one. They have not yet developed the culture required for this; and it is culture that is required. Nothing will be achieved in this by doing things in a rush, by assault, by vim or vigour, or in general, by any of the best human qualities. Secondly, we have elements of knowledge, education and training, but they are ridiculously inadequate compared with all other countries.

Here we must not forget that we are too prone to compensate (or imagine that we can compensate) our lack of knowledge by zeal, haste, etc.

In order to renovate our state apparatus we must at all costs set out, first, to learn, secondly, to learn, and thirdly, to learn, and then see to it that learning shall not remain a dead letter, or a fashionable catch-phrase (and we should admit in all frankness that this happens very often with us), that learning shall really become part of our very being, that it shall actually and fully become a constituent element of our social life. In short, we must not make the demands that are made by bourgeois Western Europe, but demands that are fit and proper for a country which has set out to develop into a socialist country.

The conclusions to be drawn from the above are the following: we must make the Workers' and Peasants' Inspection a really exemplary institution, an instrument to improve our state apparatus.

In order that it may attain the desired high level, we must follow the rule: "Measure your cloth seven times before you cut."

For this purpose, we must utilise the very best of what there is in our social system, and utilise it with the greatest caution, thoughtfulness and knowledge, to build up the new People's Commissariat.

For this purpose, the best elements that we have in our social system—such as, first, the advanced workers, and, second, the really enlightened elements for whom we can vouch that they will not take the word for the deed, and will not utter a single word that goes against their conscience—should not shrink from admitting any difficulty and should not shrink from any struggle in order to achieve the object they have seriously set themselves.

We have been bustling for five years trying to improve our state apparatus, but it has been mere bustle, which has proved useless in these five years, or even futile, or even harmful. This bustle created the impression that we were doing something, but in effect it was only clogging up our institutions and our brains.

It is high time things were changed.

We must follow the rule: Better fewer, but better. We must follow the rule: Better get good human material in two or even three years than work in haste without hope of getting any at all.

I know that it will be hard to keep to this rule and apply it under our conditions. I know that the opposite rule will force its way through a thousand loopholes. I know that enormous resistance will have to be put up, that devilish persistence will be required, that in the first few years at least work in this field will be hellishly hard. Nevertheless, I am convinced that only by such effort shall we be able to achieve our aim; and that only by achieving this aim shall we create a republic that is really worthy of the name of Soviet, socialist, and so on, and so forth.

Many readers probably thought that the figures I quoted by way of illustration in my first article[1] were too small. I am sure that many calculations may be made to prove that they are. But I think that we must put one thing above all such and other calculations, i.e., our desire to obtain really exemplary quality.

I think that the time has at last come when we must work in real earnest to improve our state apparatus and in this there can scarcely be anything more harmful than haste. That is why I would sound a strong warning against inflating the figures. In my opinion, we should, on the contrary, be especially sparing with figures in this matter. Let us say frankly that the People's Commissariat of the Workers' and Peasants' Inspection does not at present enjoy the slightest authority. Everybody knows that no other institutions are worse organised than those of our Workers' and Peasants' Inspection, and that under present conditions nothing can be expected from this People's Commissariat. We must have this firmly fixed in our minds if we really want to create within a few

[1] See *LCW*, Vol. 33, 1973, pp. 481-86.

years an institution that will, first, be an exemplary institution, secondly, win everybody's absolute confidence, and, thirdly, prove to all and sundry that we have really justified the work of such a highly placed institution as the Central Control Commission. In my opinion, we must immediately and irrevocably reject all general figures for the size of office staffs. We must select employees for the Workers' and Peasants' Inspection with particular care and only on the basis of the strictest test. Indeed, what is the use of establishing a People's Commissariat which carries on anyhow, which does not enjoy the slightest confidence, and whose word carries scarcely any weight? I think that our main object in launching the work of reconstruction that we now have in mind is to avoid all this.

The workers whom we are enlisting as members of the Central Control Commission must be irreproachable Communists, and I think that a great deal has yet to be done to teach them the methods and objects of their work. Furthermore, there must be a definite number of secretaries to assist in this work, who must be put to a triple test before they are appointed to their posts. Lastly, the officials whom in exceptional cases we shall accept directly as employees of the Workers' and Peasants' Inspection must conform to the following requirements:

First, they must be recommended by several Communists.

Second, they must pass a test for knowledge of our state apparatus.

Third, they must pass a test in the fundamentals of the theory of our state apparatus, in the fundamentals of management, office routine, etc.

Fourth, they must work in such close harmony with the members of the Central Control Commission and with their own secretariat that we could vouch for the work of the whole apparatus.

I know that these requirements are extraordinarily strict, and I am very much afraid that the majority of the "practical" workers in the Workers' and Peasants' Inspection will say that these requirements are impracticable, or will scoff at them. But I ask any of the present chiefs of the Workers' and Peasants' Inspection, or anyone associated with that body, whether they can honestly tell me the practical purpose of a People's Commissariat like the Workers' and Peasants' Inspection. I think this question will help them recover their sense of proportion. Either it is not worthwhile having another of the numerous reorganisations that we have had of this hopeless affair, the Workers' and Peasants' Inspection, or we must really set to work, by slow, difficult and unusual methods, and by testing these methods over and over again, to create something really exemplary, something that will win the respect of all and sundry for its merits, and not only because of its rank and title.

If we do not arm ourselves with patience, if we do not devote several years to this task, we had better not tackle it at all.

In my opinion we ought to select a minimum number of the higher labour research institutes, etc., which we have baked so hastily, see whether they are organised properly, and allow them to continue working, but only in a way that conforms to the high standards of modern science and gives us all its benefits. If we do that it will not be utopian to hope that within a few years we shall have an institution that will be able to perform its functions, to work systematically and steadily on improving our state apparatus, an institution backed by the trust of the working class, of the Russian Communist Party, and the whole population of our Republic.

The spade-work for this could be begun at once. If the People's Commissariat of the Workers' and Peasants' Inspection accepted the present plan of reorganisation, it could now take the preparatory steps and work methodically until the task is completed, without haste, and not hesitating to alter what has already been done.

Any half-hearted solution would be extremely harmful in this matter. A measure for the size of the staff of the Workers' and Peasants' Inspection based on any other consideration would, in fact, be based on the old bureaucratic considerations, on old prejudices, on what has already been condemned, universally ridiculed, etc.

In substance, the matter is as follows:

Either we prove now that we have really learned something about state organisation (we ought to have learned something in five years), or we prove that we are not sufficiently mature for it. If the latter is the case, we had better not tackle the task.

I think that with the available human material it will not be immodest to assume that we have learned enough to be able systematically to rebuild at least one People's Commissariat. True, this one People's Commissariat will have to be the model for our entire state apparatus.

We ought at once to announce a contest in the compilation of two or more textbooks on the organisation of labour in general, and on management in particular. We can take as a basis the book already published by Yermansky, although it should be said in parentheses that he obviously sympathises with Menshevism and is unfit to compile textbooks for the Soviet system. We can also take as a basis the recent book by Kerzhentsev, and some of the other partial textbooks available may be useful too.

We ought to send several qualified and conscientious people to Germany, or to Britain, to collect literature and to study this question. I mention Britain in case it is found impossible to send people to the U.S.A. or Canada.

We ought to appoint a commission to draw up the preliminary programme of examinations for prospective employees of the Workers' and Peasants' Inspection; ditto for candidates to the Central Control Commission.

These and similar measures will not, of course, cause any difficulties for the People's Commissar or the collegium of the Workers' and Peasants' Inspection, or for the Presidium of the Central Control Commission.

Simultaneously, a preparatory commission should be appointed to select candidates for membership of the Central Control Commission. I hope that we shall now be able to find more than enough candidates for this post among the experienced workers in all departments, as well as among the students of our Soviet higher schools. It would hardly be right to exclude one or another category beforehand. Probably preference will have to be given to a mixed composition for this institution, which should combine many qualities, and dissimilar merits. Consequently, the task of drawing up the list of candidates will entail a considerable amount of work. For example, it would be least desirable for the staff of the new People's Commissariat to consist of people of one type, only of officials, say, or for it to exclude people of the propagandist type, or people whose principal quality is sociability or the ability to penetrate into circles that are not altogether customary for officials in this field, etc.

* * *

I think I shall be able to express my idea best if I compare my plan with that of academic institutions. Under the guidance of their Presidium, the members of the Central Control Commission should systematically examine all the papers and documents of the Political Bureau. Moreover, they should divide their time correctly between various jobs in investigating the routine in our institutions, from the very small and privately-owned offices to the highest state institutions. And lastly, their functions should include the study of theory, i.e., the theory of organisation of the work they intend to devote themselves to, and practical work under the guidance of older comrades or of teachers in the higher institutes for the organisation of labour.

I do not think, however, that they will be able to confine themselves to this sort of academic work. In addition, they will have to prepare themselves for work which I would not hesitate to call training to catch,

I will not say rogues, but something like that, and working out special ruses to screen their movements, their approach, etc.

If such proposals were made in West-European government institutions they would rouse frightful resentment, a feeling of moral indignation, etc.; but I trust that we have not become so bureaucratic as to be capable of that. NEP has not yet succeeded in gaining such respect as to cause any of us to be shocked at the idea that somebody may be caught. Our Soviet Republic is of such recent construction, and there are such heaps of the old lumber still lying around that it would hardly occur to anyone to be shocked at the idea that we should delve into them by means of ruses, by means of investigations sometimes directed to rather remote sources or in a roundabout way. And even if it did occur to anyone to be shocked by this, we may be sure that such a person would make himself a laughing-stock.

Let us hope that our new Workers' and Peasants' Inspection will abandon what the French call *pruderie*, which we may call ridiculous primness, or ridiculous swank, and which plays entirely into the hands of our Soviet and Party bureaucracy. Let it be said in parentheses that we have bureaucrats in our Party offices as well as in Soviet offices.

When I said above that we must study and study hard in institutes for the higher organisation of labour, etc., I did not by any means imply "studying" in the schoolroom way, nor did I confine myself to the idea of studying only in the schoolroom way. I hope that not a single genuine revolutionary will suspect me of refusing, in this case, to understand "studies" to include resorting to some semi-humorous trick, cunning device, piece of trickery or something of that sort. I know that in the staid and earnest states of Western European such an idea would horrify people and that not a single decent official would even entertain it. I hope, however, that we have not yet become as bureaucratic as all that and that in our midst the discussion of this idea will give rise to nothing more than amusement.

Indeed, why not combine pleasure with utility? Why not resort to some humorous or semi-humorous trick to expose something ridiculous, something harmful, something semi-ridiculous, semi-harmful, etc.?

It seems to me that our Workers' and Peasants' Inspection will gain a great deal if it undertakes to examine these ideas, and that the list of cases in which our Central Control Commission and its colleagues in the Workers' and Peasants' Inspection achieved a few of their most brilliant victories will be enriched by not a few exploits of our future Workers' and Peasants' Inspection and Central Control Commission members in places not quite mentionable in prim and staid textbooks.

* * *

How can a Party institution be amalgamated with a Soviet institution? Is there not something improper in this suggestion?

I do not ask these questions on my own behalf, but on behalf of those I hinted at above when I said that we have bureaucrats in our Party institutions as well as in the Soviet institutions.

But why, indeed, should we not amalgamate the two if this is in the interests of our work? Do we not all see that such an amalgamation has been very beneficial in the case of the People's Commissariat of Foreign Affairs, where it was brought about at the very beginning? Does not the Political Bureau discuss from the Party point of view many questions, both minor and important, concerning the "moves" we should make in reply to the "moves" of foreign powers in order to forestall their, say, cunning, if we are not to use a less respectable term? Is not this flexible amalgamation of a Soviet institution with a Party institution a source of great strength in our politics? I think that what has proved its usefulness, what has been definitely adopted in our foreign politics and has become so customary that it no longer calls forth any doubt in this field, will be at least as appropriate (in fact, I think it will be much more appropriate) for our state apparatus as a whole. The functions of the Workers' and Peasants' Inspection cover our state apparatus as a whole, and its activities should affect all and every state institution without exception: local, central, commercial, purely administrative, educational, archival, theatrical, etc.—in short, all without any exception.

Why then should not an institution, whose activities have such wide scope, and which moreover requires such extraordinary flexibility of forms, be permitted to adopt this peculiar amalgamation of a Party control institution with a Soviet control institution?

I see no obstacles to this. What is more, I think that such an amalgamation is the only guarantee of success in our work. I think that all doubts on this score arise in the dustiest corners of our government offices, and that they deserve to be treated with nothing but ridicule.

* * *

Another doubt: is it expedient to combine educational activities with official activities? I think that it is not only expedient, but necessary. Generally speaking, in spite of our revolutionary attitude towards the

West-European form of state, we have allowed ourselves to become infected with a number of its most harmful and ridiculous prejudices; to some extent we have been deliberately infected with them by our dear bureaucrats, who counted on being able again and again to fish in the muddy waters of these prejudices. And they did fish in these muddy waters to so great an extent that only the blind among us failed to see how extensively this fishing was practised.

In all spheres of social, economic and political relationships we are "frightfully" revolutionary. But as regards precedence, the observance of the forms and rites of office management, our "revolutionariness" often gives way to the mustiest routine. On more than one occasion, we have witnessed the very interesting phenomenon of a great leap forward in social life being accompanied by amazing timidity whenever the slightest changes are proposed.

This is natural, for the boldest steps forward were taken in a field which was long reserved for theoretical study, which was promoted mainly, and even almost exclusively, in theory. The Russian, when away from work, found solace from bleak bureaucratic realities in unusually bold theoretical constructions, and that is why in our country these unusually bold theoretical constructions assumed an unusually lopsided character. Theoretical audacity in general constructions went hand in hand with amazing timidity as regards certain very minor reforms in office routine. Some great universal agrarian revolution was worked out with an audacity unexampled in any other country, and at the same time the imagination failed when it came to working out a tenth-rate reform in office routine; the imagination, or patience, was lacking to apply to this reform the general propositions that produced such brilliant results when applied to general problems.

That is why in our present life reckless audacity goes hand in hand, to an astonishing degree, with timidity of thought even when it comes to very minor changes.

I think that this has happened in all really great revolutions, for really great revolutions grow out of the contradictions between the old, between what is directed towards developing the old, and the very abstract striving for the new, which must be so new as not to contain the tiniest particle of the old.

And the more abrupt the revolution, the longer will many of these contradictions last.

* * *

The general feature of our present life is the following: we have destroyed capitalist industry and have done our best to raze to the ground the medieval institutions and landed proprietorship, and thus created a small and very small peasantry, which is following the lead of the proletariat because it believes in the results of its revolutionary work. It is not easy for us, however, to keep going until the socialist revolution is victorious in more developed countries merely with the aid of this confidence, because economic necessity, especially under NEP, keeps the productivity of labour of the small and very small peasants at an extremely low level. Moreover, the international situation, too, threw Russia back and, by and large, reduced the labour productivity of the people to a level considerably below pre-war. The West-European capitalist powers, partly deliberately and partly unconsciously, did everything they could to throw us back, to utilise the elements of the Civil War in Russia in order to spread as much ruin in the country as possible. It was precisely this way out of the imperialist war that seemed to have many advantages. They argued somewhat as follows: "If we fail to overthrow the revolutionary system in Russia, we shall, at all events, hinder its progress towards socialism." And from their point of view they could argue in no other way. In the end, their problem was half-solved. They failed to overthrow the new system created by the revolution, but they did prevent it from at once taking the step forward that would have justified the forecasts of the socialists, that would have enabled the latter to develop the productive forces with enormous speed, to develop all the potentialities which, taken together, would have produced socialism; socialists would thus have proved to all and sundry that socialism contains within itself gigantic forces and that mankind had now entered into a new stage of development of extraordinarily brilliant prospects.

The system of international relationships which has now taken shape is one in which a European state, Germany, is enslaved by the victor countries. Furthermore, owing to their victory, a number of states, the oldest states in the West, are in a position to make some insignificant concessions to their oppressed classes—concessions which, insignificant though they are, nevertheless retard the revolutionary movement in those countries and create some semblance of "class truce".

At the same time, as a result of the last imperialist war, a number of countries of the East, India, China, etc., have been completely jolted out of the rut. Their development has definitely shifted to general European capitalist lines. The general European ferment has begun to affect them, and it is now clear to the whole world that they have been drawn into a process of development that must lead to a crisis in the whole of world capitalism.

Thus, at the present time we are confronted with the question—shall we be able to hold on with our small and very small peasant production, and in our present state of ruin, until the West-European capitalist countries consummate their development towards socialism? But they are consummating it not as we formerly expected. They are not consummating it through the gradual "maturing" of socialism, but through the exploitation of some countries by others, through the exploitation of the first of the countries vanquished in the imperialist war combined with the exploitation of the whole of the East. On the other hand, precisely as a result of the first imperialist war, the East has been definitely drawn into the revolutionary movement, has been definitely drawn into the general maelstrom of the world revolutionary movement.

What tactics does this situation prescribe for our country? Obviously the following. We must display extreme caution so as to preserve our workers' government and to retain our small and very small peasantry under its leadership and authority. We have the advantage that the whole world is now passing to a movement that must give rise to a world socialist revolution. But we are labouring under the disadvantage that the imperialists have succeeded in splitting the world into two camps; and this split is made more complicated by the fact that it is extremely difficult for Germany, which is really a land of advanced, cultured, capitalist development, to rise to her feet. All the capitalist powers of what is called the West are pecking at her and preventing her from rising. On the other hand, the entire East, with its hundreds of millions of exploited working people, reduced to the last degree of human suffering, has been forced into a position where its physical and material strength cannot possibly be compared with the physical, material and military strength of any of the much smaller West-European states.

Can we save ourselves from the impending conflict with these imperialist countries? May we hope that the internal antagonisms and conflicts between the thriving imperialist countries of the West and the thriving imperialist countries of the East will give us a second respite as they did the first time, when the campaign of the West-European counter-revolution in support of the Russian counter-revolution broke down owing to the antagonisms in the camp of the counter-revolutionaries of the West and the East, in the camp of the Eastern and Western exploiters, in the camp of Japan and the U.S.A.?

I think the reply to this question should be that the issue depends upon too many factors, and that the outcome of the struggle as a whole can be forecast only because in the long run capitalism itself is educating and training the vast majority of the population of the globe for the struggle.

In the last analysis, the outcome of the struggle will be determined by the fact that Russia, India, China, etc., account for the overwhelming majority of the population of the globe. And during the past few years it is this majority that has been drawn into the struggle for emancipation with extraordinary rapidity, so that in this respect there cannot be the slightest doubt what the final outcome of the world struggle will be. In this sense, the complete victory of socialism is fully and absolutely assured.

But what interests us is not the inevitability of this complete victory of socialism, but the tactics which we, the Russian Communist Party, we, the Russian Soviet Government, should pursue to prevent the West-European counter-revolutionary states from crushing us. To ensure our existence until the next military conflict between the counter-revolutionary imperialist West and the revolutionary and nationalist East, between the most civilised countries of the world and the Orientally backward countries which, however, comprise the majority, this majority must become civilised. We, too, lack enough civilisation to enable us to pass straight on to socialism, although we do have the political requisites for it. We should adopt the following tactics, or pursue the following policy, to save ourselves.

We must strive to build up a state in which the workers retain the leadership of the peasants, in which they retain the confidence of the peasants, and by exercising the greatest economy remove every trace of extravagance from our social relations.

We must reduce our state apparatus to the utmost degree of economy. We must banish from it all traces of extravagance, of which so much has been left over from tsarist Russia, from its bureaucratic capitalist state machine.

Will not this be a reign of peasant limitations?

No. If we see to it that the working class retains its leadership over the peasantry, we shall be able, by exercising the greatest possible thrift in the economic life of our state, to use every saving we make to develop our large-scale machine industry, to develop electrification, the hydraulic extraction of peat, to complete the Volkhov Power Project,[2] etc.

[2] The power project on the Volkhov River was the first of the large hydropower stations in the Soviet Union. Construction on this project was started in 1918, but the work really got under way only in 1921, after the Civil War. The

In this, and in this alone, lies our hope. Only when we have done this shall we, speaking figuratively, be able to change horses, to change from the peasant, muzhik horse of poverty, from the horse of an economy designed for a ruined peasant country, to the horse which the proletariat is seeking and must seek—the horse of large-scale machine industry, of electrification, of the Volkhov Power Station, etc.

That is how I link up in my mind the general plan of our work, of our policy, of our tactics, of our strategy, with the functions of the reorganised Workers' and Peasants' Inspection. This is what, in my opinion, justifies the exceptional care, the exceptional attention that we must devote to the Workers' and Peasants' Inspection in raising it to an exceptionally high level, in giving it a leadership with Central Committee rights, etc., etc.

And this justification is that only by thoroughly purging our government machine, by reducing to the utmost everything that is not absolutely essential in it, shall we be certain of being able to keep going. Moreover, we shall be able to keep going not on the level of a small-peasant country, not on the level of universal limitation, but on a level steadily advancing to large-scale machine industry.

These are the lofty tasks that I dream of for our Workers' and Peasants' Inspection. That is why I am planning for it the amalgamation of the most authoritative Party body with an "ordinary" People's Commissariat.

March 2, 1923

station became operational in 1926.

PUBLICATION DETAILS

Leninism and the Liberation of Oppressed Peoples by Ho Chi Minh
Pravda, April 18, 1955. Published according to the *Pravda* text.

The Historical Destiny of the Doctrine of Karl Marx
Pravda No. 50, March 1, 1913. Signed: V.I. Published according to the *Pravda* text.

The Three Sources and Three Component Parts of Marxism
Prosveshcheniye No. 3, March, 1913. Signed: V.I. Published according to the *Prosveshcheniye* text.

Marxism and Revisionism
Written not later than April 3 (16), 1908. Published in 1908 in the symposium *Karl Marx—1818-1883*. Signed: *Vl. Ilyin*. Published according to the symposium.

Our Programme
Written in the second half of 1899. First published in 1925 in *Lenin Miscellany III*. Published according to manuscript copied by an unknown hand.

Where to Begin?
Written in May 1901. Published in *Iskra* No. 4, May 1901. Published according to the *Iskra* text.

What Is To Be Done?
Written between the autumn of 1901 and February 1902. First published as a separate work in March 1902. Published according to the text of the book checked with that in the collection *Twelve Years*, by Vl. Ilyin, 1907.

Two Tactics of Social Democracy in the Democratic Revolution
Written in June-July 1905. First published as a pamphlet in Geneva, July, 1905. Published according to the text of the pamphlet checked against the manuscript.

Party Organisation and Party Literature
Novaya Zhizn No. 12, November 13, 1905. Signed: *N. Lenin*. Published according to the text in *Novaya Zhizn*.

The Socialist Revolution and the Right of Nations to Self-Determination
Written January-February 1916. Printed in April 1916 in the magazine *Vorbote* No. 2. Printed in Russian in October 1916 in *Sbornik Sotsial-Demokrata* No. 1. Published according to the *Sbornik* text.

Imperialism, the Last Stage of Capitalism
Written January-June 1916. First published in mid-1917 in pamphlet form, Petrograd. Published according to the manuscript and verified with the text of the pamphlet.

Letters on Tactics

Written between April 8 and 13 (21 and 26), 1917. Published as a pamphlet in April 1917 by Priboi Publishers. Published according to the pamphlet text.

State and Revolution

Written in August-September 1917. Published as a pamphlet in 1918 by *Zhizn i Znaniye* Publishers. Printed according to the pamphlet text published by *Kommunist* Publishers in 1919 and verified with the manuscript and the 1918 edition.

On Compromises

Written on September 1-3 (14-16), 1917. Published in *Rabochy Put* No. 3, September 19 (6), 1917. Signed: *N. Lenin*. Published according to the newspaper text.

Marxism and Insurrection

Written September 13-14 (26-27), 1917. First published in 1921 in the magazine *Proletarskaya Revolutsia* No. 2. Published according to the magazine text verified with a typewritten copy.

Can the Bolsheviks Retain State Power?

Written at the end of September-October 1 (14), 1917. Published in October 1917 in the magazine *Prosveshcheniye* No. 1-2. Published according to the magazine text.

"Left-Wing" Communism: An Infantile Disorder

Written in April-May 1920. Published in pamphlet form, in June 1920. Published according to the text of the pamphlet, as checked against the manuscript.

The Immediate Tasks of the Soviet Government

Written in March-April 1918. Published on April 28, 1918 in *Pravda* No. 83 and *Izvestia VTsIK* No. 85. Signed: *N. Lenin*. Published according to the text of the pamphlet: N. Lenin, *The Immediate Tasks of the Soviet Government*, 2nd ed., Moscow, 1918, collated with the manuscript.

Letter to American Workers

Pravda No. 178, August 22, 1918. Published according to the *Pravda* text checked with the manuscript.

The Tasks of the Working Women's Movement in the Soviet Republic

Pravda No. 213, September 25, 1919. Speech Delivered at the Fourth Moscow City Conference of Non-Party Working Women on September 23, 1919. Published according to the text of the pamphlet, V.I. Lenin, *Speech at the Working Women's Congress*, Moscow, 1919, verified with the *Pravda* text.

First All-Russia Congress on Adult Education

Published in the pamphlet: N. Lenin, *Two Speeches at the First All-Russia Congress on Adult Education*, Moscow, 1919. Published according to the pamphlet.

Publication Details

Preliminary Draft Theses on the Agrarian Question

Written at the beginning of June 1920. Published in June 1920. Published according to the manuscript.

The Tasks of the Youth Leagues

Pravda Nos. 221, 222 and 223, October 5, 6 and 7, 1920. Published according to the *Pravda* text, verified against the text of the pamphlet: N. Lenin (V. I. Ulyanov), *The Tasks of the Youth Leagues*, 1920.

Speech Delivered at an All-Russia Conference of Political Education Workers of Gubernia and Uyezd Education Departments

Bulletin of the All-Russia Conference of Political Education Workers (November 1-8, 1920), Moscow. Published according to the text of the Bulletin.

The Party Crisis

Pravda No. 13, January 21, 1921. Signed: *N. Lenin*. Published according to the *Pravda* text collated with the text of the pamphlet: N. Lenin, *Party Crisis*, 1921.

On Cooperation

First published in *Pravda* Nos. 115 and 116, May 26 and 27, 1923. Signed: *N. Lenin*. Published according to the *Pravda* text checked with the stenographer's notes.

Better Fewer, But Better

Pravda No. 49, March 4, 1923. Signed: *N. Lenin*. Published according to the stenographer's notes (type-written copy) checked with the newspaper text.